Conducting Business with Professor Spice

MW01709346

DANIEL LAFFERTY

CONDUCTING BUSINESS WITH Professor Spice

To the Pommiers,
Thank you for
reading!
5/21/11

TATE PUBLISHING & *Enterprises*

Conducting Business with Professor Spice
Copyright © 2011 by Daniel Lafferty. All rights reserved.

No part of this publication may be reproduced, stored in a retrieval system or transmitted in any way by any means, electronic, mechanical, photocopy, recording or otherwise without the prior permission of the author except as provided by USA copyright law.

This novel is a work of fiction. Names, descriptions, entities, and incidents included in the story are products of the author's imagination. Any resemblance to actual persons, events, and entities is entirely coincidental.

The opinions expressed by the author are not necessarily those of Tate Publishing, LLC.

Published by Tate Publishing & Enterprises, LLC
127 E. Trade Center Terrace | Mustang, Oklahoma 73064 USA
1.888.361.9473 | www.tatepublishing.com

Tate Publishing is committed to excellence in the publishing industry. The company reflects the philosophy established by the founders, based on Psalm 68:11,
"The Lord gave the word and great was the company of those who published it."

Book design copyright © 2011 by Tate Publishing, LLC. All rights reserved.
Cover design by Lauran Levy
Interior design by Chelsea Womble
Author Photo by Rebecca Smith

Published in the United States of America

ISBN: 978-1-61777-119-4
1. Fiction, Fantasy, General
2. Fiction, Fantasy, Paranormal
11.03.17

DEDICATION

For Dad,
Without the passion for reading you inspired in me at such an early age, this book never would have been written.

And for Susan,
No amount of personal ambition, hard work, and inspired drive can compare to the gift that is the unconditional support of a loving wife.

PART ONE:

Gerald

Some stories begin with something happy. Some stories begin with something sad. Some begin with something scary or surprising or just plain bad.

Some stories leave their readers applauding and crying out for more, while other stories leave their readers cringing and trying to spit the taste of them upon the floor.

There is one story that begins with a frightened rabbit and ends with a great royal feast. There is another that starts with a loose tooth and ends with a dancing scarecrow. One story began with a peanut shell collection and found its way to a harp that knew a secret. For reasons great and small, silly and serious, joyous and tragic, stories unravel as they must, taking us down paths we may never have expected, but concluding, at last, with the only possible ending such a string of events could lead to.

For better or worse, this story begins with a pouch of pipe tobacco and ends with a falling nickel.

The pouch of pipe tobacco in question was the one Gerald had been sent for by Mr. McGulliver, the owner of the hat shop. Gerald wasn't quite fourteen years old and walked with a distinct spring in his step, his mop of blonde hair loosely swinging up and down and side to side as he moved. The boy didn't spend his days at school with the other children of West Cuttingsborough; rather, he could routinely be found at Hats for All Occasions, the only hat store in the city. The shop was owned and operated solely by Mr. P. F. Rutherford McGulliver, who employed only Gerald to sweep and straighten and run errands. It was in this capacity that he sent the boy for the tobacco on this particular crisp and ash-scented, fire-colored October morning. Mr. McGulliver had no need of other workers, you see, because no one ever shopped at Hats for All Occasions. He alone was quite sufficient man-power to run the single cash drawer, to size any customers (there was never more than one), and to maintain the cleanliness of the quaint little building. This last duty was notably easier for him than the other two, as Mr. McGulliver was horridly timid with people, yet astonishingly tidy at all times.

Even when sending young Gerald on some errand about town, Mr. McGulliver had a decidedly difficult time at expressing his wishes.

"Gerald," Mr. McGulliver said on this particular October Thursday, "Gerald…"

At this point, Mr. McGulliver paused and seemed to await some unlikely verbal recognition from the boy, though Gerald was already looking Mr. McGulliver straight and surely in the eye and nodding for him to continue.

"Gerald," Mr. McGulliver repeated, looking expectantly at him for a few more seconds before nodding uncomfortably and continuing. "Yes, well…Gerald, I'd like you…you wouldn't…or rather…an errand? You'd not mind to?"

Gerald shook his head rapidly and amiably, smiling as he did so.

"Yes," Mr. McGulliver continued. "Yes, quite well, then. Should that you…if you would…" Here Mr. McGulliver paused again to extract his handkerchief from his coat pocket as he so often did and, removing his glasses, proceeded to wipe even cleaner the already quite spotless lenses, then to perform the decidedly more necessary act of mopping the sweat droplets from his not entirely bald head.

After Mr. McGulliver had finished with this familiar ritual, he replaced both his spectacles and handkerchief (not without first mistakenly placing the glasses in the pocket where the handkerchief belonged) and began again.

"Yes. Well, Gerald, if you'd report promptly to, uh, Professor Spice's tobacconist shop and…that is to say…here is…an envelope." Here Mr. McGulliver pulled his keys from his trousers pocket and began to hand them to the boy, who looked at his employer questioningly.

"Ah, yes." Mr. McGulliver discovered the error and replaced the keys, presenting an envelope from the other pocket. "Take this envelope, uh, Gerald, and, uh, you'll receive…that is to say, a, uh… pouch. A pouch of…a pouch of…" Mr. McGulliver trailed off distantly, turning to look toward the door to the stockroom in the rear of the store and sighed heavily. He remained in this manner for what, to Gerald, seemed an uncomfortable length of time.

At last Mr. McGulliver turned again to his youthful assistant and seemed to return to his senses. "Ah, yes," he said, looking from side to side and patting his pockets, seemingly in search of something. Upon spotting the envelope in the boy's hand, he said, "Well, then. When you, uh, give the, uh…the…envelope to Professor Spice, he, uh, he'll give you…a pouch. The pouch will, uh…that is, it's…tobacco. Uh, pipe…tobacco." He seemed to want to say more, but could think of nothing appropriate or necessary. So he smiled his awkward, stiff smile and nodded shortly, turning away, apparently in the hopes that Gerald would take his cue and exit.

Gerald did take the cue, but he had his own rituals he needed to attend to before he could see to his errand. He opened the coat closet that was neatly tucked in one corner of the hat shop and removed his cap and jacket from the hanger. He pulled them on swiftly, then withdrew a small plastic sandwich bag out of the left jacket pocket, emptying the contents—a quarter-handful of bread crumbs—into his palm. Crouching down on the floor, Gerald delicately placed the bread crumbs on the floor in the back of the coat closet, right beside a tiny hole in the wall. Without waiting to see if anything should emerge from the hole, he stood up and started for the front door.

As the bell at the top of the door rang, Mr. McGulliver called from the back of the main sales room, "Uh ... Gerald?"

Gerald turned to his employer, eyes questioning.

"You ... uh ... you know the way, of course." Gerald smiled and nodded, departing the shop.

If Mr. McGulliver was awaiting any other response, he would not receive one from Gerald, neither today nor any other day. Indeed, Mr. McGulliver would never hear any words of reply from Gerald, for Gerald could not speak.

It wasn't really necessary for Mr. McGulliver to ask Gerald if he knew the way to the tobacconist; he sent the boy there every Thursday morning like clockwork. Still, that was the hat shop owner's way, and every week upon sending him, he also confirmed that Gerald knew where to go. Gerald didn't mind. The way he saw it, it would be far worse should he be sent to an unfamiliar destination without any directions.

He set out down Pucket Street, passing by several other shops similar to Hats for All Occasions. There was Buttons, Buttons, Who's Got The Buttons? which sold not just buttons, but thread as well. Then there was Pageturners, the rare and used book shop, and next came The Fourth Chocolatier, which experimented in combining unusually large quantities of different varieties of chocolate with each other. Then there was Tea Is for Teatime, which not only sold assorted exotic teas, but also provided tables and hot water so as to enjoy one's purchases right there upon the premises.

Upon reaching the corner of Pucket and Rood, he made a right turn and passed a series of restaurants, including Charles & Company's Piping Hot Griddlecake House, Sweeney's Sea Cuisine (which was shaped like a great starfish), and Lotsa The Pasta, where you could enjoy not just spaghetti and meatballs, but even meatballs stuffed with spaghetti. These were restaurants Gerald walked past every day, taking in their delicious aromas and trying not to stop and peek in at their contents. Once a month, Gerald was treated to a lunch at one of these wonderful establishments, followed by a treat from the chocolate shop, courtesy of his boss, Mr. McGulliver. That one day always proved to be the greatest day of the month for the boy, who, though he could have cleaned his plate and then some, quite easily, and still have had room aplenty for his chocolate, always requested to take half home in a box. This he took home to his father.

At the corner of Rood and Stover, Gerald encountered Scratches O'Hannigan, a middle-aged bearded man who could often be spotted on different street corners of West Cuttingsborough playing his fiddle for change. As Gerald drew close to Scratches, he could hear that he was playing a soft and sad traditional song of the region, and as he listened he felt an unwelcome melancholy wash over him, slowing his steps to a crawl.

As Scratches spotted his favorite young citizen of West Cuttingsborough, he smiled as best as he could manage with the instrument under his chin. He worked the tune to a close, then let the fiddle and bow fall to his sides, widening a yellow-toothed grin at his visitor.

"Ah, Gerald lad, how then goes the morn, son?"

Gerald responded using one signal from their library of nonverbal codes: a close-mouthed smile with a single abrupt nod, meaning to say, "All's well; business as usual."

This was one of the more commonplace codes from their repertoire, which also included:

- Slow head shake with solemn, close-mouthed stare ("Things aren't good, no sir.")
- Wide-mouthed open grin and rapid head nod ("Things are swell, and boy, have I got some news!")
- Downcast eyes and shuffling feet ("I really messed up; I hope you won't hate me.")
- Smiling eye contact with shuffling feet ("I'm so excited I can hardly contain myself!")
- Worried eyes with shuffling feet ("I really have to use the bathroom!")
- Worried eyes looking from side to side and in all directions with shuffling feet ("I really have to use the bathroom… Where's the nearest one?")

This list could go on for many pages. This was, after all, a system they'd been developing and honing Gerald's whole life.

Now, seeing the envelope in the boy's hand and the direction in which he appeared to be headed, Scratches O'Hannigan nodded slowly, raised a bushy gray eyebrow, and scratched absently at his tangled nest of a beard.

"Runnin' 'long to see the tobacconist, then, are ya?" he asked, and Gerald nodded. Scratches could read the meaning behind the nod, and not because it was part of a secret code. No, Scratches understood that Gerald was uneasy about visiting Professor Spice because he saw him this way every Thursday morning, and had done so for the past two years, ever since Gerald had begun working for Mr. McGulliver. Gerald was always at least a little uneasy about delivering the weekly envelope to the tobacconist, even if he'd done a rather dandy job of convincing himself otherwise. Indeed, Gerald would probably always feel nervous around Professor Spice, ever since the very first time he'd set foot in the tobacco shop on the first Thursday of his employment with Mr. McGulliver.

"You know, then, son," Scratches said slowly, "if yer cont'ry to goin' to that there pipe shop, ya can always tell ol' Percival ya don't mean to anymore." Percival being, of course, the "P" in P.F. Rutherford McGulliver.

Gerald shook his head rapidly, eyes pleading ("Oh no, I couldn't. That's my job, and Mr. McGulliver counts on me!").

Scratches shook his head and sighed, then nodded in the direction of the next intersection. Raising his fiddle back to his chin and placing the bow in proper position, he said to the boy, "Well then, lad, you'd best be off. Not to keep either of them gents waiting, right?" Gerald's face scrunched up into the look one gets when feeling a particular way but not wishing to admit it. At last he nodded agreement, gave a short wave, and continued on his way. Scratches O'Hannigan lowered his bow and fiddle without playing a single note, watching as the boy walked down Stover Street.

After making his way three blocks down Stover Street, Gerald made a left at Cobble Road and slowed down. The extensive and vast emptiness between homes and businesses on Cobble Road gave the impression that there were very few buildings on this block, and it always seemed to Gerald that, despite the weather and color of the sky in other parts of West Cuttingsborough, it was always gray on Cobble Road. Gray and cold. And damp. Gray and cold and damp. So it felt to him now as he stood at the corner and looked down the length of the road. There were trees here, but somehow they seemed to have skipped over the fire-red and gold phase most of the trees were in this autumn season and reached out across lawns and sidewalks with warped, bent, and contorted arm-like bare branches. The trees themselves had a grayness, and indeed seemed to feel the same chill that Gerald did, as they appeared to shiver in a breeze that wasn't there.

There was a smell on Cobble Road as well. It was a sticky, humid, stifling, sort of stale, almost-not-there-but-there-enough-to-tickle-at-the-nose-and-scratch-at-the-throat sort of smell, and it wasn't pleasant.

Still, it was nothing new. Gerald had made this trip many times. In fact, this was his ninety-eighth time bringing money to Professor Spice to pay for Mr. McGulliver's pipe tobacco. And so, with head lifted high and envelope gripped securely in hand, the boy marched his way to the dead (appropriate description, he realized) center of Cobble Road and to the front entrance of the building, whose rotted wooden sign read simply, "Tobacconist."

No bell sounded upon his entering the shop, yet the spoiled and still water smell of Cobble Road did disappear with the sudden and overpowering scent of various flavors of pipe tobacco. Pipe tobacco is a smell considered by many to be warm, comforting, and pleasant. For Gerald, however, it was no better (and perhaps even worse) than the smell outside. Every time his nose captured the scent of a burning pipe or unburned tobacco, he would get a chill that resulted in gooseflesh all up his arms and the back of his neck. He hardly even realized this anymore, though; it had been that way for him for so long.

There were two sounds in the pipe shop when he entered. There was the constant and steady ticking of the clock on the mantle over the fireplace, and the dull and monotonous tones of two men speaking of business that meant nothing to Gerald. These were two of Professor Spice's regular customers, and they looked up only briefly as the boy entered the shop, not allowing his entrance to disrupt their discussion for a beat.

"Charlton says the eastern side will be finished by January," one of the men was saying. "If Hamburg and Tuck don't stand in the way, the ownership of the Knightsbridge shares should—"

"Yes, yes," the other interrupted dismissively, waving his pipe at him and leaning in closer to him. "But the land is worthless! Any percentage is a profit so long as—"

"Degree of usefulness—" the first interrupted in return.

"Or uselessness?"

"Or uselessness, thank you, Cromby—"

"Not at all, Simon."

"—is only measurable in relation to those who deem it to be so."

This was all confusing nonsense to Gerald. He stepped to the front counter and looked around cautiously for some sign of Professor Spice, the proprietor. Professor Spice, however, wasn't in sight, so Gerald stood and waited, patiently as he could, looking around the room with feigned interest and trying (and failing) to block out the detestable noises of the businessmen.

"When Dowd died, he didn't leave the business to Groves, and it's the county that's paid the price, Simon."

"Indubitably, Cromby, but the county won't see it that way, even should the circumstances grow very large feet and tread upon it."

"We know it, of course. Masters and Oxford know it. I'd even wager that Harrison knows it—"

"And Nealy—"

"Oh, rubbish. Nealy wouldn't know his own socks in his very own sock drawer."

"Perhaps. But your point—?"

"Ah, yes. Even the most pinheaded slow-wits see the situation we're in. Why, even *he* probably could offer a halfway reasonable notion or four." At this, Cromby thrust his thumb over his shoulder at the still-waiting Gerald, and Simon released a hearty chortle.

Gerald, too preoccupied with looking around the shop at the assorted pipes and tobaccos, did not understand at first that the laughing was at his expense. He caught on, however, when, looking back in their direction, he saw them both looking directly at him and laughing. Suddenly Gerald found himself even more greatly ill at ease, and he began looking around again, in the irrational and unusual hopes that Professor Spice had emerged. He had not, and the laughing continued. In fact, it seemed to Gerald that the more his discomfort with the situation grew, the redder the men's cheeks became, and the more illustrious their laughter. Through it all, Gerald could do nothing but focus on an umbrella that was leaning in one corner of the shop. It was no sort of special umbrella, gray, tattered around the edges, and not fully closed due to the lock's being broken. Still, unremarkable though the umbrella might be, it provided something for him to look at besides the businessmen's red, laughing faces. And so he stared at it for what surely must have been a lifetime.

And then Professor Spice entered from a room in the back of the store.

Professor Anson Spice was a towering man of over seven feet, silver-haired, slender in his sleek and expensive suits, and peered down at most of the world around him through watchful and knowing eyes, catlike, many had noted before. His sleek, pointed nose was the centerpiece of an always perfectly clean-shaven, sharp-featured face, and his usually silent stares spoke volumes more than the occasions when he did choose to speak.

Spice's title was an earned one, not simply a fanciful self-decoration to draw attraction to his business. In fact, he did not much seem to care whether anyone set foot in the tobacco shop. He had earned the title of professor from his years teaching ancient history at West Cuttingsborough University until, for reasons that were still a mystery to most, he'd been forced to resign. He had already begun running the tobacco shop of Cobble Road at that point, and then was able to devote all his time and attention to it. Of his teaching years and his eventual dismissal from that position, he never spoke. Indeed, he never spoke of it, and no one asked. Few people spoke to him at all, other than to place their orders at his counter. No one ever invited Spice to their parties or even for an end-of-the-workday bite; so far as I can tell, he was rarely even asked the hours of operation of his establishment. Even the businessmen who frequented the shop spoke predominantly amongst themselves, only occasionally asking for his opinion on whatever topic was under discussion. This request would sometimes result in his providing a succinct and factual-sounding viewpoint that usually brought the matter to an immediate close. More common, however, was a brief glare of contempt followed by his turned back and removal of himself from any part of the mundane talk.

The first time Gerald had been sent with an envelope to Professor Spice's shop, he knew nothing of the man. He had trotted the same route he used now, cheerfully making his way toward what seemed to be a simple task that he was, nonetheless, proud to have been entrusted with. Upon his arrival at Cobble Road, he had been caught quite short by his surroundings. The skeletons of the trees and the nearly visible grayness which moved in sinister dances through the mist and air gave him pause and caused him even to glance up at the street sign to be sure he hadn't taken a wrong turn somewhere on the way. Sadly, though, the weather-worn, wooden, hand-painted sign clearly read "Cobble Road," and this was, most assuredly (and unfortunately) the correct place.

Would Mr. McGulliver send him to a place like this? he'd wondered to himself at the time, and what unnerved him most was his realization that he did not know. He'd only been working in the hat shop for less than a week, but his employer had treated him well so far, and for years Gerald had encountered the nervous little man around downtown West Cuttingsborough, and he'd always seemed kindly enough. This, then, was a peculiar and unwelcome turn. But, he'd resolved, it was also his job, and he had thus far done everything Mr. McGulliver had requested without question. He couldn't fail now, not so soon in his position at the store.

And so he had entered the tobacconist shop and walked directly, if with a wandering eye, to the counter, clutching that very first envelope in his hands and looking expectantly around, waiting for someone to emerge from somewhere.

There'd been no businessmen milling about that day, and the ticking of the clock was the only sound in the shop. Gerald would not forget that ticking. It would haunt his dreams that night, and many thereafter. He had listened to it as he stood at the counter, the plain white paper envelope forming distinct damp sweat prints beneath his absently clutching fingertips.

While waiting, he'd noticed a disturbingly plump and fuzzy spider scuttling across the countertop. Frozen in place, Gerald was held in paralytic fear, unable and unwilling to tear his stare from the great and menacing thing. So rapt in its travel across the counter was he that he never heard the extremely tall and silent man enter from the door behind the counter...if he did actually enter, rather than somehow materialize. Gerald often wondered about that.

It was Professor Spice's pale and bony fingers spanning the arachnid's hairy, meaty body and curving around it, taking it into a loose and confident grip that awoke the boy at last to his presence. Looking up, Gerald went through a series of alternating emotions in the span of a paper-thin slice of time. His first reaction was a start of heart-jumping proportions that there was suddenly a person here who'd not been only a second ago. This gave way to a fleeting relieved gratitude as he took the man to be disposing of the dreaded counter-spider. The following emotion lasted much longer, forever in fact, and that was a deep and stomach-churning revulsion and horror as that skeletal hand drew the spider's hairy body close to its owner's face and stroked its bulbous body with its other cold hand (Cold? How did Gerald know that? He hadn't touched it...) in a tender and loving manner.

His horror must have been reflected in his eyes, for Professor Spice smiled an amused and condescending smirk and said, quite quietly indeed, and with little animation in his voice, "It isn't fair to judge this as evil, boy. Do you think yourself so beautiful?" Then the strange, tall man did something Gerald would see in his dreams for years: he kissed the spider softly on the head. A wretched taste grew in the boy's mouth and he suddenly had an overwhelming urge to spit or to gag. He fought this, though, and as he did so, Professor Spice threw (actually threw!) the spider in what he at first took to be his direction.

Gerald started to duck but didn't have time; the ghastly thing flew over his head (Oh, he could feel it! He could feel the air—or the hair—brush the top of his head!). Turning, the boy saw for the first time a girl seated in a wheelchair in a corner near the front entrance. She was dirty, brown hair tangled and unkempt, and certainly unwashed as well, dressed in men's clothing that was far too big for her and whose cleaning had clearly been quite as neglected as her hair. The spider landed on the floor right beside her. She glanced at it, either afraid or intrigued; Gerald could not say which.

"Take her out," Professor Spice had instructed, and she wheeled over to it and (very bravely, in Gerald's opinion) picked it up and set it on the front stoop. Gerald noticed that the girl's wheelchair creaked when its wheels turned, but the sound didn't seem to give him the chill one might expect.

"Now," Professor Spice said, turning back to the small, mute customer, "what do you want?"

"That will be enough, gentlemen," Spice now declared quietly, and as if they'd been hit full-force in their bellies with cannon balls, the businessmen's laughter ceased. Instantly, the room sounded just as it had that morning on which Gerald had first entered it. The ticking of the mantle clock amid nothing else audible in the shop led Gerald unconsciously to glance to the countertop, half-expecting to see a bulging, furry spider ticking its alien legs across it.

"Gerald," Professor Spice said after he was quite satisfied that he was in total control of the room. "You have the envelope, of course?"

Gerald nodded uncomfortably, doing his best to recover from the agony he'd just undergone. He handed the paper envelope to Professor Spice, who took it gently between the tips of his right thumb and ring finger, never allowing his eyes to surrender their contact with Gerald's. "A moment," he said, turning slowly to the door and departing to the back room.

"Yes, well..." Cromby huffed, clearly perturbed at the situation. "We'd best shove off then, Simon."

"Of course, of course," his cohort replied, and they made their way sulkily out the door.

As his gaze followed them out, Gerald noticed that Molly was outside watching him through the window. Molly was wonderful. She was the only bright part of Gerald's visits to Cobble Road. She was kind to him and tender as well, though she was tough, crass, and hard and sharp as nails to the rest of the world. She was cautious around Professor Spice, though she wasn't afraid to speak up to him now and then when she felt especially wronged. Usually, however, Molly simply did as asked without question or comment, just as she had when Gerald had witnessed her dispose of the spider nearly two years ago.

The boy jumped at the sound of Spice's voice from behind him. "One pouch, as always." Gerald turned to see the tall, pale tobacconist extending the same two fingers that had claimed the envelope, now holding between them the golden drawstrings of a small, black, velvet pouch.

Gerald nodded his thanks and attempted a smile, but he found that this came with difficulty.

"Good day, boy," Professor Spice said then, with a tone that, to Gerald at least, sounded a touch ominous. The boy nodded again and departed the store.

As the door came to a menacing click behind him, Gerald attempted to rid himself of the chilled sensation the pipe shop had put upon him and managed a more confident smile of greeting toward Molly.

Molly had only been working in the employ of Anson Spice for a short while when Gerald began running errands for Mr. McGulliver. Her age was indeterminate, as Gerald was just a boy and knew very little when it came to the ages of his elders. Molly was older than he was; he knew that for sure. He guessed she may have been in high school or shortly out of it when they'd first met. Now, who could say? She was pretty, though, or at least he thought she was. Mind, he didn't find her attractive himself; rather, he could tell she looked the way a nice young woman ought to. She was also permanently seated in a rickety, creaking wheelchair.

Her face sometimes took upon itself a distant expression, as though she really were trying hard to see something very far away, like a person looking out across the ocean. He and Molly hadn't devised a secret code for communicating the way he and Scratches had, so whenever Gerald wished to know something about her, he was restricted to hand gestures, which she usually didn't understand. Gerald suspected she was sometimes pretending not to understand, however. Those mute questions she would answer were typically unimportant ones, simple questions referring to how she was feeling or what time it might be. She was secretive of where she'd been before working for Professor Spice, and Gerald didn't pressure her to share. Certainly she never let on where or when she'd lost the ability to walk, let alone how. This didn't matter, however. She couldn't use her legs; he couldn't use his voice. This commonality was unspoken between them, yet very much understood, and, to Gerald, greatly appreciated.

"How long have you been coming here, Gerald?" Molly asked the boy now, and before he could signal some sort of response, she continued, "Closing in on two years now?"

Gerald worked it out in his head and delivered a sort of "more or less" type of nod.

Molly sighed and looked in through the tobacco shop window, Gerald following her gaze. Professor Spice had seemingly returned to the back room, leaving the store vacant but for the many-colored pipes and tobaccos.

Turning back to Gerald, the young woman pursed her lips and sighed again. In her wheelchair, their eyes were nearly level. "Gerald," she said, and the boy heard the peculiar urgency of her movements make its way into her voice. "We don't have much time. It's important that you listen to me."

Gerald didn't like this side of his friend; it was making him nervous. Molly was supposed to be his reprieve from nervousness on Cobble Road. Still, he did trust her, and he listened.

"I can't tell you much right now. I don't know how much I can tell you at all. Right now, I just want to ask you two questions. Just two questions, all right?"

Gerald nodded. Simple enough, he supposed.

"But I don't want you to answer them."

Well now, he thought. *That is odd.*

"Not yet, anyway. I want you to go back to the hat shop and give Mr. McGulliver his tobacco, and I want you to think about these two questions as you do. Got it?"

Gerald nodded. Fair enough.

"When you've had some time to think it over, come and find me. Not when Mr. McGulliver sends you again. Before then. Don't come into the pipe shop either. Just hang back some in the area. I'll watch for you."

This seemed trickier. Molly couldn't know when he might show up, could she? He didn't want to argue, though, and the stench and gloom of Cobble Road was closing in on him, making him claustrophobic. He felt he might faint from the feel and reek of it at any moment. So he nodded his understanding that he might be on his way.

Molly nodded back. "Good," she said. "Then I want you to go back and think about these two things: One ... Why do you suppose Professor Spice always goes to the back room to get the pouch when all the tobacco is out there in the shop?"

In the few seconds that were open to him to process this question, the boy thought merely that this might seem curious, but hardly worrisome. This was struck from his mind with a force he nearly felt smack across his face, however, when in the very next instant Molly went on to say:

"And two ... When have you ever seen Mr. McGulliver smoke a pipe?"

The answer, of course, was never. In two years of employment and twelve preceding years passing him in the streets of West Cuttingsborough, not once had Gerald witnessed a pipe in the hands of Mr. P. F. Rutherford McGulliver, let alone between his lips. Did this fact startle Gerald? Perhaps. Confuse him? Maybe. Frighten him? Unlikely. There must, of course, be another, quite simple explanation, after all. Clearly, the boy told himself, the tobacco was for someone else.

Someone else? Really, Gerald? his mind retorted, forcing him to think on it further. *Who, then?* The only socialization Gerald ever witnessed Mr. McGulliver to be partaking of was with the odd customer in Hats for All Occasions, and those were brief, businesslike, usually uncomfortable and with unreasonably lengthy silences, and exclusively pertaining to hats.

So the boy conceded to himself as he made his way back to the hat shop that perhaps there was something more to his visits to Professor Spice's pipe shop. Perhaps. But if so, then what? What, exactly, had Molly been suggesting? Professor Spice was certainly a menacing character, and it could very well be that the addled and awkward Mr. McGulliver could be in some sort of trouble with him. But if this were true, surely there was nothing Gerald could do about it.

On the other hand, Mr. McGulliver had been very good to the boy. Gerald owed a great deal to his employer, and to suspect he might be in trouble and Gerald do nothing? The boy couldn't allow that, could he?

No . . . No, of course not . . .

But what . . . ?

How . . . ?

And here he was, then, at the door to the hat shop. He hardly recalled the journey back. Through the storefront window, the boy could see his worrisome, bookish employer taking down hats from shelves and hooks, patting them and inspecting them absently, then replacing them in the same condition in which they'd begun. When the doorway bell jingled, the little man jumped in alarm and dropped the hats he was holding.

"Ah," Mr. McGulliver sighed in visible relief. "Gerald. You're back. Yes, well…good. Yes, I, uh…good. Very well." With this, the little man took the pouch from the boy, glanced at the ornate cuckoo clock on the wall, double-checked its time against his own pocket watch, and nodded to himself. "Yes, yes. Quite right." And Mr. McGulliver scurried off to the back room of the shop, just as he always did, shutting the door securely behind him as he did so.

Well, now it seemed simple, the boy thought to himself. Clearly Mr. McGulliver enjoyed his one and only pipe per week in privacy and solitude immediately after receiving the tobacco. Thus satisfied, Gerald put Molly's unsettling remarks out of his mind and went about dusting and sweeping the shop.

Before parting for the day, Gerald bent down low at the coat closet, peering in to investigate the back of it. No signs of life appeared there now, but the crumbs had disappeared completely. He bade Mr. McGulliver "good day" with a wave and a smile (returned awkwardly but genuinely, Gerald believed) and made his way into the cool October evening.

The boy made his way through town, quite the opposite direction of the route to Cobble Road, with a skip in his step and a smile on his face. Passersby could not help but to tip their hats or wave and smile back, so engaging was the sight of this merry youth. And it did Gerald's heart good to share these glad greetings with his neighbors, some familiar, some strange to his memory, but all seemingly awoken and cheered at his evident joy of life.

Perhaps it was Gerald's own natural cheer that had him in such a fine spirit on his walk home. Perhaps it was his own love for the town he lived in, the streets he strolled, and the people he met. Perhaps it was that he understood why he spent his days not with other children in study but with grownups, learning the way of the world. Perhaps our protagonist in this little tale that started with a pouch of tobacco really was smiling for joy of life that evening.

Perhaps.

Perhaps not.

Perhaps he was merely trying to distract himself from having to determine why he had never smelled Mr. McGulliver's burning pipe, not today, nor any of ninety-seven other Thursdays before.

One person on the streets of West Cuttingsborough was not quite so cheerful. This particular individual was, in fact, quite distressed. He moved through the shadows, observing silently as Gerald made his way farther and farther from Hats for All Occasions, and when the boy was clearly out of sight, he crossed the street and entered the hat shop.

If Percival McGulliver was alarmed by the door's bell when Gerald entered, or the two other times it had announced customer arrivals throughout the day, then it gave him a genuine fright this time, when the shop was far beyond its regular hour for receiving visitors. Indeed, Hats for All Occasions never had any customers after Gerald left at five o'clock each day. That's not to say that Mr. McGulliver closed up at that time; simply no one ever came in.

"Oh!" the hat salesman exclaimed. "I..." This appeared to be all he could manage.

"Percival." Scratches O'Hannigan's voice was soft but cold.

"Ah, yes...O'Hannigan...certainly. Yes, well, right as, uh, well...rain. Indeed."

"Percival," Scratches said again, stepping closer to the timid little man. Beside the diminutive shop owner, Scratches O'Hannigan looked far more intimidating than he ordinarily would. "That boy works his fingers to the bone for ya."

"Who...boy?" This didn't appear to be feigned confusion, but Scratches stepped closer and said nothing nonetheless. "Gerald?" McGulliver said at last, brightening at the successful workings of his worried mind.

Scratches gave a single nod. He seemed now to tower over the other man. "Gerald."

"Well…I…yes! Yes, well…he's, uh…he's…a fine lad. Yes indeed, a fine lad."

"Then stop 'rewarding' him with frightening trips to the Tobacconist." He somehow managed to pronounce the capital T in the way he said this, clearly not referring to the shop itself, nor to any general unnamed pipe shop owner, but rather to Professor Anson Spice of 33 Cobble Road.

Percival Fairbanks Rutherford McGulliver's eyes widened and his head began shaking rapidly. "But, I…but…I…No, I, but, oh, I…"

"I don't know what sort of dealings you've got with Spice," Scratches O'Hannigan interrupted, "but I'm steppin' in now, Percival. No more involvin' the boy in it. It ain't right, Percival. You know that."

Percival McGulliver's face sank in frustration and imminent defeat. What could he say, his downcast eyes seemed to ask, to support his sending the boy to the most vile and despicable corner of West Cuttingsborough?

Nothing, the nod he at last delivered said in response. Nothing at all.

Scratches O'Hannigan nodded abruptly, satisfied. "Well, then. Good." He turned back toward the door. He paused with the door ajar, turning to look again at the little hat shop owner. "Are you all right, Percival?" There was reluctance in the bearded man's words, trepidation of asking the question lest it be returned with an unpleasant response.

"Oh, I…" McGulliver appeared to be startled by the question. But then, Percival McGulliver appeared to be startled by many things. After much stumbling of words and non-words, he at last settled for saying, "Yes…quite."

Did the hat salesman's eyes have a sadness as they looked on Scratches O'Hannigan for a final second before turning away? The fiddler thought that maybe they did…but he couldn't be certain. What he was sure of was that Anson Spice was trouble and always had been, even when he'd taught at the university. There had always been a shadiness to that man. Why had he been asked to leave his profession…? Scratches couldn't quite recollect. It had been rather a hushed and cryptic incident at the time it had happened, whatever it was, and it seemed now as though many had forgotten it altogether. In any case, the man could not be trusted.

And McGulliver? Ah, well now. That was something else entirely. Scratches had known Percival McGulliver his whole life; they'd been boys together. Percival hadn't changed much in his adulthood, which was to say he was as nervous and fidgety now as he had been then. This was, to many, an endearing quirk of a nice man's demeanor, but Scratches knew it could prove to be the bane of him as well. And now the lad had been dragged into…into what? Well, into whatever confounded mess his old friend had found himself in. That was, of course, the only explanation for someone like Percival McGulliver to be consorting with Anson Spice, or any of the residents of Cobble Road, for that matter.

Yes sir, there was a wrongness on Cobble Road, and Scratches O'Hannigan was determined to keep Gerald away from it.

Someone else was worried about Gerald. A teenaged girl who was so soft-spoken, one might think that she was as incapable of speech as her mute younger brother. Yes, Gerald's sister, Patty, was afraid for the safety of her sibling, and with good reason. It was she who had gone to the girl Molly in the hopes of enlisting her help in saving her brother's life.

But more on that later…

Gerald's home was quite small.

It was quite small with very few contents. Any surplus unnecessaries they had possessed had long since been sold or traded for food or new clothing. The cracks in the walls, the steady drip-drip leak in the southwest corner of the roof, the two stiff cots, the torn and patchy carpets, the peeling paint, the lukewarm (at best) water, the broken window, the dirty chimney, and the tired furnace were all things the boy and his father were accustomed to.

They were the only residents of the house, and had been for two years now, ever since Gerald's older sister, Patty, had failed to return home from work one day, not to be heard from again. Patty had worked for Mr. McGulliver in those days, performing most of the same daily tasks her brother did now. The family being in desperate need of money, the kindly hat peddler had been prompt to hire his vanished worker's brother to replace her. Schooling was a concern, of course, but with the proper documents signed by the boy's father and the required materials provided to Mr. McGulliver from the school, Gerald was able to accomplish both his studies and his duties every day in the hat shop.

There had been an investigation, of course. The local constabulary had exhausted every effort in attempting to locate Patty. As you might suspect, they had some questions for Percival McGulliver, seemingly the last individual to have seen or spoken to her. McGulliver was decidedly nervous and damp with sweat during the interview, but, as you also might guess, that did little to implicate him. Indeed, months and months of searching and questioning had led them right back to where they'd started, and still no one knew where Patty was, or even if she was still alive.

Now, as Gerald entered his home, the happy and shining mood that had followed him home found itself faltering as many of these memories crept into his mind. He couldn't remember his mother at all; she'd died shortly after he'd been born. Even Patty's recollection of her had been slight, "more like a dream than remembering," she'd told him once. And so, now it was he and his father, and the house was very quiet, for one could not speak and the other usually chose not to.

Gerald's hand gently touched upon his sleeping father's shoulder, and the man turned, eyes opening. As the boy's face came into focus, the man managed a faint and tired smile. He returned his son's touch warmly and whispered, "Gerald ... my boy ... home ..." The smile remained as the eyes closed again, and the tired man's hand fell back to the side of his cot.

The boy's smile of constant satisfaction gave way for a second, and he turned to the little house's tiny kitchen, which basically was a small refrigerator, a sink, and an old stove in one corner of the common room, which was the majority of the home. With no thought or hesitation, he set about opening a can of chowder and slicing some staling bread. As the father slept, the son warmed the soup on the stove. There was no butter for the bread, but there was a pitcher of water in the refrigerator which he poured into glasses. That would wash the bread down just fine.

When the supper was fully prepared, Gerald woke his father again with a gentle nudge on the shoulder. The man rose slowly, groggily, and brightened at the sight of the boy. "Gerald," he said. "You're home ..."

Gerald turned away and gestured to the table, uncertain if his face might be betraying his reaction to his father's failure to remember their earlier greeting. The father seemed momentarily confused by the food, laid out already upon the small wooden table, but just as quickly forgot his perplexity and sat down, picking up the spoon and beginning to slurp it noisily. Gerald touched his father's arm and shook his head, his father pausing with the spoon halfway to his lips. The boy folded his hands and gestured for his father to do the same. The man looked at the boy for a moment, at his hands, at his face, and down to his own hand, still gripping the spoon. Then he nodded, started to fold his own hands, found it difficult to do so with the spoon in the one, set the spoon in the bowl, then looked at the boy again questioningly. Gerald again gestured to his own folded hands, reminding his father of why he had set the spoon back down. Nodding his understanding, the man folded his own hands. No words were spoken, but eventually the boy unfolded his prayerful hands and nodded, smiling at his father and picking up his own spoon. The father needed not be told a second time. He picked up the spoon and began once again to slurp the thick, steaming chowder.

The father didn't speak during the meal. He slurped and crunched and gobbled and occasionally glanced at his son with an appreciative smile, at which the boy watched and smiled in return, relishing his meal less frantically than his father.

Through all of this, the two empty chairs that had once seated Gerald's mother and sister seemed almost to cry out and reach for any portions of the meal left untouched, seemed to look questioningly at the boy about where their owners had gone to for so long, seemingly never to return. Truly, Gerald knew his mother's death was a certainty from which there was no return. He expected not to see her again, or at least not for a very long time. Patty, on the other hand, he wasn't so certain about. Patty was out there, he supposed, somewhere, and the most haunting question in the young boy's life, far darker than that of Mr. McGulliver and his tobacco, was what had caused his sister to want to leave them so suddenly and unexpectedly? Or worse, what had forced her to?

He managed fairly well to forget the ominous words Molly had shared with him that morning, at least until he retired to bed that night. When that time arrived, and the lights were out, and the moon loomed overhead, there always seemed to be sounds that hadn't been there earlier, and thoughts that were easily pushed away or scoffed at as nonsense in the daylight seemed to trickle their way into the mind, prying open whatever small little gaps in the consciousness they could find and squeeze their way inside, mocking and laughing as they did so, watching as their host sweated and tensed in newfound fear and uncertainty.

Such was Gerald's state as he stared at the ceiling from his cot, covers pulled to his chin. To say that every possible scenario of what sort of trouble Mr. McGulliver might have gotten himself mixed up with was running through his mind would be untrue because he didn't have the slightest notion what sort of trouble the man could be in. He didn't like to think about Professor Spice, mostly because he felt guilty for having such bad thoughts about a person. He didn't know for a fact at all what kind of person the tobacconist was; he just knew how he felt when setting foot in his shop. The feelings of chilled foreboding, goose bumps that mocked and taunted and announced to the haughty businessmen lingering in the store that he was quite afraid, the dying, rotting stench of burning and unburned pipe tobacco enveloping him in its smoky grip, these things all told him that there was something not right about Cobble Road and its residents, this one in particular, and all he knew he could do about it was make his trips as brief as possible and attempt not to think upon them.

Lying in bed, of course, was, again, a different matter, and now it wasn't merely his own comfort that was being threatened; it was not simply the mockery and ridicule of the stuffy, over-vocabularized men of the shop. Now it was the safety of his employer that was at stake, and Gerald lay there in bed realizing in his muddied, sleep-threatened thoughts that it was his responsibility to do something about it, beginning tomorrow.

Dreams took him gently and without warning. They guided him through the streets of West Cuttingsborough, passing friends and strangers alike. There was Scratches O'Hannigan waving to him from inside the Fourth Chocolatier, calling him to come in and taste his new recipe. But Scratches didn't work at the chocolate shop, did he?

There was Mr. Olinoli, the owner of Lotsa the Pasta, dancing in mad circles and waving his arms as he clutched a spoon that somehow didn't drop the meatball that was in it.

"It's a-the biggest a-meatball ever to come out of the pot!" Mr. Olinoli was singing as he waved his creation around, and indeed, before Gerald's eyes, the meatball did seem to grow until it was larger than the restaurant it had been cooked in.

His father was walking next to him, humming a song and holding his hand.

"It's all going to be just fine, son," he was saying, and the tone of his father's voice told Gerald that it was the truth; it really was going to be okay...whatever "it" was...

And soon they found themselves turning the corner onto Cobble Road, and if it had been dark and gray and stinking of rotten death in Gerald's waking hours, it was something still less pleasant now. The stink was gone, but it had been replaced by a sound—a sound that the boy couldn't quite identify. It was a creaking sound, like a porch swing going back and forth...back and forth...and though he looked in every direction, he could not see anything that could be creating such a noise. In turning to look behind him, he saw that his father was no longer there, and neither was the rest of the town. Beyond Cobble Road, everything gave way to an empty whiteness that seemed to shake and waver like an old woman with a chill. He turned several complete circles, and every time he did, little pieces of Cobble Road seemed to give way to the same whiteness that had devoured the rest of West Cuttingsborough. Even the shops and decaying trees were vanishing, not before his eyes, but behind his back, when his face was turned away, until all that was left in the emptiness was himself and Professor Spice's pipe shop, which seemed to hover and wiggle its way from the side of the road until it was directly in front of him, staring at him, beckoning him.

Its front door was thrown wide by an unseen hand, and inside he could see nothing but pure blackness. The building itself began to fade in the whiteness, dot by dot, line by line, until all that remained was the rectangle of black contrasted against the white slate that had been Cobble Road. Within that deep blackness, the boy could see an even darker blackness of shapes moving through that black rectangle. He'd no idea what these shapes might be, but he watched in horror as they intertwined in a ghastly dance in the air. The boy couldn't pull his eyes from the treacherous sight as they gained speed, the black-within-black swirls racing, wicked and frantic. He stood there with his feet planted on nothing, his body still, staring hypnotized at the strange and ghastly sight, until at last his eyes somehow broke free of the dark boundaries of vision and could see right through the blackness and into the heart of the tobacco shop.

And there, in the middle of that tar-black pipe store sat his sister, Patty, on the other side of the writhing and dancing shapes, watching them from their other side as Gerald watched from this one, terror in her face, tears staining her cheeks, and unaware of her brother watching in the least. Gerald's attention and fear were torn between the menacing blackness and the sight of his poor, terrified sister, until he felt that he would likely explode from the tension. He felt his legs and arms tense, his teeth clench; his fists squeezed tight, and his eyes closed against the horrific spectacles before him.

He woke.

Perhaps it was the dream that slowed Gerald's pace on his way to work the next morning. Perhaps he was taking ill. Or perhaps the bread had been older than he'd thought and wasn't digesting properly. Whatever the reason, he found himself facing great difficulty in confronting the new day and didn't quite know what to do with such halting energy.

The ringing of the bell as he opened the door of Hats for All Occasions prompted Mr. McGulliver to look up from his absent-minded rearranging and situating of various hats and to smile his uncomfortable smile half-heartedly at the boy. Gerald found himself wanting to ask Mr. McGulliver if there was something the matter, if there was some sort of trouble he might be of assistance in remedying. Of course he could ask no such thing, not with spoken words, at any rate. Certainly he could have written him a note or even communicated concern through a simple questioning look. A genuinely sympathetic meeting of the eyes among friends can speak volumes more than the most stirring speech, if such is what is needed at a particular moment.

But his lack of voice was, of course, an excuse. It was an excuse to avoid exploring the realm of the unknown and of learning things he feared, of which it might be best to remain ignorant. And so he inquired nothing of his employer, but went immediately to his usual mundane morning duties.

Percival McGulliver looked on as the boy worked, still fretting about the visit he'd received from the street fiddler, Scratches O'Hannigan, the night before. He hadn't made his mind up what to do about O'Hannigan's demand, and he felt quite lost and befuddled, usually a comfortable place for his state of mind to reside, but much less welcome under such circumstances. After all, his dealings with Professor Spice were well under way. There had been much progress in their transaction and, unpleasant though the tobacco shop and its surroundings may be, the fact of the matter remained that the boy had thus far been completely unharmed. Why, the fiddler had more scratches in his own name than the boy had had on his whole body, at least any inflicted by anything on his ventures to Cobble Road. But perhaps the hat shop owner would have been less dismissive of the potential for harm to be found there had he been aware of the maddening dream the boy had had during the night.

Perhaps.

Perhaps not.

At any rate, Gerald worked steadily and quietly. The shop seemed somehow especially still on this work day, and indeed, by the end of it they'd not received even one visitor. Mr. McGulliver spent most of that time pacing back and forth, sweating, and appearing to be looking around for something he'd misplaced. When Gerald offered a helpful hand, however, the little man insisted that he was quite satisfactory. He also disappeared into the stockroom in the back of the store several times, usually only gone a few moments, but one time, it seemed to the boy, rather longer. He always ducked back there and returned in the same condition: empty-handed.

Finally, nearly an hour prior to five o'clock, Mr. McGulliver sighed and said, "Well, Gerald, I think…you'd best be off and… yes, uh, take this hour…take it to…well, uh, to yourself."

Gerald gave his employer a questioning look to be certain this was okay, and the man nodded quickly and waved his hand in a shooing manner. Gerald paid his second visit of the day to the coat closet then, depositing another meager meal of stale bread crumbs for his little friend, still unseen by his eyes but certainly in there somewhere. And with that he was off, the bell on the door announcing his departure.

After making his way partially in the direction of his home, he stopped and glanced around himself thoughtfully. He was thinking, really thinking, for the first time since last night, about Molly's words of warning and her advisement to pay her a visit when he was ready to discuss the circumstances. He felt now that his early release was disturbingly convenient, an almost prophetic gift from some unseen force telling him to use it to go see what Molly had to say. Shuddering, he turned away from the direction of Cobble Road and looked toward the way home.

Then he looked back.

He stood there for some time, trying to gauge his own feelings and get a handle on what his best course of action ought to be at this particular moment in time.

"Don't come into the pipe shop either," she had told him. "Just hang back some in the area. I'll watch for you."

That was reassuring, at least. While the idea of visiting Cobble Road voluntarily on a day other than Thursday seemed like grotesque self-inflicted misery, the notion of not having to face Professor Spice and his vilely unpleasant customers made it a bit more palatable. Gerald didn't waste another second. At the first glimpse of a motivating thought that prodded him in the direction of the pipe shop, he grabbed it and began to march forward, determined to see this through.

As the door shut behind the boy, Percival McGulliver watched as his small shape made its way down Pucket Street until he was quite satisfied that he was alone. He had intended to step into the stockroom the previous night to take a closer look at the tobacco he'd acquired, but the surprise visit from Scratches O'Hannigan had first interrupted this intent and then rattled him too much to think clearly enough to continue with it after the fiddler had gone. His lengthier visit to the stockroom that hadn't gone unnoticed to Gerald had, in fact, been for this purpose. But the contents of the pouch still must be put to use.

So now he stole quietly into the back room of the store and into his little office, where the velvet pouch was still resting silently and beckoningly on his wooden desk. Picking it up with gentle care, relishing its weightlessness, its scent, the feel of the plush velvet against his fingertips, he took it to the far back corner of the stockroom, where his small steel safe, not even two feet high or deep, stood upon the concrete floor.

Kneeling down on the cold, hard floor of the stockroom, Percival McGulliver dialed the combination that would spring open the tiny vault. His hands trembled and he swallowed slowly; it was a dry sensation and he was hurled into a wretched fit of coughing. When the spasm had passed, the little man pulled open the safe's miniature door and reached into its darkness. He groped in that blackness until his hand closed around a small iron ring that was attached to the floor, the safe itself being bottomless and leaving the concrete floor exposed on the inside. Turning the small ring between his fingers, he heard a clicking sound from inside the safe, and lifted the metal ring and with it a square of the very floor itself.

With his true hiding place thus unlocked, Percival McGulliver upturned the velvet pouch, emptying its contents into the square hole in the floor inside the safe. He paused, watching the darkness, perhaps waiting for something to happen (or not to happen) before replacing the square of concrete. The scraping sound as it dragged to its home had long since grown from a chilling one to a comfortable (and comfort*ing*) one. And even more naturally welcome was the echoing, stony clang as it dropped into place. McGulliver once again found the metal ring in the darkness and turned it in his fingers until he heard a gentle click that assured him the hiding place was again secure. He closed the door, spun the combination dial a few times randomly, and stood up with several grunts and groans, grappling for the surrounding shelves to assist him in the task.

Then he collected his belongings and went home for the night.

Cobble Road, Gerald soon discovered, was little different on a Friday than on a Thursday. The trees still stretched across the road in every bit as menacing and bone-like a manner, and the grayness that could be smelled and sensed as well as seen was no less thick than it had been the prior morning. And the buildings, well, if anything the buildings were worse. After all, normally Gerald's visits were focused on survival; his attention was set upon his goal, the tobacco shop, and little did his gaze on the line of buildings stray from that goal. Straight to it, straight back. But today he wasn't even arriving at the tobacco shop. Today he was simply meeting Molly at some unspecific, general location in the vicinity of the store, so it was necessary to look in other directions so as not to overlook her.

He noticed today the bent and twisted structures that were the homes and businesses along Cobble Road. Most of the buildings seemed to defy gravity in their ability to remain standing, so uneven and top-heavy they appeared. There were gardens in many of the yards, but what grew out of them certainly didn't appear alive, let alone appetizing. One old woman was actually tending to her patch of weedy growth, the "fruits" that sprouted from the gray and lifeless stalks wilted, warted, and discolored. With each rake of the hoe, the old lady overturned thousands of worms and grubs, whose bodies were cracked and sticky with blood and pus. Gerald felt a lurching in his belly that worked up to a not-quite-dry heave in his throat, and he promptly turned away and hurried past that house. There seemed to be little relief with each subsequent building, however, as each unveiled an ugliness of its own that spurred the boy to racing along down the street faster than before.

Soon he realized that he was close on arriving at Professor Spice's tobacco shop, and he forced himself to skid to a halt, recalling the instructions he'd received from Molly. He found himself beginning to lean against a tree in an attempt to appear casual to the locals, visible to Molly, wherever she may be hiding, and yet (hopefully) obscured enough not to be seen by Professor Spice through his windows. Indeed, on closer examination, Gerald realized that in many ways the tobacconist was the nicest building on the street. It lacked the ramshackle character of most of the structures, and where he needn't have worried about most other people seeing him from inside due to clouded and dirtied windows, Spice's windows were, if not as spotless as those of Hats for All Occasions, still quite clean.

He quickly jumped away from the tree when he felt something move in its bark against his back. Looking back at where he'd been leaning, he could see a bulge beneath the tree's surface that slithered its way in a zigzag fashion down the trunk and to the ground, where it continued its travel in the dirt and, upon arriving there, in the concrete. The concrete defied the very same laws of physics that the buildings did as it temporarily bulged to allow space for the traveling Thing underground, and it was coming right toward Gerald's right foot. The boy jumped away from it, still watching in mystified horror as it ventured on down Cobble Road until it was unseen.

Something touched his back from behind.

He jumped quite high and spun around, and had the boy been capable of speech, he'd have cried out as well. As it was, a sort of voiceless gurgle of displeasure seemed to escape from his mouth, but that was the most his mute body could muster, and upon coming to his senses and focusing in on the new Terror that had touched him, he merely saw Molly seated there in her wheelchair, smiling up at him in mild amusement and...and what? Sympathy? Perhaps. He couldn't be certain.

"You okay, Gerald?" she asked, and he nodded a brief "yes." "Good," the girl went on decisively, "because we have a lot to discuss." The boy nodded more tentatively, glancing around himself and thinking that he may not have the constitution to stand in the middle of Cobble Road for the time required to discuss "a lot." As if reading his mind (which wasn't very difficult; he was, after all, looking distastefully up and down the road with a visible chill), she quickly clarified: "No, no. Not here. Let's go somewhere. We shouldn't talk here." This last was with a quick glance to the tobacco shop across the street. "Come on," she said, and began to wheel herself in the direction from which the boy had just come.

Scratches O'Hannigan was fiddling outside the Beanhouse coffee shop when he saw Gerald approaching, accompanied by a young woman in a wheelchair. It was a curious sight, as he did not recognize the girl and Gerald was never seen out and about this time of day. They weren't even coming from the direction of the hat shop, nor were they headed in the way of Gerald's home. He lowered his bow and fiddle and watched as the odd pair neared. As they drew closer to the coffee shop, Scratches imagined he saw the boy's stride slow a bit, and that he may have glanced worriedly at his crippled friend. The girl didn't notice, however, and Gerald quickly looked back in the fiddler's direction and smiled…falteringly? Yes, there was no mistake this time in the man's mind. There was quite certainly a decided reluctance in the boy's greeting.

"Ah, good afternoon to ya, lad," Scratches said, sounding as normal and positive as he could manage. Bowing his head in turn to the girl in the wheelchair, he said, "And to you, then, lass. I don't recollect that I've seen ya in West Cuttingsborough before now, then, have I?"

Molly turned to look at Gerald questioningly, without responding. The boy nodded reassuringly, and she looked back to the fiddler, suspicious but willing to attempt to trust him. "I'm Molly," she said to him, businesslike but attempting to inject as much warmth as possible. "I'm a friend of Gerald's."

"Aye, I can see that. The lad's as good a friend to any and all as one could want, if ya ask me. Were ya heading in for a cup, then?" he asked, gesturing at the Beanhouse.

"We were," Molly said, and she said no more. There was a noticeable moment of awkwardness in which she was clearly obligated by the laws of etiquette to extend an invitation to join them, but this moment remained silent and unfulfilled.

But no worries in Scratches O'Hannigan's mind, then. He simply invited himself.

"Well, kids," he said, bending over and picking up his hat off of the ground, "I've collected more 'n enough today to treat myself to a cup of coffee and then some, if ya'd be wantin' to have me."

Molly was visibly annoyed. There was clearly more to this trip than a cup of coffee, and whatever it was, Scratches was obstructing her progress. But if the boy was involved, then the fiddler wasn't going to let go so easily; he saw it to be his responsibility to look out for the lad, and he would continue to do so, regardless of what discomfort may arise of the occasion.

"Fine," Molly said finally when it became clear that Gerald wasn't going to object, and they all entered the coffee shop. Scratches held the door open for the two youths, and he watched from behind as Molly, in the lead, went immediately for the table in the farthest, most secluded corner of the shop, almost invisible to the rest of the patrons and even to the workers, it seemed, as it took some time for anyone to notice they were there and to inquire as to whether they'd like to place an order.

In the interim between their ordering and the delivery of their food and beverages, Molly sat silently, and Scratches made several attempts to begin conversation. Gerald nodded or smiled good-humoredly, but Molly didn't speak a word in response or of her own accord.

The waitress returned with coffees and biscotti for Molly and Scratches and hot chocolate and a doughnut for Gerald. They ate their treats and sipped conservatively at their hot beverages in silence, and when the doughnut and biscotti were finished and the crumbs cleaned up, and they were sitting quietly, nursing their beverages, Scratches at last broke the silence, not with idle chatter this time but coming directly to the point at hand.

"I know ya've got somethin' ya need to be talkin' about here. I've got that, and I appreciate that." He was looking directly at Molly, seated in her wheelchair at the end of the table. Gerald looked on, but he might as well not even have been there at the moment, the other two were so fixed upon each other, completely unaware, seemingly, of his presence.

"You don't need to appreciate it," she responded.

"True enough, true enough," Scratches said, nodding amiably, "but here's how it is, then. This boy is my friend and, the way I see it, to a certain degree too, then, my responsibility. Gerald's a good lad, Molly, and I've sensed of late some danger that may be goin' on, then. I don't know if that's what this here is about or not, but if it involves the lad, then it involves me. Ya can trust me farther than ya think; I can tell that from the look in yer eyes, and lass ..." Here he paused and warmed his gaze, looking at her with a soft approval that gave her a start and some unease. "I can very much appreciate that yer tryin' to take care of him, if that's what yer doin.' I can appreciate that more than ya realize. But I want to help."

Molly looked at the man with the same guardedness as before, but with a lessened expression of distrust than had been lingering there since they'd met outside. She glanced at Gerald questioningly, and the boy smiled comfortably and nodded a very eager "yes" in return. She sighed, nodded briefly, and looked back at Scratches resignedly.

"Fine then," she said in defeat. "But this is as wide as the circle gets, got it?" She looked from one to the other, and they both nodded their agreement confidently.

"Aye then, lass," Scratches assured her. "No argument from me on that point. I'm not sure as I trust much of anyone else to let in."

"That's good," Molly said, "because the only reason I'm deciding to trust you at all is because Gerald is so confident that you're safe."

"I wouldn't have you trustin' me under any other circumstances, lass."

Molly nodded in a way that said that she was satisfied they understood each other, and sighed. She paused to take a sip of her coffee, then held it cupped in her hands upon the table, looking down at it as she began to speak.

"Gerald," she said, "what would you say if..." She paused and restarted, realizing her poor choice of words. "I mean, what would you think if I told you I knew where your sister is?"

No amount of consideration or imagining could have prepared Gerald for this announcement. His mind had been summoning all manner of outlandish possibilities or haunting threats since his meeting with Molly the day before, but no matter the height of horror of each scenario, none was in league with the question Molly actually posed to him about his sister.

Patty had been missing for two years now, and while Gerald had never surrendered hope for her return, he had come to accept her absence and the sad possibility that it may be forever. Now he was faced with a suggestion he'd been unprepared for and didn't know how to react to or to deal with, and from a person with whom he'd never even discussed his missing sibling.

Scratches clearly read all of this in the boy's face. The arched eyebrows, the gaping mouth, the widened eyes, and the drainage of color from the cheeks all spoke in loud clarity the lack of preparation he'd had for this question as well as his temporary inability to respond. The fiddler jumped in, allowing Gerald a moment to collect himself.

"Lass," he said carefully, not wanting to offend, but wanting to take care of the boy first and foremost, "that's a pretty great claim. Can ya explain it?"

"Not entirely, actually," Molly responded, not completely satisfied with the man's interjection on Gerald's behalf, but understanding of it nonetheless. "I can't tell everything, but I can tell you that she's in a place she'll never be found by anyone."

This did nothing to help Gerald's reaction, and he looked to Scratches O'Hannigan for help.

"Lass," Scratches said, a little more firmly now, "ya must be realizin' how that sounds."

Molly quickly waved off this suggestion in annoyance. "No, no, not me. *I* didn't take her, but I know who did. Well, actually, no one really *took* her away so much as *sent* her away, but I know where they sent her."

The others looked on with questioning faces, not interrupting, waiting for her to elaborate. Gerald was calming now, but was still clearly shaken.

"I can't say any more about that, except that there's something very secret going on, and if we can stop it, we could maybe get her back."

Gerald raised a questioning eyebrow, and Scratches said, "We?"

"You, him, whatever. The point is, if this thing going on is stopped before it actually happens, she could be back in West Cuttingsborough very soon."

Gerald and Scratches exchanged a questioning look, a more sophisticated signal than their usual system ordinarily called for. Gerald attempted to the very best of his ability to convey "What do you think?" but Scratches's look seemed to communicate the very same right back to him.

The fiddler turned to the crippled girl and asked, "What is this thing, then, that's so dire, lass?"

Molly pursed her lips, glanced at Gerald, then said, haltingly, "I think you need to see for yourself. If there's any evidence, that is. But I'm pretty sure there is."

"Girl, ya'd best be gettin' a bit more willing to share a few details if ya expect us to go along with ya in whatever venture this is."

Molly didn't argue; she knew that Scratches O'Hannigan was right. But she knew that if she divulged too much right away, they would simply get up and leave, and she couldn't allow that to happen. Gerald could see this frustration in her face, and though he was unable to read specifically what all of it meant, he did know that Molly didn't usually appear so helpless, so at a loss, and this was all the proof he needed that they should just trust her. The boy laid a hand gently on the fiddler's wrist to get his attention. As Scratches turned to his little friend, the boy shook his head slowly. Then he laid his other hand upon Molly's hand and nodded. He lifted his hand long enough to demonstrate a gesture that clearly said, "Lead the way," and Molly's frustration that was verging on tears began to melt into a satisfied and accomplished smile.

The girl nodded back decisively.

"Good," she said. "We need a plan. Gerald," and she leaned in as far as her wheelchair would allow her. Instinctively, both the boy and the man leaned in toward her to receive whatever information they were at last on the verge of. "We need to get into McGulliver's office. Do you think you can manage that?"

Gerald sat up straight at that, eyes widening. This abruptly gave way to an intense expression of "Why?" and he began to shake his head instinctively.

Scratches cocked his head to one side curiously. While this was sudden information dropped out of nowhere with not a touch of preface to suggest it whatsoever, the man found he was not truly surprised. "What are ya expectin' to find in there, lass?" he asked, caution lacing his words.

Molly shook her head in a determined fashion, making it clear she was still unwilling to tell more than was necessary; they would see for themselves when they were there, her face professed.

Sighing his concession, Scratches turned a questioning gaze to the boy. "Well, lad? What do ya say?"

It was Gerald's turn to look helpless. He didn't know what to think or to say. Even should he be capable of sneaking them into Mr. McGulliver's private office, he just couldn't comprehend how or why he should bring himself to betray his employer like that. Mr.

McGulliver had never done anything to harm him or cause him to want to sneak behind his back. This was more than the boy knew how to bear or to deal with.

The others looked on at him, concerned. The boy looked from one to the other desperately, hoping one of them would confess that it was all just a joke at his expense. At last, he could think of it no longer. He jumped from his seat, reached in his pocket, dropped some change on the table to cover his share of the bill, gave them each a final look of desperation, and then simply shook his head and exited the coffee shop.

At that same time on Cobble Road, Percival McGulliver was paying Anson Spice a visit.

"You're not supposed to be here, Percival," the tall man proclaimed quietly, gesturing him to be seated in the chair across from him at the coffee table in his office. They were in the back of the pipe shop, which, unlike Hats for All Occasions, was not closed. Professor Spice had no regular hours of operation, but rather opened and closed his shop based upon his own personal needs and conveniences. This was a method of business that Percival McGulliver could never have practiced. That sort of spontaneity was beyond his comprehension. McGulliver was a man of order, plans, and constancy. Change (and in particular, last-minute change) was not compatible with his character.

"I know, Anson, I . . . I . . . I . . . yes . . . I know . . . I . . . yes."

Spice shaded his eyes with a frustrated hand. He'd not spoken with McGulliver in a long time, and he had forgotten just how cumbersome it was to listen to the little man speak. "Just come to the point, Percival," he said, still looking down in an effort to minimize his frustration.

"Well . . . uh . . . It's Scratches, Anson. It's, well, uh . . . Scratches. See, he, uh, well . . . he's . . . suspicious."

Anson Spice looked up at this. "Did he say something to you?"

If McGulliver attempted to verbalize a response, he showed no signs of such; rather, he simply sputtered and flushed and pulled at his collar in a decidedly cartoonish fashion that only repulsed the professor even more so. Spice had had no tolerance for such foolish bumbling as a youth; he was far less willing to hear of it now. Of course, maturity had diffused some of the childish retorts and mockeries that he would have slung in Percival's face in those days, but what he spared the little man in spoken insult, he made up for in spades with expressions of disgust and impatience.

"Nevermind," the professor said, putting a stop to McGulliver's embarrassing display of worry and uncertainty. "He cannot know what he cannot see. He has no knowledge of our dealings, and if you continue to exercise prudence, I fail to see the problem."

"Of course, yes, I...well, certainly, of course...yes." This was either all Percival could manage or else all he decided was necessary, for not only did he not say anything further, he also clearly was not attempting to.

Spice was unsatisfied. He had as much to gain from this ongoing transaction as McGulliver did; more so, in fact, though the hat dealer remained unaware of that. It was imperative to keep the bumbling little man in check long enough simply to bring the task to its rightful conclusion. He'd managed as much thus far; it would be a fine show of slyness from the heavens to allow him this close to his purpose, only to have it snatched out from under him like a diamond in the hands of a night thief.

"Percival," he said now, his voice stern, almost a voice to be used on a child needing correction, "I won't allow you to fail this late in the operation. I'll see *you* brought to an end before this task. You do realize this?"

Percival McGulliver nodded rapidly, wise enough not to attempt speech, but communicating just as effectively without voice his comprehension of the severity of the situation.

"You expect council? On the O'Hannigan situation? Is that correct?"

There was more nodding from the feeble little hat dealer, who wrung his hands in his lap desperately, lest his ceasing of any motion actually result in his body exploding into small, messy pieces. Sweat droplets seemed to have formed on every portion of his visible skin, and Spice was quite certain he could smell it; his nose wrinkled in distaste.

"Very well, Percival. I'm not completely without decency and helpfulness. Here is what you'll do."

Percival McGulliver leaned forward, ever as nervous but fearful of missing even one word of the advice he was about to receive.

"You will continue as is normal in our businesses." He paused here, awaiting any slight sign of understanding from his peer. McGulliver nodded falteringly, attempting a half-smile. He seemed to think this was all he was going to get in the way of advice. Spice, however, continued. "Should our old cohort attempt to stand in your way, you will invite him for tea and cake in your office." Spice held up a silencing hand in response to McGulliver's opening mouth and worrisome eyes. "You don't keep the such stocked in your office, I know. But he doesn't need to know that. Simply invite him in for a chat, tell him you'll put water on while he sits and waits for you in your office, and return to him after a suitable water-warming time has passed. In this duration, you will have collected your tool of choice."

Percival McGulliver was attempting to follow this as best he was able, but the individual pieces of this very specific plan were seemingly more than his little mind could keep a hold on. "I, uh . . ." he began. His face contorted in the effort to get the question out intelligibly. "Tool?" he managed.

Anson Spice nodded slowly, a thin smile materializing on his face for the first time during the meeting.

"I don't . . ." Percival's voice drifted as a look of understanding was born in his eyes.

Professor Spice nodded, pleased that something had gotten through on its own. "Blunt or sharp, your personal preference, really," he said casually, appreciating and relishing the discomfort and dismay this suggestion was certainly creating in McGulliver's mind, quite visibly on his face. "My best guess," he continued, allowing himself to lean back more comfortably now, "would be that you'd be partial to something blunt to the head. His back will be turned to the door, of course, so it doesn't make much difference. But if you're likely to faint at the blood before the job is finished, or if you think you may lack the physical strength necessary to ascertain a mortal wound, then I should expect that blunt is the way to go. If things come to such a conclusion, lock the body in your office and send word to me. I'll assist with the disposing of it."

Percival McGulliver knew not what to say. This was more than his mind could process, and did Anson really believe him to be capable of such an act?

Seeing these thoughts in the little man's eyes, Spice stood up and made his way to the door, all the while maintaining his casually satisfied demeanor. "I need not remind you, dear Percival," he said craftily, "of what is at stake for you in this matter. You know what you want, and if you can't perform whatever may be necessary when difficulties arise, then you must determine whether you want it badly enough."

This was all he needed to say. McGulliver turned around in his seat to see the professor smiling down at him, the doorknob of the now-opened door in his hand. Nodding his understanding and his consent, the timid little hat dealer stood up, murmured his thanks, and took his leave of the office and the tobacco shop.

Once the little man had gone, Professor Spice sneered at the closed door and turned to a cupboard in the back wall of the office. Opening it, he pulled out a drawer that came out of the very wall itself. In the drawer was a lengthy row of filed white envelopes, the ones farthest in the back delivered by Patty, the last two years' worth by her mute brother, Gerald. Removing the most recent envelope, he removed its contents.

It was not money, as Gerald, and Patty before him, had been led to believe. Rather, it contained merely one unfolded strip of paper, upon which was written:

G 7 R P 92 v

He smiled softly to himself at the sight of it, of the feel of the paper betwixt his fingertips, and, stroking the paper gently and with deep fondness and appreciation, he replaced it in the envelope, securing it back in its place in the drawer, and locking it back in the wall behind the wooden cabinet.

Scratches and Molly carried on their discussion after Gerald's departure from the coffee shop, worried and discouraged at his reaction, yes, but unwilling to allow it to bring things to a halt. This was decidedly more difficult a stance for Scratches to take than the girl as he knew virtually nothing of the situation they were supposed to be discussing.

"Is there anythin' ya can tell me now, Molly, with Gerald out of earshot?" he asked, hoping that perhaps she'd been holding back on account of Gerald's closeness to whatever the situation was.

"Are you serious?" she responded, gape-jawed. "I didn't want to bring you in at all. I don't even know you."

"Aye, true enough, true enough. But I was hopin' as I'd maybe earned some more of yer trust." There was perhaps a tinge of sadness deliberately injected into this statement, in a shameless but (he felt) harmless strategy to tug at her sensitivities.

"You can't guilt me, pal. I'm not that emotional a girl."

"Fair enough, lass. But leastways there must be *something* ya don't mind sharin,' even with the likes o' me, so long as the boy's out of the room, no?"

She shook her head, not in a negative way, but rather in disbelief at how the situation had evolved into this. When she'd determined the time had come to bring the danger to Gerald's attention, she never could have predicted it would result in her sharing secret details with a complete stranger and with Gerald nowhere in sight.

"Fine," she conceded with a huff. "You must have some fears or theories. You wouldn't have been so intent on joining us today if something weren't already on your mind."

"Bright lass," he responded. "Fair enough and right enough, then. Right's rain, lass. I suspected."

"Suspected what?"

"That Percy McGulliver's gotten himself into somesuch troubles or others with Anson Spice. Percy sends the poor lad there every week to make some purchase or other, and the boy's clearer 'n crystal scared as a mouse every time. Not that he shouldn't be, goin' to that confounded neighborhood, and to see that no-good son of a lump of coal."

"Right. Well, you're half right."

Scratches O'Hannigan lifted a questioning eyebrow at this. "Which half, then, lass?"

"That there's trouble between those guys and that Gerald's caught in the middle with those stupid deliveries."

"Okay, then. Good, lass. Right, then what half is wrong?"

"That the trouble is Professor Spice."

It took Scratches a moment to process this information. He cocked his head at the girl, and for a moment, he looked remarkably like Gerald, his nonverbal cues conveying anything necessary to be said, with nary a word to be spoken. After thoughtful consideration and a returned slight nod of confirmation from Molly, he thought he was understanding her suggestion.

"Percival?" Scratches whispered in astonishment. "Percival McGulliver?" Molly nodded wordlessly. "*He's* the one puttin' little Gerald in danger?"

"The tobacco shop may not be pleasant, and Anson Spice even less so, but it hasn't been dangerous to Gerald. Not yet. But his trips there *are* going to get him in trouble. Big trouble. But that's going to come from McGulliver, *not* Professor Spice."

Gerald's father was telling the boy about his day.

This was something that occurred periodically, and had Gerald been a very different child (had he been Molly, in fact), he perhaps would not have had the patience required to listen to a man like his father relay the details of his entire day. It was a slow progress, these stories, filled with all sorts of disconnected and remarkably uninteresting details that would spur a less tactful individual to scream at the teller to arrive at the point, *please!*

Gerald, as you've witnessed already, was quite different. It was not in his nature to react this way, nor did it seem to those who knew him to be in his nature even to mind the storytelling to begin with. Indeed, if there were a fly lazing about on one of the walls of Gerald's home (and there very well may have been!), it may have been impressed with how genuinely intrigued the boy appeared to be with his father's plodding and difficult story.

Such was what it meant to be in a family, in Gerald's mind. After all, he'd lost a mother and a sister; he was *fortunate* to be able to listen to his father talk to him, wasn't he? And truth be told, it was often so difficult maintaining his father's attention that on those days when Dad wanted to share every mundane detail of his day (many of said details quite possibly being completely made up, born out of the man's childlike imagination), Gerald was quite eager to receive that kind of attention.

"It was fun, Gerald, but it's more fun now that you're home," the man concluded, and the boy smiled warmly, his way of thanking his father for the compliment. "Where were you, Gerald? I didn't know you were leaving all day, and I thought we were going to take a walk together."

Gerald made a gesture as if to be adjusting a hat on his head, his signal for his job at Hats for All Occasions. The man responded with an expression that shouted "a-ha!" but could just as easily have been entirely feigned remembering. Gerald wasn't sure, and he didn't much care.

After putting his father to bed and going through his own evening rituals in preparation for sleep, Gerald sat himself down on the edge of his bed and let his face fall into his hands. As always when faced with solitude in the darkness, difficult thoughts were much more difficult to be buried away.

Not that he'd successfully buried them so far. Though he'd been trying his best to absorb every word of his father's stories earlier in the evening, he couldn't seem to keep his mind from continuously returning to the things Molly had said at the coffee shop, and his mind was still just as muddled in confusion at how to go about making a decision.

That he may have already made a decision hadn't particularly occurred to him, but later in pondering the events of these days, Gerald would manage to confess to himself that he knew exactly what he intended to do even when he was standing up to leave the coffee house earlier in the day.

And so it came to pass that Gerald managed to remain in Hats for All Occasions on his next work day after-hours completely undetected. The weekend had been mostly uneventful, though his thoughts had rarely strayed from the events of the previous two days. He had stayed away from the town, allowing himself to believe himself completely safe within the confines of the four walls of his modest home. There were attempts at games of cards and checkers between the boy and his father, but those resulted in the same frustrating confusion as they always did, and the conversation fared little better. All in all, Gerald was decidedly torn between a desire to escape the restless tedium of the quiet weekend and the fear of what awaited him at the end of it. When eventually Monday came around, however, he found himself confidently yearning for the achingly dull hours of his safe two days at home.

The workday was no different than most, but it seemed quite as though it dragged far more slowly than any he'd been a part of before. He knew quite well what he intended to do, though he hadn't stopped to sit down and specifically formulate a plan. It was the only logical course of action, really, and it had been circling a just-out-of-reach corner of his brain since his departure from the Beanhouse the day before.

In all his dealings with his employer that day, he felt he repeatedly failed to achieve the necessary demeanor of normality that would keep all suspicion a safe distance away. But he didn't notice any unordinary behavior on Mr. McGulliver's part, no nerves that apparently exceeded the usual ones, and so he continued in the same manner for the remainder of the day, still in his own mind failing miserably at exercising nonchalance.

And so, he dusted shelves, organized back stock (there was much of this, as the merchandise on the sales floor moved at a deceased snail's pace), and left his daily bread crumbs in the back corner of the coat closet, performing the regular duties as the hours seemed to stand perpetually still.

His guilty conscience and worrisome paranoia were only solidified and worsened when lunchtime came.

"Uh…Gerald," Mr. McGulliver stammered, nearly too quiet to be heard. Gerald looked up, nervous at what might be coming, but painting a look of casual curiosity and cheer upon his anxious face. "Uh, yes.…I, uh, well…Today is the day, I think…yes, indeed. Today should be, uh, that is, our…our lunch. Together. Out. In the, uh, the town. Yes. Quite right. Our monthly…lunch. Together. Collect, uh, your things…my boy…and we'll, uh, that is…be off. Yes, off."

As has already been mentioned, once a month the hat dealer treated Gerald to a lunch at one of West Cuttingsborough's eateries, usually outside the boy's means and thus, otherwise unattended. Gerald felt his stomach lurch with guilt as he realized that he was about to be treated to a fine meal and dessert at the expense of his employer, the man whose privacy he was secretly planning on violating come closing time. What could he do? He certainly could not turn down the lunch; he never had before, and it would certainly be far too suspicious, wouldn't it?

And so they attended Lotsa The Pasta for their lunch, where Gerald picked half-heartedly at a giant, cheese-stuffed meatball and a Caesar salad served with the sweetest, most unique croutons one could not begin to imagine. If Mr. McGulliver noticed Gerald's lack of enthusiasm for the meal, he showed no signs of it. There was no conversation, though the boy did manage to smile at his employer a couple of times, simply to convey his thanks and to attempt to alleviate some of his guilt. There was little luck in the latter.

Mr. McGulliver did try to speak once, and his words chilled Gerald through to the bone. He was moving his meatball around on his plate, gazing down at it thoughtfully when the bespectacled little man declared, alarmingly close to stammerless, "Uh.... Gerald. You know you can always trust me. I do my best to look after you since... well... since your sister's... disappearance."

Gerald would have loved to have been able to look back down at his plate to avert the uncomfortable gaze of Mr. McGulliver, but his eyes were held secure in the hat dealer's, and he feared that his employer may see something of a look of doubt while looking back at him. Indeed, it would hardly have been astonishing had there been such an expression, as the look on Mr. McGulliver's face communicated something far from reassurance. In fact, the eyes seemed coldly detached to any of the meaning connected to the words being spoken, and Gerald couldn't help but think that the true meaning behind the man's words was that he could *not* actually trust him. And the only thing that kept his guilt intact and held him from complete emotional detachment from Percival McGulliver in that moment was the further impression that Mr. McGulliver just may have *known* that his eyes were betraying his meaning, and that this may have been his intent all along: to warn the boy.

Upon leaving Lotsa The Pasta, Mr. McGulliver led the boy, as was the custom, to The Fourth Chocolatier, where Gerald selected a sandwich consisting of two massive chocolate chip cookies held together by a nearly two-inch layer of chocolate buttercream. He kept this in the box, not opening it so much as to look at it, and put it in the bag containing the remains of his stuffed meatball.

They walked back to the hat shop in utter silence. Gerald could almost feel that Mr. McGulliver now had an impression that something had changed in the boy and in their rapport with each other. Granted, they had never been bosom associates, but there had been a silent comfort in their days together, and now that comfort was trickling away into nothingness. Gerald felt confident that the rest of the day promised it to get no better.

As closing time approached, Gerald plotted out the details of his plan in his mind, and when the time came to put these details into motion, he found them fall into place with disturbing ease. Mr. McGulliver instructed Gerald to begin gathering his things and call it a day's work, and Gerald did just that. He placed some bread crumbs in the back of the coat closet (he was fairly certain that his employer had never even noticed him perform this act of charity, but he was willing to take no chances, and although he intended to be around the shop a good deal beyond its closing, should Mr. McGulliver have noticed anything amiss, he would be given up), and he put his broom and dustpan back in the stockroom where they belonged. When he did so, his eyes settled upon the small cubic metal safe that was tucked away in the corner next to the shelves of hats. He had seen this safe many times before, of course, but today he was looking at everything in the hat shop with a different eye. He'd never seen it opened, and come to think of it, he'd no real notion of what was contained inside. He supposed he had assumed it to house Mr. McGulliver's money, but suddenly the clarity crystallized in the boy's mind of the inaccuracy of this; Hats for All Occasions had a bank account in town, and all but the cash drawer money required for the next business day was deposited in that account daily, and that money was kept securely locked beneath the cash register itself.

He forced himself to turn his attention away from the safe; there was no time or need to fixate upon it now.

That evening, while Mr. P. F. Rutherford McGulliver was preparing a deposit for the West Cuttingsborough Community Bank at the desk in his office, little Gerald bade him farewell, ventured out to the front of the store, opened and shut the door convincingly, then hid himself quietly in a cupboard on one side of the sales floor beneath a display of derbies. From this extremely snug and sightless hiding place, he eventually heard the sounds of Mr. McGulliver stepping out of the office, collecting his coat and hat from the closet, and setting out into the brisk West Cuttingsborough evening.

Gerald waited decisively and deliberately some time before venturing out of the cupboard. He didn't like the idea that he would be so late in arriving home; his father would be hungry, if not fully aware enough of his tardiness to be concerned or confused. He needed to see what there was to be seen, though, and dinner would have to be served a bit later than was customary tonight.

When he felt sufficient time had elapsed, he opened the door to the cupboard very softly to induce as minimal creaking as possible. As he did so, it crossed his tensed and anxious mind that Mr. McGulliver could have had every awareness that he was hiding here, that he could have used the same false exit ploy Gerald had to trick the boy in turn. The cupboard door was half-opened, however, and he couldn't close it now. And if he had, what good would it have done? He couldn't very well hide in a cupboard all night, waiting to see if the voice of Mr. McGulliver made itself known from outside of it, could he?

There was no one else in the room.

With a sigh of relief, he climbed out of the tight little cupboard, taking care to shut the door behind him, and with that he returned to the back room of the store. It wasn't until this time that his mind pointed out to itself that he truly had no idea what sort of thing he should be looking for here. Of course, that was his own fault for not having heard Molly out, but he knew that if this was going to be done, it had to be done by him alone, not with others accompanying him. The fewer people involved, the less dirty with sneakiness he would feel; this was the best way.

He started with the safe in the stockroom. He had never thought anything of it before, not until today, and now that he had, he was certain that its contents were important. Of course, he had no idea what the combination to unlock it might be. He randomly spun the dial back and forth a number of times, not really expecting anything to happen, but somehow suddenly wishing to feel the turn of it between his fingers, to hear the faint clicking of the dial as it sought its purpose, however unsuccessfully. He started to stand up and step away from the safe, and as he did so, it occurred to him that this was a rather curious place to keep it, right out in the open, set upon the floor. Why was it not in Mr. McGulliver's office, behind his desk or in some equally personal, private location? He bent down and grasped its sides with his hands, thinking to test its weight. To his surprise, the box wouldn't budge. He lifted harder, mute grunts building in him but unable to make themselves heard. Finally, he surrendered, let go, and cocked his head at the little vault. He wasn't quite certain whether it was very heavy with its mysterious contents or actually permanently affixed to the floor, but he had a feeling it was the latter. Perhaps, he thought, it was both.

Moving on to Mr. McGulliver's office, Gerald picked up papers, moved around knickknacks, and looked around at the quaint little wood-paneled room with a forced casualness that allowed him to postpone the inevitable. But he could only do this for so long, of course, and at last he made his way around the wooden desk and closed his fingertips around the brass knob on its long main drawer. He breathed in deeply, closed his eyes, and pulled.

There was next to nothing in the drawer—a couple of pencils, a pad of paper, some sales receipts, and a photograph. Gerald removed the photograph and studied it. It was of Mr. McGulliver, much younger, with a woman Gerald vaguely recognized to be Mr. McGulliver's wife. Gerald had never really known Millicent McGulliver, but he did recall that she had been his wife before she'd died several years earlier. How had she died? Gerald couldn't quite recall; Mr. McGulliver never spoke of her. Quite literally never, in fact. Gerald could not remember his employer mentioning his deceased wife a single time in his nearly two years working at the hat shop.

He replaced the photograph, reached deeper into the farthest-back portions of the drawer, felt them to be empty, and closed it again. He attempted to search each other smaller drawer in the desk as well, but he found those to be equally unexceptional.

The boy seated himself in Mr. McGulliver's chair and looked around the room in frustration. There were no other shelves, tables, drawers, or anything where something might be obscured. This and the safe were the only private locations Mr. McGulliver had. Gerald knew every inch of the shelves of the stockroom as well as he knew his own home, and he was willing to stake his life on the certainty that there was nothing odd or suspicious in any of those places. No, with every second that he looked around at Mr. McGulliver's small and empty office, Gerald grew more and more certain that the secret lay within the safe.

Then his eyes fell upon it.

Had it been there all along?

His head cocked, curious at the possibility that he'd overlooked it before.

It was so visible.

It was so clearly in the open and extending invitation to be inspected.

Three thin lines, two vertical and parallel, connected by a horizontal one at their tops, were cut into the bottom of the wall next to the desk.

A door.

Gerald swallowed nervously, feeling his muscles tense and his palms moisten.

Then he leaned over and tucked the very tips of his fingers into the top crack. There was, to his vision, no knob on this "door." It was, quite simply, three lines waiting to be pried from their surroundings.

A gentle tug proved to be unsuccessful.

A slightly more forceful one felt a budge, but nothing more.

A two-handed solid pull of strength, backed with a foot planted firmly on the wall beside the door freed the loose rectangle from the wall.

Gerald got down on the floor and peered inside.

In the small, carved-out piece of wall were all of the little velvet pouches he'd brought back from Professor Spice's tobacco shop over the course of the last two years, as well as all of those delivered by his sister, Patty, before him. They were strewn about in a messy, disarrayed heap, and they had all clearly been emptied of their contents.

There were other items in the secret compartment with the pouches as well. There were more photographs of the late Millicent McGulliver, a little black book, and a nickel. He picked these last two items up curiously. He studied the nickel and found it to be quite ordinary, but for a reason he couldn't have explained, found himself sliding it into his pocket. He thought for a moment that he had seen it before, that it may have been . . . but it was simply a nickel, as far as he could tell. It did, he noticed, emit a foreign odor that suggested exotic oils and ancient blends of plant life.

Then he turned his attention to the book and found it to be a journal. He thumbed left and right through the pages, and as he did so, he realized that he knew the hand-writing. He skimmed over a line or two here and there, taking proper care not to read too much too carefully, not yet at least. If this was what he thought it was, he didn't want to read anything too closely until he was mentally prepared to do so.

With a shaking hand and a ready gasp of tears caught in his throat, Gerald turned to the very first page of the journal. On the first page was the publisher's inscription reading, "This Book Belongs To," and on the printed line beneath that, the owner's name was hand-written clearly and legibly in all capital letters:

"PATTY"

It was his missing sister's diary.

Gerald turned to the first page and checked the date. It was from her fifteenth birthday. He remembered when she'd received the diary as a birthday present, and well he should have. He'd been the one to give it to her.

He turned to the end and found many blank pages. Then he began flipping back until he arrived at the last entry.

It was dated the day she had disappeared.

Gerald felt hot tears marking his cheeks and rubbed them absently with the back of his hand. He was shaking and had chills that were cutting through his whole body and soul. He collected himself as best he could and returned to the first entry of the diary and began to read.

PART TWO:
Patty

When Patty began working for Percival McGulliver, her first thoughts were about how much she was going to miss her school. She was in her third year at West Cuttingsborough High School, and all of the teachers there (including those who had never taught her) were in full agreement that she was destined for a bright and shining future. Patty was quiet as cotton at her desk and in the halls, prompt as punch with her assignment deadlines, and respectful as rain to her teachers and peers. Her academic work was a glowing example of what every teacher dreamed of seeing and what most students never dreamed to strive for, but she was shy about discussing her work and shier still about the accolades she received from the teachers.

You might expect that she would have difficulties with the other students, be teased out of jealousy, ridiculed out of a lack of understanding, or simply ignored because of her silence and solitude. This wasn't the truth, however, as the other students could hardly find fault in someone who was so genuinely considerate and optimistic, remote and quiet though she may have been. Furthermore, they could never mock or scoff at someone who came so utterly to life on stage.

Yes, Patty was an actress. In every school play, every musical, she never ceased to stun the directors with her auditions and everyone with her performances. She had made them weep, laugh, blush, gasp, and every other physical or emotional reaction an ambitious person of the stage could dream of evoking in her audience. Indeed, with the lights down and the music loud, costumed as another person in another place, Patty was free to speak as loudly, defiantly, hysterically, and absurdly as she pleased. And the best part? She was making others happy.

It was generally believed amongst the faculty and student body of West Cuttingsborough High School that Patty would secure an impressive scholarship to the university and pursue a successful career in the theater. She would enrich her mind through a diverse load of courses, somehow find the time and energy to perform in every campus production, perhaps even become involved in some other extracurricular clubs or activities as well. They envisioned her working at the university library, tucked quietly in a corner, shelving books unnoticed except, perhaps, by a single modest and equally introverted boy who would admire her from afar, too afraid to approach her and speak. This young man would eventually be unfortunate enough to be stumbled into in the cafeteria, thus spilling his tray of food all upon the floor. And he would be fortunate enough to have this beautiful and mysterious young lady of the library passing by to notice and help him to clean up the mess. They would go on to eat together, to take a walk, visit, share, laugh, and eventually to share their lives with each other. The young man would go on to become her biggest fan, watching from a different seat in the theater every night, never wishing to be a distraction yet forever unwilling to miss a performance. And their lives would continue thus happily ever after.

At least, that's how everyone envisioned that it would go.

By the time Patty was a junior at West Cuttingsborough High, her father's mental state had taken a sad turn for the worse. It came rather out of nowhere and was astonishing to many. He had always been a simple man of few words and many smiles, but he'd been a strong and supportive father as well. As his mental health continued to decline, however, more and more did Patty see the outward change in her father, less the quiet and strong man who'd raised her, and increasingly the childlike individual who relied on his children for the simplest of daily tasks. Patty had very little memory of her mother, and her father had been the parent who had seen her get to where she was today. Alas, he was no longer the man he once was, and it wasn't long at all before he was asked to leave his job of postal carrier. Patty knew what she must do. She must set her ambitions aside and leave school. She would have to go to work.

There was no "Help Wanted" sign in the window of Hats for All Occasions. In fact, there were no "Help Wanted" signs in any of the windows that Patty walked past in her search for employment. She entered every business, filled out the required paperwork, met with the appropriate people, and went on her way to the next place, fearing more and more as she pressed on that the applications were being promptly tucked away into a file drawer somewhere only to be forgotten.

"Well, we're not looking for help at the moment, but I'll certainly see that she gets this and has a look at it," said the girl at the register in the book shop.

"I'm afraid we just filled our last position," she was told by the manager of the Fourth Chocolatier.

"Have you tried next door?" little old Mrs. Sumkin of Tea is for Teatime asked her. "I believe Mr. Olinoli could use extra hands making pasta."

"I don't have anything right now, young lady," Mr. Olinoli declared. "Why don't you try the tea place? Maybe Mrs. Sumkin can find something for you."

And so it was wherever she went.

Well, almost.

Mr. Percival McGulliver of Hats for All Occasions offered her a job on the spot. There hadn't even been a "Help Wanted" sign in the window, but she had entered just the same, in the hopes that perhaps her showing interest might plant the seed of an idea that he could use some help in his head. As it happened, this was seemingly exactly what occurred.

"I...uh, that is...I can, uh, you see...I would like help...cleaning? I suppose cleaning, yes, and...errands. There are often... errands to be...run. That is, if you'd wish to."

This was followed by a more-than-sufficient quantity of ums and ers until Patty managed to smile her way backward out of the store, assuring him that she would consider the option and return the next day with an answer. Of course, there was the possibility that she might receive a better offer after the next day, but she didn't feel she had that sort of time to toy around with. Her father had spent many years delivering mail in West Cuttingsborough in order to support the family, and now it was her turn to do the same.

She had left the hat shop with a feeling of trepidation, not certain she trusted the funny little man with the stammer and sweaty scalp. She had seen him and spoken to him many times before, of course, and she knew his reputation about town to be a good one, most finding his uncomfortable demeanor and his nervous twitches to be nothing more than an endearing if a decidedly irksome trait. Patty had never questioned this interpretation before, but now...

Well, how was it that nobody in all of the town could be hiring except for one? Why was Mr. McGulliver so eager for her help if he hadn't even had a sign in his door?

These were questions she mulled in her mind quite on her own, not wishing to burden her father or her brother with such thoughts and decisions. They, of course, would have been quick to assure her that she should wait for a job more suited for her or, more likely, they would have told her she didn't need to work at all, that she should be finishing school. But she knew in her heart that what was best for her wasn't necessarily what was best for the whole family, and with her father sick and her brother still a boy, she could easily see that she was now in charge of the household.

And so, when nothing else panned out, Patty made her way nervously but confidently (at least as much so as she could manage) back to Hats for All Occasions to announce to Mr. McGulliver that she would gladly accept his offer.

"Ah, yes, well, I…uh, that is to, uh, to say…splendid. Yes, splendid." It wasn't an exclamation of delight; Percival McGulliver never raised his voice nor displayed too celebratory of joy. Rather, he looked almost relieved, his body seeming to collapse into a state much more relaxed than was typical for the man, nodding quickly as it did so. "Yes, indeed. Splendid."

McGulliver had never taken on an employee before. He'd never had the need as there was rarely much business. He made quite enough money to remain in business, but not nearly so much as to allow much of a life of extravagance. As Patty would later discover, however, the hat shop was merely a time-passing project amid a life that truly was quite luxurious. McGulliver, in fact, was the wealthiest man in West Cuttingsborough. But in his cardigan sweaters and with his thin, wispy, unkempt hair, and in his tattered and patched work shoes, he wasn't quite an advertisement for riches, and he quite preferred it that way.

Never having had an employee, he wasn't certain how to correspond with someone he found himself alone with for many hours a week. He found himself sending Patty on errands simply to be rid of the discomfort of conversation. Not conversation that he initiated, mind you, but always that begun on her end of it. Patty's initial qualms with the notion of working for McGulliver seemed to dissipate rapidly, and she was soon laughing at her own discomfort, calling it silly and unfounded nonsense. As awkward as the man might be, her days working for him were relaxed and quaint, and more importantly, they were putting food on the table.

And so life's transitions go, insisting upon changes we are certain we will always abhor, only to find upon waking one morning that we've accepted them, and another morning some time later we find that we've perhaps even come to love them, and we ask ourselves how we ever thought that our old lives were truly what we were destined for. So it was for Patty, who found herself with each passing month more engaged in her duties at the hat shop, always striving to do beyond better than her best work, always hoping that one day her enthusiasm and efficiency might induce a genuine grin upon Mr. McGulliver's face, something more open, honest, and joyous than his typical half-smile of discomfort and anxiety.

She saw that smile once. It was the day she first was sent to the tobacco shop on Cobble Road.

"Uh...Patty," Mr. McGulliver said to her that Thursday morning, a look of nervousness painted clearly upon his face, and yet, she imagined, not the usual nervousness. This morning her employer seemed more, well...perhaps more immediately...concerned? Anxious? Possibly. She couldn't quite seem to place how the look was different. It would only occur to her much later that it seemed as though it was the first time Mr. McGulliver looked as though he actually had something to be nervous about.

"Yes, sir?" the girl responded dutifully, standing before him with perfect posture and a proper smile, hands clasped neatly behind the back of her yellow dress.

"You, uh, wouldn't...that is...I need an errand. If you wouldn't, uh, mind? Too terribly much? Perhaps?"

Smiling and nodding reassuringly, the young woman assured him of her glad compliance.

The hat shop owner relaxed only a very little, and as quickly as his demeanor would permit, continued on to explain the nature of the errand. "Yes, well, I...thank you. I'm...well, that is, I am... grateful. Yes, grateful. It is...that is...you'll need to go to...you'll go...to Cobble Road." The hat salesman's voice became little more than a whisper on these last two words, and though he'd been looking down at the floor or around the shop for most of the time he'd been speaking, his eyes found their way slowly to her after he said this, appearing to assess Patty's face for a betrayal of her sudden refusal or at least distaste or fear at the prospect of journeying to the least respectable part of West Cuttingsborough.

But if these feelings were felt, betray them her face did not. She simply nodded officially and said, "Yes sir. And where on Cobble Road shall I go?"

And so it came to pass that Patty began the tradition of the delivery of the paper envelope in exchange for the velvet pouch full of pipe tobacco, a weekly excursion that her brother would pick up in her stead after her mysterious disappearance.

Cobble Road was every bit as horrid in Patty's eyes as it would eventually be through Gerald's, but at the same time, it did not instill the fear in her that it would in the boy, and indeed, that it would in most residents of West Cuttingsborough. She heard people speak of it, and she'd seen her boss's face when he first instructed her to make the trip to the pipe shop, and had she taken the time to step outside her own mind and attempt to examine herself, she may have credited her lack of paralytic fear for the dread corner of town to the many plays in which she'd performed. Entertainment always required a good degree of evil, of danger, or else where would be the story? And so her constant surrounding of herself in these imaginings, these horrors, these darknesses and sinister goings-on had perhaps numbed her to the shock of a place like Cobble Road. Indeed, the street merely inspired her imagination. She would walk down it and feel inclined to write a play of her own, telling the tale of the eccentric shopkeepers who resided there and of their fiendish plots to take over the rest of the town through their black magics and cunning deceptions. And, of course, Anson Spice would be the principle antagonist to lead the bunch.

At the time of her disappearance, she had still not found the time or opportunity to put the idea to paper.

The ever-loyal and optimistic young lady never said a word of her ventures to Cobble Road to her father. Feeble-minded though the man may have appeared, this state of mind was something that remained unspoken of between Patty and her brother. They needn't have spoken of it; they both knew the other was aware of it. They certainly didn't ignore the problem; they simply didn't call each other's attention to it. And so, despite the fact that the father may have been entirely incapable of processing just what his daughter meant when talking about errands to Cobble Road, she chose not to take that chance. Worrying was to be her responsibility now.

That's not to say that she didn't speak of it to Gerald, however. One shouldn't be fooled by Patty's secretiveness from her sibling when she'd set upon the streets of West Cuttingsborough in search of employment. That had been a rare instance of one or the other of the siblings withholding valuable information from the other, and Patty had paid for it. If she thought she was accustomed to the boy's inherent silence, she was given quite a shake by the many-day *active* silence he treated her with when he'd realized she'd not included him in the decision or the process.

Yes, the two were closer than any pair of good friends could be, and then some. And who better to speak of the haunting neck of her hometown to which she was made to travel once a week than with her younger brother? Gerald, of course, being a young boy, absolutely gobbled these stories to pieces. They were, after all, delivered as such: stories. Consider the source: Patty wasn't genuinely afraid of Cobble Road, nor of Professor Spice, and when she told the stories of them to her brother, unaware though she may have been how therapeutic the telling was for her surprisingly afraid and disturbed subconscious, she told them in the voice of a narrator, of a storyteller, in the safety of home and comfort, with the Voice of the Fantastic.

Once, Gerald asked her to take him along to work one day, and in particular on a Thursday, that he might witness these mysterious sights for himself. It was in the evening on Wednesday, after their father had retired to bed for the night, and Patty was speaking absently about some of the things she needed to get done at the hat shop the next day. When Gerald collected her attention with a touch on the arm and then pointed to himself and then to her in a "take me along" gesture, the girl merely interpreted it as a sweet and generous offer of assistance, which she promptly dismissed with gracious thanks. When the boy shook his head adamantly, pointed to himself and to her again, and then folded his hands in a sign of plea, she was a bit more taken aback to come to the realization that her brother really did *want* to attend the work day with her, Cobble Road and all, that he wasn't simply offering his assistance out of courtesy and familial duty.

This disturbed Patty, though she wasn't quite certain why. Could it be that she realized then how she'd sugar-coated the makeup of her days, and her trips to Cobble Road in particular? She supposed perhaps she had, and that now her brother's caution had suffered at the hand of a taste for adventure. Who could blame the boy? Of course he wanted a change in routine, a day away from classes, as most young people do. Patty wasn't unaware of how extraordinary her perpetual, undying love for classrooms and textbooks was, and it pained her now to think of how much she envied her brother, who didn't even seem to understand what a good thing he already had.

Touching Gerald's arm in return, Patty said as gently as she could, "I really appreciate your wanting to help, and I completely understand your curiosity, but trust me when I say that you're much better off at school. My work really is pretty dull most of the time, and there are times when . . . well, when I'd rather you not see . . . certain things."

She hadn't wanted to say that last part, knowing that the concern would escalate in him and make him even more persistent on seeing what went on during her days, but she just could not bring herself to allow Gerald to believe that she was snobbish enough simply not to want him along; it was important that he realize there was a reason for her refusal to have him there.

Gerald certainly wasn't weak or cowardly, but he was by all means respectful of his sibling's maturity, wise judgment, and especially her authority over him in the household, and he let the matter drop, unaware that with just a little patience, he would indeed witness the goings-on of a day of work at Hats for All Occasions and the weekly visits to the tobacconist on Cobble Road.

Patty's closest friend was a girl by the name of Madeleine, and it was through her that Patty managed to remain apprised of the goings-on at West Cuttingsborough High School, where she'd left her studies, her friends, her teachers, and her performing behind.

"Denise Caffagil is playing Hippolyta in *A Midsummer Night's Dream*," Madeleine told her in disgust, "as though she even understands what she's saying when she says her lines!"

Patty wouldn't display the same disdain that her friend was quick to feel; she was more patient with people and things that Madeleine had little tolerance for. You might suspect that this quick-tempered disgust and intolerance in her friend may have been an unattractive quality to Patty, but this was hardly the case; she accepted Madeleine's difficulty in this area just as she accepted Denise Caffagil's inability to perform well on stage. After all, she had befriended Madeleine as Madeleine was; why should she want her to behave differently now? And didn't Denise Caffagil have every bit as much right to a part in the play as anyone else? She, too, was a student at the high school, and awkward and misinterpreted though her acting parts might have been, no one could deny Denise's ambition and love for performing.

"Well, I can't wait to see the show for myself," was all Patty would reply.

"Patty," Madeleine replied, the same disbelief in her eyes as with every other reaction her friend demonstrated to the news of what she was missing at school. "Doesn't it kill you? Doesn't it absolutely eat you alive for dinner?"

To these sorts of pointed questions, Patty would pause and reflect, seem to chew the question contemplatively for a couple of moments, but would always respond with a comparatively similar answer as the last time.

"What is *is*, and what may have been isn't for us to assume. It didn't happen the way I'd planned for a reason, and all I can do is press forward on the path that's been chosen for me."

"But it *wasn't* chosen for you, Patty! You chose it yourself! Don't you see? It all could have been prevented! And it could still be fixed! That's what I really can't understand, Patty, is why you let it happen this way, why you don't turn right around and come back to school."

"I have responsibilities, Maddy. You know that."

"Everyone misses you, Patty."

"And I miss everyone right back; you *know* I do. But I can't come back. Not as long as I'm in charge of the household."

Of course, even Madeleine had no response to that, as that was the determining factor, was it not? She wasn't willing to throw the matter of a sick father in her best friend's face, not even in the attempts to win her back in her company in the grueling days at West Cuttingsborough High. Rather, she could merely silently concede and move on to other news with less commentary on what she felt Patty ought to do.

As for Madeleine's claims of Patty being missed, well, that couldn't have been truer. Her name was always surfacing in conversations amongst both faculty and the student body, finding its way into such remarks as "When Patty was here" or "That's not what Patty would have thought" or "Oh, how Patty would have loved to have seen that!" Each day that she was away grew not easier for those she'd departed, but only more difficult.

She still saw many of them in town, of course, but her time in town was limited due to her busy days at the store. Once she'd been relieved for the evening, it was customary for her to make her way straight home (unless groceries needed to be purchased first) in order to prepare dinner and clean the house. But many visited her at Hats for All Occasions when they had the opportunity, teachers and students alike. Indeed, the hat shop saw more traffic in Patty's days working there than in any period prior or since. That they didn't enter the establishment for the purpose of finding a hat hardly seemed to matter; many, while there, found themselves discovering one to their liking anyhow, and while Percival McGulliver was usually stifled and overwhelmed by the increased number of visitors to his store, he was grateful for the increased profits the young lady seemed to have brought to him.

What of the boys, though, you may be wondering? Certainly a young woman of Patty's influence at the school must have received a good deal of attention from her male peers. Actually, as you may or may not have noticed in your own lives, often someone as good and humble and private and soft-spoken as Patty draws less attention in the way of love interests, for the simple reason that such people's apparent perfections are intimidating to those who feel they can't possibly live up to such a high standard, never realizing that girls such as Patty never hold anyone to unreasonable expectations.

There was one young man, however, who loved Patty dearly and who would suffer her disappearance probably every bit as much as Madeleine and her other friends. This boy's name was Stuart Freeley, and he was the student stage manager for Mr. Batchley, the high school's drama director. In all the school musicals and plays, it was Stuart who helped with such things as organizing props, prompting students with their lines, fetching necessities, and seeing to all the smooth goings-on backstage during the rehearsals and performances. He was an awkward boy, Stuart was, and what confidences he did have came entirely from the positive treatment he always received from Patty.

Whether Patty was romantically interested in young Stuart or whether she was simply bestowing upon him the same kindly treatment as she'd give any of her high school peers (or any adults, for that matter), no one was quite certain, and no one ever found out, as it had still remained unclear at the time of Patty's vanishing.

"Stuart's hardly said a word during rehearsals without you there, Patty," Madeleine informed her one Saturday as they walked with ice cream cones through the streets of downtown West Cuttingsborough.

"Stuart never said much, Maddy. You know that," Patty returned, with a lighthearted laugh and a lick of a drop of mint chocolate chip that was preparing to fall from the materialized hole in the bottom of the cone.

"No, it's different. He's ... I don't know ... sad, I guess." Madeleine took a taste of her own blue moon ice cream cone and looked at her friend to gauge her reactions to what she was telling her. If there was anyone who knew truly how Patty felt about the bashful stage manager, it was Madeleine, though many suspect that on this subject, even Madeleine was in the dark, as she seemed every bit as curious and frustrated by it as everyone else.

Patty stopped walking and turned to study her friend's face with care. After a moment of this scrutiny, Madeleine became uncomfortable and looked around her and back at her friend. "What?" she said, more defensively than she'd intended. "What is it?"

"I just wonder, Maddy," Patty said thoughtfully, "why it is that everyone else, including my very best friend, seems to be more interested in whether or not I'm interested in Stuart Freeley than I am!" And with a laugh and an appreciative shake of her head, she continued on her way down the street, leaving Madeleine as perplexed and unenlightened on the matter as before.

While no one could be certain what went through Patty's head with regards to Stuart Freeley, it was no secret to anyone that Stuart Freeley was very much in love with Patty. Perhaps this was partly another reason why very few boys expressed an interest in her. Many assumed that if Stuart and Patty weren't a couple already, that they would be some day, or that they certainly ought to.

Without Patty to help draw Stuart into the spotlight now and then, he would have gone through four years of high school virtually unnoticed. In fact, it was Patty who first landed him the position of stage manager during a school production of *Brigadoon*, when Katrina Katsbury, who'd served as exclusive stage manager for three years, suddenly and unexpectedly had to move away due to her father's job.

"Patty," Mr. Batchley asked her as he pulled her aside on the way to lunch one day. "If you know of *anyone* who might be proper for the job of stage manager, *please* give me their name. I'm at a loss. I think Katrina's done more work in preparing the last several shows than I have, and I'm in a panic to be without her."

Unhesitatingly, Patty smiled and proclaimed, "Stuart Freeley would be wonderful, Mr. Batchley. I think it'd be good for him, and he'd do an outstanding job. You have my word."

The drama teacher stared at the girl dumbfounded for a moment, then cocked his head, peered more closely at her, and said, "Who?"

At this the girl laughed her trademark laugh, which seemed unfailingly always to throw her whole head back in genuine amusement, and she repeated with delight, "Stuart Freeley. He sits next to me in my Geometry class."

"Oh. Well," the man said, uncertain, but reminding himself that he'd asked for Patty's opinion for a reason; he trusted her. "If this… Stuart has your seal of approval, then consider him hired. You'll ask him?"

"I'll tell him," she responded and went on her way.

This, as it turned out, was a significant correction, subtle and undetected by Mr. Batchley though it may have been. For once Patty reported to the cafeteria, before entering the food line, she scanned the large room in search of her shy friend. She found Stuart seated with one other boy, Duncan Morley, equally awkward and silent, both of them eating their respective lunches in shared solitude, seemingly aware of each other but not choosing to share in each other's company.

"Hi, guys," Patty said as she approached their corner table. Both boys looked up in surprise and fear, then attempted to turn back to their meals, but found themselves unable to look away from the pretty girl's smile. "Stuart?" she said when it became clear they weren't going to verbalize any sort of greeting. (This didn't bother the girl, however; obviously she was accustomed to being around a silent teenaged boy.) "Mr. Batchley needs you to take over for Katrina as stage manager for the show."

That was all. There was no further explanation, no inquiry whether this was okay with him, no waiting for a response of any kind (not that any most likely would have been quick in coming). The girl merely stated it as a fact, declared that she'd be looking forward to seeing him at rehearsals, and went on her way to the lunch line, where she proceeded to fill her tray with fruit salad and granola cereal.

Such was the way of Patty, and where some people acting in this manner would be insulting, tiresome, and anything but attractive, it was this simple acceptance of life as it came to her and the assumption that everyone around her was equally easy-going and optimistic that made everyone love her, especially Stuart Freeley.

Of course she knew what she was talking about. Stuart became almost as good a stage manager as Katrina had been before him, if he was a little time coming to that status. Timid and uncertain at first, by the time Patty found herself having to leave West Cuttingsborough High School, Stuart was a confident expert at all the inner and outer workings of a live stage production.

"I don't know how you knew, Patty," Mr. Batchley told her once after a smashingly successful opening night of *A Christmas Carol*, "but you were absolutely right about Stuart. You certainly have a good sense about people, don't you?"

Alas, not quite good enough, as it would turn out.

When Patty announced her departure to her classmates and teachers, most everyone attempted to talk her out of it. They all had their own reasons for wanting her to stay, and they all had their own suggestions of why it was a mistake for her to leave. It became somewhat of a competition amongst the students and teachers to try and be the one who would find the magical words that would change the girl's mind. Of course, in the end they realized to their mutual surprise that there were no magical words, and there was no changing her mind.

During that period, Stuart was one of the few who remained silent on the issue. Not once did he declare what a mistake it was for her to leave, or how negatively his life would be altered in her absence. He uttered merely one statement on the issue, and that was on the evening of Patty's final performance on the stage of West Cuttingsborough High School's auditorium, a comedy written by Mr. Batchley himself entitled *The Fantastic Culinary Caper*, in which a group of chefs at a baking contest are hurtled into the middle of a murder mystery when the head judge turns up missing.

"Wonderful show, Stuart. Great job!" she commended him after the curtain call.

Stuart smiled his gratitude and said in his tender and gentle voice, the blood rising to his cheeks, "You were really great, Patty. That was a terrific French accent. I can't believe you can play mean so well."

She laughed her head-throwing laugh and thanked him, and he said, with the greatest sincerity, "I'm going to miss you, Patty. I'll miss you very much." And before she could respond, he picked up his belongings, waved his goodnight to Mr. Batchley, and made his way to the exit. It's possible that in that slight moment, Stuart Freeley witnessed more disarming of Patty than anyone ever had. She was taken aback by Stuart's frank honesty and its lack of any hunt for personal gain attached to it. It was, perhaps, at that moment that Patty first realized just how much she was going to miss being at the school. It was, perhaps, also at that moment that she fell in love with Stuart Freeley.

As Patty and Madeleine continued to make their way through the streets of West Cuttingsborough, still attempting to eat more of their mint chocolate chip and blue moon than ended up on the sidewalk, Madeleine became aware that she had been following Patty's lead through the streets for some time now, and that they weren't walking in the direction of any of their usual points of interest in the city. In fact, she realized, they were drawing uncomfortably near to Cobble Road.

Stopping in her tracks, Madeleine said, "Why are we going this way?"

Patty stopped, staring blankly, and turned to take in her surroundings, as though she'd had no idea where they were or toward what they had been going. "Oh," she said, coming to the realization of just what part of the town she'd been leading her friend. "Wow, I…I don't know, Maddy."

There was no doubt in Madeleine's mind whether or not to believe her friend; Patty was clearly as surprised as she was to find where they'd come to be.

"I guess…it must have been habit." She didn't usually like to speak of her travels to Cobble Road with Madeleine, as she knew very well the judgmental and disapproving looks and remarks she'd receive. She'd seen and heard them before, and she'd put a stop to them by pointing out that Madeleine had never even set foot in that part of town, and how could she judge what she hadn't seen for herself? But Patty knew quite well that this defense would only hold up for so long, that it was only a matter of time before her friend retorted with "I don't need to go" or something of that sort, to which there would be no response. Cobble Road, after all, had earned its reputation over a course of many decades, and it was common knowledge in all of West Cuttingsborough that it was a neck of town from which to veer away.

Now, however, she was thrown off-guard by her unconscious route to that dark part of the city, and her defenses were down.

"Listen, Patty," Madeleine said urgently, "I know you do some weird things for the hat guy, and I don't like it, but I don't bug you about it either. You've made it clear that you're happy doing what you're doing and that you want to be left alone, so I don't say a word, do I?"

Patty nodded approvingly and sincerely. "Yes, that's true, Maddy."

"So just because I don't say anything doesn't mean I suddenly approve of the whole thing. So don't think that just because you're suddenly okay with being…over there," she said, gesturing vaguely with a hand in the direction of Cobble Road, "that I'm suddenly okay with it too. 'Cause I'm not."

Patty nodded firmly to show her complete understanding. "I know, Maddy. I know that, and I'm very sorry. Come on; let's go back downtown to Page-Turners. I want to see if they'd be willing to stock copies of Mr. Batchley's plays. I always told him to ask, but he never would."

She started back in the direction toward downtown, but Madeleine was slow to follow, uncertain what to make of her friend's unexpected detour, and perhaps even more concerned with how surprised Patty had been herself with it. What was the job doing to her, that she found herself walking to Cobble Road without any care and completely unaware that she was doing so?

With a shudder, Madeleine followed her to the bookstore.

As would later be the case with her brother, Patty never questioned her employer's weekly purchase of seemingly unused tobacco. Unlike Gerald, however, Patty did notice on her own the peculiarity of his sending her for tobacco at the same time of the same day every week; she simply didn't see any sort of threat in that. In all fairness, though, most likely neither would Gerald if he hadn't been forced to by Molly's cautionary words. Patty, however, simply saw it as another quirk of her loveable and eccentric boss, and she certainly didn't see that asking him about it was any of her business.

And so she pressed on with the deliveries, remaining oblivious, for the time being anyway, of Mr. McGulliver's treacherous plans.

When Mr. McGulliver one day asked Patty about her family, and showed particular interest in Gerald, Patty was quite delighted to find that the meek little man appeared to be drawing further out of his shell. It pleased her to know that she'd helped to accomplish this, and she satisfied his questions with detailed and unfiltered information.

In all fairness to the poor girl, she probably didn't tell McGulliver anything he didn't already know or suspect, and had she suspected something was afoot and thus chosen her words (or lack of words, as the case may be) with greater care, in all likelihood the outcome would still have been the same.

"He's, uh, that is ... your brother ..."

"Gerald," she helped him, while spraying a glass shelf and wiping it clean, relishing the squeaking sound of the washcloth as it spread the spray across the glass, a sound she'd always adored.

"Uh, yes, then ... right. I, uh, yes, Gerald. He, uh, well, he ... how old now, did you say?"

"He's eleven now, sir," the girl replied dutifully, attentive and responsive, but never once slowing down in her work.

"And, he, uh ... he has ... uh, no sense of ..."

"Speech. That's right. Gerald has never been able to speak. He does a good job communicating without a voice, though. I feel like I know his voice just as well as if he did have it, just because his communication is so clear, and so ... well, so *him.* If that makes any sense."

"Oh yes, yes, quite, uh, yes, quite," the little hat salesman assured his faithful helper, and he went back to his own mundane duties, spending more time appearing to be busy than actually accomplishing much at all, and Patty more or less forgot that the conversation had even occurred.

To say that Stuart Freeley was silently accepting of Patty's departure from the school, and from the performing arts department in particular, is not precisely accurate. While that may have seemed the case, being that he bade her farewell without so much as a syllable of protest, once she had taken her leave, he immediately began his venture to bring her back. Stuart started what he labeled the HOP fund, standing for "Help Our Patty." Of his own accord, and with no assistance, Stuart Freeley collected what he could from every teacher, student, and administrator at West Cuttingsborough High School, and indeed, even from neighbors and local establishments who had virtually no stock or interest in the local high school. They did know of Patty, however, and to know that Patty was in trouble was sufficient information to donate to the HOP fund.

The HOP fund did a bit to bring some more visibility to Stuart Freeley, and he certainly did become more known amongst the staff and student body than he ever had been before. Of course, many thought it funny that one of the most well-loved and well-known young ladies in the school should be defended and heroically assisted by someone they'd rather failed to notice. Once someone informed these people that the lad with the box and the clipboard making rounds was none other than Stuart Freeley, the quiet lad whom Patty had always seemed to take such a liking to, they required no further explanation.

Did Patty know anything of the HOP fund? Perhaps; it's difficult to say for certain. But I rather would guess not, as her brother attended the junior level high school and Madeleine uncharacteristically took care to practice a degree of discretion on this one subject and determined it wasn't her place to announce it to her friend; Stuart should be the one to present her with whatever was raised, she felt.

"I think this is a great thing you're doing, Stuart. I'm kind of jealous I didn't think of it myself," Madeleine proclaimed one day in the hallway as she passed by him on their way to lunch.

The shy boy shrugged and may have blushed just a smidgen, but he truly did not show much outward sign of bashfulness or pride. Only one young lady in the world had the power to affect him that much, and she was the one he was doing this for.

It is likewise uncertain whether Stuart Freeley and all who had contributed to the HOP fund were aware of the existence of Patty's brother, Gerald. What is certain is that once Patty mysteriously disappeared, word of her vanishing act spread through the town quickly and the HOP fund was brought to an immediate stop. The possibility that the money could still be used and appreciated by the girl's surviving brother and father hardly seemed to matter. The purpose had been to bring Patty back to school, and that purpose (for the moment, at least) had been rendered useless by her disappearance.

What became of the money wasn't quite clear either, though no one expected it back. No one believed it had been spent, as they chose to consider that Stuart was keeping the money stored safely until the day on which (they hoped) they would hear of the young lady's return.

And so the boy Gerald was perhaps not quite as known or cherished by all as his sibling. Indeed, he had his share of friends and admirers at his own school, but certainly he did not hold the legendary status that Patty did, and so the HOP fund remained a stagnant and temporarily suspended cause, and the notion of altering it to the HOG fund never occurred to anyone.

The events which directly led up to Gerald's stepping in for Patty as the lone employee at Hats for All Occasions did indeed begin with Mr. McGulliver's then seemingly innocent questions about him to his sister.

As has already been noted, she thought nothing of these questions at first, other than that they were indicative of her employer's becoming more comfortable with her presence and the art of conversation.

"Oh, Gerald is just fine," she would reply. Or, "No, he isn't in high school yet." Or, "Crippled? Oh, I don't really tend to think of it as that at all."

Patty would never be quite sure when exactly she'd thought the questions had crossed the line from pleasant and polite conversation to uncomfortable and unwelcome interrogation. Perhaps she only noticed that evolution in hindsight. For when one day Percival McGulliver invited Patty to come with both her brother and her father to his home for dinner, she gladly accepted, and only later after she'd gone away did she think that this was perhaps a mistake.

"Come in, uh, yes, I, uh…yes, indeed…uh, come in," the little man stammered nervously as he gestured into his astonishing abode. The young lady and her silent brother and befuddled father entered into McGulliver's lavish and expansive mansion that gleamed with unmatched upkeep and unfathomable riches.

Patty's first thought on entering her employer's home was that she couldn't comprehend how the ploddingly unvisited hat shop could have yielded the wealth for something like this. Almost as soon as she'd thought this, however, she realized the answer: Mr. McGulliver didn't need the hat shop at all. It didn't matter whether anyone ever bought anything; he was clearly rich beyond her own mind's possible comprehension, and whether he owned and operated Hats for All Occasions to keep himself from becoming idle or as part of some crafty scheme on his taxes or for another reason entirely was beside the point. Suddenly she had difficulty placing her role in the world. As a student, she'd learned wonderfully. As an actress, she'd performed admirably. But in her role as the assistant to a hat shop owner, she suddenly understood just how unimportant she was.

Just as was the case at the hat shop, McGulliver appeared to enjoy endless solitude in his giant home. The meal was already upon the table, seemingly placed there by himself as no servants were anywhere to be seen or heard. The notion of Mr. McGulliver having cooked and set the place settings at the table struck young Patty as an entertaining vision, but she stifled her giggles, chose to view it as endearing, and seated herself before a grand feast of turkey, biscuits, beef stew, cheeses, wines, steel-cold ice water, and wild steamed vegetables.

The meal may have been awkward with the silence had everyone not been eating so greedily and perpetually. Only Patty attempted to begin any topics of conversation, and in those, she seemed repeatedly to be the only participant, so she ceased trying rather promptly.

Mr. McGulliver did attempt to speak to his guests after unveiling dessert, an enormous and rich chocolate custard pie with cherries, strawberries, and coffee.

"I, uh …" he began, and trailed off in his normal confusion and disorientation.

All eyes turned to him, Patty's reassuring, Gerald's curious, their father's only seeming to notice the presence of the little man for the first time that evening.

"I," Mr. McGulliver continued, attempting to secure more confidence, "I thank you …all for …coming. Tonight. Yes, yes …thank you. Yes, thank …you …" and his voice trailed off yet again as his eyes settled curiously upon the boy Gerald and a thin, appreciative smile presented itself upon his face.

"Thank you very much for having us, Mr. McGulliver," Patty said, formally yet sincerely, on behalf of the family. "Your house is just beautiful, and this meal is simply delicious."

Patty's father sat staring at the still uncut chocolate pie lustily, but hearing his daughter's praise of the food brought him to the discussion instantly. "That's true," he said loudly. "We haven't eaten like this in a long time. Patty can't cook this good at all."

Patty noticed Gerald snap his head in her direction, his face concerned for her feelings. She quickly and subtly shook her head and smiled, assuring him that she was fine, not to worry, and she nodded to Mr. McGulliver in agreement. "It's true," she said after a moment to compose herself. "This really is wonderful."

"Oh, well…I, uh," McGulliver managed, and then he promptly nodded decisively and stated, astonishingly clearly, "It was my, uh, pleasure, Patty…everyone."

After dinner, Mr. McGulliver led his guests on a tour of the impressive home, making his best attempts to narrate the contents of the rooms and corridors as they made their way.

"And, uh, this is my, uh, map room, you…you see," he managed when pushing open a door to a room that was not only covered on every inch of every wall with maps of countries, territories, bodies of water, and mysterious forests, caves, and palaces, most of which none of Patty's family had ever heard of before, but also tables and racks and desks containing and covered in more maps, of every size and color, every texture and material, some seemingly rather young, others decisively old, or even ancient, as well as exotic and elaborate charts and magnification tools to assist in the reading and deciphering of the assorted documents.

Another room revealed wall-to-wall shelving filled with vials and bottles containing many-colored potions, some stagnant, some bubbling, others actually containing unidentifiable tiny organisms, swimming, darting, and swirling in hypnotic formations and patterns. "I, uh…like to, well, I, uh…experiment, I suppose? Yes, uh, experiments and…tests…yes, quite right."

There were rooms with animal heads on the walls, rooms with elaborate costumes, gowns, and masks, and rooms with thousands of books and scrolls. "Research is, uh, a…passion of mine," he explained with flushed cheeks.

And there was a room that astonished them all into a skidding halt. Gerald in particular seemed practically bewitched by its appearance. This room was actually missing one wall, where the floor extended to the outside in the form of a balcony. Upon this seemingly inadvertent balcony was situated green wrought iron table and chairs and a fully stocked matching wine rack. This balcony looked out over the meadows, hills, and fields to the south of West Cuttingsborough, a beautiful territory that neither Patty nor her brother had ever had the pleasure to explore, despite its close proximity to their home. It wasn't at all certain whether this missing wall was a planned portion of the building, or whether it was the result of some sort of accident, storm, or even if it had simply never been finished.

The hat salesman could hardly help but notice the awe-filled expressions on the faces of all three of his guests. "It is, uh . . . I don't, uh, sit here . . . very, uh . . . often. I, uh, don't particularly care for the, uh, the . . ."

"The heights?" Patty offered helpfully, turning her gaze from the view to meet his appreciative eyes.

"Indeed. The heights."

"It's high!" the father shouted in amazement, and they all turned to watch as the simple man stared gape-mouthed at the homes, cottages, farms, roads, and very tiny people that hardly seemed real at so great a height.

"It certainly is, my friend," Mr. McGulliver said somberly, and Patty found herself snapping her head back in his direction, certain that there was something sinister or threatening in the voice. Perhaps it was simply that she was so accustomed to the little man stuttering and stammering that when he spoke clearly and confidently, it carried an unintentionally ominous tone.

When she saw his face, however, it was not her father that the hat salesman was looking at; it was Gerald. He was looking down at the mute little boy with a sideways gaze, studying his face as he looked out serenely beyond the rolling green hills, where the elevation grew them higher into the sky in the form of snow-covered rock mountains that were at the same time unwelcomingly cold and distant and temptingly beautiful and majestic.

Mr. McGulliver's expression when watching Gerald on the balcony was one that, while not the threatening menace his voice had sounded to Patty, still offered a suggestion of predatory satisfaction for just a second, and then it was gone. The man turned to see his young assistant watching him intently and promptly came back to himself, straightening up, smiling, and waving them back into the house for the remainder of the tour. "Still more to, uh, to see. Yes, more to see," he said, and shuffled off ahead of them in the assumption that they'd be following right behind, which, of course, they did, the father first, eager and impatient to be on. Patty hesitated, looked at her father and Mr. McGulliver moving back toward the corridor, then back at her brother, who was still staring entranced at the distant mountains.

"Gerald? Hello?" Patty said, and he started at the sound of her voice. Turning to her, he smiled, nodded, looked back once at the horizon, and then moved back indoors. "Are you okay?" she asked as he passed by her. "Did you see something?"

The boy merely shrugged, gestured toward the view, smiled, and went on to catch up with the men. Patty nodded to herself, looked back at the view that had so engaged him, and whispered, "Yes, it certainly is beautiful," and she too went on to see the rest of the mansion.

If the evening was curious, it was also admittedly more enjoyable than one may have expected. After all, to suggest that three very modest people who share one impossibly small home might spend an evening in an equally impossibly extraordinary home with a man less than adequate in the art of conversation does not sound altogether promising. Yet we are often attracted to the unfamiliar, and such was the case with Gerald and his father. Both left the mansion that evening with a newfound appreciation, the boy for all things naturally beautiful, the father for all things elaborately luxurious.

Indeed, Mr. McGulliver noticed these delights in their eyes and sent them on their way that night with an individualized gift for each. The little man, as he was seeing them to the door, appeared to pull a small wooden box from nowhere ("When did he pick that up?" Patty wondered to herself. "I should have seen!") and handed it to Patty's father. The presentation of the gift was carried out with McGulliver's occasional ability to present himself with little or no difficulty, as he proclaimed in as esteemed a voice as was possible from such a small and meek character, "Thank you, sir, for your visit tonight, and for your appreciation of my home. I treasure your opinion." And when the father lifted the lid of the wooden box, he drew forth from it a golden pocket watch on a shining gold linked chain. The father didn't exactly thank the little man, but the look of astounded awe and inexpressible, unrestrained joy conveyed all the appreciation one could expect, and infinitely more sincerely than mere words might have accomplished.

Next, Percival McGulliver turned to the boy Gerald, and with a smile and a nod of approval, he extended his hand toward him. The boy began to extend his in return, and Patty was just beginning to admire her little sibling's confident manners in returning an apparently manly handshake, when she realized that this was not the case at all. Rather, the extended hand that had only a second ago been empty was now passing into Gerald's hand a wooden box quite the same as the one that had just been opened by her father. Whether the boy was as surprised as his sister by the suddenly materialized object, or whether he had seen it there before she had and extended his arm with the full intent on receiving it, Patty was uncertain.

When Gerald lifted the lid of his box, he found that his gift could not be removed from it. This was hardly a disappointment, however, as what he was looking at brought an unprecedented grin across the boy's face: it was a very small scale model of the hills, fields, and mountains to the south of West Cuttingsborough, the same scenic view he'd been admiring upstairs earlier in their visit. Patty looked quickly to her employer, astonished that he could have something so clearly perfect for her brother, and that he would so promptly gift it away as though it could be replaced at the general store the very next morning for pocket change. Indeed, Patty had never seen anything like this at any shop in town.

Gerald nodded his thanks sincerely, and Percival McGulliver nodded warmly in return. "You're, uh, quite, uh, welcome . . . Gerald." These were the only words during this gift-giving ritual that came to the little man with some difficulty, and Patty was sure that his voice came more hoarsely upon uttering her brother's name. She had just enough time to think to herself, *I don't want anything. Whatever the purpose of these presents is, and wherever he's pulling them from, I don't want one.*

And no sooner had this thought crystallized as a sort of prayer in her conscious than was a third wooden box being held before her, waiting to be taken and opened.

The girl swallowed and looked to her employer questioningly, her newfound, inexplicable fear clouding her thoughts and making the situation only more difficult. "Mr. McGulliver," Patty finally managed, "I don't need anything, really. I appreciate my job, and the dinner was perfect. That's more than enough, really." Only then did she realize that she was holding the box in her hands. When had she taken it? She was quite sure she hadn't.

The little man simply smiled at her expectantly, as did her father and brother. They were all waiting to watch her reveal what little secret wish of her own was hidden inside the wooden box.

"Really," she tried again, attempting to extend the box back toward Mr. McGulliver, but she found that to move it away from her came with far greater difficulty than it rightfully should have. It felt as though a magnetic force was pushing the box right back to her, and before she even knew what she was doing, and certainly before noticing that she'd even begun to lift the lid, she was holding in her hand a single nickel.

She looked at it for a moment, studying it, finding it to be no more spectacular than any other nickel she'd seen in her lifetime.

"It's very nice," her father said with a smile, and Patty turned to Mr. McGulliver questioningly.

"Sir?" she asked, and the little man once again smiled warmly at his assistant, then stepped uncomfortably near to her, the better to explain.

"Patty," Mr. McGulliver said tenderly, and the quiet of his voice was, to the girl's ears, not the ordinary uncertain and meek sort of quiet Mr. McGulliver's voice was known to communicate, but rather a knowing and secretive quiet, one that warned her through every sense she possessed not to trust it, but to leave there promptly and not look back. But she was frozen, the nickel betwixt her fingers and a coldness across her skin.

Mr. McGulliver continued, "That may not seem an extraordinary gift at first examination, but this coin contains great luck for whoever possesses it, as I've been witness to. I'm quite certain that you will find the same to be true of it."

She managed a hoarse murmur of thanks, and before she pocketed the coin (Had she meant to do that? She thought not; ah well, she'd remove it and discard it as soon as she left the mansion), she caught a peculiar scent that wafted from the nickel, an exotic scent, not one of metal and dirt, but one reminiscent of the aromas that drifted from the ventilation of Lotsa The Pasta in downtown West Cuttingsborough.

As they departed the mansion, their feeble host waved from the rectangular yellow light that was his doorway against the night, and Patty's reservations and trepidation seemed to rise like a veil lifted off of her of their own accord. She walked with her father and brother through the streets of the town, toward their waiting home, the lucky nickel resting already forgotten in her pocket.

Now, as has already been suggested, Patty felt little fear in her visits to Cobble Road. While she would openly acknowledge, should someone have inquired, that there was mysterious eccentricity about Professor Spice, and that there was a less-than-ethical air about his dealings, that was the extent of it. As she trekked the streets of

West Cuttingsborough en route to the tobacconist shop the first Thursday after the curious dinner at the McGulliver mansion, she crafted lines and scenes in her mind from her imaginary play-to-be about Professor Spice and his circus of notables from Cobble Road, and thought to herself that perhaps Mr. McGulliver deserved to figure into the story as well. While the nervousness that had hovered over her at the mansion had disappeared, forgotten, she still found herself fully aware of his unusual behavior as of late, and credited her employer with being less ordinary than she'd previously believed.

And so it was that this curiosity, when mixed with her disturbingly high comfort level with Anson Spice, led her to ask the tobacconist a question that day.

Professor Spice's left eyebrow arched as he looked down at the young woman across the counter. The businessmen in the tobacco shop silenced their conversation immediately and looked with intrigued disbelief at Patty, who ignored them with effort and continued to look on Anson Spice, awaiting a response to the question she'd just posed.

"What did you ask me?" Spice said in a voice nearly quiet enough to be categorized a whisper, yet intoned enough to contain a clearly detectable bite.

Businessmen Cromby and Simon exchanged glances with each other, but wisely said not a word.

Patty refused to be derailed.

"I said, 'Why does Mr. McGulliver send me here every Thursday?'"

Silence ensued.

Uncomfortably, clearly thinking that the towering shop owner had no intentions of replying, the businessmen awkwardly resumed their discussion.

"Anyhow, Simon," the other began, "my only point is that the profits to be gained are neither outweighing of, nor incomparable to, the deficits to be suffered at the expense of the board."

Simon, at first hesitant to fill the void of silence with his own voice, was nonetheless baited into responding.

"The board?" he said in defiance. "The board wouldn't support a venture of that magnitude if it meant an early retirement in a tropical paradise for each of them!"

"Really, Simon, exaggeration is unflattering."

"Indeed, but I hardly think it exaggeration to make note of certain individuals' tendencies to fear all things costly. And what's more—"

"And what's more is that my own son is one of those men you're speaking of now!"

During this, Patty and Professor Spice held each other's expectant stares, the girl forced to contend with the man's hauntingly certain presence as it awaited her inevitable flight from the tobacco shop, and the man, in turn, challenged by the young lady's determination to see her curiosity satisfied.

Simon chuckled musingly, shaking his head in apparent thought.

"What?" his cohort retorted in disgust, holding his pipe at arm's length, gesturing to his friend's laughter. "You're acting the fool there, old bean. Stop it and explain yourself at once."

The other man gathered himself and explained, "My wife. She's suggested that I give my stepson an apprenticeship."

"What of it? Too young?"

"No, no, certainly not. The boy is in the high school. But he's as simple a lad as you've ever been witness to. He can't find the wits to tie his boots without tying himself to his chair."

"Indeed."

"Indubitably."

"Silence." This last was, of course, from Professor Spice, and it was obeyed immediately. They looked back at him aghast, faces flushed from the icy reprimand. They watched and waited as the tobacconist continued to eye young Patty.

"Very well," he said at last. "I will divulge what I can, though I hardly believe that will constitute enough to satisfy your inappropriately heightened curiosity."

"That's perfectly fine, sir," the girl said with genuine sincerity, and the tobacconist nodded.

"Allow me first to assume that you've likely perceived the fact that he does not burn the tobacco, for smoking or any other purpose?" Patty nodded. "And let me next consider that you've noticed that he keeps and collects these samples?" Here the girl faltered. She actually hadn't noticed anything of the sort. She knew he didn't smoke the tobacco, but she had never witnessed what was done with it after she'd turned it over to him.

Professor Spice's face lit with clarity. "I see from your expression that you haven't." She admitted the truth of this with a reluctant shake of the head. "Well, then. I think all the answers are there for the finding for anyone eager enough to find them. Allow what I've unintentionally shared to be the extent of my sharing for today. Good day."

And the girl gave her thanks, nodded politely (if a bit put off) toward Misters Simon and Cromby, and set off with the velvet pouch of tobacco to the hat shop.

Upon her departure, the businessmen attempted once again to break the menacing silence.

"That was . . . interesting, there, Professor," Cromby stated, hoping it would be received as complimentary.

"Quite," the other quickly put in. "She'll be decidedly confounded by an answer like that, good man."

"Out." Anson Spice's voice contained the same cold threat as it had when speaking to Patty, and the men did not need to be told a second time. They departed, chuckling about Simon's incompetent stepson's would-be apprenticeship.

Patty would hardly recall the discussion of the inept stepson, but she may have put more stock in it, had she realized that the stepson in question was none other than her long-time admirer, Stuart Freeley.

It was true. Innocent and pure-hearted Stuart had been adopted at a tender age by businessman Simon, and from the start, the stepson would generate nothing more than hostility and disgust in the man. First of all, the lad enjoyed the outdoors, which was a concept foreign to Simon and all his peers. Simon could have accepted some fashion of rough-and-tumble outdoorsiness that consisted of such tasks as chopping wood and whitewater rafting, but this was not the sort of outdoor behavior young Stuart demonstrated. Stuart would instead sit for countless hours atop a hill or in the shade beneath a tree, or on a large rock in the center of a river's current, staring into the distance with a contemplative air that Simon could only label as "unproductive daydreaming."

Additionally, Stuart had always been partial to studious, artistic activities such as literature and painting. He would often have a book open when he sat beneath a tree, or paper and pencil would be in his grip, for the purpose of someday creating a masterpiece of his own. This had not happened yet, though he never gave up trying.

"Of course, if his scrawlings and scribblings were devoted to the end of something worthwhile," his stepfather would emote to Stuart's mother, "I could get behind such an endeavor!"

Simply and with true interest, his wife would return with the question of what sort of endeavor he had in mind.

"Well, I, why, he should," he would sputter from his spot by the fireplace, arms waving in elaborate waves of frustration, "a business plan, of course!"

That a young man still in high school, and clearly not destined for a path in the business world, should be spending his recreational time devising a strategy for a business he hasn't even imagined yet confused Stuart's mother, but she yielded to her husband's evident expertise and would quietly and secretly suggest as much to her son when Simon wasn't near.

"Have you ever thought about writing a business plan, Stuart honey?" she would ask in feigned curiosity, secretly hoping the boy would find it a perfectly natural wondering to come from his unschooled mother.

"A business plan?" he would ask uncertainly and never disrespectfully. "Why would I do that?"

"Well," she would confess with little pressuring, "I know it would make your father very happy."

Stuart would never play the *step*father card in response to a comment like this. He knew that it meant the world to his mother to think of his having a father who wasn't absent, and he wouldn't hurt her for all the treasures in the wide world and beyond. He would simply shrug and look away, mumble something about "never happy with me," and his mother would leave him alone again, forcing back the tears that were naturally emerging without invitation.

That Stuart's stepfather knew nothing of the Help Our Patty fund is most assuredly a fact. That such a sum of cash and coin could be secreted in his own home and he remain unaware of it would have left him flabbergasted, but more importantly, that money would have immediately been intercepted and deposited in a more "safe and sensible" location, which would inevitably have borne a striking resemblance to Simon's personal bank account.

But the boy kept the money quite safe and secret, and his stepfather never learned of it. Simon may have been less hasty to remark of Stuart's lack of business savvy were he to discover just how much he'd accumulated from others with little effort put forth at all. This, however, would have been, obviously, an erroneous estimation, as the people's generosity spoke less of the boy's skills of persuasion and more of Patty's still fresh imprint on the hearts of the townsfolk. That is not to say that Stuart's fundraising was without its merit, however. The collection spoke volumes of his good heart and desire to help someone in need.

As Patty made her way back to Hats for All Occasions, part of her felt a shade guilty for having asked suspicious questions of Mr. McGulliver behind his back. If she'd wanted to know something, why had she not asked him rather than sneak around, attempting to collect clues from shadier characters?

The answer, of course, lay in Mr. McGulliver's questions and comments as of late. His growing interest in her family, and in Gerald in particular, left her with considerable distaste in her mouth, and she was determined to get to the root of the whole thing so she could simply report to her job every day with no doubts or questions.

Now, when we find we are feeling guilty for something we have done, there are several ways we might react to our own feelings. For instance, many people will promptly reverse the behavior as best they can and press forward on their best behavior in an attempt at remedying whatever it is they've done. Alternately, some people may feel that if they've crossed a line so far already, they may as well cross a bit more while they're at it. This is the logic Patty's mind was rationalizing as she made her way back to the hat shop, and it was this incentive, the drive to know what she might discover before settling back down to normality, that caused her to stop at the corner of Rood and Stover and loosen the drawstrings on the velvet pouch she was carrying.

Patty had never peeked inside one of the pouches before, and she didn't intend to take or keep anything she saw in there now. She merely felt she *needed* to verify the contents.

She looked.

She sniffed.

She looked again.

She sighed. Tightening the drawstrings, she allowed her mind to concede; the pouch contained pipe tobacco, for certain and surely. It was much richer and tempting a scent than simple ordinary tobacco, true, but it was tobacco nonetheless. Feeling foolish and still guiltier than she had at the start of the journey back, she returned to Hats for All Occasions to deliver the pouch to Mr. McGulliver.

She froze in her tracks when she reached the front of the store.

Through the window, clearly and without any possible mistake, Patty saw Stuart Freeley speaking with Mr. McGulliver. Stuart was holding a clipboard and a small, white, cubical cardboard box. It appeared that Stuart was doing the talking, and Mr. McGulliver seemed less than ecstatic about whatever it was the boy was saying.

Without thinking about what she was doing, Patty ducked around the corner and pressed herself tightly against the brick wall.

After a moment of this, she found her own voice of reason in her mind, speaking in disgust and disbelief, demanding to know why exactly she was hiding. She couldn't seem to provide herself with a reasonable response. Just as she was preparing to sneer at her own silliness and remove herself from the wall, she heard the bell above the front entrance ring and Stuart's footsteps as he exited the shop, and she immediately and unconsciously pressed herself back against the wall even tighter. She waited for a moment, but no one approached in her direction. She hazarded a peek around the corner and saw Stuart in the distance; he'd turned left rather than right out of the shop and had gone away from her rather than toward.

Again, as she stood up straight and neatened her mussed clothing, she was forced to face the question of what she could possibly have been afraid of. Still she could not begin to imagine. With a shake of the head and a sigh, Patty entered the hat shop and presented Percival McGulliver with the velvet, tobacco-containing pouch.

"Ah, yes," Mr. McGulliver said, his eyes darting to the door. "Quite good, quite good, uh…Patty, yes. Yes, thank you, uh, Patty. Yes."

The rest of this particular Thursday passed slowly for Patty. She attempted to make conversation with Mr. McGulliver so as not to appear any different than usual, but regardless of whatever mundane and unimportant topic they discussed, she couldn't wrest her mind from the one thing she really itched to know: Why had Mr. McGulliver been showing so much interest in her brother?

Now you may be wondering just where Scratches O'Hannigan fit into the picture in these days of West Cuttingsborough, when Patty was working at Hats for All Occasions. True enough, they certainly did encounter each other in the streets, and courtesies were always exchanged. But if Scratches felt a certain degree of responsibility for protecting young Gerald, he felt no such thing where Patty was concerned. It was not that Scratches O'Hannigan didn't care for Patty, and nor was it that she deserved assistance any less than her brother later would. It was simply that Patty was so renowned as being such a responsible young woman that it never even occurred to Scratches that she may need extra help in avoiding danger. As it happened, the events that followed those I've just related directly led to the heightened sense of danger that kept Scratches O'Hannigan keeping close tabs on Gerald in the two years to follow.

When uncertain how precisely to capture the personality of a certain role she was playing, when struggling with placing the contents of her history class in "real-life" contexts, when itching to get to the root of where the mathematical theorems she was required to memorize had come from and to identify the workings of the minds of the men who concocted them, Patty always knew where to turn, and the public library had never failed to assist her in the past. And so it came to pass that on Saturday, when she had the day off of work and managed to catch up relatively well on the work about the house, Patty ventured to the library to see if she could gather any clues that might decipher the mysterious goings-on in which she'd appeared to have become involved.

Once facing the card catalogue, of course, the girl realized she had very little to go on. She drew open a tiny wooden drawer at random and sifted through the little cards, relishing the old, musty smell that clung to them. Subjects, titles, and authors swept past her eyes, all as interesting, intriguing, and frustratingly irrelevant as the last. When Mrs. Daly, the head librarian, saw the girl appearing to have difficulty finding what she needed and offered to help, she briefly did attempt to explain what she was interested in, only to discover almost immediately that she really had no idea what it was she was interested in.

In frustration and apparent defeat, she sat down in one of the orange, soft-cushioned chairs and attempted to gather her thoughts. Her mind began to pan over the things that had stood out as being unusual to her in the recent weeks. *Hat shop, brother, hat salesman, mute, dinner, mansion, model, questions, tobacco, tobacconist, pouch, envelope, gifts, mountains, balcony, view, stammer, no stammer, pocket watch, wooden boxes, nickel…*

She gave a start and sat bolt upright in the chair.

Leaping to her feet, she reached into her pocket and felt for the coin. Her fingers closed around a cold, metallic object, and she drew forth the nickel she'd received from Mr. McGulliver. How had she forgotten about it? She had intended to dispose of it immediately. Somehow that had escaped her mind the night of the dinner, and here it had remained since then.

Patty examined the nickel more closely, hoping to find some characteristic trait that would set it apart from an ordinary coin. Mr. McGulliver had claimed it would bring luck, which she hardly believed to be true. There were no unusual markings or anything of the sort on the nickel, but the scent she had noticed on it the night she had received it was still present and strong. She attempted to place the exact aroma. It seemed a mixture of some exotic oils and herbs. The same scent burning in incense or streaming from an oven that boasted a special holiday feast would have brought water to her mouth and warmth to her heart, but somehow coming off of the nickel, it only made her sick to her stomach. She pocketed the coin again and thought to herself that perhaps this was a starting point. It was as good of one as any, she supposed.

Returning to the card catalogue, Patty sifted through the cards again until she found books on coins. She jotted down the general call numbers that signified that topic and sought out the corresponding shelves. When she arrived at the books on coins, Patty ran her fingers along the spines of the volumes, eyeing the titles in the hopes that one might spring from its owner and shout at her, "Here! Open this one!"

Such was not her luck.

She pulled off one, two, three books, placing them delicately in a stack at her feet. A fourth, fifth, and sixth appeared to have equal potential, and she set those atop the others. When she had a stack of thirteen books, she determined she would need to be more selective.

She looked back through the titles she'd found: *A History of Coinage*, *The Mint and the Economy*, *Ballard on the Significance of the Monetary System*, *On Coin Collecting*, etc. On second look, none of them seemed to be what she was looking for. She scanned the indexes and the tables of contents, thinking perhaps one of the subcategories would feel or sound appropriate. Still she found nothing.

She ignored the sign that read "Please Do Not Re-Shelve Books" and placed all thirteen of them in their correct sequential location, then she sat down with a huff and felt her whole body slump with discouragement. As she sat there staring at nothing in particular, a certain title seemed to float off of the shelf and meet her gaze. Her eyes came into focus curiously, and she cocked her head as she at last settled on the title that had captured her attention:

Coins and the Like and Their Role in Luck and Magic

She reached out and drew the book from the shelf.

She opened the extensive volume to the table of contents and ran her finger down the chapter titles: "When Coins Are More Than Money," "Controlling the Power in Your Change Purse," "Chants and Rituals Applicable in Coinage," and the title that slammed her heart hard and strong into her throat:

"The Anointing of Coins for Extraordinary Purposes"

Her fingers thumbed to page 337 and she scanned the pages, hunting for key words, pictures, anything that would indicate she was looking in the proper place. She didn't see anything as such at first and was growing close to admitting total defeat when a word caught her eye:

Seasonings.

Arching an eyebrow and situating herself more comfortably on the floor with her back to the shelves, she backed up to the beginning of the paragraph that had drawn her attention:

> The notion of coins as ritualistic charms dates back almost as far in history as the monetary system itself. Its credibility grew in the late 18th century, however, when revolutions in technology and industry threatened to detach people from their spiritual heritage. In the hopes of securing a hold on the vanishing qualities of the past, village elders, clergymen, advisors to nobility, and others of such social standings began to keep records of encounters, experiences, and recipes involving coins that had been known to see effective results in the supernatural realm. Many of these rituals involved the anointing of the coins themselves with various kitchen oils and seasonings, the concept being that the marriage of the kitchen ingredients with the symbol of the monetary system would birth an object of traditional but profitable good fortune.

Patty looked up thoughtfully from the page. So far, all she had read could only point to Mr. McGulliver's having spoken truthfully. She was shocked at her own reaction, finding that she felt somehow disappointed. It was highly out of her character to look for the worst in people, but in the last few weeks she had become so certain that Mr. McGulliver was up to something, that he was being deceitful and self-serving, and that at least she, if not her brother or even her father, were just pawns in an unsettlingly real and complex game.

She returned her attention to the page and moved on to the next paragraph:

> With time, the inevitable departure from many traditions ancient and spiritual that had been the cause of such records in the first place did transpire, and it was that very departure that drew those who had familiarized themselves with the rituals of coins and other such charms to stray from the righteous path of honorable magic-making and luck-spreading. It was, perhaps, imminent that these groups would, in fact, turn these spells and enchantments to the acts of darkness and destruction that they are now widely agreed to be. One such ritual, known to very few living people, was reputed to call for a single anointed nickel as a key ingredient to unlocking a trans-dimensional portal that would serve as a sacrificial medium for victims of soul exchanges. As the legend goes, should a person wish to revive a loved one from the dead, they may do so with the proper spell components. They would be required, however, to make an exchange, sending a pure and innocent soul to whatever otherworldly dimension the resurrected soul had inhabited. Typically these exchanges demanded the sacrifice of someone who suffered some form of handicap, someone who would be considered something other than "average," be it a mental disorder, an inability to use one's limbs, or the lacking of one of the key senses. While little is known of the required ingredients for such enchantments anymore, it is widely believed that this transaction required the bestowing of an anointed nickel to one of the sacrifice victim's loved ones.

Patty's breath had halted several sentences earlier. Her flesh was erupted in millions of chilled goose bumps, and her eyes were dry with wide, unblinking astonishment. Her hands were gripping the book painfully, and her neck was stiff with not moving. She reread the same two paragraphs again to verify everything she'd just absorbed, and upon finishing it the second time, a choking sob caught in her throat and tears welled into her eyes with the sudden force of a water valve that's been smashed with a sledgehammer. Shakily, she rose to her feet and made her way in a trance-like state to the circulation desk.

The girl didn't remember checking out the book. Nor did she remember exiting the library or walking back through the streets of West Cuttingsborough. She did not remember arriving at the hat shop either, and she most certainly did not remember letting herself in with the key she owned. Mr. McGulliver would never entrust her brother with a key, quite likely in reaction to this very incident, but Patty's renowned responsibility and maturity had led him to give her one almost immediately after hiring her.

No, she did not recall doing any of these things, but she had done them just the same, for she found herself in the back room of the hat shop, making her way stealthily through the shelves of back stock, allowing her gaze to fall on every bit of every place, uncertain what it was she was searching for, but quite positive that there was, indeed, something to be found.

As she searched the premises, her mind played through what she had read in the library book, which was still tucked under one arm. Clearly she was the loved one who had been gifted with the anointed nickel, implying that she had a loved one who was meant to be sacrificed for the sake of a ritual, some sort of exchange for someone who had died. Her mind was moving faster than it was fashioned to operate, and the thoughts were becoming jumbled in her head. She tried to slow her thinking down. "One thing at a time," she told herself. The book had said that the ritual called for the exchanged person to have some sort of…deficiency? Was that the word it had used? No, no, that wasn't it. A handicap! That had been it. A person with a handicap. And that perfectly fit both her brother and her father, did it not? So which of them was McGulliver after? Well, certainly his excessive interest in Gerald as of late would suggest that he was the subject of the little man's plans.

Patty shivered with the thought. She had been working for Mr. McGulliver for two years now, and to think of the things that had been going through his mind during all of those hours they'd spent together was unnerving. Had this been his plan all along? Or had this only come up since she'd begun her services here? Grudgingly, she recalled how eager Mr. McGulliver had been to hire her on, despite the fact that there hadn't even been a sign in the window announcing a position. Had he hired her simply as a means to get to her brother, knowing fully well that the mute boy was a perfect candidate for his dark needs?

She didn't like to think on this, but telling herself that she knew nothing for certain was fruitless; the pieces were all simply beginning to fit too perfectly.

"Ah!" Patty shouted in pain as she stubbed her toe on the little safe that sat directly on the floor in the back corner of the stockroom. As would be the case for her brother some time later, regardless of how many times she'd set her eyes upon the safe, it had never looked unusual until now. She didn't bother attempting the lock; she wouldn't know where to begin to guess Mr. McGulliver's combination, and she didn't care to waste time on something she knew would result in failure. Instead, she ventured into her boss's office.

Patty was not fortunate enough to locate the secret compartment her brother would uncover two years later; in fact, upon entering the office, the first thing she did was pull her journal and pen out of her pocket and sit down at Mr. McGulliver's desk. She looked back over some of the entries she'd written in the last month, reviewing some of her passing conflicting emotions regarding Misters McGulliver and Spice, her brother Gerald, the odd gifts, and the mysterious velvet pouches of tobacco. As she read, things crystallized in her mind in ways she hadn't expected. She would occasionally cross-reference something she'd noticed or felt with the information available at hand in *Coins and the Like and Their Role in Luck and Magic*. Time after time, her fears were confirmed, and the evidence stacked itself up against Mr. Percival H. Rutherford McGulliver, owner and operator of Hats for All Occasions.

Patty thumbed the pages to the first blank one and commenced writing what would become her final entry. She wrote feverishly and tight-fistedly, pausing only to copy appropriate quotations from the text. She didn't know for certain how safe she was. She knew the hat shop was closed on weekends, but she did not know Mr. McGulliver's weekend habits, and to assume that he would never possibly show up was recklessly unsafe, in her estimation. Still, she needed to write this down while it was fresh, and when finished, she would swiftly inspect the little office. She wasn't certain she would find any evidence there. After all, Mr. McGulliver had an entire mansion at his disposal inhabited by no one but himself for more than adequate hiding places.

Still…she had a hunch, and searching the mansion would be infinitely more challenging. She would do so, of course, if it came to that. She would find a way. But for now, she would accomplish what she could here in the office.

The shadow that spread across the desk and darkened her diary brought a chill to her blood and threatened to squeeze her heart in her chest until it silenced itself forever.

She didn't need to look up. She knew who was standing there.

"I know what you're planning," she said, her attempt to sound brave and challenging failing miserably; for once, the great actress Patty was unable to master a role, and undoubtedly, despite the attempt, her audience was unconvinced.

"I can see that," came the calm and clear voice of Percival McGulliver. His hand brushed lightly over the open pages of the book, and when Patty hazarded a glance at his face, the scowl it harbored was wicked and loathing.

Sobs choked her, but she managed to implore of him, "Why? *Why?*"

Mr. McGulliver sighed and began to stroll circles in the small room. "Oh, 'why, why, why?' It's such a pointed and fruitless question, isn't it? Dear Patty, this was not a personal vendetta against you or your family. This was a business transaction into which I entered, and you and your delightful younger brother just happen to be useful tools in those dealings."

"But I don't remember asking to be 'used'!" she challenged him, and the anger was steely in her voice.

"Mind yourself, young lady," Mr. McGulliver said softly, stopping his wandering to peer closely down his nose at her. "Watch your tone, as I am presently considering what is to be done with you, and I trust you'll want it to be as painless as possible."

She struggled to control the anger in her voice, but her eyes still betrayed her true emotions. With care, she slowly asked him, "The tobacco is part of it, isn't it? You said this is a business transaction, and you have a business deal with Professor Spice. You buy tobacco from him every week, and you never smoke it. The book said that spells like this call for ingredients; the tobacco is a spell component." She looked to his face for any sort of confirmation, but the little man merely continued to study her fearful and angered stare. "Right?" she prodded, demanding a response.

He nodded guardedly, his face demonstrating a "more or less" expression.

"Very perceptive," he said at last, and he began to step toward her.

"What do you pay him?" the girl demanded to know. "Just how much is my brother's life worth?"

At this, Mr. McGulliver laughed aloud, and Patty realized with a shudder that this was the first time she had ever heard the hat salesman laugh, excluding all of those forced and insincere chortles of discomfort that had been such a sadly endearing defense mechanism. He clearly needed no such defenses today.

"Silly girl," her employer said, shaking his head at what he evidently viewed as her own naiveté. "Professor Spice does not collect a monetary fee for his ingredients. He charges us with knowledge."

His word choice did not go unnoticed; she corrected him instantly.

"Us? *Us?* This is not an 'us' situation! This is *you*! *You* have done these things, and *used* me to do them! You make a deal with someone on Cobble Road, and you don't even have the courage to visit it yourself? So you sent me?"

McGulliver sneered.

"Speak what you wish, little girl, and think what you believe. But the end of the matter is that I *helped* your family. I hired you when you needed a job and no one else would give you one. But as I was saying, all I have that Anson Spice could ever want from me is certain…information. He wishes assistance with, well…with… well, I'll just demonstrate."

Mr. McGulliver gestured to the clock that hung on the office wall, and Patty watched as the minute and hour hands danced back and forth across its face. She glanced at him suspiciously. "How did you do that?" she demanded.

Mr. McGulliver chuckled again and shook his head.

"That's not the impressive part, Patty. What was unclear from that demonstration was what was going on outside as I was exercising it. You see, I was not merely manipulating my own clock; all time itself was bowing to the whims and fancies of my own little finger. Dark, light, early, late, evening, morning. Many are the times I have altered the state of time itself. Why, your very work days are a perfect example. Attempt to recall specific moments of your days *other* than when you were cleaning or running an errand." She did try to think on this, and was alarmed to realize that his suggestion proved quite right. When it came down to it, she had precious few memories of all her time at Hats for All Occasions. Mr. McGulliver smiled as he read the realization on her face. "Indeed. I myself would have gone mad had I been required to live out the gruelingly depressing days here in actual time. You may recall your confusion when you found the wooden box with the nickel in your hand?"

She did. Her eyes widened as she recollected her certainty that she had never extended her arm and taken the box into her grasp.

Chuckling again with a mischievous quality that grated at every nerve in Patty's body, Mr. McGulliver shrugged an almost embarrassed guilt.

"You never did take it from me, my dear. I paused the passing of time long enough to place it there myself. In fact, you and your family stood there for quite a length of time as I set about the business of finding those gifts for you. Well, not for you. Yours was prepared already. But the others ... those took some searching to locate."

She eyed him warily. She thought she saw what he was getting at, but she was also sensing the satisfaction he was experiencing at watching his plans unfold in her mind. Thus, she sat silently and waited for him to speak again.

At last, he concluded. "Well, as you can imagine, Professor Spice is aware of my, uh, abilities, and he, uh, well ... arranged a, uh ... trade of sorts." Patty's eyebrow arched unconsciously; was she imagining, or had his stammer only just returned? "For every required specimen of tobacco you bring back, you take to him one series of letters and numbers that serves as one portion of a code that controls the very essence of time. With that code, one can control, twist, bend, move, shift, or erase time altogether quite simply."

"You're sick."

"I'm talented. And I'm a widower."

Patty's face executed a few seconds of befuddled perplexity. How in the world could those two thoughts be connected ...? Then realization clicked and understanding came into focus.

So that was it. Mr. McGulliver was looking to resurrect his wife from the dead. From what she recalled, this was certainly a credible wish; Millicent McGulliver had been a beautiful, kind woman, full of love and life. Patty couldn't quite recall the circumstances of her death ...

"How does the code work?" she asked, trying desperately not to sound frightened, but she was, after all, simply attempting to win herself some extra time. But was that possible? Could she win a game of time with someone who could apparently win as much of it for himself as he wanted?

"Oh, any way at all, really. One can, uh, type or handwrite the, uh, characters in the proper ... uh, sequence, or speak them aloud, or any other of a number of possible things. But, uh, well, it must, uh, be done properly, with care, well-paced, not too fast, uh…not too slow, and with confidence and, well, uh, authority."

"But you didn't say or write anything when you made the clock change."

Mr. McGulliver tapped his head. "It's, uh…well, all in here, my dear. It would take a novice much longer, of course, but, uh, I've managed rather to, well, shall I say, to…well, uh, to *imprint* the code in mind?" He shrugged modestly, and it struck Patty that the return of his stutter seemed perfectly in tune to the trickling away of the confidence he'd exuded only moments before.

He was becoming nervous. Why?

As if reading her thoughts, Mr. McGulliver sighed and declared, "Well, young lady, I do, uh…believe that I, uh, have…uh, well, that is, I, uh…have determined what, uh, that is…what I shall, uh, well, be…doing with you."

Patty's muscles tightened, and the tears welled in her eyes. There was no hiding the fear now, and she sat there in her wicked employer's chair and awaited whatever wretched fate was to befall her.

"Yes, uh…well, that is, I, uh…I do believe I shall, uh…send you. Away."

Patty turned her head curiously, waiting for the inevitable explanation.

"I, uh, well, I do believe…Patty…I shall be sending you to, uh, to a, uh, well, to where you can't, uh…do any, uh, well…damage."

"Where?" she choked out, and the gasp she managed was dry and hoarse, the word barely audible.

"I, uh…rather," Mr. McGulliver amended, "I ought to, uh, to, uh, say that I shall…send you to, uh, well, that is…to *when* you can't do any, uh, damage. Yes. When."

He seemed satisfied. Nervous, true, but satisfied nonetheless.

"Goodbye, Patty," he said softly. "You were a good helper."

And with the same casual gesture of his finger, Patty quite literally vanished into thin air.

There was, as has been stated, an investigation, but no evidence was unearthed to suggest that Patty may be deceased. Thus, there was no funeral. There was a memorial of sorts, in the West Cuttingsborough auditorium, appropriately enough, in which anyone who cared to stepped onto the stage and shared what they loved about Patty. Some sang songs, some led prayers, some shared stories, memories, or well-wishes for the girl, wherever she may have been, and others stepped up front and center merely to cry and fail to get the first word out. Many spoke of the girl as though she had been their closest friend, which, of course, led their true friends who were in the audience to feel certain resentments and offenses. Others told stories that some would question the validity of, and then those who questioned felt immediately guilty for being so dark-mindedly suspicious, which prompted them to share their own stories. Sadly, their stories were every bit as suspect as the ones that had led them up there in the first place.

Altogether it was a decidedly horrendous affair, as Gerald and Stuart Freeley and Madeleine Piper all suspected it would be. None of them were in attendance. Mr. Batchley, the drama teacher, had his suspicions regarding how tasteful (or tasteless) the memorial would be, but felt an obligation as a member of the faculty to be there anyway. He regretted it almost immediately.

The HOP fund was hidden away permanently and would not be spoken of or seen for some time, and when it would eventually surface, it did not help Patty in the way it originally had been intended to. And all of those people who *were* in attendance at the memorial managed somehow to move on quite quickly and thoroughly the next day, missing young Patty, true, but accepting her as gone forever.

Those who knew and loved Patty enough not to attend the dreadful memorial weren't so swiftly convinced.

One evening shortly thereafter, a knock came at the door of Gerald and Patty's house. The father was asleep early, exhausted from crying for his inability to understand where his dear Patty was, and the boy was washing dishes and putting away the remnants of their dinner. He strode to the door and opened it, and was only mildly surprised, but greatly pleased, to see his sister's boss, the kind Mr. McGulliver, who had given him the spectacular wooden-box model of the southern landscape standing on the stoop.

Gerald smiled warmly and welcomingly, gesturing an invitation for Mr. McGulliver to come inside.

"I, uh ... well, I, uh, thank you ... Gerald. I can't stay, uh, too long, but ... yes. Yes, indeed, I suppose I shall for a minute or, uh, or two."

Mr. McGulliver seated himself at the kitchen table, and Gerald gestured to the coffee pot questioningly. Mr. McGulliver smiled and nodded, sweat droplets covering his scalp. "Yes, yes, uh ... coffee would be, uh, well, uh ... delightful."

The boy proceeded to brew the coffee as Mr. McGulliver sat in silence. It would have taken a very perceptive person to detect any reason the encounter should have been awkward, and Gerald served the little man his beverage and sat down next to him without even the shadow of a suspicion in his mind.

"I, uh ... Gerald," Mr. McGulliver began as he sipped his coffee carefully. He started at the hotness of it, took a second to blow on it, and then set it down gently on the table. Folding his small hands as if to pray, Mr. McGulliver leaned in closer to the boy. "Gerald, I am dreadfully sorry about your sister. I shall miss her greatly."

Gerald nodded his thanks and understanding and touched his hand to the man's in a sincere show of his sympathy and mutual sadness.

"I wonder, Gerald, if you wouldn't want to come and work for me in your sister's stead."

Patty stood on the street corner, holding the newspaper in her hands, staring at it in disbelief.

"Miss? You gonna buy that?" the man at the newsstand said as politely as he could manage.

She looked at him, shook her head slowly, overcome with what she had just seen. "No," she managed, and the hoarse choke of it sounded just the same as when she'd attempted to ask "Where?" to Mr. McGulliver only moments before.

Patty turned and walked away in a general direction, not certain where she was going or what she was to do, but still seeing, printed firmly on her mind's eye, the date on the newspaper that had revealed her to be walking the streets of a West Cuttingsborough of over twenty years ago, some five years before she was born.

PART THREE:

Molly

The day Molly met her daughter, Patty, they were both seventeen years old.

She'd started the day at school, of course, and that, Molly believed, was always bound and destined to be the onset of something horrid. West Cuttingsborough High School was a large stone building; four floors with several little turrets, which, on the inside, were the restrooms, but on the outside gave the structure a grand and historic appearance. Not grand in a merry and joyous style as one would expect to find in fairy tale storybooks, but rather in a stuffy and daunting, perhaps even menacing manner, the type of building that appeared to stare at you as you approached it and which you could feel watching you as you left. Its rooms varied in comfort, some cold and dark with concrete floors and water-stained walls, little light, and no heat. Others, the same at their core, had been altered into something more welcoming and quaint by their resident teachers, who had added rugs and wall hangings, bookshelves and aquariums. Most of the rooms had a fireplace, and the same teachers who'd brought their own décor were the ones who would build a fire in the hearth to lighten and warm the atmosphere.

West Cuttingsborough High School was one of the oldest buildings in the entire city, and had indeed stood as the exact same structure with the exact same purpose substantially longer than even the oldest West Cuttingsboroughians could recall. The school had seen its rotation of administration and faculty, and the demeanors of these, as you might already have guessed, could be estimated within seconds of entering and taking in their classrooms or offices.

Our young Molly, however, in these days quite prior to her destined permanent seating in the wheelchair that Gerald would know her to inhabit, was decidedly bored and (in her viewpoint) inconvenienced regardless of the level of warmth and welcoming that was to be found in a particular classroom. Indeed, while her heart of hearts would certainly loathe the tedium and low tolerance that went along with the cold and uninviting teachers' classes, a personal desire to maintain a certain image would often call for her to proclaim her even greater annoyance at the *nice ones* (this phrase emphatically spoken with clear and unmistakable disgust) for the simple fact that, the way she saw it, "They're the ones who are just trying too hard, determined to be *liked*."

For a teacher to be "liked" was a concept significantly beyond young Molly's grasp, and when her peers retorted that they had their favorites (Mr. Gorflinder, who provided treats every Friday from The Fourth Chocolatier for their enjoyment as they took their weekly test, or Miss Libbitz, who managed to bring in the most fascinating and engaging guest speakers for every imaginable topic to be discussed in her classroom), Molly would simply roll her eyes, nod in a patronizing fashion, and declare knowingly, "What's really sad is that it seems you actually believe that."

This particular morning, Molly's day began in one of the less than comfortable rooms, dim and damp and quite chilled, a room that housed Mr. Grondknot's western civilization class. Trouble came almost immediately this morning, mostly because Mr. Grondknot had misunderstood her remark about how it didn't really matter what long-ago philosophers did or didn't say, as that was a very long time ago anyway, and philosophy can't possibly be meant to last very long since the world is always changing and people couldn't honestly expect the abstract notions and ideas of someone who'd lived hundreds of years ago to apply just the same today as they had back then.

Indeed, Mr. Grondknot had not managed to reply with much more than a sputter, a flushed face, and a finger pointed toward the door. Molly knew fully well what this meant, and with the typical eye roll and huff of annoyance, the girl slowly stood up and slung her backpack over one shoulder, taking her time as she exited, sensing the rest of the students in the class staring awkwardly down at their desks to minimize their discomfort with the situation as much as possible.

That they didn't seem to care whether *she* was uncomfortable was the sort of irksome characteristic of her peers that compelled Molly to lead a significantly solitary teenage existence.

This was not an unusual manner for Molly to depart the classroom. In fact, most weeks saw it occur at least once or twice. She would sit in the stiff and creaky wooden chair in Vice Principal Anglehanger's office, slouching as much as the unfortunate chair would permit her while she attempted to master an expression upon her face that fell somewhere in between careless boredom and disgusted perplexity. Most of the teachers, and Mr. Anglehanger himself, would have offered the opinion that she'd mastered that look years ago and the last thing anyone needed was for her to practice it more now.

Vice Principal Anglehanger was what one might refer to as a "business-as-usual" sort of personality. Speaking in a drab monotone and rarely making eye contact with the person he was doing business with, he inspired the imagination and passion of no one but, perhaps, his pet guinea pig Henry, whom he kept in a cage on the bookshelf in his office above a dozen or so shelves that housed no books at all, in fact, but merely stacks and stacks of blank paper. ("You never know when you'll run out," he would say on the rare occasion in which someone showed enough interest to comment on the unusually high quantity of paper. What was most perplexing to Molly, however, was that he never seemed to use paper at all, and the stacks appeared quite the same as they had when she'd begun her attendance at the high school three years ago.) Even Henry, however, rarely seemed very inspired.

The décor of his office was true to Mr. Anglehanger's personality as well, not the reeking and echoing dungeon-like chamber that Mr. Grondknot's classroom was, but devoid of any personal touches but for the immobile lump of a guinea pig. The walls were white as white could be, the shelves empty but for the notorious collection of paper, his desk clean of everything but a pencil. No paper on the desk, mind, but rather just a lone and idle pencil. (Molly would often wonder if the pencil had remained unchanged all these years as well; in fact, there was no sign of a pencil sharpener anywhere in the office.)

Today, though, despite the drear surroundings, the vice principal was acting differently from his standard behavior of interviewing and doling out of disciplinary measures. Today, well, today he seemed to care. This didn't accomplish much in the way of making Molly feel any better. Of course, had she pointed this out to him, the vice principal would have interpreted this as a sure sign that he was doing a smashing job.

"Molly," Vice Principal Anglehanger sighed, looking up from the report on his desk to her sullen face. "Well, I just don't know what we're to do with you anymore. You're, well, potentially one of the brightest students at this school, and your creativity, well…if half of it went into your writing or some sort of extracurricular activity instead of constant outward defiance, well…"

Usually it was a silent game for Molly to count in her mind how many times during his speech Mr. Anglehanger used the word "well." She attempted this now, but the unusually consistent eye contact was putting up a wall of distraction in her mind.

"Molly, I think we need to, well…to take a new direction in dealing with these little, well…indiscretions."

Molly stared back silently, waiting for him to continue, not for the sake of politeness, of course, but rather simply in the hopes that the end may be in sight. If he were waiting for her to show some kind of curiosity or interest, he'd be disappointed rather quickly, her mind mused.

"Do you hear what I'm saying, Molly?" Mr. Anglehanger prodded. The girl shrugged briefly. Mr. Anglehanger sighed a faint disappointment and then seemed to determine that this was response enough. He himself shrugged, less defiantly than his young interviewee, and more as if to concede that there was no other avenue of opportunity than the one he'd been attempting to avoid.

He said as much: "Well, I didn't want to do this, Molly. I'd really, well, hoped to see some sign of…well, of remorse, I suppose." He sighed again and continued, "But, well…I see that's not going to happen."

Molly wasn't too concerned. Adults, in her experience, had a fondness to give the impression that something bad was about to occur, only for the exact opposite to occur in the end. How else could she get away with the things she did? The consequences were unfailingly always laughable.

"We're going to remove you from your, well, afternoon classes," the vice principal went on slowly, watching the girl's face for any signs of revolt.

Molly didn't react right away, though. Not entirely, anyway. She did sit up a smidgen and furrow her brow, clearly paying more attention now. She didn't say anything outwardly, however.

"Well, it just seems that perhaps, well, what you need right now isn't, well, what you're getting from us," Mr. Anglehanger went on, and Molly felt that she would erupt with frustration with the very next "well."

"Now wait a second," Molly said crossly, leaning forward and planting her hands firmly, flatly, face down on the administrator's desk. "Those are the classes *I* picked. You can't take me out of all the classes I picked to stick me, what, in some extra math class?"

"Yes, well...you misunderstand, my dear. We're not putting you in different classes. We're simply, well, removing you from your current ones."

Suddenly the situation looked brighter. She sat back slowly, cautiously. "Wait. You're saying I can leave at lunch?"

"Well..." The man thought for a moment before shrugging again and saying, "Well, yes."

"And I'll be free. To go wherever. Do whatever."

"Well, now, let us not forget your studies, Molly."

The girl fought the instinct to roll her eyes.

"And, well, you won't be, well, *free* to go wherever you wish." A single dark-haired eyebrow arched on the young lady's face. Mr. Anglehanger continued, "You will, well, you'll be...apprenticed. You see? You'll have, well, a, shall we say, cooperative venture between the school and a local establishment. You will leave here either immediately prior to or following your lunch period and report directly to the butcher shop on, well, Cobble Road."

It was unmistakably apparent by the expression on Mr. Anglehanger's face that he was expecting an outburst, and perhaps that he believed one was warranted as well. His face had frozen in a cringe, as though he expected an actual physical altercation to ensue. As for Molly, she didn't disappoint. She'd developed a reputation for speaking her mind at the school, and she wasn't going to stop now.

"Cobble Road? You're joking," she said, dumbfounded and gape-mouthed, incapable of taking on a tone of true disrespect or anger, occupied as she was with shock at what she'd just heard.

"Well, no..." Vice Principal Anglehanger looked uncomfortable now and made a half-hearted attempt to avert the girl's stare. She had reason to react this way, he knew. Cobble Road was rarely visited unless it was absolutely necessary, its residents famed for dark arts, treachery, and unspeakable deeds. It was often wondered but rarely verbalized by many West Cuttingsboroughians whether Cobble Road's dismal appearance was a result of the people who lived and worked there, or whether those people had been drawn to it for its dark nature. No one knew the solution to this chicken-or-egg riddle because even the longest-residing people of the town could not remember a time when Cobble Road had not been the way it was now. "Let me remind you, Molly, that, well, you did rather bring this on yourself."

The girl fought the instinct to counter this remark. "And there's no place in the whole town that needs help that *isn't* on Cobble Road?" she retorted instead.

With a reluctant shrug, Vice Principal Anglehanger said, taking time to select his words with care, "Well…there *are*, but…well, they don't seem to want…well, *your* help, my dear."

Molly wasn't sure what was eating at her more, the "wells" or the "my dears." What he said was inarguably valid, however. Just as her daughter would one day acquire a reputation around West Cuttingsborough to be one of the finest, most respectable young ladies to grace the town with her residence, Molly had managed to acquire one that spoke quite the opposite. Indeed, many in the years to come would proclaim that it was in part her mother's teenage personality that made Patty's very different one all the more impressive.

There was nothing more to be said. Mr. Anglehanger reached into his breast pocket and pulled forth a business card, which he handed to Molly across his desk. "Well," he said, "take this with you. It has, well, the name and address of the, well, the establishment. Your parents, well, they have already been contacted and informed of this change, and they've provided, well, their full support. Mrs. Swither, well, she will be expecting you beginning tomorrow afternoon. And Molly," he said, focusing intently on her and awaiting an acknowledgment of some sort.

She managed her best "Yes?" face without actually verbalizing anything.

"Well, be careful."

The butcher shop on Cobble Road was much what one might expect a butcher shop on Cobble Road to be. The meats that hung from hooks and were displayed prominently in the store window seemed grayer and more wilted than a proper cut of meat should appear. There weren't necessarily living organisms that were visible upon them, but strange discolorations and odd little wet or dark patches suggested the markings of something that called the food its home. The odor, which may have been a very brief relief from the one outside, would promptly be identified by anyone with a sense of smell as a far more atrocious bouquet. The floors were dirty, not merely with dirt, but with poisoned insects, used napkins and tissues, the dripped blood of the hanging meats, and dried up messes from Mrs. Swither's cat, Tin Pan, who choked up hairballs regularly.

All in all, it was the last place a respectable person would want to visit, let alone to spend his or her days. Hence, it should be little surprise that Mrs. Swither was far from decent in her own appearances. She was a frighteningly skinny woman, bent forward from the waist up, with one lazy eye that lingered in one's direction long after her conversation with that person had ended. Her fingers were long and bony, the yellowed cracked nails at their ends jagged from being the victims of her gnawing, crooked teeth. Her cheeks sagged in lumps of grayish flesh, and black hair was tangled in webs of knots and cross-stitches in the places where she wasn't bald altogether.

Mrs. Swither was actually the co-owner of the butcher shop, her partner being her husband, Mr. Swither, who was a beast of a specimen himself. Over 450 pounds and splotched over every inch of his skin with dark pockmarks and welts, which fought for space on his skin with oozing pimples that nested in the greasy creases of his body, Mr. Swither was only seen when he managed to pull himself up from the couch in the back room of the butcher shop to hunt for food. Where Mrs. Swither was disturbingly thin and frail for lack of eating ("I sells it, me deary, but I've not an inclinations to *eats* it!" she would later explain to Patty), Mr. Swither lived solely on the cuts of meat sold in the shop. As he would tear them from their resting places and take them back to his couch in the back room for his dining pleasure, no one but Mrs. Swither could be certain whether he actually cooked the meat before ingesting it, though Mrs. Swither did very little to speak up for him if he did.

Molly had never been to the butcher shop before, and nor, in fact, had Vice Principal Anglehanger, who didn't fully comprehend just what sort of vile punishment he had administered in sending the girl there. There were precious few people (students and faculty alike) who had even set foot on Cobble Road itself, let alone conducted business in one of its many disagreeable establishments.

Molly had, in fact, been to Cobble Road, however. It had been on a mutual dare, and she had been accompanied by one of the few students she attended school with who actually rather enjoyed her company. This young fellow's name was Jefferson Gladwell, and while he was a far cry from the defiant and troublesome teenager Molly was, he shared her passion for free-spirited loving of life and adventure, finding difficulty in the tedious imprisonment that schooling seemed to administer, far preferring the open air and the vast expanse of the world that surrounded him. Why study the world, he reasoned, when it was out there to be experienced, after all? In fact, there was many a Saturday that saw Molly and Jefferson sprawled out in the sun atop one of the very hills or on one of the very mountainsides whose view would so enrapture young Gerald many years later.

The two adventurers' one-time visit to Cobble Road consisted of little more than touching base on the street itself ("It doesn't count if we don't actually stand on it!" Jefferson proclaimed with a grin), taking in an astoundingly vivid and bleak view of the street's landscape, and turning quickly around and walking away very fast. Still, it had been more than enough time and experience to convince the girl that some adventures were best left unattended.

It was with these thoughts that Molly stepped upon the sickly, crumbling concrete of Cobble Road. She looked both ways down the street, wondering if the direction she'd seen when last here would look somehow less offensive than she recalled, or if perhaps the opposite direction held more optimistic promise. She was quite disappointed on both counts.

Drawing the business card from her pocket, she checked the address, looked up at her surroundings again in an attempt to locate a number on one of the decrepit, lopsided buildings, saw none, and chose a direction to begin walking.

Patty had been watching her mother from a distance for several days now.

Finding her hadn't been all that difficult. She knew, of course, that, based on the date, Molly would still be in high school. What she didn't know, however, was that her mother had been such a delinquent. Patty had never once been called to the office for anything other than accolades, thanks, and rewards. Her mother, on the other hand, seemed to make it a regular habit to get sent there for disciplinary action.

Patty had registered herself in the high school and managed to, thanks to only the dumbest of luck, find herself sharing two classes with her mother, one of which, as it happened, was Mr. Grondknot's western civilization class. Thus, Patty had been sitting just two rows away and three seats back from Molly when she had been sent out for sharing her feelings about philosophy.

Since Mr. McGulliver had sent her to this time period, she had done her best to stretch what money had been in her pocket for food and shelter. She was currently residing at the least costly inn in West Cuttingsborough, with the exception of the one located on Cobble Road, and she was taking advantage of the free donuts and cereal the inn provided each morning. Still, her life had tumbled into one of discomfort and want, and what she desired most of all was to be back home again. She was determined to do what she could to make that happen.

Molly had located the butcher shop. She was standing at the sidewalk still, staring wide-eyed at the windows of the shop, which boasted the lumpiest, greasiest, bloodiest, most discolored, and most unwelcoming cuts of meat she had ever laid eyes upon. She was thus far doing an admirable job of keeping her lunch down, though the smells that wafted from the shop's vents and commingled with those that permanently resided in the air of Cobble Road and built homes in the nests of deformed birds atop craggy and stretching, sprawling, yawning, begging, dead trees were fighting her greatly on that.

The girl was just beginning to ask herself how she might ever muster the courage to enter such a foul structure when a voice at her side made her jump and cry out, yanking her abruptly from her hypnotic appraisal of her would-be new job.

"Hi," was all the voice said, and when Molly had sufficiently recovered to examine from whom it had emitted, she was surprised to see a familiar face.

"You," Molly replied warily, looking back up at the butcher shop and then again to Patty. "I know you."

Patty's face betrayed both shock and fear, and she managed to choke out with trepidation, "You do?"

Nodding slowly, doing her best to avoid giving the impression that she was being friendly, she responded in as accusatory a voice as she was capable of, "You're the new girl. I don't know your name."

Patty nodded her understanding and confirmation and shared her name with her rough new classmate.

"Whatever," Molly said, turning back to the butcher shop. When Patty showed no signs of departing, she turned back grudgingly and demanded, "What do you want?"

"I just thought maybe I could help you," Patty offered brightly, smiling in such a manner as to leave Molly gagging on it nearly as much as she already was on the stench.

"Help what?" she said, perturbed. There was something about this girl that was disagreeing with her, something about her that didn't seem right. She couldn't put her finger on what it was, but there was something in the girl's mannerisms, her face, and her body language that didn't fit.

"Well," Patty said tentatively, realizing more every second how much she would have to feel Molly out and take special care with her choice of words and tactics in getting close to her, something she had not expected to have to do. "I've spent quite a bit of time here, and I'm pretty used to it. I thought if you want, I could pretend to be you and work here for you."

Molly didn't know whether to be ecstatic or repulsed, and was just about to berate the girl before her for what surely must have been a sickness for actually seeking to work in this vile place when it struck her that this was exactly what had been bothering her about Patty: she wasn't showing the least signs of discomfort at her surroundings, and Patty was clearly not of the rough and tough nature that Molly was. That she, Molly, could be so repulsed and physically ill over the sights and smells on Cobble Road while a prim and proper little sugar-sweetheart like Patty should be standing there as nonchalant as if she were standing in line for an ice cream cone was just plain offensive. Still, an offer was an offer, regardless of how revolting the motives may be.

"How do you know I'm supposed to be working here?" she demanded.

"Well, word's gotten around. I left at lunch today to meet you here. It'll be a while before they realize I'm missing."

Untrusting of Patty's unfounded consideration, Molly spat back at her, "And why would you want to do that?"

"Well," Patty said.

"That's the second time you've said that," Molly accused, sudden realization dawning on her. "Did Anglehanger send you here?"

"Who?" Patty's face showed genuine signs of bewilderment. "What? No. I. . . . I said what?"

"Well."

"Well what?"

"Just 'well.' You said 'well.' Twice. V.P. Anglehanger says it after about every third word. I figured you were, you know, mixed up with him or something."

Patty's head began to shake back and forth vigorously, panicked denials pouring from her mouth faster than she should have been able to speak.

"Fine," Molly interrupted as Patty rambled on. "Fine, fine, fine, *fine*! So what? Why are you actually offering to go into that rotten place for me?"

"Well," Patty said, and realizing what she'd done just as Molly's eyes widened in anger, she quickly continued. "I need the job. And I know you don't want to work here. Like I said, I have experience here; I know how it can be when you aren't used to it."

"Here? Here, like the butcher shop?"

"Well, no," Patty admitted, looking with obvious distaste at the meat shop. "Cobble Road, though. I run errands here a lot."

Molly assessed the girl's face, looking for signs of trickery or deceit, but could find none. "It's not a paying job, you know. It's just in place of afternoon classes. You won't get money, *and* you'll get caught leaving school early every day."

Patty smiled knowingly, and shook her head. "Don't worry about that. I think I can take care of both of those problems."

"Fine then. What about me? You're just going to do my work while I, what, go sleep under a tree somewhere?"

Patty was becoming more comfortable. She seemed to have picked up a rhythm of how to talk to Molly, and as far as Molly could tell, she was enjoying it far too much. "I'm going to take care of that too," Patty explained. "I'm going to talk to the vice principal about allowing me to do the same sort of thing. I figure that because I'm doing it on my own, I can maybe get a job somewhere nicer, and we could then trade."

Molly was impressed. She hadn't given this girl an ounce of notice or credit when she had joined her western civilization class almost a week ago, but she was proving to be pleasantly sneaky and conniving. Still not without reluctance and a certain degree of distrust, but wanting to believe the girl and thinking that the plan just might succeed, she determined to go along with it.

Patty nodded, satisfied, and sent Molly on her way. When Molly reached the corner where she was to turn off of Cobble Road, she turned back and watched Patty enter the butcher shop. Then she turned around and walked with an uncharacteristic spring in her step to the park, thinking that this would be a perfect afternoon for a nap.

If Patty was just a tad dishonest, or not entirely forthcoming with the whole of her plan, it was simply to win Molly over. In fact, she did visit Vice Principal Anglehanger for the purpose of discussing an afternoon apprenticeship position for herself. And true, she did fully intend to trade positions with Molly. What she'd failed to mention was that she already had a position in mind, one that would place Molly right where Patty needed her to be in order to accomplish what needed doing.

"An apprenticeship?" Vice Principal Anglehanger asked skeptically, peering at Patty over his horn-rimmed glasses.

She nodded agreeably, and went on to explain, "Like Molly Noggett has. I think it would be a good experience for me."

Mr. Anglehanger chuckled mildly and shook his head with unmistakable condescension. "Ah, well, my dear, I don't think that being like Molly Noggett is something you'd best be, well, striving for here."

"I know what you're thinking," Patty assured him, fighting the temptation to speak angry words of defense on her mother's behalf. "But it doesn't really matter *why* she's working at the butcher shop, does it? It's still a good experience, isn't it?"

Mr. Anglehanger's face demonstrated the expression of a man who'd just been knocked in the head by a very large object. Clearly, the notion of doing *anything* on Cobble Road was not something he had ever considered "a good experience."

"Well..." he began, and looked at Patty's serious, unsmiling face. The girl was clearly sincere. Sighing, Vice Principal Anglehanger started again. "Well, young lady, I have no objection...currently. At present, well, I don't believe this could do any harm. But mind you," and here he held up a single index finger and allowed his eyes to bulge from their sockets, "the first sign that I think, well, that it is anything other than a valid, well, learning experience, you'll be sitting right back in, well, your afternoon classes. Am I understood, my dear?"

Patty nodded her understanding and expressed her thanks profusely, and when Mr. Anglehanger began to search through his drawers for a directory of local businesses, she craftily requested that she simply take the necessary forms and see if she could find the perfect position for herself. Seeing no reason to object to this any more than to the parts he'd already agreed to, he handed her copies of the same paperwork he'd given to Molly the previous day and wished her the best of luck in her venture.

It wasn't much of a plan, true, but still, it was under way.

"McGulliver? I don't know who that is."

"He owns the hat shop in town." They were seated in a small café sipping lemonades and nibbling on butter cookies. Patty continued quickly before there was an opportunity for Molly to misunderstand her. "But that's not where you'll be working."

"Where, then?" Molly asked. While there was still a degree of impatience and annoyance in her voice, her edge had dulled markedly since their initial meeting the previous day.

"His house," Patty said with a grin. "You'll be his housekeeper. His wife's, actually."

This news was received with less enthusiasm than that with which Patty delivered it. "Housekeeper? A maid?"

Patty shook her head adamantly. "I know how it sounds, and I know you think it's not in your personality, but just wait until you see his house! He lives in that giant mansion on the other side of town. It has the most exotic rooms, and it's almost immaculate to begin with. No doubt you won't need to do anything more difficult than brew the occasional pot of tea or coffee, or set the table settings or make the bed."

Molly couldn't help but feel that the girl was overselling the housekeeping position. Had she known that there was, in fact, no position to be filled, at least none that Mr. McGulliver knew about, she may have determined that Patty was perhaps a bit too strange for her tastes and abandoned the endeavor altogether. But as it happened, the café where they were meeting at present was not all that far away from Cobble Road, and when Molly looked out the window and imagined having to set foot upon that ground, walk past those trees, inhale those fumes, and then spend her afternoons in that revolting butcher shop, she dismissed any reservations she may have had.

"Fine," she said. "Whatever. I'll do it. Okay."

Patty seemed satisfied. She was, of course, gambling on the chance that Mrs. McGulliver would accept that there had been some sort of mix-up at the school, or that her husband had failed to tell her about his participation in the school's apprenticeship program, but would be kind enough to allow Molly (or Patty, as she would know her) to come to work as her housekeeper.

To say there was some confusion when the girls showed up at the door to the mansion would be an understatement, but Patty was confident that her experience as an actress would guide her to success.

"Just let me do the talking, and you follow my lead," she said. Molly let this go, unclear about what sort of "talking" should need to be done. She had learned in the last two days to accept that she had met someone more eccentric than herself.

Good fortune was with them that afternoon. One can only speculate how the events of this tale may have turned out frighteningly different, had Percival H. Rutherford McGulliver been a more communicative spouse to his wife. As it happened, it was quite clear from Mrs. McGulliver's reaction that it would have been completely true to her husband's character to make arrangements such as this without informing her.

"Well, in all fairness to Mr. McGulliver, ma'am, the high school has made mistakes like this before; I wouldn't be surprised if it was their fault, actually." Patty's fashioned excuse seemed to be perfectly sufficient for the lady of the house.

Welcoming them in and directing them to a seat in a warm little parlor, Mrs. McGulliver spoke with an air of amusement. "It's good of you to defend him like that, not that the old crackpot deserves it."

Mrs. McGulliver was a beautiful woman. To say that she was a beautiful woman, however, hardly does justice to the physical presence that was the wife of the hat salesman. Indeed, even on her own or beside a handsome prince of a man with striking good looks of his own, Mrs. McGulliver would have stood out in a crowd. One could only wonder at how her beauty must have radiated and magnified when standing next to a mouse of a man like Percival McGulliver. Mrs. McGulliver's hair was less than shoulder length, and it bounced and flowed in a silky chocolate splendor even as it framed an olive-skinned face with a nose just pointed enough to be characteristic without being a distraction. Her coffee-colored eyes had a penetrating knowingness that bored through to one's soul, and her curved figure and stylish yet simple clothing (she was currently wearing a flowered cocktail dress that would have flattered a woman with a less desirable frame than hers) would have led Molly to demand tactlessly of her just what she was doing with Percival McGulliver had she ever laid eyes upon him. Indeed, watching Mrs. McGulliver now, Molly would have assumed that her husband was of the svelte and muscular nature, complete with a swirling mass of perfect hair and a smile that could blind with its glowing whiteness.

"Thank you for taking Patty on, Mrs. McGulliver," Patty said politely, not bothered by the woman's biting words of her husband, but wishing to direct the conversation back to the matter at hand. She did, after all, need to get to work at the butcher shop on Cobble Road before Mrs. Swither became suspicious and contacted Vice Principal Anglehanger.

"Millicent," Mrs. McGulliver replied. "Call me Millicent." Then she turned to Molly, a questioning bemusement evident upon her face. "Can't you speak for yourself?" she put forth directly.

Molly peered at Millicent McGulliver down her nose, taking no heed of any potential disrespect she may have been conveying.

"Yes," she said in a tone that suggested this should have been the plainest fact imaginable.

Mrs. McGulliver nodded her satisfaction, seeming simply to be confirming what she's suspected already. "Very well," she said with a decisive sigh that communicated a desire to get down to business, as though Molly's questionable sense of speech was the one determining factor in her hiring of the girl. "I suppose, Molly, that you should be reporting to your own assignment, yes?"

Patty, nodding and rising to her feet, responded, "Yes ma'am. I really should be going. Best of luck to the both of you in getting acquainted." And she saw herself out the way she'd come in, venturing back to the Cobble Road butcher shop.

After she'd gone, Millicent McGulliver turned to Molly and instantly graced her with a knowing, businesslike expression.

"All right, young lady," she said in a voice to match her face. "What is really going on here?"

Molly, not to be taken aback (at least not visibly), took her chances at her best nonchalance. "What do you mean?" she asked in a voice that didn't quite manage to sound as ignorant as she might have wished.

"Come, come," the beautiful woman said with a smirk. "Clearly there is more to this whole...*arrangement* than you or your little cohort are willing to let on. I've hired you; I've determined to take a chance upon allowing you into my home for fifteen hours a week, and I can quite easily change my mind. Now, I'm willing to overlook certain...specifics, but not if I don't receive sufficient reason from you as to why I should. In other words, if you want me to go along with this charade, I'm going to need full honesty from you."

Molly told Millicent what she knew, though admittedly that was very little. All she knew with any amount of certainty was that she was supposed to be working at the butcher shop, that Patty was there in her place, and that Patty had finagled this job, and the two had traded positions and names. She knew her own motive for doing so, and the desire *not* to be working on Cobble Road was hardly an alibi whose validity Mrs. McGulliver could contest, though Molly had no understanding whatsoever of what *Patty's* motive might have been for desiring to work on Cobble Road.

"Hmm," Millicent said thoughtfully to herself, working out the details in her mind. At last, after a good deal of staring down and biting her lower lip, Millicent McGulliver determined, "I'm not certain she does want to work there, in fact. It seems much more likely that her wish was for *you* to work *here*."

Few things ever surprised Molly, and it was perpetually the frustration of her peers and superiors at school that she was so constantly unimpressed or moved to emotion by anything. This, however, clearly perplexed her, and she showed as much on her face as well as through the simple fact that for once she had no verbal return to offer.

"Don't ask me why," Millicent declared before Molly had a chance to regain her train of thought and express the inquiry. "I haven't the foggiest notion. For the time being, though, we shall humor her, you and I. But keep a close watch on her. If our young Miss Patty has reasons for bringing you and me together, she's kept them secret deliberately. The question that remains is who that secret might be protecting? Her? Us? Someone else? All of us?" She shrugged her own lack of an answer, and then stood up, indicating for Molly to do the same.

"She knows the truth," Molly expressed in her deadpan voice, as if to say that she didn't care one way or another, and if Patty did, that was her own issue to deal with. The bottom line in her estimation was that they'd struck a bargain that kept her off of Cobble Road, and she didn't intend to allow Patty to renege on that deal. Patty, however, showed no signs that she would allow Millicent McGulliver's wit and insight to derail her plans.

"As long as she's willing to go along with the whole thing, I don't mind what she knows. All the better that she does know, in fact."

It may have been Molly's imagination that Patty was enjoying harboring some secret knowledge that Molly wasn't privy to, but she didn't think so. Molly leaned forward, her hands palm down on the table between them.

"Listen here," she said, a coldness in her voice that somehow Patty had managed to melt away over the past few days. Really, Molly found herself wondering, what *was* it about this girl that seemed to soften and break Molly's hard edge the way that few others could? She couldn't have answered if she tried. "You're going to need to start being straight with me about what you're up to, or *I'm* going to stop keeping your secrets for you."

Patty appeared to examine Molly's face closely, seemed to be considering her words and assessing her sincerity as she'd said them. "I want to," Patty said at last in a hushed voice, sounding less in control than she'd managed so far. "I really do, Mo—" Patty's voice ceased completely. Molly looked at her, wondering if she was about to start crying. "Molly," Patty finished. "I want to, and I have to. I will. Soon. But right now, just trust me. It's important."

"To who?" Molly shot back, and Patty stared back pleadingly.

"Just trust me. For now." Her voice reflected the plea that was in her eyes. Molly was unaccustomed to being begged, and she wasn't entirely certain it agreed with her now. And yet, there was something in this girl's face, something in her mannerisms and the way she acted and spoke around her that screamed in loud and reassuring tones that she was to be trusted.

"Fine," Molly said to her daughter, not for the first or the last time.

The following weeks saw Molly exhibiting a stronger work ethic than she ever previously had. Millicent never left home, and as Patty had described, the mansion was normally in pristine condition and required very little effort on Molly's part, which allowed for much time spent between the two women. Molly would seek out additional responsibilities, due neither to boredom nor to a newfound enjoyment in the duties of a housekeeper, but rather in an effort to please and impress her supervisor. Molly saw Percival McGulliver very rarely, only on the occasions that she was still at the mansion when he arrived home from the hat shop, though that only typically occurred when she either had been running errands that took longer than anticipated or when she and Millicent were so engaged in conversation that the girl lost track of the time.

That Molly's parents noticed a difference in her since her work at the McGulliver mansion had begun is undoubtedly true. The same could be said for her teachers and peers. Indeed, were Vice Principal Anglehanger the type of man to think upon and consider a student when the child was not seated directly in front of him at the moment, he too would have realized that a change had been under way almost from the start. But, alas, being that Molly had not been sent to his office since her work for Millicent McGulliver had begun, he actually hadn't thought much about her.

The afternoons at the mansion were filled with meaningful conversations, hearty laughter, and even, from time to time, wrenching tears and comforting hugs. Molly's parents were neither negligent nor nurturing. They simply didn't understand their daughter and, for lack of a better idea, kept her at arm's length for fear of losing her completely. Millicent seemed, though she was greatly different from the girl, to understand her with no effort at all. She could relate to her feelings, identify her motives, and usually figure out what was on her mind or why she was speaking or acting in a certain way, but she also wasn't afraid to criticize the girl and put her in her place when she felt she was acting inappropriately or unfairly. In a nutshell, though Molly never could have thought to label it as such, she had at last found a strong and supportive parent figure in her life in the form of Millicent McGulliver.

Likewise, Patty had grown to be like a sister to her, though that wasn't quite it, she thought. They had a strong, solid relationship that grew every day, and they equally supported and aggravated each other, but Molly couldn't help feeling, though Patty certainly kept things from her and wasn't entirely forthright and honest, that she, Molly, had a certain responsibility to look out for her and to take care of her. When it seemed to Molly on certain occasions that Patty's secrets may be getting dangerous, she would watch and listen extra carefully, looking for signs that the girl was in trouble or was somehow asking for help.

"Have you made any progress in getting to the bottom of your friend Patty?" Millicent would ask occasionally, and Molly would be forced to confess that she hadn't tried very hard.

"I just figure she'll tell me what's going on when she wants to," she explained on one such occasion.

Millicent curled her lips and furrowed her brows. "Hmm ..." she said, trailing off without expanding the thought at all.

When prompted by the girl to explain what was turning over behind the thoughtful face, Mrs. McGulliver suggested to her, "Perhaps she believes that she will. But she may be afraid to tell you the truth."

One thing that Patty did not appear to be was fearful, and this theory seemed ridiculous to Molly. Still, she had gotten to know Millicent McGulliver fairly well in the last several weeks, and she had proven herself to be a decidedly intelligent and insightful woman. The thought stuck in Molly's brain and gnawed at it until her next meeting at the local diner with Patty.

Patty attempted all the ordinary avenues of conversation, and some new and unexplored ones as well, but Molly remained silent, barely touching her sandwich and staring intently at Patty's face, searching for the slightest sign of a betrayal of whatever secret she'd been harboring.

"The butcher shop isn't really that bad," Patty attempted. "I mean, the Swithers are ...well, strange. But they haven't been *mean*, exactly. I'm not even sure Mr. Swither has noticed my being there. He comes in sometimes, sniffs around at the meat, takes something, grunts at his wife, and goes back into the back room. I'm not allowed back there. I can go into the bathroom, of course, but not into the room where Mr. Swither is all day. I have to stay in the sales room. I take care of customers mostly. Mrs. Swither puts out all the cuts of meat when the deliveries arrive. You'd be amazed what size cuts of meat she can lift with her tiny little body. It's scary, almost."

Patty had so impressed Mrs. Swither with her positive attitude and willingness to work under her that she had managed to persuade the woman to allow her to work on past the ending time of her apprenticeship each day for actual pay. It wasn't good pay, mind, but rather pay to be expected from someone of Cobble Road, and certainly as shady an individual as the butcher lady. But it was enough to pay for Patty's room at the inn, and to buy her meals, which was all she was looking to accomplish until she'd managed to return to where she belonged.

Molly finally couldn't tolerate the endless stream of babble that was trickling from her friend's lips. "Stop it," she said, her annoyance plain. "What is going on?"

Patty stopped short and only for a second attempted to feign ignorance.

"Just stop," Molly repeated, and softened her voice just a touch. "You basically admitted weeks ago that there was something you were keeping from me. Why you have no problem working on Cobble Road, why you really wanted me to work for the McGullivers… There's a reason behind it all, and you've been keeping it from me. I'm through. Just tell whatever it is. Now."

Well, she'd been wrong about one thing; that was now evident. Patty was indeed afraid. The look upon the girl's face was unmistakable, and though they were the same age, Molly saw a youth and an innocence, a pleading look in her eyes that conveyed, quite alarmingly, a need for reassurance, a look that said that Patty needed Molly to understand and feared her rejection of whatever story she was about to share. Once again, Molly was overcome with the feeling that she was responsible for this girl, the feeling that she wanted to take care of her and protect her in a way she'd never felt about anyone but herself, except perhaps for her friend Jefferson Gladwell, whose own innocence and desire to bring joy to her life dulled the edge of resentment she'd carried for the world for so many years. She didn't know what Patty was going to say to her, but she resolved to herself at that moment that she would have an open mind and do her best to accept whatever words she heard next.

"I'm your daughter," Patty said, her voice trembling and catching, but being forced from her mouth with visible effort, unwilling to allow the one-second window of courage to escape untaken.

Molly's head bent forward as her eyes bored into Patty's, awaiting the explanation, but somewhere, somehow, deep beneath this waiting, deep beneath the common sense that cried out that the girl was either speaking figuratively or else was insane, there was another voice that hushed her thoughts and whispered to her to remember the promise she'd just made to herself, to hear out what Patty had to say with an open mind, and this voice, as clear as crystal in a shining sun, was indeed calling Patty her daughter.

And so Patty explained it all. To say there were no tears would be an apparent lie, but to say that there were none on Molly's part would be equally untrue. Molly said nothing, but sat attentively listening to Patty as she related how she'd been working for Percival

McGulliver for two years, and how she would make weekly deliveries to Professor Spice, the tobacconist on Cobble Road, which was what had so desensitized her to the unsettling nature of that stretch of West Cuttingsborough. She explained about her mute younger brother, Gerald, and the danger he'd turned out to be in. She explained about Mr. McGulliver's secret code for manipulating time, and she explained about the anointed coin and the required sacrifice to raise the dead. She explained how the sacrifice required someone who suffered some disability, a person more vulnerable than others, and how McGulliver had perceived Gerald as the perfect candidate for this sacrifice. And then she explained that where she came from, Mrs. Millicent McGulliver had been dead for several years.

At last, with a breath, the girl rested her voice, looked to Molly, and awaited her response. She hadn't said everything, but she knew she'd said enough for the moment.

After a rather lengthy silence, Molly took a sip of water, looked down at the table, cleared her throat, looked around uncomfortably, and rested her eyes on Patty once again. When she spoke, her voice had the same catch that Patty's had had when they'd first met. "And where are you from?" she asked, though Patty had been correct; enough had been said already to piece it together.

Patty's reservations were gone. Either her mother believed the story or she didn't, and there was no going back now. With no hesitation, she declared, "You'll marry Jefferson Gladwell about a year after you both graduate. You'll have me three years after that, and Gerald will come later. Mr. McGulliver sent me here when I discovered what his plans were."

Molly's eyes were wide, yes, and her mouth hung open with what could only have appeared to be disbelief. Tears stood in her eyes to represent what Patty was certain was the sadness at the tragic apparent mental collapse of her friend. "And," Molly managed softly, her voice no more than a hoarse whisper, "when did he send you here?"

Certain now that Molly was simply gathering all the evidence that she was out of her mind and that none of what she was saying was going to help to save her brother *or* help her to get back to the time where she belonged, Patty answered simply, "Just about a month ago. Just a few days before I talked to you outside the butcher shop."

Molly said nothing, but nodded shortly. Her face looked thoughtful, her emotions torn. The waitress approached during this silence to refill their waters and to inquire whether they were interested in dessert. Their awkward short head shakes sent the poor woman shuffling away in discomfort, and Molly turned back to Patty with a look of resolve on her face. Patty braced herself for what was to come, fighting back the outpouring of tears that were standing by awaiting their trigger of release.

"Okay," Molly said simply. She nodded, tears of her own welling and streaming. She brushed these away angrily, embarrassment overshadowing whatever other emotions were gripping her now.

Patty cocked her head with confusion. She looked carefully at the other girl, not wishing to misconstrue anything she saw or heard. Hesitantly, with great caution, she repeated, "Okay?"

Molly nodded more decisively now, quickly and solidly, at the same time forfeiting her battle against the tears that were so persistent to be shed. "Okay," she said again. "Okay."

Patty's smile was the truest, broadest, most Patty-like smile she'd displayed in many weeks, and it was the first such grin that Molly ever witnessed on her daughter's face, and it was in seeing this smile that she finally, concretely *knew* Patty's story to be the truth. Her widened eyes and sharp intake of breath told Patty as much, and they both burst into newer, cleaner, happier tears, laughing and reaching uncomfortably but determinedly for each other's hands across the table.

"Help me," Patty choked through the emotion. "Gerald needs us. Please, help me save him."

And again, Molly nodded, gripping her daughter's hands tightly and mirroring the grin she was seeing in her face, the same one that was on her own face, the one she would be gifting to her five years later in her birth.

"Okay," she said.

Millicent wouldn't know the details, but Molly saw to it that she would know as much as she needed to. She took a couple of days (with Patty's assistance, of course) to devise a version of the story that would be sufficient in accomplishing their goal while not losing Millicent's trust or risking her judgment that they were both out of their minds.

"It's all about your husband," is what Molly determined in the end to tell her. What she would say next, if anything, hinged upon the woman's response.

"Ah, well, that doesn't surprise me one bit," was Mrs. McGulliver's less than surprising reaction. Millicent didn't speak of her husband with any frequency, but on those days when she did, it was not with what one would call affection.

Molly waited before explaining further, silently hoping that this was sufficient enough explanation to satisfy her employer. She didn't think this was completely out of the question.

Sighing, Millicent strode closer to the girl and, with resolve in her eyes and body, went on to explain. "Percival spends . . . a *lot* of time," she said, choosing her words with care, "behind locked doors, researching or experimenting or . . . well, I don't know what. He's never let me in on his private study sessions, and I stopped expressing interest years ago."

Molly nodded slowly, considering the situation. Relief was in order, certainly, but it pained her to witness such a clear soreness of heart in the woman who had grown to be, well, rather the mother figure in her life. She hadn't considered it to be so before, but now that she thought about it, she felt more part of a loving family now with Patty and Millicent than she'd ever felt with her own parents. How fine it would be, she thought briefly, if Patty could have spent more time with her and Millicent; that would have been a true family indeed.

She started when she felt Millicent's hand upon her shoulder, rousing her from her thoughts.

"Where did you go?" the woman asked with a smile. Molly shook her head with a smile of her own, dismissing her moment of dreamy lapse. "Well," Millicent went on, "I suppose the less I know the better?"

Molly shrugged, not wishing to admit as much to her boss, but knowing that this was the truth; ignorance was Millicent's best position in this case. It was bad enough not to share all the facts with her friend, but to cause her any further pain or resentment toward her husband was something she could not bring herself to be a party to.

"It's truly fine, Molly," Millicent reassured her with a comforting smile. "I long ago accepted that Percival has a whole life apart from me behind closed doors, one in which I have never been welcome." Molly looked down, eye contact during this confessionary moment of sharing too painful to bear. "What's more," the woman went on in a conclusive voice that gave Molly a chill, "it's never been a secret to me that it was that life he preferred. Sometimes I wonder whether he would notice if I just left one day and didn't return."

Molly's blood turned to ice with this admission, for she knew she couldn't share with Millicent the sickly truth that Patty had brought to light, that Percival McGulliver very much *would* notice her absence, and would attempt to come to grips with it in a frightfully extreme manner.

"Very well," Millicent said with an air of decisive finality. "Clearly your friend has been crossed or wronged in some way by my husband, she or her family or someone. I trust you can admit to that much?"

Molly nodded briefly. "Yes, ma'am," she managed.

"Fine then. What does she want from me?"

What Patty actually needed at that moment was the good grace of God to bless her with the loss of her sense of smell. The beastly odors that filled the sales floor of the butcher shop were especially offensive today, and Mrs. Swither's own natural scents were giving them a good challenge in a competition of stenches to match none Patty had ever been subject to. Still, she put on her happiest face possible and tried not to think about the seedy customers who actually purchased the foul meats. In fact, it hadn't yet failed to alarm her how much foot traffic the butcher shop actually did receive, and how few of those people (truly next to none of them) left the shop empty-handed. Of course, one does not enter a butcher shop with the intent simply to browse; one most often has an objective in mind, and that includes departing the establishment complete with a specific cut of meat. These people left with the meat, true enough, but Patty found it difficult to imagine that it was the sort of meat they actually had their hearts set upon eating.

"There, dearie," Mrs. Swither screeched, her voice almost metallic in its naturally high pitch. "You forgots to try and sells that last one a nice lamb shank, see? Don'ts be tryin' a do's thats agains, me dearie."

Before Patty could respond, the door to the back room swung open and Mr. Swither was standing there with his whole frame slouched forward, as if merely holding up his body from falling to the ground like a sack of wet dirt was a task requiring great strength. He stared unseeingly at no certain focal point in the room, or perhaps through the window to the street outside, and then shuffled despondently where the links of sausage hung from hooks in the ceiling. He reached up, and with one very gentle tug, managed to bring down every sausage that was there. He darted a challenging look at Patty, his eyes daring her to say anything to him, anything at all, and then, satisfied that no one was going to disrupt his sausage thievery, nodded, grunted, and returned to his room, shutting the door with a conclusive *click* behind him.

"There thens, dearie. Does ya hears what I says?" Mrs. Swither demanded, a bit instigated by the attention her husband had received from the girl while she was busy reprimanding her.

"Yes, ma'am," Patty acknowledged, and returned to her work.

The truth of the matter was Patty had always struggled more on the inside than she'd ever been willing to allow people to see on the outside. In her days at West Cuttingsborough High School, she'd seen every day what an inspiration her high ambitions, her perpetual smile, and her ever-positive attitude had been for her peers and teachers. When she was lacking the confidence to perform a certain role, when she scored less than she felt she'd been capable of on an examination, when she simply felt she needed a moment alone to sit someplace quiet and allow herself to be sad, she never took the opportunities to feel this way; she maintained the persona people had come to expect of her.

In fact, it had been somewhat of a relief in some ways when she'd decided to leave school. Oh, she missed all of the people, certainly, and being on stage had always been what made her happiest, and even though she'd promised herself that she would never stop learning, that there was an entire world to be discovered, whole histories to be unlocked, her duties at the hat shop and at home had kept her occupied and she found she greatly missed her studies. Still, to have to appear happy and positive to hundreds of people every day was quite taxing, and the notion of only having to be that way for one person (Mr. McGulliver) and the odd customer who wandered into the shop, well, that was a load off of her shoulders, and she could not deny it.

Molly had been unable to come to grips with why Patty had been so eager to work on Cobble Road. In fact, aside from the need for money and the wish to place Molly strategically alongside Millicent McGulliver, Patty also considered that working in a place where *no one* was happy, where *all* was gloom and despair would allow her to go through her days without having to put on a happy face that simply was not in her spirits anymore. She was banished from where she belonged, her brother was in grave danger, and, as wonderful as it was finally to develop a real relationship with her mother, knowing it was doomed to come to a tragic end made the time she spent with Molly quite bittersweet.

Indeed, Patty never did divulge *all* the information of the future, namely the fact that Molly would die when Patty was still quite young. And sitting upon such a weighty slice of the truth while looking into her young mother's eyes was something that turned out to be far more painful than she'd expected. When Molly asked her questions about their future, about what kind of relationship they shared or what fond memories Patty had that Molly could look forward to, Patty would dismiss the question lightly, smiling and assuring her that it was best for everyone if she just wait and experience it all firsthand. Molly never argued with this, though she was clearly curious, and it wore poor Patty down more every day.

Sadly, as you may have noticed in your own life, despite our best intentions, our own natures are a difficult thing to alter, and no matter in how utter of despair Patty found herself, she still could not dismiss her need to demonstrate the happy, positive face for the benefit of others, even if those others were the dismal Swithers of Cobble Road. With every berating, every criticism, every snide remark or ruthless sneer, Patty returned it with a smile and a nod and a job well done. And it was breaking her inside a little more every day. Though she could not have recognized it herself, Molly's success in helping her defeat Percival McGulliver was becoming every bit as much integral to her own life as to that of her brother.

"What does she want from me?" Millicent McGulliver had asked of Molly. As it turned out, what Patty really wanted (or needed, as the case may have been, for the time being anyway) was information. Of course, she knew she needed access to the secret code that would allow her to control time, but that would take some time and craftwork. In the meantime, she had suggested to Molly that they might be able to uncover some information about the alleged dead-raising spell that Professor Spice evidently had knowledge of. This, Patty reasoned, would at least give them some further understanding of the transaction that was leading to her brother's doom.

Now, Millicent McGulliver knew a thing or two about Anson Spice. Being a bit younger than her husband, she had actually been a student at the university during the professor's brief time there, and she had been unfortunate enough to be one of his very own students.

Being a student under Professor Spice was a position that none at the university strove to achieve and that fewer still envied of those unlucky ones who had no choice. His standards were unreasonably high, his expectations were unfairly low, his moods were cloudy at best, and his voice injected acidic venom directly into the hearts of any who were made to stand at the receiving end of it. In short, Mrs. McGulliver knew about as well as anyone in West Cuttingsborough (or anywhere, for that matter) just what an unpleasant fellow Professor Anson Spice was.

"Spice? Oh yes, I know Spice," Millicent informed Molly one afternoon when Molly had mustered the courage to broach the subject with her. Millicent was sitting upon a wooden stool on the patio outside the back of the mansion, her attention on an easel set up in front of her, on which was a canvas that boasted a half-completed painting of a village scene in the winter. Molly was pulling weeds from the vegetable garden that thrived right next to it.

"Is he very bad?" Molly asked. Patty had been rather vague on the matter of Anson Spice. Of Percival McGulliver, Molly was quite versed in Patty's opinions, but his mysterious partner in this little matter of business was still just the foggiest of phantoms in Molly's mind.

Millicent stopped painting, and looked to Molly thoughtfully. She lowered her brush and bit the inside of her lip with the delicate care of her attention to the question that had been posed.

"Bad?" the woman repeated at last. "No, no, I don't believe he is bad. He is quite intelligent, though I'm not at all certain that he's very wise. He is perceptive and powerful and probably harmless to most. But," she said, her mental cogs still working to bring forth the best estimation possible, "I do trust that he could be quite threatening to anyone who stood in the way of his ambitions. Or anyone who could be useful in meeting them, for that matter." Millicent McGulliver nodded, satisfied with her summing-up of the man, and turned back to her painting. After several strokes and stabbings with the brush, she lowered it again and turned once again to Molly. "As a matter of fact," she said, "I don't know that he's all that different in that respect from Percival."

This shouldn't have surprised Molly, what with all the cold-hearted things she'd heard the woman say of her husband, but it captured the girl's attention nonetheless, and she paused in her work and lowered herself from the uncomfortable stoop to sit right on her bottom in the dirt to listen.

Millicent McGulliver stood up from the stool, laid her materials down upon it, and wiped her paint-smeared hands on her smock. Her delicate and flattering figure seemed contradictory to the crackling and snapping of her knees as she straightened them.

"Some men," she said as she strode toward the garden, "have ... shall we say, difficulty, figuring out who they really love. There was a time," she went on, a wistful smile materializing on her lips, "when Percival would have uprooted mountains if he thought it would make me happy. Now?" She simply shook her head and turned back toward the easel, picking it up along with the brushes. "I think you've done splendidly for today, Molly. Why don't you quit early and meet Patty? Ask her what evenings she's free from the butcher shop; it would do well for all of us to sit and have a chat together. Tell her not to worry about encountering Percival. I'll secure us a private chamber for the occasion."

Molly felt a warmth come over her at this suggestion. She had only just been thinking of how good it might be to spend some time with both of her newfound friends at the same time, and here one of them was putting it forth as a suggestion. Nodding vigorously, the girl thanked the woman and she went inside to wash her hands and be on her way.

The meeting of the three ladies occurred in the game room of the mansion three nights later, not entirely to the excitement and willingness of Patty, who had decided that the further from the McGulliver home she remained, the better.

"Mr. McGulliver and you don't know each other in the future, not the way he knows me," Patty protested. Molly assured her friend of Millicent's promise that Mr. McGulliver would not be anywhere near them, and took the liberty of elaborating, sharing the other details of the McGullivers' suffering relationship. This didn't put a rest to Patty's concerns; it did, however, ease them enough to allow Molly to convince her (grudgingly, of course) to accompany her to the mansion.

They were seated closely to each other on three different antique sofas, a coffee table at their center, offering chocolate cake, milk, crackers and jam, and coffee. They sat quietly, filling their plates and cups and munching and sipping at them, the girls nodding their approval and taking in the sights of the room. There was a pool table in one corner; a wooden card table complete with chips, cards, and dice in another; a rather large and ornate chess set; and various other tables throughout the room of indeterminate nature, with the sofas situated at the center of it all.

"Do you ladies know," Millicent asked at length, "how Percival came to have this great wealth?"

The girls shook their heads, wide-eyed and attentive. This was something they'd both been aching to know since their respective first visits to the McGulliver mansion. Though they had never discussed it with each other, they had both individually wondered if Mr. McGulliver had married into Millicent's own fortune.

Millicent's nod of the head said that she'd suspected as much. "Well," she said, her voice soft and guarded. She had assured them that her husband was far too distant to hear any of their discussion, and that she had not informed him of where they would be. Still, even she seemed to fear that he was right behind her at the moment. "It's something I'm not altogether proud of," she began.

Patty and Molly managed a quick glance in each other's direction. What each saw in that split second wasn't enough to know exactly what the other was thinking, but it was time enough to realize they were both understanding that they were both fully aware that they were sharing their first meaningful moment as mother and daughter. Molly smiled warmly at her future daughter.

"Percival was always the timid and insecure man he is now," Millicent continued.

At this, Molly stole a quick glance at her daughter, not questioningly, exactly, but showing recognition that Patty had more knowledge of what Millicent's husband would be like in the years to come than Millicent herself did. Patty returned the glance just enough to show that she wasn't going to interject any sort of contradiction, and Molly watched her for a moment to see if the girl's face would betray anything, found her to be consistent in her silence, and nodded her understanding.

If Millicent noticed any of this exchange, she did a fine job of hiding it. She simply continued, "Well, he didn't always own the hat shop. And, of course, we didn't always live here." She gestured elaborately at their surroundings, allowing her eyes to reveal a slight disapproving annoyance at the glamour of the mansion. "Percival worked at the store at first. It was owned then by Miles Garrish, who now runs the clock shop in town. They have a sort of collaboration of minds in the planning, organizing, and running of the businesses downtown. The Council, they call it. Percival would attend the meetings, but he wouldn't speak at all; he would sit by and allow the important decisions to be made by the others. Of course, he wasn't officially a Council member, being a worker and not an owner and all, but that wouldn't stop other underlings from offering their opinions and suggestions. Percival just wasn't comfortable being seen and heard."

She paused to refill her china cup with milk and to take a bite from a sugar cookie. She chewed it with relish and allowed it to melt gently on her tongue and take a cool, slow sip of milk before continuing.

"What he really wanted, I suppose, was to own the hat shop himself and mind his own affairs. He doesn't like taking orders or being at someone else's command, not because he wants to be powerful, you understand. He simply feels he knows what's best for himself and would rather be left alone."

Molly couldn't have spoken on this, not being an authority on the man, but to Patty it sounded reasonable enough to match her former employer's demeanor.

Mrs. McGulliver took another moment to nurse her glass of milk, and then went on, seemingly with a degree of effort, reminding herself that she felt these were things that needed to be said. "The men of the Council would hold regular card games, here in this very room. Of course, this wasn't our home then; in fact, it belonged to Miles Garrish."

Millicent McGulliver took this opportunity to glance warily at her audience, seemingly to gauge their reactions to this revelation, but the girls' expressions hadn't changed.

"Well. Percival was never much of a gambler; he was too nervous to put money on the line, especially with as little as we had." She shrugged, forced a smile, and cleared her throat. For a second, her face nearly seemed to reflect fondness for her husband. "Such recreation just wasn't in his nature. He would sit by and watch, sit on the side, fetch food and beverages for them. He never actually sat in on a game, though. But," she went on with a sigh, "one day, without even telling me, he decided to play in the game for the whole of the evening, from start to finish. That game lasted longer than any they had ever played in before. Percival was gone the entire night and most of the next day. In those days, we were still close, or at least I thought we were. Looking back, I've recalled how he'd already begun to pull himself away from me, but I thought it was a phase, something that would end eventually and that things would go back to the way they'd always been. I was worried out of my mind when he didn't come home; I hadn't expected him to be gone past eleven the night before. When he finally arrived home, well, he had wealth beyond anything I'd ever dreamed of, and the deeds to both the hat shop and the mansion. He insisted we move in immediately."

"How did he do it?" Molly asked in awe. Patty didn't have to ask. She didn't know the details, but she had a pretty strong idea of how he might have accomplished such a feat.

Millicent shrugged. "I honestly don't know. He never told me. He told me he had had a lucky night in the Council card game, but he would say no more than that. The truth is, girls, I didn't really care to know. Percival was not good enough at card games or betting to have won such wealth. I knew there was more to the story; I still do. But I don't know what it might be, and I'm not sure I ever will. Or want to."

They were all silent for some time, the only sounds the clinking of cups and the crunching of cookies and crackers. At long last, Patty broke the quiet. "Thank you, Mrs. McGulliver. For telling us."

Millicent smiled gently at the girl. "Well, Patty dear, I just thought you both ought to know. I'm not certain why, but it felt right telling you. You should probably also know that you two are the first people I've ever shared that story with." The girls did look surprised at this. "It's true," she said with a smile. "I don't know what compelled me…I think…well, I think I just feel…at home with you both. Thank you, Patty, for bringing us all together."

Patty looked down, embarrassed, but the others could see that her cheeks were red and her face was broken into a grin.

Their evening gathering had certainly done the job of forging a bond between the three of them that would last beyond the bounds of this little tale. Some connections cannot be severed by something as small as time or death, and from that moment forward, regardless of in which time they were residing or in what heavenly or earthly realm they dwelt, Molly, Patty, and Millicent would consider each other family, the family that they sadly never would have the opportunity to bask in as much as they should have.

When Patty had suggested to Millicent that there might be valuable information to be gleaned from a meeting with (or observation of) Professor Anson Spice, Millicent had tensed and looked away, the most vulnerable either of the girls had seen her to appear yet.

"Is that really necessary?" she asked, her voice hushed.

Molly turned to Patty, questioning. She didn't feel qualified to answer this question and secretly hoped that her friend would let Millicent off the hook; she didn't like seeing her so fearful.

Patty, however, spoke with resolve. "Well, ma'am, with all due respect, nothing is really *necessary*, but that doesn't change the fact that it would still be a good idea. Your husband is going to do some very bad things, and it's his dealings with Professor Spice that are going to make those things possible."

Molly noticed Millicent's arched eyebrow as she heard Patty speak in the future tense. Millicent didn't acknowledge it, however, but simply thought quietly, studied Patty's face, and shrugged. "Very well," she said. "If it would be helpful, then it should be done." The woman turned to Molly. "Dear, eat your lunch at school tomorrow. I'll be prepared to leave directly once you've arrived here, and we will go straight to the university to see what we can uncover."

Percival McGulliver was every bit as oblivious to his wife's little gathering as she'd said he would be. All the time the women were conferring in the game room, the hat dealer was in his study, sitting hunched over his desk, peering by dim lamplight over the dense lenses of his spectacles, studying the numbers and letters of the time manipulation code.

The walk to the university was a long and dreadful one. Millicent said few words, and Molly's attempts at conversation to rid her mind of their destination did little to prompt her. They walked the streets through the October gray and chill, barely noticing the emptiness of the city. The only noises that accompanied them on their journey were the whistling of the haunting autumn wind and their footsteps on the rocks beneath their feet.

Not until the university's massive, towering structure was looming above them and Molly unconsciously hitched a breath with tears that were forcing themselves into her eyes did Millicent manage to shake herself out of her distant thoughts, alarmed to see the girl's fear and ashamed that she'd only now realized it.

"Don't fret, Molly dear. This is going to be far more painful for me than for you. Trust me."

Molly's breath came in choking gasps as she looked up at Mrs. McGulliver, her eyes pleading for more of the same promises.

"Molly..." Millicent drew herself closer to the girl and put a soothing arm around her shoulders. "The man we're about to go and see is...dark. He's very dark and very sinister. I've never had a doubt, even when I was his student—yes, that's right, he was my teacher here—I knew that his purposes were cruel ones. But Molly, he will *not* harm you if you can do two things: Do not stand in his way, and do not show weakness. If you can manage those things, and you *can*, as we will *not* be here any longer than we need be, *and* I will be here to take care of everything, then you need not worry about Professor Spice hurting you."

Molly swallowed her sobs to explain her emotion to her friend. Shaking her head fiercely, she gasped, "I'm *not* worried about him hurting me!" Millicent's brows furrowed and she examined the girl's face as her explanation continued. "I'm worried about what he might do to Patty."

Millicent's head cocked in a curious manner, and she shook her head in perplexity. "I don't understand. Patty's not here. What are you talking about, Molly dear?"

Molly's brain raced in circles in a struggling effort to determine what she could tell Mrs. McGulliver. "I...I can't explain. I just...I don't know. I just..." Suddenly Molly had an impressive admiration for her daughter's ability to say what needed to be said on the spot, despite the circumstances. If she could live to see her daughter's natural gift for performing, she would not be surprised.

Millicent accepted Molly's emotions for what they appeared to be. Clearly, she thought, the girl's changes in her life, the newfound familial relationships that she'd always lacked had caused her irrational fears of loss. It would be, she reasoned, fruitless to try to comprehend such fears, let alone to attempt to hush them. She simply held the girl in her arms, rubbing the back of her head silently, allowing her to have her moment of fear.

When the moment had passed, they both entered the giant university building and made their way to the marble directory that was mounted on the wall near the staircase. Scanning the alphabetic listings, they learned that Professor Anson Spice's offices and laboratories were in the H wing of the eleventh floor. Looking at each other and taking in the support each needed that was to be found in the other's eyes, they began their climb up the stairs

Professor Anson Spice had made a discovery. Oh, certainly, he had made plenty of those in his years walking the earth, but this was different. This was extraordinary. In his view, all of his naturally given talents, all his abilities that set him apart from other people had been in preparation for this.

He had spent the past several months studying, practicing, and perfecting this particular art, this "craft" as he murmured of it when alone in his office or laboratory. The practice sessions, seventeen of them altogether, had used assorted creatures, as small as a ladybug and a tadpole and as large as an elk and a bear cub. He had even used a couple of specimens of plant life as well. While the specific results varied from one test subject to another, after the fourth attempt, at which point he had perfected the formula, the final product was always the same.

He was ready to move on to a larger sort of specimen.

Through no small amount of deceit, trickery, and stealth, he had managed to secure a human corpse from the medical school at the university, and this was now laid out upon one of the long, black-topped tables in his private laboratory. Professor Spice, before getting to work on the project (he could hardly refer to it as an "experiment" when he knew perfectly well what the outcome would be), spent what ought to have been an uncomfortably lengthy time examining and admiring his test subject.

He was far too enamored with this latest endeavor, with the relish of the rush of exhilaration he was preparing to undergo to pay any heed to the seventeen caged creatures around the perimeter of the laboratory, making assorted sounds that provided a chilling penetration of ominous darkness to the room. They were alive and awake, potential witnesses to the unseemly violation of the laws and wisdoms of nature about to be displayed. They squawked, they howled, they hissed, and they cackled. The human body, though, his latest specimen, lay upon the table, still as the calmest lake, silent as the most peaceful forest, and dead as the feelings of goodness and cheer in the heart of Professor Spice.

Such were the goings-on in the only occupied room in the eleventh floor's H wing when Molly and Millicent made their way stealthily through its corridors, searching for a sign of life, a light, a sound, anything. There was no light to be seen, but there was, of course, sound. Molly insisted in an intense whisper that she heard a snake, while Millicent was certain they were hearing a squirrel. The nearer they drew, the more dense, detailed, and defined the noises became, and they followed them all the way to the door labeled Prof. A. Spice–Laboratory. The long room was filled with assorted lab tables, and countertops with instruments and tools scaled its perimeter.

Spice's acquisition of the laboratory had been through pleas to the dean of the urgency of careful and studious examination of ancient relics and archaeological artifacts; it had since come to be the home of far darker deeds and unsavory practices.

Millicent beckoned the girl up against the wall while she peered through the door's window, uncertain of whether or not she hoped to see Spice in the room.

The laboratory was unlit, and the curtains were drawn to keep out the afternoon sunlight. Millicent's eyes came into focus, however, thanks to numerous small fluorescent lights attached to the cages that circled the room.

"Is he in there?" Molly whispered, her hushed voice quaking and catching.

Millicent nodded rapidly and stole a glance at her cohort. "Yes, yes he is. He's standing at the back of the room. He's . . . I'm not sure. He's looking at something. He's . . . I think he's smiling."

"What's he looking at?"

Millicent shook her head, looking back through the window. "I can't tell. It's too dark. Do you smell something?"

Molly started to shake her head, but stopped abruptly, eyes widening. "Yes," she nodded. "It's . . . What is it?" Her brows furrowed, her eyes crossed thoughtfully, and she looked up at Millicent curiously, her head shaking slowly in perplexity.

"Tobacco," Millicent said with confidence. "Very strong tobacco. Different kinds, I think. And unusual . . . exotic."

Molly nodded her gradual recognition, and her eyes widened as she remembered the patchy but informative account of the future she'd received from Patty, recalling Spice's reputed occupation-to-be.

Spice had begun to walk circles around the laboratory table, the thinly visible smile Millicent McGulliver had observed still sitting delicately upon his lips.

He had never been one to talk to himself; indeed, he had never been one to talk to others unless it couldn't be prevented. It was much more Professor Spice's style to savor a moment such as this in silence. Why sully a perfect experience, a turning point in one's life and career, with mere words?

On the burner at the other end of the room, the various exotic tobaccos were slowly roasting over the blue flame. Unaware of the pair of eyes peering through the window, the towering, shadowed professor plucked a very small creature from his coat pocket and placed it upon a tray on the back counter. The creature was a yellow fly Spice had found outside the university. The fly was moving in unproductive circles, one of its wings having been lost.

Professor Spice smiled down at the creature and began reciting the words he had perfected.

Millicent saw only pieces of what was transpiring in the laboratory, her view obscured by objects in the room, Spice's position in it, and the dimness of the laboratory all alike. Molly, still pressed with her back against the wall in the corridor, saw none of it, relying solely on Mrs. McGulliver's barely audibly whispered descriptions of what she could decipher, which was really very little.

"What's he doing now?" Molly demanded. She was frustrated at being at Millicent's mercy to know what was happening in the laboratory, but even greater than her frustration was her fear of what she might see if she dared look through the window.

The girl glanced to her left to see the woman shake her head slowly, her expression clearly one of confusion. "I…I'm not sure…I don't know *what* I'm seeing…"

"Well, *try* to explain!"

"He took something out of his pocket…something very small. I couldn't see what. He put it on some kind of tray on the counter and…I don't know. He's just looking down at it and…I can't see what he's doing…He's…I don't know…It looks like…Oh!"

The woman jumped with a start and focused again on the sight on the other side of the door.

"What?" Molly urged her. "What is it?"

"There's . . . I don't know! It's . . . a hole. In the air."

"What?" Molly was very close now to looking for herself, and she wrestled with her emotions in a vain attempt to determine her best course of action. "What?" she demanded once again. "Tell me!"

"A hole just *appeared* . . . hovering . . . in the *air*! It's . . . it's . . ."

Molly could take it no longer. She pushed Millicent McGulliver out of the way and pressed her own face to the glass. As the woman had described, Spice's back was to them as he looked down intently at something on the back counter. Next to him, above the counter, floating in wrinkles and liquid motion was a hole. It shook and waved, shuddered and bent, and it certainly seemed to change size, seemingly unattached to a permanent one. At first it appeared no larger than Molly's own hand, and at another moment she would have insisted that Professor Spice himself would have fit inside of it. Its unseen depths were inky blackness blended with kaleidoscopic rainbows, gelatinous greens oozing and dripping into heated oranges, and dwelling in those swirling lights was a flickering, glowing shape that seemed both to beckon and threaten simultaneously; it was fire. Clearly the girl could see an angry, vile, menacing, and powerful fire raging deep inside the hovering emptiness.

Anson Spice drew the crippled insect close to him as he finished whispering the words that had made the swirling, stretching, breathing portal materialize. With a sneer, he cast the fly into the black vortex's fires, and he turned once again to the corpse that still lay frozen on the table. Stepping closer to it, the professor began speaking a different series of words, meaningless to anyone else, had anyone been there with him to hear it. Still oblivious to the observers in the corridor, he lifted his long arms over the body and raised his voice to one of command and urgency. He felt the tremble of excitement seize his body, prompting him to keep going, working toward his ultimate goal.

Molly slammed herself immediately back against the wall where she had been the second she realized that Professor Spice was turning back in their general direction again. Millicent ducked down a bit as well, though remained peering through the window. Both immediately regretted their sudden movements, fearful that Spice would glimpse them and they would be caught. They had, by this time, both determined that whatever strange ritual they were witnessing was infinitely more telling and valuable than anything the professor would speak of through an interview, and they wanted to see this sight through to its finish.

"What was that?" Molly hissed through clenched teeth. "What was that he threw in there?"

Millicent shook her head, still looking intently through the glass. "I'm not sure, but I think it was whatever he took out of his pocket before."

They stood in silence save for their intense heavy breaths for what seemed to Molly like many minutes but may have been mere seconds. When she could stand the silence no longer, she whispered through interjecting, gasping breaths, "What now? What's he doing now?"

"He's turned back to the thing on the table. He's saying something to it, and…I don't know what…he's…his arms are raised over it…What *is* that on the table?"

But Molly knew. She had only seen all the images in the laboratory for a moment, but that had been time enough to identify the mysterious, darkened lump that lay motionless on the lab table. She closed her eyes, breathed in the air she needed to speak the words, and barely spoke them to her friend:

"Body," her voice managed in a barely audible hush.

"What?" Millicent looked over at her, her face demanding and urgent. "What did you say?"

The girl turned to the woman, her face pleading and scared.

"What, Molly?" Mrs. McGulliver insisted. "Did you see what it was?"

Molly nodded slowly and whispered again, "A body. It's a body. A human body."

Millicent turned at once to the window, her eyes resting anew upon the before-unidentifiable mass, and once they did, she gasped, throwing her hand to her mouth.

"Did he…do you think he…*killed* that person?" Molly wanted to know. Millicent didn't respond; she simply looked down at the girl, returning her frightened expression.

As Millicent turned her attention back to the professor, Molly saw the woman's head cock in a newly curious, uncomprehending manner.

"What?" Molly demanded. "What do you see?"

It took a rather lengthy time for the woman to respond, so long in fact that Molly hissed even more loudly, "What *is* it?"

"I'm not sure," Millicent responded slowly. "Something is… different. I can't…something…" Her eyes widened. Her jaw slackened. "No…" she attempted, but it came out as a dry and soundless hitch. "No…"

The words came like liquid velvet, chocolate sunrays dripping from his tongue and resting upon the ears of the unseen forces that feasted on these dark enchantments. He could feel the power coursing, his blood boiling, his body aching. His arms, tedious with exhaustion, begged to be lowered, but his will was greater than that; aloft they remained, filling the space above his deceased experimental prop.

Grasping onto consciousness with all his might while refusing to miss a beat in the delivery of the spell, he managed to break through a wall in his mind and revive with newfound energy. A grin spread across his sweaty, reddened face, and his arms found new life as they straightened themselves with conviction above the corpse. Behind him, the hovering portal remained, having collected its fee but watching with an intent and hungry eye to see the task through to its finish.

And as the seething, scathing power escalated to new heights within Professor Spice's soul, as blinding light and uncompromising darkness threatened to seize his consciousness forever, something began to happen. In fact, this was the same something that caught Millicent McGulliver's attention in such a painfully horrific manner outside the room. The human corpse's right arm began to rise slowly off of the table.

Inspired by this apparent onset of his success, Professor Spice declared the words even more loudly, his grin terrifying in its thirsty madness. The fire in the portal intensified, sharing in the professor's triumphant pleasures, throwing sparks in every direction, many of them striking Spice himself on his bare skin. Heedless and unfeeling, he pressed on in his endeavor, watching as now the left arm joined the right and the head began to jerk back and forth, uncertain of its desire: assist itself in its return to the living . . . or push the darkness away and return to peaceful slumber?

Such forces as that which Anson Spice was now wielding have power that can dwarf even the greatest souls, the strongest fortresses, and the barrier around the body's heart, the shield that protected its immortal soul from these sinister tasks began to crumble before the confident, massive spectacle that was Professor Spice. Somewhere, hovering in a realm unseen to the mortal eye, the corpse's soul attempted to cling to its surroundings, made every effort to scream at its former self to deny the bewitching effects that were settling in on it and permeating themselves into its most private and hidden crevices. But the power was great, the struggle was painful, and the surrender was inevitable. The soul, in its misty white space, let go and laid down for the professor to seize it. The body jerked and arched in responsive obedience, accepting the soul back inside to share its fear with the body.

It rose.

Millicent's scream may have been inevitable, but many would ponder later on how events may have unrolled differently had it simply not been so piercingly *loud*.

Professor Spice's head jerked up instantly, and in more than enough time not only to see the face that lingered in his door's glass window, but to identify it as well, before it vanished from view. He may not have spent any time near the cohort of his youth, Percival McGulliver, in many years, but that didn't mean he was ignorant of his comings and goings. Indeed, McGulliver would have been unsettled to have known just how much Anson Spice saw of his life, just how much he knew; likely he wouldn't have been *surprised*, mind you, but nor would he have been pleased.

Spice made an instant break for the door, realizing in the scant seconds that were lapsing how critical a moment this was. He dismissed his tendency not to talk to himself to curse himself for becoming careless. This shouldn't have happened, and in previous ventures he had even had the foresight to pin a curtain over the window. Now, however, he had gotten arrogant; he had developed a naïve sense of invincibility, and now if he didn't catch up with the McGulliver woman, he would pay for his imprudence.

There was nothing to argue, nothing to compromise. He must catch the woman.

Millicent McGulliver was astonishingly quick. Though she had never been one to engage in athletics, only her beauty surpassed her natural skills as a runner. She took only a second to hiss through her teeth at Molly, "Go back the way we came! He didn't see you; he only saw me. I'll go the other way."

Of course Molly started to object to this, but she'd barely parted her lips before Millicent was snapping, "Go! Together we're lost! Go!" And the woman ran off before the girl could respond. In fear and defeat, Molly did as she'd been told, bolting as fast as her legs would permit back in the direction they'd come. Hearing the door of the laboratory swinging open, she dove through the open air for the stairway.

Spice turned immediately in the direction he'd seen Millicent McGulliver flee, never taking a second even to glance in the direction to which young Molly had retreated, unbeknownst to him.

He was aghast to see how far she'd gotten in so few seconds. He broke into as fast a run as he was capable. His unnaturally long legs on his slender, insectile body took him by bounds through the corridor, closing the space between himself and his intruder by the second.

Determined, filled with ire, he lengthened his strides to their greatest capability, and he watched with certainty as his speed drew him ever nearer to her.

She could hear him growing closer. Tears flew from her eyes, mixing confusedly with the sweat that was soaking her face. The stairway at the end of the corridor grew closer, as did the threatening, stomping footsteps behind her. Their rhythmic landings seemed to chant to her from behind:

We…come…give…up…clo…ser…al…most…

She could hear the stomping much closer now, right behind her it seemed. She felt something behind her that may have been his hand or his breath, or even the immediate rushing of air from the space he was now occupying directly in her tracks.

And then she reached the stairway.

Leaping down several steps at once, bouncing off of the one she landed on and taking even more with the next stride, she took all ten flights of stairs in no more than twenty leaps from one step to another, and as she arrived in the lobby, she bolted for the exit as she heard her pursuer still on the last set of steps.

She had escaped. The blasted woman had seen what he could do, and now she had escaped. For just a moment, Spice considered following her outside and pursuing her through the streets of West Cuttingsborough, but he knew if anyone witnessed that, he would have to answer for such behavior. Perhaps if he let her go, she would simply choose to forget what she had seen. Spice knew very well how people were too often incapable of comprehending and dealing with talents such as his, things they would refer to as "unnatural."

Yes, he thought to himself, most likely the woman would erase the unpleasantness from her mind, scoffing at it as mere fancy, and he would be left to conduct his projects in peace.

Still, there were concerns he could not ignore. There was, of course, the uncertainty of whether she *would*, in fact, forget what she'd witnessed. What if she told someone? Would they believe her? Probably not. But even so, her reputation around the city far surpassed his in the way of honor, and he couldn't deny that if she did say something, her story would have his lack of good humor to support its credibility.

And then there was the much more irksome question, the one that tempted Spice to march directly to the McGulliver house that very evening and uncover the answer: Just what had she been doing spying into his laboratory in the first place?

Once Millicent's feet hit the pavement, she continued to run, not allowing herself to lose speed by the slightest degree. She ran, of course, in the direction of the door through which Molly should have exited. But when she found it, Molly was not waiting there for her. Millicent looked around her surroundings, anxious that Professor Spice could be rounding the corner at any second.

With great reluctance, she pulled open the big door of the university and cried out at what she saw. Molly was lying at the foot of the stairs in a messy contortion of limbs. Her face was sticky with blood and her eyes were closed and unseeing.

Millicent ran over to her, feeling for a heartbeat, listening for sounds of breathing. "Oh, Molly," she wept over the girl. "Oh, Molly, I'm so sorry." With many grunts and curses and tears of agony, she managed to half-carry the girl from the university and to the nearest shop, a tuxedo rental business by the name of Friar Tux. The sign depicted a portly man with a monk's hair wearing a tuxedo and smiling cheerily. Millicent scowled as she dragged the girl into the building; she had little tolerance at the moment for such frivolity.

As it happened, Molly's desperate lunge for the stairway had resulted in a loss of footing that saw her tumble down four flights of steps. When she attempted to get to her feet to make her way gingerly down the remaining stairs, the pain was excruciating and incomparable; it sent her plummeting down another three flights. Again she picked herself up and managed to walk with great pain down the next two flights of stairs, at which point she lost consciousness and tumbled down the final flight, collapsing into the tangled heap Millicent discovered only seconds later.

With the assistance of Toby, a teenaged errand-runner for Gorman Dillworth, the tuxedo shop owner, a doctor was brought to the scene and Molly was transferred safely to the McGulliver mansion, where Millicent insisted she be treated in comfort. There was only the slightest contesting from the doctor that she required the facilities of the West Cuttingsborough Hospital; after all, one didn't argue with one as wealthy as Millicent McGulliver. He had no doubt that Mrs. McGulliver would pay whatever sum was necessary to see that any and all equipment he required would be available to him in her home.

And so she did.

The tragic accident did not cloud or evict Millicent McGulliver's vivid memory of what she'd witnessed through the window to Professor Spice's laboratory. In fact, she became less and less horrified by the offense of what she had seen, and only angrier due to the harm it had caused her friend.

Millicent knew that action needed to be taken, not simply in healing Molly, but in avenging her seemingly permanent infliction as well. She spent many hours mulling and deliberating how best to see justice served against the vile and impure act she had witnessed Professor Spice partaking of, but it wasn't until she saw the newspaper article that she knew for certain what was to be done.

The article appeared the day after the accident, and it concerned the mysterious disappearance of a human biology study corpse from the university's medical school. Looking up from the paper, Millicent McGulliver instantly made the connection between the missing body and the one she had seen rise from the black-topped table in Anson Spice's laboratory. She knew what she must do about it; justice needed to be served.

She didn't discuss it with Molly or with Patty; she simply made the decision on her own. She could have spoken to Molly about it had she chosen to; the girl was again conscious and was recovering very slowly in one of the guest chambers of the mansion. She was unable to get out of bed, of course, and Dr. Unsky had made no secret of the fact that she would most probably never walk again.

It seemed to Millicent McGulliver that during this horrific stage of the girl's life, she need not be burdened with thoughts and dilemmas to do with the foul Professor Spice; it was, she had decided, her own responsibility to see that his actions were brought to light and that he answered for this evident dabbling in dark and sinister arts. She could have gone to Patty about the problem of Professor Spice, of course, but somehow, without any degree of certainty why, she had no doubt that Patty would try to stop her from doing what it was she knew she had to do.

Why did she know she had to do it? She had never had such a strong conviction on something before; that was certain. And particularly something she knew so little about. She had always been uncomfortable around Anson Spice, but now she possessed valid reasons to detest him, and she had a personal need, a *craving*, an *ache* to bring the man falling to his knees.

And so, in solitude in the library of the mansion, she stole away and sat herself down at one of the room's several typewriters. She stared at the blank page before her for some time, drafting thoughts in her mind, making mental scratches and edits as she crafted the letter to the dean of the university. Eventually, when she had a fairly solid grasp on what it was she wanted to say and how best to say it, she set her fingers to the home keys and began to type.

> Dearest and Most Esteemed Dean Topper,
>
> It is my sincere regret to inform you of immoral wrongdoings being performed by one of your respected faculty members.
>
> One Professor Anson Spice has been entering into the dark arts, and on the university's very premises no less. It was my genuine displeasure inadvertently to be a witness to the instance.
>
> After reading of the recent disappearance of a certain valuable and sensitive study aide from the university's medical school, I have connected pieces of evidence in my own mind and have come to determine that Professor Spice was likely in recent possession of this item. I feel it is my civic duty to the city of West Cuttingsborough and my personal responsibility as an alumnus of West Cuttingsborough University to come forward and share what I have seen.

> I don't feel comfortable stating exactly what I witnessed, so this will have to suffice. If I am correct about the missing "item" from the medical school having fallen into the possession of Anson Spice, then you can be assured it was put to use for dark and sinister purposes in his laboratory. Whether he still has knowledge of the item's location I cannot say, but it would not surprise me in the least if he has, shall we say, lost track of it. I will inform you that the dark magic to which I referred at the onset of this correspondence was an act that prominently featured and revolved around this missing tool of the medical school.
>
> Should I be incorrect about my theory that the missing "study tool" is one and the same as the item I witnessed in Professor Spice's possession, then please at least trust me when I say that there was still an unnatural ritual taking place in Professor Spice's laboratory recently and that it involved something he had no good reason to be in ownership of.
>
> Thank you for your time and consideration; I trust you have many pressing matters to tend to daily. Do with this information what you will.
>
> Regards,
>
> A Concerned Citizen

Once this letter was received and an investigation begun, it didn't take long to confirm what "A Concerned Citizen" had claimed. While Dean Topper and the rest of the university faculty and student body never fully knew or understood what exactly Anson Spice had been doing with the missing body, only a few days shed enough light to allow for little doubt that Spice had been responsible for its disappearance. It seemed that one of Spice's own students worked evening hours in the medical school in a night security capacity. This student, one Colin Howe, was struggling greatly in his world history course, taught by none other than Professor Anson Spice. Interestingly, a scant two days after the corpse had gone missing, young Master Howe's abysmal history grade had found itself transformed into a solidly passing one. At the same time, he found himself, a constant dormitory resident, with enough money to be able to afford a decidedly respectable campus apartment. After these clues had been upturned, it took little interrogation on the university's administration's part to pry the truth out of young Colin. Spice, of course, denied everything, but the evidence with Howe's testimony appeared in Dean Topper's opinion to be grounds enough for dismissal. No charges were pressed in an effort simply to move beyond the ugliness promptly, but Anson Spice was asked to vacate his offices immediately. As for what inappropriate or "unnatural" uses Spice had put the body to, this was, of course, a concern, but merely further negative publicity to add to the severe enough case of the stealing of the body.

"I don't particularly want to know what he did with it or to it or why he was interested in it in the first place," Dean Topper told the newspaper. "What a world history professor would want with a corpse belonging to the medical school is too disturbing for my mind to want to explore. He took it; that's solid enough ground for his removal from the university."

And that is how it happened. Millicent McGuillver, loved by many, admired by all, single-handedly (and *anonymously*) saw to the dismissal of Professor Anson Spice, and, of course, when the firing occurred, Spice's anger and bitterness intensified to new dimensions, and when he began to crave a taste of revenge, the list of suspects who had brought about his downfall at the university (not to mention the severe limiting of his immediately accessible resources for his projects) was a very brief list indeed. It had been limited to one name, in fact. Yes, Professor Spice knew immediately and never wavered from that belief that he had been cast out of West Cuttingsborough University by none other than Millicent McGulliver, wife to his childhood rival, Percival McGulliver.

Millicent could not have been a better nurse to her recovering housekeeper, and Millicent couldn't have hoped for an easier patient. The girl didn't ask for much, but on the occasion that she requested something, be it food, beverage, a book to read, medicine for her pain, a friendly face to talk to, or the peace of the room to herself, it was provided with promptness and perfection. What was truly remarkable was that it was all done completely without Percival McGulliver's ever being aware that she was in the house. Indeed, if McGulliver even knew that his wife had taken on a housekeeper, it was certain he couldn't have identified Molly as she in even the most desperate of times. The knowledge that this same housekeeper was currently laid up in bed in one of his own guestrooms was something he never achieved.

Molly responded with astonishing calm to the news of her future off of her feet. Millicent presented her with the finest wheelchair available for purchase, assuring her that it was the very least she could do to assist her in the transition, as she eventually would rise from her sick bed. Molly was gracious in receipt of the gift, quiet in her opinions of never walking again, and had been (at present, at least) overcome with a peaceful air that none who had known her had ever witnessed. In fact, the expensive wheelchair had but one possible fault, which became apparent in these moments of heightened introspection on the girl's part. Its wheels squeaked when turned overly slowly, and Molly, when caught in moments of deep thought, would absently wheel herself forward a little and back a little, forward a little and back a little. At these times, the wheelchair sounded quite like a porch swing creaking softly on a summer evening.

Millicent attempted to remain calm about this change in the girl. She chose to view it as progress; the tragedy had softened her, brought a peace that she had been unable to achieve in her life before now. Whether Millicent was able to convince herself of these truths is uncertain. What she did know was that she was relieved that her friend hadn't been killed in her fall, and that if her life had been, in any small way, changed for the better, she was honored to have had even the briefest and most insignificant of hands in it. Still, aside from the dismissal of Professor Spice and the crippling of Molly, Millicent recognized in her own mind that their little escapade at the university had truly accomplished nothing. There was nothing to help guide them toward whatever it was that Patty needed from them. In fact, Millicent was still ignorant of what, exactly, they were *supposed* to have accomplished. Suddenly she was very angry with Patty. Obviously this would never have happened had that girl not expected them to act as her spies to achieve whatever end it was she was after.

But blaming Patty would do no good; she knew that. Patty had never specifically stated who should visit the professor. Besides, if she was to lay blame on Patty, she knew she would have to lay blame on Molly as well, for she was quite knowledgeable of the fact that Molly knew a lot more of Patty's situation than Millicent did, and she had gone along with the venture to the H wing of floor eleven of the university fully of her own accord.

The girl received a couple of visitors while in bed. Patty, of course, was very quick to come and see her after being relieved from her duties at the butcher shop each day. They would sit in silence or they would discuss the goings-on at the high school or at Patty's own job at the butcher shop. Millicent had called the high school, feigning to be Mrs. Swither of the butcher shop (Patty had to impersonate the woman to give her a taste of what she sounded like, at which both Molly and Millicent laughed at great length) to inform Vice Principal Anglehanger that Molly had been injured and would not be at school or at the butcher shop for weeks.

Millicent notified the girl's parents of the accident, of course, and they did pay one silent and awkward visit, to which both Patty and Millicent were witness. Saying little, and looking lost, confused, and sad, Molly's mother only wept while her father mumbled that he didn't know why his daughter had become so secretive that she should be nursed to health in a mansion by a woman his daughter by all rights shouldn't even know. Molly fought to maintain composure during this uncomfortable visit, but she was unable even to conjure up a fabricated reason for her being there in the mansion.

Millicent stepped in to rescue her friend with a story of her own. “Well, Molly and I have met when she’s made deliveries here for the butcher shop, you see, and…well, I’ve taken quite the liking to her. This is a wonderful young lady you both have raised. You should both be quite proud of her.”

Molly looked to her parents hopefully at this explanation, certainly wishing both for them to accept this story as well as perhaps to see her in a new light based on Mrs. McGulliver’s kind words. Her parents, however, just looked at her like she was a stranger, her father casting a sideways sneer toward Millicent, shaking his head in disbelief. They left with little more than a goodbye, and Patty was left hurting on behalf of her mother and friend, suddenly aware why she could never remember meeting this pair of grandparents.

As you might expect, the students of West Cuttingsborough High School didn’t exactly flock to the mansion to see their classmate, but one of them did come to see her, and this, as you may already suspect, was Jefferson Gladwell, Molly’s closest lifelong friend and, according to Patty, her future husband. Jefferson, of course, knew nothing of where Patty had come from or what the whole business of McGulliver and Spice was about, but Patty had pulled him aside at school one morning to inform him of their swapping of afternoon apprenticeships. Jefferson, being the easy-going boy he was, didn’t question this information or demand more details; he simply smiled, nodded, thanked her for sharing that with him, and went on his way.

When Jefferson paid his visit to the mansion, he was visibly and openly impressed with the abode, oohing and ahing over every detail, great and small. Molly rolled her eyes as she listened to him gush, and she would scold him for his lack of tact. Millicent, however, would throw her head back in laughter and encourage the boy, assuring them that there was nothing healthier in her opinion than a positive attitude and the willingness to let it burst out.

"Nothing," she said, "should be bottled inside of us where it can burst at any time. If you see something you like, Jefferson, by all means, shout to the mountains about it."

The weeks passed thusly, with Molly's health climbing steadily toward the plateau that it was destined to reach, and those around her who cared about her competing with each other's efforts to bring a smile to her face and hope to her life. The girl was afraid to get out of bed, she was terrified of showing herself at school, and she was most afraid of the inevitable repercussions that would surely result from the firing of Anson Spice.

"What can I do for you, Molly?" Millicent asked as she sat on the edge of the girl's bed one afternoon.

"I'm fine for right now," was the girl's innocent reply. How she had changed since she had first come to work for her, Millicent noted to herself.

"Well, Molly dear, I'm not simply referring to what you need at the moment. I don't want what's happened to you to be in vain. We went to that university and watched Professor Spice for a reason. True, I don't really understand what that reason was, but I know that you and Patty are in need of…something. Tell me what I can do to help."

Molly considered this at length, studying her friend's face and internally judging how she thought it best to respond. After careful consideration and a deep sigh that hitched in her throat as it delivered a jolt of pain to her legs and back, she settled her gaze at last upon Millicent's hopeful, concerned eyes.

"There is something I need," she said quietly.

"What is it? Just tell me, Molly, and I'll see that you get it."

Molly's intent stare deepened as her voice lowered to even softer hushes. "It's not simple, Millicent. It will take some cleverness and…" She drifted, hesitant to say more. An overwhelming rush came over her head and she lay back, her eyes closed, breathing deeply and rhythmically to regain control of her senses.

Millicent leaned forward, concerned, and reached out to touch the girl's forehead. "Molly? Molly, are you all right? Molly dear?"

The girl nodded abruptly, her eyes still closed and turned toward the ceiling of the guest chamber. Millicent sat and watched in horror. Such attacks seemed to strike Molly often, and each time was just as frightening as the last. A deep and buried part of Millicent silently feared that one of these times, Molly wouldn't recover from it.

At last, the girl opened her eyes and turned them awkwardly toward Millicent; she didn't attempt to sit up.

"Take your time, dear," Millicent assured her, her voice trembling.

"I was saying…" Molly's voice was coming in difficult gasps. "I was saying…it will take some cleverness…planning…and…and you need…to be willing…to deceive…your…" Here she was overcome with a bout of coughing that wracked her body and jolted her forward and backward. The coughs turned to voluminous belches that threatened to purge her insides. "Your…your…" the girl still attempted to communicate.

"Hush," Millicent repeated, over and over, rubbing the girl's back and waiting for the fit, she hoped, to pass. "Hush…hush…"

At last, pass it did, and Molly's face was stained with streaming tears. She closed her eyes and appeared as though she was preparing to attempt to finish her thought again. Millicent interrupted before she had the chance.

"My husband?" she asked, looking expectantly at Molly for verification. The girl looked momentarily surprised, then smiled and nodded. Millicent sighed, not with disgust or annoyance or sadness or uncertainty, but with a conviction that might as well have said, "Very well."

Millicent McGulliver had not exaggerated the distance between herself and her husband. The two of them had begun their life together in a closeness beyond compare. People all over West

Cuttingsborough would see them together, hand in hand, all smiles, and without any care at all, and their jaws would drop and fingers would point.

"What could a woman like her *possibly* see in a man like him?" they would cry at each other, seemingly offended by their happiness, as though it violated their own most personal and clearly defined understandings of how the world operated. And the only responses they ever found from each other were dumbfounded shakes of the head and equally gaped mouths and wide-eyed stares. Alternately, the only response they would receive from the McGullivers themselves were the gales of head-throwing laughter from Millicent and a timid blush from Percival.

On the rare occasion that someone had the nerve to confront her personally and demand an explanation for the union, she would draw them close in a conspiratorial manner, peer around for potential unwanted eavesdroppers, and then she would whisper ever so delicately and sincerely, "I so desperately wished to have an alliterative name!" And she would smile and wink and signal them with a hushing gesture as she backed away, relishing the confounded look upon the poor fool's face.

Yet somewhere along the line, things between the happy couple changed, and as has been told by the fairer McGulliver, the love faded to little more than a distant recognition. Their time spent together shriveled to mere encounters here and there. Percival ate all his meals at Hats for All Occasions, as he was the sole person working there and was away from the mansion from before breakfast until after dinner. When Percival had been the assistant manager of the hat shop, working alongside the owner, he would eat his breakfast with Millicent before leaving for work, wait until he'd arrived back at home to join her for dinner, and would even travel home during his lunch hour so they could dine together at that time as well.

And so, it was far from difficult for Millicent to act, as Molly had suggested, deceptively toward her husband. It took a few days for her to decide upon a time and place to approach him. What she must propose was of such a sensitive nature, was indeed so vitally important (of course, still for reasons that remained a mystery to her) that to rush into the endeavor without properly adequate preparation was certainly not an option.

And then an opportunity managed to present itself to her of its own accord. Perhaps the stars were in perfect alignment that evening. Maybe a greater force was smiling down upon her in fine favor. Maybe it was simply one of those eerily frequent coincidences that lead many to believe that they are not in control of their own lives. Regardless of the reasons, Millicent McGulliver, who would ordinarily have been in either the library or her own sleeping quarters by the time her husband returned home from the hat shop, was actually stealing into the kitchen to scavenge a leftover pudding she remembered to be in the refrigerator. And Percival McGulliver, who, under regular circumstances, would have enjoyed his dinner at the hat shop before closing up for the evening, had for the first time since he had taken to eating all his meals there, forgotten to bring his lunchbox.

Ergo, both McGullivers found themselves each in the kitchen of their vast mansion at precisely the same time with the purpose of enjoying a bit to eat at the table.

They both attempted, at first, to disregard and feign oblivion to the awkward discomfort they were each feeling in the other's presence. Mr. McGulliver chose to try his hand at small talk, discussing the mundane goings-on at the hat shop and the whimsical humor of his forgetfulness of his lunchbox. This endeavor took some time, of course, as he battled the stammering that came so naturally with his own voice. Mrs. McGulliver remained silent, smiling good-humoredly at her husband's stories and observations but offering little response of a verbal nature.

Then she threw caution to the wind and brought the agonizing talk to an abrupt halt.

"I know what you can do, Percival, and I want you to let me in on how," she demanded in an even, cool voice, her eyes locked on his.

Percival McGulliver's eyes fixed themselves in a piercing comprehension and accusatory stare that chilled Millicent through to her heart. It was true, she had been distanced from her husband for some time now, but to see a look in his eye that put on display his true nature, the depths to which his morality and good will had sunk in the time they'd been apart, that was something she had been unprepared for. She held her ground, though, staring him down with only the faintest swallow in her throat, her stare unwavering, and the tears that stood behind her eyes held at bay.

"What...do...you...know?" McGulliver was clearly pacing his words in an attempt to tame his nervous stammer, which appeared to be more willing now than ever to make its presence known. Despite this strained effort, his voice was icy steel.

"You know what I'm talking about," she forced her voice to respond. Her husband stared at her with a suspicion she was unused to witnessing upon his features, even in these days of darkened, shrouded mystery that clouded their less-than-tender relationship. He studied her, searching desperately for signs of a bluff, evidence of ignorance, but he found none; her resolve was solid.

"Very well," the little hat salesman said after this lengthy silence. "What...makes you...think...that I...would...share..." At that moment, he became the first of the two of them to forfeit the eye contact. Mr. McGulliver's eyes closed for the slightest second, and there was more frustration in those closed eyes in that one second than they had communicated to her when opened over the course of many years.

"I'll make it easier for you," she said, interrupting her husband's struggle to overcome his uncooperative speech, which was every bit as uncomfortable for her to watch as it was for him to undergo. Once upon a time, she had listened to his stammer and watched his uncomfortably contorting face with endearment and loving support. Many were the times she had stepped up to defend him from mocking taunts and misunderstanding intolerants of West Cuttingsborough. Now, however, it was simply painful.

"You," she went on, gathering strength in her confidence, though her voice was still on the verge of cracking completely, "have never changed our will. It is still in the safe in the library where it's been since we wrote it when you inherited the mansion and hat shop. If something were to happen to you, every bit of this, including whatever notes might be tucked away in your study or in your office at the store, will become mine."

Percival's eyes widened. "You . . . would . . . never . . ."

"Don't be so certain," she said, forcing a levelness into her voice that would communicate what she needed to: that she had absolutely no fear or emotional restraint to keep her from taking his life. "It's your decision, Percival. I learn your secret with you alive . . . or dead."

And she watched his wicked little face as it melted from one of stony coldness into the troubled, uncomfortable, meek man she had fallen in love with so many years ago.

"Oh . . ." his voice trembled as tears welled in his eyes. "Oh dear . . . oh Millicent, my Millicent . . ."

More than any other possible result of this discussion, this was the most unexpected, unforeseen possibility of all. Millicent watched in shock and disbelief as her husband crumbled before her, his hands folded on the kitchen table, his eyes pleading with hers.

"What, I . . . oh, oh my, I . . . oh dear . . . what . . . have I . . . done?"

Millicent McGulliver didn't know what to think or how to respond. The husband who had grown to be such a stranger to her, the man who had fallen in love with his secret projects and out of it with her, was now realizing the extreme to which his ambitions had taken him, and he was begging for a fresh start.

"I . . . the things I've . . . I've seen . . . the things that I, I can . . . I can do! I . . . oh my . . . oh dear, but I should have . . . I should have been . . . sharing those things with, well . . . with . . . you! But I lost myself. Oh, I . . . oh my dear . . . oh dear, how I . . . lost myself, and I . . . oh goodness, my Millicent . . . I . . . I somehow forgot . . . I forgot my . . . my love . . . I forgot . . . you!"

The man was trembling and weeping, and Millicent found that despite herself, she was joining him. They cried together, they laughed together, and they retired to the bedchamber they hadn't shared in a very long time together.

It was a fresh start for the love of Mr. and Mrs. McGulliver, and it was one that was built upon honesty. Well, his honesty, at least. With great excitement and rediscovered love and trust, Percival McGulliver led his beautiful bride into his study, where she saw great stacks and towers of papers, the product of years of study and discovery. With a smile and a wink, he pointed his finger and demonstrated the same altering of the clock in his study that many years later he would demonstrate for Patty in his office at Hats for All Occasions.

Millicent McGulliver was alarmed, to be sure. But when he led her to the window of the study and indicated the clock tower that rose from the town hall at the heart of West Cuttingsborough and she saw how his own gestures and whispers were altering the time on it in the very same way, her hand nearly rose to her open mouth. She promptly stopped it and closed her mouth tight when she remembered that, as far as Percival knew, she was already aware of his ability to do this. Was this what Patty was after? Was this the secret about her husband that was destined to ruin and destroy Patty and others? It certainly might be! To think that it was games such as this that had kept her husband secluded upstairs in the mansion, away from her all those years, it was nearly more than she could stand.

"How do you do it?" she asked him, and he ushered her back to his desk, piled high with countless stacks of notes. In the midst of the chaotic disarray of paper was a far smaller stack. About ten sheets of paper were piled neatly atop each other, and each page contained lines upon lines of seemingly random letters and numbers.

Millicent looked to her husband and raised a questioning eyebrow.

"It's a, well, a, uh, a . . . code, my dear. A, uh, a . . . code."

The woman looked back to the letters and numbers and attempted to make sense of them, but as far as she could determine, they were completely random. "What do you do with them?" she asked. She was treading a fine line between seeking information for secretive purposes and expressing genuine interest in something she found curious. No matter, she thought; so long as Percival didn't pick up on the fact that she had other motives for wishing to know about this, she was safe.

Smiling endearingly at her, he nodded his understanding at her confusion. "Recite them. Uh . . . memorize them, or, uh, to . . . well, think them, uh . . . meditate on them."

Her expression only appeared more perplexed.

Percival chuckled lightheartedly and tried again. "The, uh, sequence is the . . . the key. The sequence, well . . . it, uh, exists for the . . . well, for the . . . the sole purpose of, well, unlocking and, uh . . . of wielding time itself. By acknowledging the, uh, the significance of the, uh, the code's sequence, be it through, uh, spoken word, writing, or, uh, mental concentration, or . . . well . . . any of a number of other possibilities, one has the, uh, the ability to . . . to determine the . . . well, the, uh, the course of time itself."

"For how long?"

"Ah!" Percival's index finger sprung up as his eyes lit with excitement. "So long as, uh, well, as the *user* has the, uh, the ability to . . . well, retain, yes to retain the, uh, well . . . the *essence* of the sequence without, uh, outside . . . distractions."

Millicent nodded slowly. It didn't entirely make sense, but she thought she had a relative understanding of what he was trying to say. Believing as much, she thought she had thought of a reasonably appropriate question. "How long can you maintain it in *your* mind?"

His smile was only slightly and very briefly almost a return to the devious one it had been when Millicent had first broached the subject of the time code. Then it seemed to melt into one of bashful humility. "Well…I, uh, I have learned to, uh, well…quite long, I should say."

Millicent McGulliver could see her husband's joy at bringing her into this part of his life. In many ways, his mannerisms, the light in his eyes, and the smile on his lips were all reminiscent of the man he'd once been in the love they'd once shared. But Millicent would not be swayed; as she looked into his eyes and listened to his words, she realized that it simply was not the same. There were things about Percival that had changed; no matter how familiarly he was speaking to her and looking at her, he was not truly the man he'd once been, whether he realized as much or not. She was touched to witness his reborn love for her, his need to include her in the things he deemed important, but she could not let him into her heart again, not fully. She would not leave him, she decided, and she would do her best to ascertain his surety that his love was requited. But in her heart, deep down where things mattered the most, she would know that it wasn't real; she would always be suspicious of him, and she would never be able to trust him fully again.

"Teach me," she said, and everything in her voice and expression screamed of sincerity, of love, and of the desire to share something that was of importance to him. "Share it with me."

His smile was instant and joyous, and she knew in that moment that she'd been victorious.

Molly and Patty stared in awe at the papers in Millicent's hands. After all the time that Patty had spent trapped in this time period and all of the doors that had been opened in Molly's eyes and experience, they couldn't process the truth of the fact that they had accomplished what they had set out to do. Millicent held in her hands the key to returning Patty to where she belonged and to beating Percival McGulliver at his own game. For the first time, the girls began to think that just maybe everything would turn out all right. Of course, knowing now what Millicent knew, there was no fear in sharing more details of the whole endeavor with her. There were many things Patty and Molly had agreed would be best if kept secret, but to hear that Patty had been sent here from the future by Mr. McGulliver seemed innocent enough, and Millicent certainly seemed to have very little difficulty believing as much.

"How does it work?" Molly asked, afraid of the eerie pages filled with nothing but random combinations of characters. They were seated in what had become their accustomed meeting place, around the coffee table in the game room, Molly in her new wheelchair and Patty on the couch beside her. They were glancing at the clock more frequently than in the past, as Mr. McGulliver had taken to reporting home directly from his work day what with his rekindled relationship with Mrs. McGulliver. They didn't wish to be caught unexpected by him and were making every effort to bring their discussion to a close before his arrival.

Millicent's smile was very faint, but it was there nonetheless. "It's quite simple," she said. "He's been teaching me, and I've been practicing. You don't realize it, but for eleven minutes yesterday, time reversed and went backward, then at the end of that eleven minutes, it leaped back to where it had been before the reversal."

Patty and Molly exchanged an impressed glance with each other. "Where?" Patty asked.

"Everywhere," was the woman's reply. "It changed everywhere in the world. I didn't want it to change for myself, so it didn't; you can control that. But for everyone else…well, no one realizes what happened."

"But how does it *work*?" Molly repeated. "What do you have to *do*?"

Millicent spent the next several minutes demonstrating the way she could maneuver the hands of the clock simply by reciting the letters and numbers at a steady pace. Then she went on to explain how any recognition of the numbers, thinking them, reading them silently, writing them, singing them, whatever one could think of, would result in the same way: by maneuvering anything with regards to the time dimension in whatever way one desired.

They all sat in silence for some time, each afraid to be the one to take the discussion to the next phase. At last, Patty said, "Okay, well, I guess I can head back any time, then..."

Molly turned to her daughter and pursed her lips. Her face reflected genuine fear, but she swallowed, nodded once abruptly, and said, "I'll go with you."

Patty's eyes said all the gladness and thanks that needed to be expressed. They glistened a moistness that said that a mother's love was present, and her smile made clear her willingness to accept the offer. Patty had not even begun to try to express her gratitude when Millicent spoke up.

"No...no, you won't." They both looked to her questioningly. With a reluctance to have to be the bearer of bad news, the woman explained. "This takes practice...lots of practice. I've been spending hours every day perfecting just the littlest of experiments. If either of you tried to send yourself through the currents of time without the same kind of practice...well, it could be very dangerous. You'll need me to send you back to where you belong, Patty." She turned to Molly, and her expression conveyed the greatest of sympathy. "I can't in good conscience send you someplace not knowing if I can bring you back. I've successfully sent small things into the near future, but I just have to wait a few minutes for it to show up. But I can never know if I can successfully send something to the past without going there myself. It's all just too risky, and I don't want to strand you in an unfamiliar time, Molly. I sincerely hope you'll understand."

Molly was crestfallen, to say nothing of Patty. They looked from Millicent to each other to the floor. After a few moments like this, during which Millicent allowed them the time they needed to be sad, Molly said quietly to them, "I was sure that was what I was supposed to do. You know, Anglehanger was always getting on me about not contributing anything, saying how selfish I was and how the only thing I was succeeding at was dragging down Jefferson."

The others looked at her, their hearts going to her; Molly wouldn't look up from the floor. "I thought this time I was really going to do something for someone who wasn't me."

"It's really fine, Mo—" she cut herself short as she'd done once before, reevaluated what she was about to say, and finished more appropriately, "Mom."

Millicent gave a bit of a start; this was one of the details they had omitted from their narrative. Other than a slight jump, however, she said nothing and truly didn't seem all that astonished. The girls smiled at each other, and Molly took Patty's hand and squeezed it gently.

Millicent watched them sharing their moment of closeness, and when she felt it appropriate, she asked softly, "May I offer a suggestion?"

They looked to her questioningly, saying nothing. Their inquisitive eyes were question enough.

"Molly, if you really want to go, you could go alone," Millicent continued.

"But you just said you might not be able to bring her back," Patty objected.

"I don't care if I never come back," Molly argued. "What does it matter? I can be happy there."

"But if you don't stay here and marry my father, then I'll never be born," Patty argued.

Millicent interjected with a firm clear of the throat. "May I finish?" she asked, the most motherly she'd been toward either of them since they had all met. The girls nodded silently, humbled. "Thank you. As I was saying, Molly, you could venture into the future alone. In the meantime, I could train Patty in the art and you yourself could practice it in the future. We may be able to test our abilities by sending messages to each other once you've developed the skill." She turned to Patty. "In the event that Molly is unable to pick it up on her own without someone to assist her, you can send yourself to find her when you've become proficient and you can aid her in returning.

In the meantime, whatever business needs attending to there can be performed by Molly."

She looked from one to the other, awaiting criticism or acceptance. The girls stole a glance at each other, each hoping the other's face would betray her personal feelings about the plan, so as to make her own decision simpler.

Finally, Patty said softly, "I don't know how I feel about sending you into that whole mess alone."

Molly grinned at her. "I think I can handle it. Besides, it's probably risky to send you back there until things have calmed down. If Mr. McGulliver was angry enough with you to send you here, who knows what he'll do if he sees you've managed to return?"

Her daughter nodded her agreement. "That's true enough," she said with a sigh. "Well, I suppose ..."

"I think it's worth a try," Molly said.

"It may be the only hope," Patty conceded. "You'll take care of Gerald? Watch over him?"

Molly nodded with a smile. "I must be the only high school girl in the world to get to meet both my own children before they're born," she said. "How should I find him? I'm too old to enroll in his school the way you did at mine."

Patty thought about this for a moment. She was about to tell Molly where their house was, but she feared this could lead to a devastating result if she ran into Jefferson. Not only would it be difficult to explain things to Jefferson, but also Patty had chosen not to tell Molly about the tragic mental deterioration that he would undergo in the future. After thinking on it another moment, she said, "You know...I can't be sure, but I have a very funny feeling he'll be working for Mr. McGulliver."

Millicent seemed startled at this; Molly knew better than to be alarmed by anything anymore. Nodding carefully, she said, "But I can't go there, can I? Mr. McGulliver has seen me here. Not a lot or for much time at once, but he *has* seen me."

Patty shook her head. "No, you shouldn't go near the hat shop. You're right; that would be too dangerous. Believe it or not, it would probably be more dangerous than where I think you'll need to go." Her mother looked at her questioningly with trepidation at what might follow. "You're going to have to go to Cobble Road. You have to work for Professor Spice. If Gerald is working for Mr. McGulliver, he'll be sending him to the tobacco shop every Thursday morning. Just like he sent me."

Millicent crossed her eyes at this. "Percival doesn't smoke; why would he send for tobacco?"

Patty looked at the woman for a moment, and then, as sincerely as she could manage, silently praying for Millicent's understanding, she said, "I think it's probably best you don't know that part, Mrs. McGulliver." She turned to Molly. "But," she said thoughtfully, "it would probably be a good idea for you to remember that about him. It may be useful information."

Molly's expression was dry, as was her tone. "I suppose I can't say too much since you've already saved me from working there once. What if Professor Spice won't hire me, though?"

Patty smiled. "You can make it happen; I have confidence. Just . . . be yourself."

Molly couldn't help but sputter with laughter at this advice. "If only old Anglehanger were here now to hear you say that. I think he'd fall over himself."

"I love you, Mom."

Molly blushed and looked down. After a few seconds, she looked back up with a smile, tears standing in her eyes, and nodded.

Millicent smiled at her success, and jumped up decisively. "Very well," she said. "Say your good-byes. Molly, go and gather anything you need; you may be gone a long time."

PART FOUR:

McGulliver and Spice

As boys, Percival McGulliver and Anson Spice had been less than enthusiastic acquaintances. Their distaste for each other's methods of entertaining themselves and their distrust of each other's loyalties and motives led them to keep each other at arm's length, even at such a tender age as eleven. Of course, there was nothing present then so greatly sinister as they would involve themselves with in their later years, but what dilemmas or frustrations children of such an age may face, they did, and in spades.

Once, when playing a game of checkers at a picnic table in the West Cuttingsborough Community Park, young Anson managed to jump two extra checkers in a masterfully skilled and covert manner. It wasn't quite covert enough to be executed without his opponent suspecting anything, however. Although the youthful McGulliver had actually seen nothing, somehow the result of the jumps was not what he had expected to happen when his opponent's move had begun. His first instinct was to doubt his own senses, but upon studying the board for a moment, he began to suspect he had been deceived. Sadly, Percival McGulliver was every bit as timid and uncertain at eleven as he was as an adult, and when his head snapped up to meet Anson's eyes, he could see the challenge that waited in them: "Say something," the eyes seemed to say. "Go ahead; I dare you. Say something." And of course, Percival did not.

Anson Spice was, quite certainly, a bully. He never fought with his fists, but his challenging stares, his condescending words, his manipulative coercion, all of these made him, in every sense, the meanest and most loathsome psychological bully in all of West Cuttingsborough. And no one feared him more than Percival McGulliver, mostly because no one was his target as often or as fiercely as he. Spice always knew when to stop, though. He never pushed Percival quite too hard, and it never once occurred to McGulliver that this may have been because he was powerless too, or that perhaps Spice was a little intimidated by McGulliver himself.

Indeed, Anson Spice knew potential when he saw it, even as a boy, and he saw all along that Percival McGulliver was, beneath the nervous exterior, the uncertainty, the worrisome tics, and habits, a most impressive manipulator of the very elements and principles that bound the world together. Spice had witnessed McGulliver do things that could only be defined in the mind of a boy as magic, things that defied all reason or sense. And the miracle of it was that often, while Anson Spice knew exactly what he was witnessing, Percival McGulliver had little idea that anything had happened at all.

In their early days of high school, they found themselves laboratory partners in their biology class. History and the sciences, and particularly those specific areas dealing with life and death, not only appealed most to Anson, but they were the ones he excelled in best as well. This was quite distinct from his rival, who was quite knowledgeable in the various branches of mathematics, but struggled with the sciences in a way that Spice found repulsive and inexplicable. Spice would take control of most experiments, allowing McGulliver very little opportunity to learn from them. This always earned good marks for Percival without having to put forth much effort, but it made examination days most frightful for him.

On one particular testing day, Anson could practically smell the nervous sweat that saturated the skin of his seatmate. He could feel the vibrations of anxiety leaping off of Percival, and as the time of the dismissal bell drew closer and Percival's paper was far from complete, he noticed something else as well.

Anson Spice noticed that it appeared to remain 11:19 for a remarkable length of time.

It remained 11:19, in fact, long enough for Percival McGulliver to complete the final thirteen questions on the test as well as to look back over several of the more confounding problems. Just as McGulliver's muscles relaxed, the classroom clock's minute hand shifted to meet the four, and the bell dismissing them to the next period rang out. Anson Spice sat and stared, wallowing in a mixture of envy, bitterness, bewilderment, and admiration. In this flood of emotions, he failed to recognize something very significant:

No one else in the room had noticed the phenomenon occur.

Why any of this should be, please do not anticipate for me to reveal. To attempt to understand why one young man should be able to manipulate time itself, while another should have heightened senses of perception and comprehension of the world beyond that of any others would be no different than to question why one person should excel at painting and another at singing. Such is simply the way, and so it was for both Percival McGulliver and Anson Spice.

These boys had another schoolmate who possessed his own mysterious talents, and while he practiced solitude and interfered little with others' affairs, Anson Spice may have resented him even more so than he did Percival McGulliver. This young man's name was Scratches O'Hannigan, and he could read, write, and play music of any sort and any instrument with no thought, practice, or study whatsoever.

The real trouble came in their senior year of high school. Anson Spice had planned to astound all at the graduation ceremony by using his talents to summon animals of every sort into the auditorium just as the names were finishing being called out and the graduating class was announced to the audience. What was the point of this? Well, of course, it was a prank. It was meant to wreak havoc and chaos, not to mention to add a dose of excitement to the otherwise mundane ritual, and it would show everyone once and for all just what sort of useful skills Anson Spice had been born with and had honed in his eighteen years since birth. Most of all, though, he simply thought it would be fun.

Percival McGulliver had his own plans for the event, and those were to get through it as quickly and painlessly as could be done, mustering the courage to walk across the stage and to do so without taking a nasty spill along the way. Of course, the madness that Spice intended to unleash upon the ceremony would frighten his rival to new heights, and this was certainly also a motivation in the planning of the Summoning of the Wild, as he had come to think of it in the weeks leading up to it.

Graduation was a smashing success. The ceremony was lovely, the decorations were dazzling, the faces were bright and shining, and most of all, the music was spectacular. No, not spectacular. What is greater than spectacular? And whatever word that might be, let's say that the music was quite significantly greater than that. It was, truly, outside the realm of existing vocabulary. The music was unlike anything anyone had ever heard before. Its flows of melodies and hypnotic cadences drifted in and out of the audience's ears at all the right moments. It was as though the music itself knew when, based on who was walking the stage or what was being said, to be grand and booming, and when to be softly lilting. It knew when to evoke smiles and when to evoke tears. Often it accomplished both at the same time and, indeed, this seemed equally by design. No one ever would have dreamed of suggesting that the music distracted from the ceremony. In fact, once it was over, no one would have been able to imagine anything other than that which resulted from the marriage of the ceremony to the music. For that is exactly what it seemed to be to one and all: a beautiful, lovely, compromising, shared blend of two elements to create the ultimate experience.

Well, perhaps this wasn't the sentiment of *all.*

Anson Spice watched and listened closely as this went on, studying the eyes and faces of all those around him, in every part of the hall. What he saw both confounded and outraged him. It was the precise opposite of the reaction he'd planned on receiving from the Summoning of the Wild. Everyone was at peace, basking in a warm glow that could only be called bliss. There was no fear, no confusion, certainly no uncertainty or dismay. All was well with everyone, and Anson Spice was displeased. And he blamed the music.

Shooting his gaze through the auditorium, he tried to locate the source of the sound. It was clearly somewhere near and being played by an orchestra at that very moment. He could see no orchestra, no instruments anywhere in the vast room. There was an orchestra pit in front of the stage, but it was completely empty and unused at the moment, devoid even of chairs or music stands. He trained his ears to filter the sounds in the music, to identify each individual instrument. There were flutes and pianos, yes, and violins, he thought. A harp? Yes, he thought he heard a harp. Certainly those were horns blowing as well, and xylophones were tinkling out their happy notes while bagpipes seemed to be heralding the time for mourning years past. At a certain point he lost all count and concentration and forfeited his attempt to pinpoint every sound in the music. Clearly this was an orchestra of massive proportions, and its beauty was robbing him of the opportunity to make his own statement. The attention was on someone else now, and it was someone who didn't even care to be visible to receive the credit for it. In fact, the credit seemed all to be going toward the ceremony and the graduating class itself, not to the sound of the music.

Clearly, Spice determined, this was unacceptable, and something must be done to stop it. This should have been an ordinary, dull ceremony, his for the taking at precisely the right moment. Now all of those plans were ruined. Even if he were to go forth with his plan and summon the animals into the auditorium, it would not have the effect he had envisioned. In their eyes, it would go beyond a prank; it would be the killing of this beauty they were in the throes of.

And perhaps, just a bit, he couldn't bring himself to destroy that beauty either, though that was something he was unwilling to confront in himself.

Anson Spice made his way stealthily from his seat in the auditorium to the eastern corridor. This was easily done. Since his game with Percival in the park seven years prior, he had learned how to sneak things much bigger than checkers undetected, including himself. When he entered the corridor, he found it abandoned, though the sound of the music was distinctly louder here. He followed the sound down the corridor until he reached the meeting of another hallway. Here he believed the music seemed to come from this new direction, and he turned, edging his way quietly, listening carefully to be certain he had taken the right direction.

Indeed, the music's sound continued to grow as he drew down this corridor, and when he was nearly at the end of the hallway, which came to a certain dead end with a doorway to the outside, he saw that, at the very end of the hallway, on his right, was a door. The door was solid wood with no way to see inside. He gripped the handle with surety and silence and, turning it in his angry fist, pulled the great, solid door slowly toward him.

The explosion of sound was immediate. Despite the solid, full sound that had permeated every portion of the auditorium, opening this door seemed to free a sound that had been stifled until now. Anson Spice stepped into the room and looked around at his surroundings.

The room, had it not been for the source of the music, would have been entirely empty. It was white on all sides, as well as the floor and ceiling, and there was nothing whatsoever to decorate it. There were no windows either, and the whole thing, had it been completely empty, would have given the feel of a place in which to lock up the mentally disturbed. There was coldness in the room, and a smell that seemed to signify ammonia and mildew, suggesting that the room had been closed up for some time and only reopened and cleaned for the purpose of hosting the orchestra.

But there was no orchestra.

The instruments were all there, yes, every one that Spice had identified with his own ears and more. There were snare drums, clarinets, zithers, harps, flutes, panpipes, saxophones, xylophones, theremins, psalteries, ocarinas, didgeridoos, lutes, pipe organs, lyres, maracas, tambourines, bongos, and pianos. There were guitars, violins, piccolos, harmonicas, banjos, accordions, French horns, cornets, and slide whistles.

They were all placed strategically in some part of the room, some on the floor, some hanging from the ceiling, others placed on a shelf or a platform, some actually supporting each other. And each in its place seemed to be attached to some sort of cable, tube, pedal, or other such supplement, and these all met together on a switchboard of sorts, where a single person was clearly controlling all of them simultaneously. Many of the instruments, most, in fact, had more than one cable or pipe or such implement attached to it, so that even those requiring multiple tasks at once were somehow manipulated. Small contraptions blew air into pipes that somehow managed to reach the mouthpieces of the wind and brass instruments with just the right strength at just the right moment. Pulleys worked the trombones and accordions back and forth at a steady and calculated pace. Plastic fingers tapped down on keys and strummed strings and covered holes.

And at the center of it all, controlling all of these mechanisms from the handcrafted switchboard was Scratches O'Hannigan, either oblivious to or uncaring of Anson Spice's presence, and Spice watched as his prodigious peer used his talents and his ingenuity to create the marvelous sound that was driving the graduation ceremony elsewhere in the building.

It was the most impressive sight Anson Spice had ever witnessed, and he simply stood and watched, the frustrated fury now intermingling with an overwhelming admiration. He watched and listened, and he never once tried to follow along and learn to pick up on what Scratches was doing, nor did it occur to him to sabotage the structure and put a stop to the music. He was bitter, true, and he was quite envious, certainly, but beneath all that was the simple truth that when someone's talent was used to create something, it was only for that person to determine when and how it should end. Just as Anson would have fumed at someone who would have put a stop to the Summoning of the Wild prematurely, he knew that it would be wrong to stop the music before its composer, conductor, and player had decided it was complete.

When the music had ended, Scratches O'Hannigan looked immediately to his visitor and said, "I hope ya enjoyed it, then, Anson. I hope they all did."

Anson Spice took a moment to collect his thoughts, studied O'Hannigan's face, then swallowed and said, "It was perfect. How did you do it?"

Scratches shrugged briefly and then made a vague gesture at the giant structure of instruments.

Anson nodded impatiently and started closer to his peer. "Yes, yes, I can see that, but *how*? How could you even know where to begin or how to construct it? How could you have known it would work?"

Again Scratches O'Hannigan shrugged, took a moment himself to think about the question, then, nodding to himself thoughtfully, he said, "I suppose it's not much different, mate, than when you brought in the winds and the rains the night of the East Cuttingsborough game, when Charlie Mott had broke his arm. You just knew what to do and ya did it, then, right?"

Anson Spice arched an intrigued eyebrow. While he was usually quite pleased to announce his involvement with anything impressive and to take as much of the credit as people were willing to give him, he had remained quite silent on the issue of the tornado-strength winds and rains the night of the game. That could have brought trouble to many, himself included, had he announced his role in the cancellation of the event. Yet somehow Scratches had known all along it had been him.

"Aye, I knew," Scratches said, nodding at Anson upon seeing the brief betrayal of his surprise pass across his face. "And I'd reckon I may not be the only one to either. Ya didn't talk about it none, true enough, Anson, but you had a look in yer eye that night. Ya had a look that said all that needed sayin' and it was clearer 'n crystal what ya'd done."

Anson was still very much torn in his emotions, unclear on whether to be furious at his classmate's evident ability to trump his every move, his every thought even, or whether to be inspired and moved. Surely he was both, but Anson Spice had never once straddled two varying realms of thought or emotion; he was always clear and decisive on his stance, no matter the occasion. Until now, that is.

At this point, Anson Spice made a decision. He saw before himself a crossroads, and the options were quite clear. Either he must band with his peers that they might pool their talents for a greater good, or isolate himself from this unmatchable competition. He chose the latter.

At the last minute, Anson determined that he would leave West Cuttingsborough for his university education, thus ensuring no encounters in the following years with either Percival McGulliver or Scratches O'Hannigan. In that time, he studied all manner of arts, crafts, and histories. He attended the University of East Cuttingsborough for nearly ten years, securing countless degrees and certifications in any and all fields of interest to him, culminating in enough qualifications to allow him to profess to college students himself. When this time arose, however, no openings suitable for his credentials presented themselves at his alma mater. One position was there for the taking, and it required him to venture back to West Cuttingsborough. He had little taste for this at first, but promptly reminded himself that his rivals were certainly long since departed from the school, and if for some reason they were not, that would simply place him as their superior on campus, and this induced in him a fiendish delight.

And so, Anson Spice became Professor Spice.

During his short-lived career teaching world history at the university, Professor Spice fell desperately in love with a colleague, young Janine Van Alderdash, who was working as a clerk in the school library while pursuing her graduate studies in mathematical theory. This young lady was much similar to what the future Miss Patty of our tale would become. Inspiringly beautiful, ever filled with optimism and good cheer, Miss Van Alderdash was known and cherished by many at the university. Sadly, whereas Patty's goodness and infectious cheer were genuine through to the bone, it was, perhaps, rather less so for Janine Van Alderdash.

Of all of the relationships forged during her years there, one in particular was of singular depth and sincerity. This friendship was with a certain Millicent Cotton, a third-year student majoring in classical art. This pair of young ladies found free-spirited joy and youthful fun in the most unpredictable and unlikely of places, and frequently at the most inappropriate of times.

Once, the young ladies had dressed in their finest clothes and paid a visit to the recently opened Lotsa The Pasta to masquerade as overly-critical food inspectors, much to the worry and chagrin of proprietor Salvador Olinoli, who was, at that time, quite the unconfident and easily shakable young man. Another occasion saw our Miss Cotton freeing all of the livestock on the Trotter brothers' farm while Miss Van Alderdash distracted the simple men in their farmhouse, convincing them to purchase a set of limited edition maps depicting ocean currents through the ages. The fact that these maps were purchased for rather less than a dollar apiece from a general store a few towns away and had mysteriously inflated to some forty-odd dollars in value (with the exception of the "autographed" ones, which called for quite a bit more) was a minor detail that somehow became omitted from the young lady's sales pitch. By the end of it all, the animals were roaming all parts of West Cuttingsborough (a couple made it beyond the town limits) and both the pair of young ladies and farmer brothers became a bit wealthier, one pair in cash, the other in oceanic maps.

In lieu of any more shady and character-depraving narratives, dear reader, please suffice it to say that these two painfully endearing young ladies were less than innocent when it came to youthful pranksterism. Was anyone ever hurt as a result of these shenanigans? Certainly not. Well, rather, no one that anyone specifically became aware of. A few people who may have been squeamish of livestock were sufficiently frightened to see cows and pigs crossing their paths, and Mr. Olinoli took for truth some very peculiar tips regarding health codes at his restaurant, including the conservation of water by merely dry-toweling the dishes after they'd been used. But if these were the worst of the results, then the future Mrs. McGulliver would be right in her later philosophy that so long as her husband and Anson Spice walked the earth, her own impish actions remained harmless.

Now it happened that Janine Van Alderdash had a cousin by the name of Percival McGulliver, and it was through her friendship with Millicent Cotton that the bookish man and the vibrant young lady met and fell instantly to devastatingly swoonish adoration of each other. That Millicent was merely playing another prank by appearing interested in Percival seemed obvious to Janine, who was markedly astonished (and perhaps a bit appalled) to come to have to accept that the feelings were, indeed, genuine.

In the end, they were married, of course, and Janine conceded to the marriage, standing as maid of honor for Millicent, while the shy and meek Percival McGulliver appealed to none other than Professor Anson Spice to stand as best man. That Percival didn't ask the far more palatable Scratches O'Hannigan was simply because he had designated the prodigy to be in charge of the music for the ceremony. Of course, had McGulliver witnessed the backstage phenomenon at graduation that Spice had, he may have understood more accurately that if anyone could have been standing at the altar as best man while simultaneously performing the music at the other end of the chapel, then that person was Scratches O'Hannigan.

But alas, Percival did *not* fully comprehend his school chum's talents, and so Anson Spice stood as best man. Why would such a solitary and cold human being such as Professor Spice agree to such a cheerful frivolity, you may ask? Of course, it was as self-serving as any other action he'd ever performed, and it was merely in the hopes of drawing closer to Maid of Honor Janine Van Alderdash that Spice consented to be a member of the wedding party.

"Ah, Miss Van Alderdash," Anson Spice purred from his towering place heads above the young woman as they prepared to go to their proper places before the ceremony. "Your beauty is only surpassed by your evident potential for wicked conspiracy."

Miss Van Alderdash's arched eyebrow spoke for her supposed ignorance of Spice's meaning.

"Please, my dear," the giant man went on. "Surely the fact that the Trotter brothers have fancied themselves experts in the realm of oceanography is hardly without your assistance." His knowing smirk less alarmed the young woman than perturbed her. So what if she'd swindled the Trotter brothers? It was all in innocent fun, and she'd done her best to hide her identity from the farmers and from anyone who'd heard about the event. Indeed, the Trotters did seem enriched by their purchase of the Complete Library of Maps and Charts of the Oceans Mysterious, and they'd managed to collect the majority of the escaped livestock (and, simple as the brothers were, they had never even thought to attach a connection between the sudden appearance of the map-seller with the sudden *dis*appearance of the animals). So who was this man to condescend to attempt to frighten her with his knowledge?

What Janine Van Alderdash did not realize was that Anson Spice was not being facetious; when he claimed to admire her mischief, he was being perhaps more sincere than he ever had been or ever would be. This was simply his way of expressing affection.

"Why the devil did your fiancé choose that creepy Professor Spice to be his best man?" Janine demanded of her friend during the wedding reception later that evening.

Millicent attempted (granted, not very hard and with little success) to stifle a giggle with her hand to her lips. With a shrug, she said, "He was your cousin before he was my husband."

"Oh, fine," her friend retorted. "You may think it's amusing, but you've put me in company with a very strange character, Millie."

"Oh yes, I know," Millicent agreed promptly.

"He was mocking and taunting me! He knows I sold the Trotters the ocean maps!"

Millicent McGulliver nodded her belief at this. "Hardly a surprise to anyone who knows him. Anson Spice is ...surreal."

Janine Van Alderdash was unimpressed. "He'd best stay away from me the rest of the evening," was the only further thing she had to say of the matter.

Of course, Anson Spice *did* stay away from her the rest of the evening, but hardly due to the fact that he'd perceived her distaste for him. Quite to the contrary, he, knowing very little of the fairer sex, assumed that he had said all that was required to communicate his affections to the girl. Not realizing that he'd done quite the opposite (not to mention that there was probably little hope in turning such a negative impression around, at least not in one evening), he simply stood in the shadows, sipping at his wine and awaiting what he assumed was her inevitable approach of him.

Does the fact that such an approach never occurred that night really need to be stated, fair readers?

That Janine Van Alderdash had shown no interest in reciprocating his advances was an abomination that was not to be tolerated in Professor Spice's mind. The rash and heated portion of his demeanor desired to take action against such insolence and ingratitude immediately. The colder, more calculating, and far more devious part of the man determined that it would behoove him to wait until the opportunity had ripened. For the time being, he let the matter pass. His infatuation with the young Miss Van Alderdash, however, only strengthened with his every move and step.

If Professor Spice was chagrined by the slighting he received from Miss Janine Van Alderdash, his bitterness was only intensified by the flagrant cheer that the newly wed McGullivers seemed to trickle behind them wherever they went.

Indeed, there were few in all of West Cuttingsborough who did not become familiar with the glowing and joy-filled faces of the two McGullivers walking side by side through the streets. Whether browsing through the shops or peeking at least through the store fronts downtown or sitting in front of their quaint cottage at the foot of the mountains, waving to the outdoorsy folk who ventured through the pastures and hills or attempted to climb the highest mountains, they were always visible and spreading their good humor. Love had seized them and was showing no signs of releasing them.

Whoever once claimed that all good things must some day come to an end may very well have foreseen the lives of Percival and Millicent McGulliver. As their love blossomed and grew, so did Mr. McGulliver's attention to his unique abilities. Times in his life when he had managed to slow time or quicken it or stop it altogether gnawed at the back of his brain, until he was forced to bring the thoughts to the forefront of his mind, where he focused on them with curiosity and intent study. The series of numbers and letters that Percival silently and personally referred to as "The Code" came to him quite subconsciously. Several of the sequences were doodles he'd scratched on his papers when he'd been in school. More recently, he'd found himself writing entries in his journal that were nothing but seemingly randomly placed numbers and letters. As his focus on his peculiarities increased, so did his attention to these characters that imposed themselves on his mind at the oddest or most inexplicable of times.

Whether his wife ever noticed anything peculiar when they were together, he was uncertain; he could remember times when he had, in fact, caused things to happen in her presence, but until he started truly considering these little mishaps, every episode was brief and more or less inconsequential. In other words, the things he'd done before were hardly worth noticing. The greater question which, perhaps, he may have benefited from asking himself would have been why, exactly, he'd thought it best to keep these things a secret from her. The fact that Anson Spice had noticed these occurrences from an early age was probably merely due to his own irregularities; Spice had possessed an eye and a nose for the fantastic for most of his life.

As Percival McGulliver's desire to understand his talents grew, he inevitably spent more time behind closed doors in his workshop in the back yard. At first this was once or twice a week at the most, and for only very brief quantities of time, or after Millicent had fallen asleep for the night and thus never even noticed his absence at all. But as is the case with obsessions, the more Mr. McGulliver learned of what he could do, the more time he needed to harness those abilities and practice them. He was not long at all in these studies before drawing the connection between the abilities and the sequences of numbers and letters that had haunted him most of his life.

And, of course, with the mastery of certain skills, the door opened to altogether new ones. He first discovered that he was capable of transporting things through the dimensions of time by pure chance, when he became infuriated at a pen that had stopped writing. When shaking it, tapping it, licking its nib, and pounding it against his desktop had proven fruitless, he found himself cursing at the poor inanimate implement, and in the event uttered words to the effect that it should "get itself gone," at which it did. He was alarmed, of course, to be holding nothing when only a second earlier he'd been quite certainly gripping the pen, but after careful consideration and a little bit of experimentation, he concluded that the pen had somehow been sent into either the past or the future. The following items he attempted to send deliberately to the very near future, and sure enough, after a few moments had passed, the items would re-materialize where he'd left them.

From that day forth, when Percival McGulliver was not at work at Hats for All Occasions, he was rarely seen outside his workshop, and he and Millicent grew further and further apart. One evening, when Millicent had prepared a special meal for dinner and found her spirits deflated when her husband failed to show up to the table, she made the mistake of visiting him in the workshop.

"Woman, go!" McGulliver screamed. His face turned instantly bright red, and his eyes were the wide and hysterical sort you might expect to see on one who was simultaneously outraged and terrified, one who'd been caught in the act of some indecency and was both furious and ashamed for it. Whether his anger was directed toward his wife or himself remains unclear, but in Millicent's viewpoint, it was never a question. She fled the workshop in shock too great to allow tears to shed and threw the meal away without so much as giving it another sniff.

It is impossible to say whether the wealth that the McGullivers soon afterward stumbled into was a blessing for the neglected missus or whether it only further weighed her burdens. That it changed each of them and drove wider the wedge that had come between them even more greatly is, however, quite incontestable.

With the discoveries that McGulliver had undergone came an ever-increasing sensation of invincibility. That he could achieve great things with few obstacles and even fewer failures, he was confident. And as we all know, such an irrational and inflated self-confidence can often cause tragic events to occur.

In most people's minds, winning untold fortunes in less than a day would hardly qualify as a "tragic event," but it was just that accomplishment that all but ended communication between the McGullivers until the arrival of Molly and Patty. The Council card game, held weekly in Miles Garrish's mansion, was something that Percival McGulliver had observed but never participated in for years. He attended mostly due to the fact that Garrish was his employer, being the owner of Hats for All Occasions.

Let us speak for a moment of Miles Garrish. He was an eccentric by most people's definition of the word, and in West Cuttingsborough both the word eccentric and the name Garrish were more or less synonymous. Yet Garrish was loved by many, at least by those who were amused by him, even if they didn't understand him. Those who saw no amusement in his nature saw little point in association with him at all, but those who had taken the time to make themselves acquainted with the hat seller were living proof of the benefits of such a relationship. For Miles Garrish was, quite possibly, not only the wealthiest man in West Cuttingsborough, but perhaps also the most generous. He threw lavish parties the likes of which few people in the region had ever attended. Complete with full symphonic orchestras, elaborate costumes made available for the guests to change into, foods brought in from mysterious chefs in other parts of the world, and gifts and prizes for any and all that were not only of significant monetary value, but also of a specific sentimental significance for the recipient, each event never failed to surpass in greatness and legend its predecessor.

How often did he open his mansion to these festivities? There was no real rhyme or reason to that, which, of course, frustrated the people who always wanted to know when to expect the next one. There were gaps of several years and others of mere weeks. It was all based on Miles Garrish's own whim, fancy, and personal observations of the needs of the residents of West Cuttingsborough. Such "needs" may sometimes have been difficult economic troubles descended upon the region; other times it may have been something simple and isolated as the death of one person's pet. Indeed, when Garrish heard that little Jonathan Widdle's cat Dinkerton

("Dinkie") had died, he immediately determined that it was time for cheer and hearty laughter administered as medicine upon the souls of the community.

"And music!" he declared to Patrick Sticklivid of the Goatsbridge Tavern, whose establishment he had been visiting when the news had reached his ears. "Nothing like loud and massive music to lift the spirits of a depressed village such as this!" And off he had been to begin the arrangements.

With charities and frivolities alike, Mr. Garrish's purse strings were forever loosened. But those who made themselves scarce when he was around never did find themselves invited to the mansion whenever a party occurred. It wasn't that Miles was coldhearted toward those who didn't make an effort at his friendship; nor was it that he was biased in favor of those who were nicest to him. He simply figured (quite logically, some may have believed) that someone who was opposed to being sociable in an everyday setting would just as likely act similarly at a formal gathering, and Miles Garrish had no interest in spoiling everyone's fun with a downhearted grouch who was forever in a slump.

The weekly card games were Miles's idea. Wishing to create a more sociable, less stressful and businesslike setting for the members of the West Cuttingsborough Businessman's Council in which to become better acquainted with one another, he arranged the first game as a smaller-affair party in much quainter fashion than the grand celebrations he'd already become famous for throughout the city. Responses to the initial invitations were mixed, some of the men fancying the idea as a welcome change in their humdrum routines, others rolling their eyes at what was clearly Garrish's inappropriate attempt to continue to purchase others' affections and political support with his obscene quantities of money.

Percival McGulliver's reaction was unique. He chose simply not to respond. The formal, gold-script invitation arrived in the mail (the route that would later be filled by Jefferson Gladwell, father to Gerald and Patty and husband to Molly), and McGulliver placed it on the table in his workshop, disregarding it and convincing himself he'd never even seen it. When his employer confronted him about his failure to respond, Percival simply didn't say anything.

"Well, I hope you plan on attending!" the cheerful man proclaimed in his usual voice that was often louder than necessary (and according to some, louder than appropriate; indeed, there were many people in need of hats who ventured to other towns or even did without, simply to avoid the high volume that habitually emitted from Garrish's mouth).

Percival simply stood silently looking back at his boss, blinking once or twice.

"Well then, I'm putting you down as a 'yes,' my boy!" Garrish determined with a laugh.

Percival didn't consent, but he certainly didn't object either. He simply went on watching and blinking. Had someone asked Miles Garrish on the day of the first card game whether he anticipated his assistant to make an appearance, he would most likely have confessed to being entirely without a clue. In fact, he was mildly surprised when he opened the door to reveal the bookish little man.

"Percival! So glad you decided to attend!" he expressed, stepping aside and gesturing for his friend's entrance. "Welcome, welcome. We're meeting in the game room. If you'd like to wait right there in that corridor while I step into the kitchen and collect a couple more of the hors d'oeuvres, I can show you the way in just a moment."

When Miles Garrish returned with the shining silver platters holding mysterious bite-sized puffs, pastries, cakes, sausages, rolls, sandwiches, and skewered meats, all emitting an overwhelmingly welcoming aroma, Percival followed him obediently to the game room and immediately seated himself in a corner, set apart from those who had already arrived; there he remained for the duration of his stay, which came to an end long before the games had finished and the others had said their goodbyes.

So it was and continued to be every week at the Garrish mansion. Percival rarely spoke but always observed. Gradually he began assisting in little ways in order to better serve a function at the gatherings. The others certainly didn't make him feel unwelcome, never said a disparaging word, and often went out of their way to attempt to involve him in the conversation. Certainly they tried more than a few times to get him to sit in on the game for at least a hand or two, all to no avail. Of course, after he'd left for the evening, it was a different matter. Once he was safely distanced from the game room, they would all turn to their host and begin with their theories and commentaries.

"Is that what he's like all day at the store?"

"Why does he even bother to come?

"At least I haven't had to refill my glass lately; he's started doing it for me."

"Is it just me, or does he make anyone else uncomfortable?"

"Oh, definitely. I think I'd be playing much better if he weren't distracting me what with his general unpleasantness. It's unseemly."

"You'd be playing poorly regardless," Miles would interject, voicing an opinion for the first time. He would find tactful little ways to guide the talk back away from Percival McGulliver and would never offer a negative contribution to the gossip. In fact, more than once he threatened to cease the games altogether if these little complaining sessions continued. Of course, he probably enjoyed these evenings himself far too much to terminate them, so he simply continued with his own subtle methods of defending the odd little man.

What of Scratches O'Hannigan during all of this?

Sadly, Scratches's post-high school successes were fewer than those of either of his old schoolmates. What Anson Spice hadn't realized upon his decision to leave West Cuttingsborough to escape Scratches and Percival for his university years was that Scratches O'Hannigan would not be attending *any* college institution. The musical prodigy had been raised by his grandmother, who, by that time, had found herself in a desperate situation with regard to finances. She'd managed to provide for her grandson adequately in his upbringing, but when it came time for him to leave high school, it also came time for him to leave home. He spent his first three years out of high school traveling to various surrounding towns and countries, performing his music for money and sending as much as he could to his grandmother in West Cuttingsborough.

It had been a sad and lonely time for Scratches O'Hannigan, but these solitary travels proved to be far less painful than his return. He arrived to find that his grandmother's health had declined rapidly in his absence, something he'd been ignorant of in his time away as he'd held no permanent mailing address to allow her to correspond with him. Of course, it wouldn't occur to the guild-stricken boy that she likely wouldn't have informed him of her health problems even if she'd been able to. The way she saw it, he was on his own, doing what he loved and making money at it. That the vast majority of his already meager earnings were being given to her, she had no idea. She was certain her beloved young grandson was living a thriving and exciting life, and that made her very happy.

Her savings had taken quite a battering over the years in her caretaking of Scratches, and thus she'd been unable to keep up with the payments on her house. Willa O'Hannigan being a known and loved resident about the city, the Bank of West Cuttingsborough allowed for some leniency. Still, even the kindest of little old ladies must eventually succumb to the bounds of the law, regardless of the circumstances. Unbeknownst to her grandson, Willa O'Hannigan began making personal sacrifices in order to pay more to the bank, including her own medications.

The money sent to her as regularly as Scratches could manage always went unfailingly toward payment on the little house, in the hopes that one day, when she was gone, her grandson would be able to own the house and settle down in the city of his youth with no obligations, surely living healthily and happily on all the riches he was accumulating on the road performing his wonderful music. This was to be her final gift to him.

When Scratches O'Hannigan at last returned, he was aghast to find his grandmother's health greatly deteriorated and even more greatly aghast to learn where the money he'd been sending had gone.

"Scratches, my boy," the old woman whispered from her bed on her last day in this lifetime, "I am . . . so proud . . . of you."

Scratches O'Hannigan had to look away, grief already overcoming him, but he was also angry, angry at himself for leaving, yes, but angry also at her for being so frustratingly selfless. He wanted to thank her, to tell her that he was even prouder of her, that she'd been his hero and inspiration and would continue to be, but he couldn't speak. He sat there by her bedside, tears standing in his eyes, which were turned away from her as she breathed her final breaths.

Of course he couldn't bring himself to go on living in the house. He left it as it was, hired someone to tend to the yard periodically, and took to the streets. He rarely left West Cuttingsborough after that day, unless tight finances made it absolutely necessary, and he walked the streets by day playing his favorite instrument of all that he'd ever played, the fiddle his grandmother had given him that had belonged to her own father. He owned a small piano and a harmonica as well, both of which he'd left in his bedroom in the house. Perhaps someday he would return to the house and those other instruments, but he didn't think so.

Percival McGulliver had been studying. Of course, he'd been studying his abilities, but that was not all. When he was at the weekly Council card game, whether he was refilling glasses, fetching food, or sitting quietly in the corner, he was studying the players and their techniques. He was studying their strategies and their signals, all without any single one of them suspecting a thing.

That he intended to use his abilities to assist himself in taking everything he could in the card game was something he'd determined silently to himself some time ago. That he wanted to use it as minimally as possible in order to allow himself to feel somewhat more ethical was, if entirely absurd, at least moderately sensible to himself. Yes, it was important to Percival that he not simply transport himself through the dimensions of time into the past in order to gamble on a game he already knew the outcomes of. Besides, this could have been dangerous and very likely may have been fruitless. First of all, he wasn't entirely confident that he could bring himself back to the present. He was rather confident, but *rather confident* simply isn't confidence enough when considering something so drastic. More certain was the fact that the cards simply would not be dealt the same way a second time around in an already-existing game due to the fact that he hadn't played in it the first time; an extra player would have led to entirely different hands.

No, there was only one way to do it; of that he was certain. He needed to master their signals and habits, know what to expect of each of his opponents, and then use that knowledge to his own advantage. Of course, he could just plan to bring time to a complete halt and use that time to examine their cards, perhaps trade a few of his for what was remaining in the deck and the such, but…well, that would have been cheating!

"You playing tonight, Perce?" Miles Garrish asked cheerfully as the men took their seats and he began dealing out the first hand. It was a question he always posed to the little man.

"I, uh, well…yes, I think perhaps, yes…tonight," came the unanticipated response. The cards' movement ceased abruptly in Miles's hands. Those who were there would later swear that they'd seen a card actually freeze in midair. Mouths agape, eyes widened, they all stopped their eating, their conversing, their examinations of the cards they'd received so far, and their heads all swiveled toward Percival McGulliver.

"Seriously?" their host replied, a questioning eyebrow being the most he was willing to appear unusual.

McGulliver simply nodded and took a seat, feebly nodding his greetings to the members of the Council seated around the card table. Uncomfortable glances darted this way and that amongst the others, conspiratorially confirming their own individual concerns with this disruption of the status quo. But one shooting glare from Miles and they each knew better than to bring voice to those concerns.

The game was a popular one among men in the region. It was known as Divisor, and it not only involved mathematics, but it also required a sharp mind in that realm in order for a player to have any sort of hope of success. Depending on the particular round and the dealer's choice of branch, the cards were played based on anything from basic addition to (usually only in the severest of high-stakes games) advanced calculus. Some of the more creative hands even managed to incorporate geometric proofs. It could be the simplest of games, and was indeed often enjoyed by children of the area, engaging only the barest and most basic of rules. Divisor was even occasionally used by teachers in West Cuttingsborough to help teach mathematics (though, sadly, not usually at the primary level, as those teachers felt the game's association with gambling made it inappropriate for a grade school setting; the high school teachers, on the other hand, didn't seem disturbed by this). Yet Divisor could also be a complex dance of wit and strategy, as coveted as a sign of true possession of wisdom and intellect in West Cuttingsborough as chess was in other parts of the world.

Miles Garrish, as host, was the first to deal and to choose the particular form of mathematics to be used during this hand of play. After dealing five cards to each player including himself, Miles turned over the top two cards remaining in the deck. These were revealed to be a two and a nine. After examining these two quantities and the cards in his hand, he declared, "Addition!" Now, this, in reality, had very little to do with the cards in his hand and more to do with courtesy and tradition. Miles was not only always the first dealer; he also always unfailingly called addition for the first hand, thus easing the players in with the most basic of mathematic principles.

Smiling and sitting back in his chair, Miles's part to play was over for a moment. In Divisor, the dealer took his turn last. Play moving clockwise around the card table, the person to Miles Garrish's left, Duncan Chessler, examined his own cards and the two on the table. The task of the players was now to find in their hand a card with the value closest to the sum of the two cards on the table. With reluctance, Duncan Chessler threw down a six. With a difference of five between this and the sum of two and nine, Duncan knew very well that this round was most likely already beyond his reach.

The play continued through the next two players, who, in turn, played an eight and a seven, at which point the play came to Percival McGulliver. Whether it was fate or the oddest luck that was having its hand in McGulliver's cards that night will, in all likelihood, remain one of those unanswered questions of the universe. Whatever the reason, Percival McGulliver held in his hand all three of the remaining twos, one of the threes, and an ace, which, when playing an addition hand, served as a one. Even playing his highest card, Percival McGulliver was a dismal eight points away from the target quantity.

The other men, decidedly relieved by the realization that McGulliver posed no threat, made decent efforts to laugh lightheartedly of the poor hand and to lift his visibly dampened spirits.

"Ah, Perce, no good getting discouraged this early in the game; we've still got a long way to go!" Miles attempted to cheer his assistant.

As the play continued, Desmond Willard, seated to Percival's left, smugly laid down a jack on the table. When playing an addition hand, the jack served as an eleven. There were times when the face cards served as different values or as wild cards, but in this case, Desmond had claimed at least a portion, if not the entire pot for the first round of play. Had someone else had a jack to lay down and one of the two jacks matched the suit of either the nine or the two that were laid down at the start of the round, that person would have claimed the entire pot. If both of their jacks matched suits with either the nine or the two, they would share the pot. As it happened, though, in this particular round of play, Desmond Willard claimed the money to himself.

Percival McGulliver's luck fared no better in the next round of play. Desmond Willard, being the victor of the first round, became the caller of the next round of the hand. Turning over an eight and a king, he had a choice to make. Either he could determine that the king would hold a value of thirteen and call the round as addition, subtraction, multiplication, or division, or he could call the king a wild card and claim it as an algebraic equation.

Desmond concentrated carefully on his own hand and took a moment to examine his opponents' eyes as they studied their own hands in relation to the overturned cards. Finally, decisively, he declared, "Let's have an equation."

It was rather a stray from the path of tradition in the Council card game to leap from addition all the way to algebra, but Desmond Willard had been known to be less than decent in business, and he was downright vicious when it came to gambling. Max Trot led the first card in this round, and he was in a very important position. The next top card in the remainder of the deck would reveal the remainder of the algebraic equation that the eight and the king had begun. Max, being to the left of the caller, had the advantage of being able to look at that card and play his choice without sharing what he saw on the card with the other players. It was then their job to try to guess what that card read based upon what card Max played. Of course, there could be multiple valid algebraic equations created out of three different values, but whichever card came closest in value to an actual functioning equation would be deemed the "correct" equation, and all other players' scores would be calculated based on their proximity to that equation's value for the king.

Though he had observed many games and had witnessed the game play of countless algebraic rounds, Percival McGulliver was still significantly overwhelmed by the intensity of the game play in this round. This, combined with his unfortunate hand, led to his failure once again to collect any money.

And so it went for the remaining three rounds of the first hand (the final hand of a round left the players with no choice but to play the one card that remained in their hand and hope for the best), and, if possible, his fortune only worsened throughout the second and third hands.

It was at this point in the evening that Percival McGulliver determined that he had no choice but to use his ability to his advantage. Clearly he was incapable of accomplishing anything through his own luck and skill, and he intended to leave this game nothing less than the wealthiest man in West Cuttingsborough.

In the meantime, Professor Spice had not neglected mentally attending to the matter of Janine Van Alderdash and her insolent rejection of his advances. Distaste turning him from any of the more obvious reactions that were certainly beneath his stature, he had let the matter brew and foster in the back of his mind until he had decided how best to proceed.

Just as Percival McGulliver had been working in solitude to unlock and perfect the mysteries of his natural abilities, Anson Spice had been doing the same. He had been performing many experiments in his laboratory at the university, but he was well aware of the danger of such a public venue for his studies. His campus apartment was no more discreet, what with its paper-thin walls and shared ventilation system. He needed a place of his own, a secretive place that would be unwelcoming and out of the way enough to keep potential whistle-blowers at a distance. He knew exactly where he needed to look, and throwing his overcoat on as he exited his office in the university, he turned his steps toward Cobble Road.

Perhaps it was due to his distracted state of mind, or maybe it was a result of his having ventured to this particular appendage of the city before, or just possibly he was so cold, dark, and dismal himself that he simply possessed an inherent immunity to its nature, but whatever the reason, Professor Spice strode Cobble Road entirely unmoved by its menacing sights and curdling smells. Anyone else would have sworn they could feel the very street *breathing* on the back of their neck, could feel its tree-limb fingers and its sidewalk-crack-weed legs writhing and stretching and weaving themselves around their arms and legs. Spice, however, noticed none of this; he simply walked on toward his destination.

If it was real estate he was seeking, there was plenty of availability on Cobble Road; there always was. But it was not these residences and establishments Professor Spice was interested in. He knew exactly what he wanted, what he *required*. With a purpose that drove his stride at twice what it ordinarily was, Professor Anson Spice led himself to the one place in all of West Cuttingsborough that he knew would perfectly suit his needs.

He had always been an admirer of the tobacco shop, even if its proprietor was a sniveling ignoramus who knew nothing about his own line of work. The delicate substances that were imported from all over the world (and indeed, some that were reputed to be from other worlds as well) for such a simple purpose as to be savored through a wooden pipe in one's hand were things of beauty, as Professor Spice saw it. Spice's own purposes often called for special...ingredients; oftentimes exotic and foreign tobaccos made for just the proper ingredient in seeing a task correctly executed. To have such a trove of components at his fingertips was a delicious notion. And what's more, he would appreciate the wares that were under his command, more so than Oliver Booth, the shop's current owner.

Anson Spice entered the tobacconist shop and instantly seethed at the grinning face of Booth, who was standing behind the counter with his palms pressed down flat upon it, standing at the ready for anyone to step through the entrance. Spice observed that he looked like an overly friendly bartender who'd been waiting all evening for a potential drunken sod to burden him with his life story in the hopes of his bestowing the wisest of sage advice. The professor shuddered with annoyance.

"Why, Professor! Welcome to the tobacco shop!" Oliver Booth declared, displaying a mouth full of glistening white teeth.

"Booth," Anson Spice returned with a formal nod.

"What are you in the market for today, Professor Spice?" Booth asked with an interested sincerity that all but dripped of sugary substance. Oliver Booth, you see, was a different sort of dark than the other people of Cobble Road. Booth's self-serving cunning and evil were masked under a pretense of being, quite literally, The Most Friendly Man In The World. The Most Friendly Man In The World disguise was one that the deceitful and backhanded Oliver Booth wore with pride. Of course, Spice saw right through it. He could not be fooled by the mirages that Cobble Road had to offer, be they the truly sinister appearing ones, or the overly welcoming ones. It confounded Booth that the arrogant and clearly powerful Anson Spice had never succumbed to his trickery and fallen victim to his bait.

"Your business," Spice responded, engaging in a lock of stares that, once Booth understood the true nature of Spice's visit, would break him with astonishingly rapid speed.

"Of course, of course! How can I…" Booth began, but Spice's voice was abrupt and cruel, enough to stop the man short.

"Your *business*, Booth. You are finished as tobacconist of West Cuttingsborough. You're a disgrace to the product you deal in."

Oliver Booth attempted a chuckle and a scoff, but something in his eyes said he wasn't so confident of his station. "You…you want to buy the shop?" he managed to inquire, feigning disbelief at the notion, though it was no surprise at all. Oliver Booth knew very well that Professor Spice was his superior in knowledge of the various tobaccos of the world.

Spice's sole response was to maintain his loathsome stare into Booth's eyes.

"The shop isn't for sale, Spice." Booth was changing gears, allowing his Most Friendly Man In The World disguise to fall back just a touch, trying his hand instead at mild annoyance. After all, it worked for Spice, didn't it? Why not poison him with his own medicine?

There was no poisoning Anson Spice, not with annoyance or with any other medicine of treachery.

"I have no need for anyplace else, Booth. You know that very well. And you also know that any sale is negotiable." Spice's voice, filled with resolve, was unwavering.

Now Oliver Booth was intrigued; Spice was implying that he had something to offer, something he would want. But what could possibly be an adequate exchange for the building, its stock, and its ownership other than a fair quantity of money? Rather than ask, Booth continued to watch the professor, waiting for him to explain. Spice, however, recognized this maneuver and saw it as Booth's attempt to gain control of the conversation. Unwilling to allow a feeble mind like Booth's to gain the upper hand on him, Spice simply stared back and said nothing.

An observer would have been uncomfortable, certainly. They also would have noticed, however, that Oliver Booth was even more greatly discomforted. Anson Spice, on the other hand, remained as cool as he had been upon his entrance. At last, Booth crumbled and demanded an explanation.

"Well?" he wailed, his arms flailing in what may have been a comical manner had someone other than the humorless Anson Spice been present to witness it. "What is it you're proposing, Spice?" Booth stood there huffing and puffing, his cheeks red with a difficult mixture of embarrassment and fear.

Without moving so much as half a step closer or farther from the tobacconist, Anson Spice whispered softly, "I can grant you your dearest desire."

Booth turned a suspicious, questioning glare at the professor and demanded with a hiss, "What are you talking about?"

For the first time in the conversation, Anson Spice stepped closer to the little weasel of a man. In a steady voice, trickling with purpose and confidence from his lips like liquid rock, Professor

Spice declared, "I can take care of the Swither boy for you, for good and final."

Carlisle Swither, sixteen-year-old son to the married owners of the Cobble Road butcher shop, had been a thorn in Oliver Booth's side for months. Physically, the boy favored his wraithlike mother, but in manners he was like neither of his parents. Outspoken and perpetually on a mission of supposed good-doing, young Carlisle detested his parents in the way that those teenagers less loved or loving than those like Patty and Gerald tend to do. Carlisle was what some would call an activist, or, more accurately, he was a misguided and uninformed adolescent who strove to be an activist, and he had chosen human health as his pet cause.

That his parents were the proprietors of the unhealthiest food enterprise in all of West Cuttingsborough no doubt contributed to (if not outright determined) their son's uncontrollable need to speak out for people's health. He would stand outside the butcher shop and cry to the street of the vile and unforgivable things he had seen for himself in his parents' shop. The irony, of course, was that those who shopped on Cobble Road had little interest in health or cleanliness and disregarded the boy altogether; in order to collect a more discriminating audience, he took his act to the streets of downtown West Cuttingsborough, forgetting that few of the people patronizing those streets would ever be resorting to purchasing meat on Cobble Road. The final result was that Carlisle Swither was a lad with a lot to say and no audience who cared to listen. Needless to say, perplexed though they may have been by their son's actions, repulsed though they may have felt of the way he'd turned out so unlike them, neither of the Swithers ever felt the least bit threatened by his demonstrations.

Oliver Booth, on the other hand, had markedly less patience. Though the boy never actually stopped anyone from entering his tobacco shop and making purchases, his cries of the dismally horrific effects Booth's wares would have on their health never failed to vex the irritable tobacconist. Booth, of course, had attempted to be The

Most Friendly Man In The World to the boy in the hopes of winning his trust and friendship and thus be rid of him, but to no avail. Carlisle Swither had no interest in whether or not he was liked by Oliver Booth; he cared to make known the dangers of pipe tobacco.

It was no surprise to Booth that Spice knew of his loathing of the Swithers' son; Spice frequented the tobacco shop enough to have witnessed firsthand many of Booth's awkward reprimands of Carlisle Swither. That something could "be done" about the boy was something that had been beyond Booth's capacity for thought. Thus far, the boy's public outcries in front of his store had simply been an unfortunate fact he'd been forced to deal with in his own limited fashion. Now it was suggested to him that this bane might be stopped; Booth was intrigued.

"I cannot tell you the details of his . . . disposal," Spice warned, "but you have my word that it would be handled delicately."

"Can't tell? Or won't?" Booth demanded.

"Does it matter?"

This only silenced Booth for a moment. "Now wait a second . . . why would it matter to me if I'm rid of the Swither boy if the tobacco shop wouldn't be mine anymore anyway?"

For the first time, Spice allowed the trace of a smile to flicker across his face. This, like the rest of this meeting, was entirely by design according to the professor's plan.

"Dear Booth," Spice chuckled, "first of all, you know as well as I do that your hatred for that boy runs deeper than any effect he does or doesn't have on the success of your business. Furthermore, you would remain a partner in the store."

And here it was. The Swither boy had been mere bait on the hook; it was the enticing promise that had captured Booth's attention and made any sort of transaction possible at all.

"A *silent* partner," Spice amended, also by design. Not only was Oliver Booth completely without adequate knowledge of his own business; he was also dreadfully lazy, and Spice was aware of this valuable fact. To be able to sit in his hovel of a home on Cobble

Road, devoid of any responsibilities, never required to show up at the tobacco shop again and still collect payment from a business that would undoubtedly be far more successful and draw much more money when run by Anson Spice, well, that vision was far too promising to pass up. The grin on Booth's face spoke volumes.

Spice nodded his satisfaction. "Very well. Then we shall draw up the papers while we wait for the Swither boy to pay his inevitable visit."

The game was faring much better for Percival McGulliver. Currently, all of his opponents were sitting quite still, as were the hands on the clock on the game room's mantelpiece. As the men sat there, unconscious of any movement around them or of their own stationary state, McGulliver stole stealthily from one of them to the other, examining their hands with care. There was no need for such stealth, of course; time had completely stopped for as long as he desired to keep it that way, or at least for as long as he could hold the sequences of the Code in his mind, which, when studying numbered playing cards, was rather a difficult task. A man of lesser talents would hardly have been very successful.

Once he'd gained a good memory of each of the other player's hands, Percival picked up the remainder of the deck from the table and, based on his prediction of how the next round would play out, he exchanged the cards in his hand for the ones that would be most advantageous from the deck. It had briefly crossed his mind to exchange a couple of cards from his opponents' hands, but he determined that the risk would be too great and that, if this first round played the way he anticipated, there would be little need to sabotage their hands. With what he intended to win through the rest of this game, he could afford to share a pot with a fellow winner here and there.

When he felt satisfied with the cards he was holding, he situated himself exactly as he had been and allowed his mental hold on the

Code to slip from his grasp; the clock began to tick and everyone at the table fell immediately back into the actions they'd been performing twenty-some minutes earlier.

Max Trot overturned the top two cards from the deck, a three and a ten. "Hmm," he said thoughtfully, observing his hand. "Let's go with . . . subtraction," he determined. This was, of course, expected by Percival, who had seen that Trot's hand held an eight, a difference of one when playing subtraction. Had Max called addition, his best card would have been a Jack, which would have been a difference of two. Each man played the cards Percival knew he would, and when he laid down a seven on the table, it was met with groans. There was no doubting that McGulliver's luck had turned around since the beginning of the game, and the other men were divided in their silent theories of whether they'd been hustled or it had simply taken Percival some time to get into the rhythm of the game. Whatever suspicions some of them may have harbored, they all remained silent on the issue.

Carlisle Swither was shouting his cries of death and disease outside the tobacco shop.

Oliver Booth, who was moving frantically around the shop, was flailing his arms insanely as he had been doing earlier. He was repeatedly darting expectant glares at Spice, who was casually walking the sales floor, observing the various pipes and tobaccos on display and snorting his disgust at the irrational locations Booth had chosen for each of them. "Desert Night on display with a Coriander #4?" he said in disbelief, shaking his head at Booth. "The #4 should only be used with something weaker than Clouds of Arabia. Fool."

"Fine, fine, Spice! You've made your point well enough! You can do whatever you want to the displays or to the back stock or the prices or whatever else you disapprove of! But the boy is *out there*! Aren't you going to do something? It's your business now too,

Spice! It's not just my welfare he's stomping around on anymore! One would think you'd care about that!"

Spice's offer to handle the Swither boy had, in his plan, held three purposes, none of which had the slightest bit to do with the boy's storefront protests being detrimental to the business. The first purpose had already been fulfilled; this had been to attract Booth's attention and open his eyes to the possibility of a business transaction in the first place. The second reason to deal with the boy was simply to accomplish in mere moments what his new business "partner" had been incapable of doing from the start; this would cement his role as the genuine owner and manager of the tobacco shop, and thusly as Booth's superior. In frightening Booth and demonstrating what he could do (in reality, what he could do *to him*) at any time he wished, he would manage to rid the shop not only of the nuisance of Carlisle Swither, but also that of Oliver Booth. Thirdly, he felt he needed practice for his true purpose, which was to exact his revenge upon Janine Van Alderdash.

Tension had risen drastically in the game room of the Garrish mansion. All but three players (Miles, Desmond, and Percival) were out of the game, but the others had remained seated around the perimeter of the room, observing with bated breath and more than mild interest. What they had witnessed throughout the night and most of the morning had been the single most exciting game of Divisor West Cuttingsborough had probably ever seen. Had they been aware of Percival's decidedly unethical means of success and his even more decidedly questionable methods, they probably would have been no less interested.

Miles Garrish had made a fine effort to maintain his usual hostly demeanor, though his losses thus far had been significant. Those in the room who knew him best could see the new pursing in his lips, the subtle darting of his eyes back and forth from his cards to Percival McGulliver. Percival himself may have seen the changes in his employer, but if so, he hadn't let on. McGulliver's behavior was every bit that of the nervous and seemingly incompetent fool the men of the Council had always taken him to be; he simply now seemed to be a nervous and incompetent fool with marvelously good fortune.

Miles Garrish, having taken the latest round, was considering his cards carefully. Percival could easily have ensured his privilege to call the branch every round by ensuring that he'd take the pot every round, but he feared this would be suspicious. The only reason, truly, that the other two men remained in the game was because McGulliver had taken care to stack the deck in their favor periodically for good measure.

"Well, Perce, you certainly have had a lucky first night, haven't you?" Miles remarked as coolly as he could manage through closed teeth. Someone with their eyes closed who didn't know Miles very well might have been convinced he was still in good spirits despite how much he'd lost throughout the night. Of course, everyone's eyes in the room hardly so much as blinking, they could all see clearly in Garrish's face the seething frustration and bitterness that was surfacing, and for most of them it was the first time ever to see him in such a state.

"I, uh, well…I guess I suppose…well…yes," Percival stammered, and it struck the other men in the room that it was wondrous that a man who'd become so greatly wealthy in one night and who so clearly held the control of the game could sound so devoid of confidence.

"What's your secret, then, Perce?" Miles pressed on, taking a moment to lay his cards upon the table and fold his hands atop them; he looked as though he was preparing to say a prayer.

"Miles…" Desmond began in warning tones. Usually an instigator and fairly dirty player himself, a cautionary air of maturity was an awkward fit for him.

Miles ignored Desmond, continuing to fix his gaze on his assistant across the table. "Tell me, Perce. How does someone who's never played cards, let alone gambled his own money, win tens of thousands in one night of play? Have you been hustling me, Perce? In my own home? Your employer, your friend, your *host*?" Miles's tone was lifting steadily, his eyes taking on a new look that did little to suit his usual Good Host persona. "Just *what is* the great Percival McGulliver's secret to this rare success?"

Whether Percival's responsive discomfort was genuine or feigned must, fate would dictate, remain one of the unanswerable questions of this tale. Suffice it to say that the not-so-innocent little man squirmed and smiled and stammered and sweated adequately enough to persuade Desmond and the other men in the room that he was simply the fortunate recipient of Lady Luck's whimsical touch.

"Really, Miles, let it go. The guy's just lucky is all; let it go," Desmond urged, but the only answer he received from Miles Garrish was a darting glare that spoke more than any words could have.

"Well, McGulliver? What do you say?" Miles continued, looking back to Percival. As far as Percival or any of the other men in the room could recall, Miles Garrish had never addressed him this way before; indeed, Miles was a first-name-basis sort of friend and host, and the arguably disrespectful use of Percival's last name with no "mister" to preface it was indicative of their host's changed demeanor.

"I, uh, really, I don't . . . I couldn't begin to . . . well, I, uh . . . I just don't . . ." Percival drifted off, unable to finish his thought (or unwilling to).

"We're going to finish this, McGulliver," Miles Garrish hissed.

Desmond stood up abruptly and dusted off his clothes. He spoke in loud, authoritative tones. "Fine! Yes! Finish whatever you need to—"

"'*You*'?" Garrish repeated, looking up at Desmond. "What about you? You're still in this!"

"Fine, fine, yes, *we*, then, *we*! *We'll* finish this. But I believe we need to take a break, refresh ourselves, perhaps get a drink, have a bite or a short nap . . . I think I'll shower. Let's go our separate ways for the remainder of the morning and reconvene here after luncheon to finish this . . . this *game*."

This time there was no argument from Miles Garrish, or from anyone else. Percival appealed to the reactions from the other, more experienced men in the room; if a break was needed, how would Percival McGulliver know? It didn't seem unreasonable; they *had* been at it for a rather long time.

Garrish was slow to respond, but in the end he conceded as well. He pushed his cards away, inhaled deeply, looked up at Percival McGulliver, let his breath out very slowly, and closed his eyes. There may or may not have been a trace of humility and shame that snuck across his face as he did so. Finally, he nodded. "Yes, right, then. A break it is."

And they all stood up and shuffled out of the game room in awkward silence.

"He's going to leave!" Booth was shouting. "The little weasel is going to leave before you get to him!" For Oliver Booth to refer to another as a weasel may have struck someone with more humor than Professor Spice as amusing.

Carlisle Swither was engaged in his usual repertoire of chants and spiels. He was no less passionate when the streets were empty than when he actually did see a potential audience, and he certainly did not wait to see someone approaching the tobacco shop to start emoting at them. In his youthful opinion, someone headed to his parents' butcher shop or the clock shop or the weapons and arms shop was every bit as worthy a recipient of his valuable information as anyone who was entering the door behind him.

"Death! Death and dismal darkness for all who enter the tobacconist!" the boy was yelling madly at no one in particular. Spice had noted in the past that the Swither boy had a tiresome fondness for alliteration. No doubt some insipid teacher at the high school had convinced Carlisle that repetition would win attention.

What followed had less to do with Spice's having been moved by Booth's pleas for action and more to do with his own impatience to be rid of Booth altogether.

"Very well," he sighed. "Fetch me these items immediately. A pinch each of Song of Sorrow, Darkened Paths, Treasures of the Ages, Blackberry Rain, and Wistful Script."

Booth was appalled. "Those aren't cheap tobaccos, Spice!" he objected.

"*Professor*...Spice, and I don't care an ounce of your blood for the monetary value of the ingredients. Their *magical* value, on the other hand, I respect highly, and I've little doubt they will assist in the task at hand. If you'd prefer the boy to stay, so be it."

Oliver Booth hesitated only long enough to steal another glance out the window just as the Swither boy was shouting something about "the Great Doom for those who turn a deaf ear to my message!"

"Fine, fine!" Booth sputtered as he began scurrying around the sales floor dropping pinches of each of the required tobaccos into little paper pouches.

Spice huffed in scorn when he was presented with the ingredients. "Paper," he seethed. "That will be one of the first things to change under my direction. Fine tobaccos with mystical properties deserve nothing less than to breathe and thrive in velvet; if this spell comes up anything short of perfection, the blame can be placed directly upon your own stinginess, Oliver Booth."

Booth looked away in shame, but not for long. He eyed Spice carefully as he set to work with the contents of the paper bags. "A candle," he said without looking up as he spread the tobaccos in an exotic pattern upon the countertop. "And a match."

While Spice was continuing to swirl and sweep the little mounds of tobacco on the countertop, Booth fetched the candle and match, thrusting them overly eagerly in the face of Professor Spice.

"Do *not*...break my concentration, fool!" Spice hissed, and Booth flushed a deep crimson, slinking away against a wall to watch from a secure distance. "Light the candle," Professor Spice murmured in command, and Booth nervously did so. As he hadn't been told to dispose of the burning match, he held it uncertainly, afraid to disrupt the towering professor again, and shrieked in pain when the flame reached his thumb and forefinger. Dropping it to the floor and hopping in pain, he stamped on the already extinguished match repeatedly as though it was a gruesome living creature.

Paying Booth no further heed, Spice pushed open the door to the tobacco shop and smiled pleasantly at the Swither boy, who was caught off guard and left with his mouth disturbingly wide open in mid-cry, giving the appearance of one who was at the mercy of his dentist's tools.

"Young Master Swither," Professor Spice purred gently, "won't you join me inside for but a moment?"

Carlisle Swither was taken quite off guard. The only regards he'd ever received during his acts of protest were Oliver Booth's frantic shrieks and shouts, which were more laughable than threatening. The boy looked cross-eyed at the tall man, clearly forgetting that his mouth still hung open as if awaiting the entrance of some very small creature into it.

Spice held both his smile (with some effort, certainly) and the door, gesturing him inside. Not without first glancing from side to side in evident suspicion of the unanticipated invitation, Carlisle Swither grudgingly, unsmilingly made his way into the shop.

"What's this about?" he demanded in a tone that shamed his years. He noticed Oliver Booth in the corner, whose face gleamed with a disturbingly hungry grin, his hands clenched together in visible suspense.

"About...about," Spice repeated thoughtfully. "Well, young Master Swither," he said in as comforting a voice as one may have heard from Miles Garrish as he invited the people of West Cuttingsborough to one of his lavish affairs. "Well, son, this is about your...tendencies."

"My what?" For someone who professed to have all the answers humanity could desire, Carlisle Swither was less than proficient in actual conversation.

Spice chuckled softly. "Your *habits*, Carlisle. Your insistence upon passing your hours of leisure on Mr. Booth's property. You see, your efforts to drive business from the tobacconist are hardly what one might call ethical."

"I'm being ethical by sharing the truth with the people!" Carlisle shouted. Evidently he'd merely been awaiting a comprehensible cue that would prompt one of his memorized mantras.

This time, Spice's chuckle was with less humor and notably more edge. "My boy," he said, laying his long, bony fingers delicately on Carlisle's shoulder. The boy glanced at the hand in alarm; one observing would have sworn that Carlisle could actually feel the coldness of the professor's skin through his clothing. "What would it take to keep you distanced from this establishment from this day forward?"

Carlisle Swither's scowl would have been more appropriately placed on the face of a child half his age. "Why should I stay away?" he spat at Professor Spice.

Spice chuckled once more, his fingers gliding undetected from the Swither boy's shoulder. He turned away from the lad thoughtfully, leaving him to worry over what might be about to follow.

"See, Master Swither," Spice's silky voice intoned as he paced the floor of the sales room, "certain societal behaviors and courtesies are to be expected from all of that society's members, but particularly from its youth, who've not yet come to be true contributors to the society's success or failure." The tall man turned to steal a glance at the boy, who was listening intently with wide eyes and a half-open mouth. "Sadly," Spice continued, "when certain individuals fail to uphold their role in *supporting* their fellow man in societal enterprise ..." Here Spice paused to click his tongue and sigh in disapproval. "Alas, those individuals must be dealt with."

Oliver Booth emitted an involuntary chortle of glee; Carlisle Swither's head snapped in the tobacconist's direction in dismay, perhaps even with a pleading fire in his eye, hoping, evidently, that the very subject of all his pursuits of sabotage would actually intervene and put a stop to whatever vile punishment Anson Spice had in mind.

Professor Spice's pacing came to a halt with his gaze fixed intently upon the boy. Feigning to consider what was to be done with the lad, he tapped his skeletal finger to his cheek, chewed at the inside of his lips, and furrowed his web-like brows. The whole while, poor young Carlisle's face became more and more saturated with nervous sweat, his cheeks flushed with fear, and his body fidgeted constantly in helpless frustration. In fact, he looked remarkably similar to what Gerald would look like in the future when signaling to Scratches O'Hannigan that he desperately needed a bathroom.

At last, the professor nodded decisively and declared, "Ignite the tobacco, Booth."

Anson Spice wasn't looking at the tobacconist to see his look of dismay. "But…the counter will burn!" the little man shouted in protest.

Without once turning away from Carlisle Swither, Professor Spice demanded in tones to be reckoned with, "Obey! Ignite!"

The little coward of a tobacco dealer reached a trembling hand to the burning candle and bent it over until its flame barely touched the swirling tobacco patterns Spice had created on the countertop. Astonishingly, the flame immediately claimed the entire pattern, every fleck of tobacco igniting into flaming swirls of light. The countertop, however, inexplicably remained untouched by the flame. Booth's eyes widened and he backed away from the phenomenon in horror.

Spice was finished with the pretense; he stepped to within an inch of Carlisle Swither and began whispering foreign words that were unfamiliar to the boy and Oliver Booth. Carlisle attempted to turn away, but Spice's hand gripped the top of the boy's head and rotated it to meet his waiting eye. The words continued to trickle from Spice's lips like sap from a maple, and like the tap waiting to catch it and turn it into a delicious treat, Carlisle Swither's eyes and ears were there to catch the power of the incantation; his body began to convulse.

Oliver Booth bent low behind the counter, his eyes peering attentively at the unnatural sight going on in his own store. Anson Spice stood tall and proud, his eyes never leaving the boy's, his lips never ceasing their rapid movement as the unintelligible words flowed with rhythm and grace; the words themselves, though, *sounded* evil. Their purpose seemed of things impure and their origins of someplace far away and darker even than Cobble Road.

And the boy? Ah, well, I would like to say that the boy lost consciousness rather quickly and knew little of the metamorphosis that followed. I would like to say that he didn't see, as well as feel, his own bones contort, hear them snap in places and groan in others. It would please me greatly to inform you, sympathetic reader, that young Carlisle Swither knew nothing of the bristles that forced their way through his flesh to surface all over his body. If I could, I would tell you that he didn't notice that the room seemed to grow around him as he dizzyingly sank closer to the floor, or how his arms steadily pulled themselves down level with his legs, begging to be used on the floor rather than in the air. I wish I could tell you that he didn't feel the burning sensation in his bottom that exploded in an eruption of flesh, pushing out of him into a slinking, slithering appendage that swung this way and that even as his own ears seemed to crawl farther up on his head, and to grow rounder. I would like very much to claim that poor Master Swither knew nothing of the hard, thin whiskers that jutted suddenly and with maddening force beneath his nose, which had shrunk to a twitching, almost invisible dot of pink. I wish I could tell you that he knew little or nothing of these occurrences as they were happening, but sadly, he knew every second of it with clarity and incomparable intensity of excruciation.

The mouse uttered a squeak of horror and ran circles around the tobacco shop. Oliver Booth also began to scurry in terror, he and the mouse coming within an inch of each other more than once, to each of their respective horrors. The poor, confused creature made a dash for the front door, which Professor Spice strode toward and pushed open obligingly so it could pass. Darting onto Cobble Road, stumbling between protruding weeds, upturned stones, and pieces of garbage that had been littered along the way, it made its way frantically toward the butcher shop. This was no easy task, its mental sense of direction being skewed and having some difficulty adjusting not only to moving on all fours but also to the increased length of time it took to get from one point to another; its legs were quite small.

When the little mouse arrived at the Cobble Road butcher shop, it found it could squeeze under the closed door quite easily (it was unheard of to find the store's door propped open; the Swithers were far too satisfied with trapping in the heat and stench of raw meat to have even considered it). Upon scurrying into the familiar territory of his own parents' place of business, the little mouse attempted for the first time (unless one were to count the shrieks of terror all the way from the tobacconist) to speak. Of course, the little mouse could not see his parents; all it could make out was a wall that appeared to be hundreds of miles long; that would have been the counter, of course. Even all the hanging cuts of meat were too far up and out of the mouse's vision to see, though he could most assuredly smell them.

Trusting that his mother was somewhere in the room, the little mouse opened his mouth and cried out to her. "Mother! Oh, mother! It was horrible! There was a man at the tobacconist and he ... he ... well, you can see what he's done! Mother, are you there? It's me! It's Carlisle! Mother?"

Alas, all that emitted from his mouth were squeaks and squeals, and he went entirely unnoticed by Mrs. Swither, who was, in fact, lingering behind the counter, cutting up a loin of some sort. However, the little mouse did not go unnoticed entirely. The sound he heard was deafening, too strong and overpowering to be discerned, though it contained a degree of familiarity as well. The mouse paused in his shrieks to attempt to identify the shrill noise, but before he was able to, the noise identified itself to him; Mrs. Swither's cat, Tin Pan, came darting from behind the counter, hissing and roaring as it galloped at an impossible speed toward the little mouse.

His mother screamed in turn as the cat bolted past her, and her voice was equally painful to the poor creature's eardrums. The little mouse took only another half a second to be afraid before taking decisive action and turning around the way he'd come and bolting for the door. He squeezed his way under it just as Tin Pan was pouncing at him, and he sped his way down Cobble Road, turned off toward downtown West Cuttingsborough, dodged the trampling feet of all the passersby, nearly stumbled through the grate of a sewer, caught himself, allowed himself now less than half a second to recover from that scare, and raced his way through the streets, darting into the first open door he saw, weaving his way between the legs of the person exiting that door, and squeezed himself through the crack under the door to the coat closet in Miles Garrish's hat shop, nestling himself to the very back of it, and beginning to make himself a hole, that he might hide himself even farther away.

And, of course, as you are well aware, he hides there to this day.

Things had become quite serious at the card game.

Miles Garrish had returned from the morning break reasonably refreshed, new perspective helping to calm his nerves. He still wasn't himself, however, and what truly vexed him and stood in his way of the internal cleansing he needed in order to turn this game around was the fact that Percival McGulliver's demeanor hadn't changed one bit from the beginning of the card game until now. The little man had remained every bit as nervous despite each hand he'd won and every dollar he'd gained. The man who'd always been Miles's simple and harmless assistant had somehow transformed into someone who held the power to infuriate him more than anyone else in the world.

Desmond Willard was glaring at his cards and wiping a gleam of sweat from his brow; Desmond had abandoned any attempts to appear nonchalant. Unlike his host, he recognized when he'd been bested and, though a sore loser, he was a realistic one. With a sigh of resignation, he grumbled, "Subtraction," and scowled at his four. The target quantity for subtraction was seven, and he knew that between his two opponents, at least one of them would be able to come closer to the mark than his unfortunate difference of three.

Indeed, Miles immediately laid down a six and looked across the table at Percival to see what card he had in his possession. McGulliver, not without an awkward pause to smile guiltily at his employer, shrugged and set down a seven upon the table. Miles threw his arms up and uttered a sound that could only be called a growl. And, of course, when they saw what value Desmond's best card bore, Percival swept the money toward himself.

Desmond pushed the cards away from himself and shook his head with visible conviction. "I'm through, men. McGulliver," he said, turning to Percival with a feigned look of good sportsmanship upon his face which was, in truth, a thinly masked tolerance, "you've absolutely tapped my funds for this week. I'll be back next week ready to respond in kind." The tone was certainly more parts threatening promise than humorous playfulness. Clearly the confidence the man had in his ability to return with a sufficient sum of money in the passing of a mere week was a reminder to Percival of his own station above him.

Percival nodded humbly, smiled, and turned back to Miles questioningly. "Uh, I...Mr. Garrish...I, uh...could stop as well if, well, if you...that is, if you're ready to, uh, well...to stop?"

Miles Garrish glared at Percival McGulliver and leaned across the table. The other men around the perimeter of the game room watched with bated breath, more uncomfortable than they'd ever found themselves in a gaming situation.

"McGulliver," Garrish whispered, his voice all venom, "you will *not* put an end to me. Not in my own home."

Percival nodded uncomfortably. "Yes, well, very well…sir," he managed, and Miles flashed him a suspicious glare, certain that the hesitation before "sir" had consisted of more than his assistant's blasted lack of social skills. McGulliver began to draw the next two cards off of the deck when he suddenly stopped, looking back to his opponent thoughtfully. "I, uh…could, uh, well…that is…if you…would like, I could…well, uh, I could…give you odds?"

The ire in Miles Garrish's face was incomparable. "What?" he demanded. "I don't need your help!" he spat with disgust, but the others in the room would whisper later amongst themselves that a glimmer of hope seemed to twinkle in Garrish's eye at that moment.

Max Trot stepped forth from his place by the fireplace and interjected before events could proceed any further. "Now hold on a second, both of you." Miles glared up at Max, his face a painting of threat. Max held up his hand. "Just a moment, Miles. Just hear me out." He gestured to Percival, seated at the table with a look of perplexed melancholy in his eyes. "Clearly," Max went on, "Percival has luck on his side today. It is not unreasonable to consider evening the playing field. But…I think, in all fairness, it should be by a method proposed by an objective bystander. Myself, for instance."

Miles Garrish was not above delivering an elaborate eye roll. "Fine, fine, Max, and what, pray tell, would you propose?"

Percival McGulliver simply turned his gaze from one man to the next, following the conversation with little care in the world.

"Well," Max said slowly, thoughtfully, "what if you, Miles, were to hold…say, a double hand?" At this, it became painfully clear that Max knew not which of the two opponents' reactions to gauge at this suggestion, as he was rapidly looking back and forth from one to the other, as though he were a very engaged tennis spectator.

Miles glared back and forth between Percival and Max, then huffed in annoyance, "I'm not accepting charity! I'm perfectly capable of managing my own game!"

Max smiled gently and said, "Actually, Miles, you're not. You've already put in well more than your week's Divisor fund, and luck just isn't with you today."

"Fine. Fine!" Miles Garrish burst out, "but it's still charity, and I won't accept it!"

Percival McGulliver alarmed all by invoking his own suggestion. "Uh…" he began, and all eyes in the room turned to him. "What if, well, uh, we were to…well, that is, to, say, raise the stakes? In my favor?"

Miles Garrish looked suspicious at this, but Max Trot's face lit with excitement. "Yes!" he said, shaking an admiring finger in Percival's direction. "Yes, that's brilliant, Percival!" Max turned to Miles Garrish and explained. "Miles, you see? By doubling your hand, the power of chance will be evened in your favor. But…by upping the stakes on your end, you maintain your integrity *and* give Percival the incentive to stay in the game!"

Miles Garrish thought for a moment and looked with caution to Percival McGulliver. "I suppose that would be…acceptable…for me, anyway."

Percival was nodding slowly. "I, uh…well, that is to say, yes, I'm willing to if…well, that is…if, say, I were to, uh, well…to choose the, uh, the…stakes."

Max Trot looked immediately to Miles Garrish to seek approval on his face. Miles sat momentarily, considering Percival's proposal. With a sigh, he asked, "What are the stakes, Percival?"

The only thing more stifling in the game room than the tension was the menacing silence. Miles, for all his efforts, could not sit still in his seat; he fidgeted and squirmed, folded and unfolded his hands, darted his eyes from Percival to Max, from Max to Desmond, from Desmond to the clock, from the clock to the card table, and back to Percival again.

Several times, both Max and Miles were desperately near to shouting at McGulliver to answer the question, but they managed to contain themselves. What was particularly infuriating to them was that by the appearance of McGulliver's face, he already knew his answer; he was simply attempting to work up the courage to formulate the words that would construct it. With difficult patience, they watched the little man's visible struggle with himself, each contemplating just what he might ask for…how much could the little shop assistant want?

"Well," he began at last, and it may be tricks of their memories, but the men who were present all claim that everyone simultaneously leaned in closer to hear what Percival had to say. "I…well…I should say that, well…I think I'd like…Hats for All Occasions."

Max drew in a sharp breath. This had never been amongst the agreed-upon wagers. In the past, little trinkets and heirlooms were the furthest wagers beyond those of cash that the Council card game had ventured to accept. To demand an opponent's livelihood? That was unheard of.

Miles was clearly equally taken aback. He seemed, in fact, almost moved to tears. Of course, he could have backed out of the game at this point. He could have put down his cards, shaken Percival's hand, and wished them all a fine week. But that was not Miles Garrish's way; Miles Garrish was a winner, and he wasn't about to fold to a newcomer, and his assistant at that.

"Fine," he said. "I can accept that."

Max Trot smiled. "Good! Good! Then we have a deal, I dare say?"

But Percival McGulliver had other ideas. "Would you care to… uh…*triple* your hand, sir?" he asked, the same timid voice still dominant, but…was there something else there? Was there an arrogance in that voice that hadn't been there before? Max Trot and Desmond Willard thought there might be.

An arched eyebrow revealed not only Miles's suspicion, but also his curiosity. "At what cost, Percival?" he asked with care.

"The mansion," Percival McGulliver declared with the certainty of a man who need not stammer in the least.

And though his eyes were wide and his face was flushed, though his luck was all but nonexistent and his fear was great, though he was tired and frustrated and wanting of nothing more than his bed to sleep in for a couple of hours, Miles Garrish said, "Fine."

It is remarkable how we alter our own destinies for the worse with such little words.

Anson Spice was pleased with himself. Though he had transformed things before, he had never attempted, let alone succeeded, to change an actual human being. To have metamorphosed the Swither boy so completely, so perfectly, so beautifully (for the little mouse, in Professor Spice's less than humble opinion, truly was a thing of beauty), and with such rapidity...well, it did little to stifle the professor's already excessive regard for himself.

He was alone in the tobacco shop now; Oliver Booth, as Spice had predicted, was less satisfied with what had happened to Carlisle Swither and more disturbed and frightened by it. It wasn't that he felt remorse for his accepting Spice's offer, certainly not. And neither was it that he felt sympathy for the boy's new form. No, it was simply that Oliver Booth realized with a sudden surety he'd been too blind to possess earlier that Anson Spice had no use for him and could do something similar or drastically worse to him at any moment. In the moment that Booth came to understand this, he also understood that as Spice's partner, his role would be nothing more than to stay out of the way. There was really nothing he could even do to ensure that Spice would pass along his share of the profits in the business. Of course, immoral and deceitful as Professor Spice may be, he was still a man of his word, and he did, in fact, pass along everything that was rightfully Booth's. In fact, business thrived so much more with Spice's taking of control that Oliver Booth, in simply his share of the profits, took in fairly close to what he always did when running the business on his own.

Now was Anson Spice's time for careful planning. Carlisle Swither, again, had merely been practice for his true objective, the pet project of his recent days, the one thing he wished above all else: to punish Janine Van Alderdash for her disregard for him.

He knew already what he intended to do to her; he had known that for some time now, certainly before he had taken care of the Swither boy. What he'd yet to determine was how to arrange a meeting with her. His skills were not yet of the degree that would allow him to perform his arts upon her without close proximity. So the question posed to him was, quite simply, how to get Janine Van Alderdash to visit him? The more he considered it, the more he convinced himself that the tobacco shop was out of the question for a meeting place. He must be able to persuade her that his intentions were still those of one in love, and any decent person would know better than to ask the object of his affections to venture to Cobble Road.

A letter, of course. A written invitation which she, a lady of good manners, would not have the option to decline for some fabricated prearranged commitment upon the spot. True, she could, of course, respond through a letter of her own, courteously explaining the unfortunate circumstances that detained her from paying him the requested visit. Still, Spice had a confidence in himself that more modest men detested, and he held in his mind a certainty that Miss Van Alderdash would be far too intrigued by his proposal not to investigate it.

Sadly, he was quite right. The letter he wrote was of such eloquent good nature, was of such flattery yet comfortably shy of any sort of threatening over-familiarity, that when Janine Van Alderdash read it, she found herself, well, as the professor had predicted, intrigued.

Too much was happening at once for Millicent McGulliver. The shock she was finding herself in by her husband's announcement that they would be moving into the Garrish mansion immediately was too overwhelming in itself to allow her to deal with Janine's frantic visit, waving Professor Spice's letter erratically in her face.

Janine knew nothing of the game of Divisor other than the fact that Percival had remained at it for an unprecedented duration of time. Nor was she aware of his alarming winnings, and for the time being, Millicent determined it best not to say anything. She supposed she could set her own crisis aside for the time being. Attempting to don a rational frame of mind, she took a breath and took the letter from Janine.

As Millicent McGulliver read the letter with care, Janine Van Alderdash hopped around in distress, her arms waving in nonsensical gestures of desperate pleading. When at last Mrs. McGulliver had finished reading, Janine allowed herself to take a breath and calm down enough to demand, "What is this about? Why would he want to see me?"

Millicent was torn between her amusement and her sympathy. This, at least, was a good distraction from her own situation. "Well," she managed after stifling her chuckle with only moderate success, certainly detected by the poor Miss Van Alderdash.

"Laughing!" Janine shouted. "You're laughing! How can you be laughing?" She turned away in frustration, Millicent allowing the humor she saw in the letter to flow freely now.

"Really, Janine, I don't think it's that serious. It's no surprise that he admires you, right?"

"But I don't admire him!" Janine retorted. "I never gave him any reason to believe I was interested, and I thought the matter was buried and done with!"

"Well, you never exactly said as much to him, dear. Perhaps the professor took your silence as potential interest."

Janine Van Alderdash shuddered at the thought, repulsed beyond words. "What do I do?" she cried in desperation. "You have to tell me what to do, Millie!"

Millicent McGulliver allowed herself to collect her thoughts and put her humor at bay. "I think," she said at last, "that you should go." She ignored Janine's look of revolted terror and pressed on, explaining, "I think you should go and put it to rest at last. You chose to ignore him before, and clearly that didn't work. You need to stand up straight, march in there, and simply explain that you aren't interested."

While this hardly appealed to Janine Van Alderdash's sense of how a pleasant and sunny afternoon might be spent, she couldn't argue with her friend's logic. With a scowl and a whimper, she sulked her way out the door, none the wiser that this would be her final visit with Millicent McGulliver.

If Miles Garrish was angered by his gigantic loss to Percival McGulliver, he didn't show it. Miles left his bitterness and resentment at the card table that day. He relinquished the deed to the mansion and ownership of the hat shop to his assistant with few words, but with little emotion either. Indeed, the broken man appeared to many to be walking his days in a trancelike state, only vaguely aware of what he was doing and what was going on in the world around him. Some attempted to speak to him, to ask him if there was nothing he could do to regain his stature, and of course they wished to know whether he had sufficient funds in his savings account to stay on his feet, if not high above the rest of the residents of West Cuttingsborough. These inquiries were met with grunts and mutters that held no malice and no intelligibility. Miles Garrish simply moved along about his business in what very well may have been a permanent state of shock.

Certainly if Miles intended any harm to Percival, such intentions were unknown and unsuspected by his friends and neighbors. Alas, many of the tragic events of this tale might have been prevented had someone considered such a likelihood more carefully.

Meanwhile, Percival McGulliver was coping poorly with his new wealth. Mentally, he was quite aware that he was taken care of for life. He had no intentions of carrying on the Council card game in the mansion's game room, or of participating ever again. If the other men wished to continue that frivolity, then let them find another place to do so, he rationalized; he would not be attending, he proclaimed to himself, oblivious to the fact that, in all likelihood, he would never again be invited. Indeed, the tradition survived in a manner of speaking, with certain highly evident modifications. The location was no longer a permanent one, but rather floated from home to home based upon whoever was doing the inviting, and it was far from regular. On average the men met once a month, but occasionally a month would slip by with no game held, and there was always at least one formerly regular attendant absent. Miles Garrish never played again.

Emotionally, McGulliver was less secure. His wife would hardly notice this; they saw each other rarely enough these days as it was, and since the fateful card game, he had made himself even scarcer. Once they had finished moving into the mansion (left furnished in many rooms, simply due to Garrish's lack of any place to keep such a quantity of possessions), Percival rarely emerged from the room he referred to as his study. This name, on the rare occasion that it was uttered in the presence of Millicent, would strike the fairer of the McGullivers as an odd choice of name, being that she couldn't begin to hazard a guess as to what her husband may be "studying" in there behind closed doors.

Percival didn't offer his former position at the hat shop to Miles Garrish, not that Garrish would have accepted it, nor would he have needed it. He had been a savvy enough businessman and practical enough person to accumulate a respectable sum of savings, which he used simply to enter into a new business venture. In a part of West Cuttingsborough less reputable than where Hats for All Occasions was located, but not nearly so lowly as Cobble Road, Miles Garrish purchased an abandoned building and opened a clock shop, which he named (perhaps foolishly, if a little too quaintly) Garrish Timepieces. The implications of the name didn't stop people from entering the establishment or from making purchases there. The business succeeded just fine, though it was not the hat shop, and Miles Garrish never forgot or forgave his former assistant for stealing his life so unconscionably.

Percival, however, remained oblivious to all of this. In fact, he was so oblivious that he even once actually stepped into Garrish Timepieces to find a new pocket watch. Miles stared from his station behind the counter in mute offense, never allowing his suspicious gaze to stray from the little man; McGulliver merely smiled and nodded at Miles in seemingly genuine surprise, asked a question or two regarding the watches on display, apparently failed to notice Miles's one-word, venomous responses, made his purchase, and went on his way.

With Anson Spice, Percival had very few dealings anymore. He knew perfectly well the levels of wizardry his former schoolmate was capable of, and should he be in need of such services, he was well aware of where to go for help. Likewise, Anson Spice knew what McGulliver could do, what stunning acts he must now have mastered since his unconscious school years' manipulation of the classroom clocks. The difference, however, between McGulliver and Spice was that, should Professor Spice find he needed the services of Percival, he would be far less likely to approach him for his assistance and far more so merely to wait patiently until Percival approached him. That time, he was certain, was imminent, and if he needed something from him, well, then he would make his fee known to him at the appropriate time.

As it would happen, some time later they would each be in need of the other's talents, and each in response to the same tragic incident.

Janine Van Alderdash should not have taken Millicent McGulliver's advice. It was a sad truth with which Millicent would live for the rest of her years. Though she would never know her best friend's fate, exactly, she would live with a tormented guilt that would forever tame her youthful mischievous nature and paint a permanent sadness in her eyes that Molly would one day know as Mrs. McGulliver's *most* recognizable trait during her months of service to her.

But as stories go, even those with relatively happy endings, turns of sadness and tragedy must appear, and such was the case on the day that lovely Janine chose to turn up at Professor Spice's office at the university.

It was winter, and the roads of West Cuttingsborough were slick with ice and the grasses were piled high with cottony white, billowing in hillocks and paths that had been glistening in the splendor of afternoon sunshine only hours earlier. As Miss Van Alderdash made her way through the streets toward the university, however, the clouds had covered the sky in a dark grayness that hid the sun from view, and the hills of snow and ice had begun to appear far more dark and daunting than they had before.

The university itself was a building of character. Having spent better than two-hundred years standing in the same place, with the city growing, changing, and moving about it over the years, it held the appearance of a wizened village elder or an ancient and solemn god, looking constantly over its people with care, concern, and a judging eye. In fact, it was tradition since the almost simultaneous deaths of the school's first dean and one of its original professors to leave the two neighboring offices they'd occupied during their tenure vacant and with their lights always turned on; these offices happened to be at the top and center of the front of the university building, and beside each other as well, suggesting the appearance of two eyes staring down at West Cuttingsborough and keeping vigil in the silent hours of the night.

As Janine approached the watchful structure, she had a fleeting inclination to turn around and make a dash for home. This thought, however, trickled into nonexistence as an invisible hold seemed to grip her shoulders and turn her to the entrance of the university; she found herself, willing or not, stepping toward the doorway.

How could she have known that another pair of eyes besides the two lit windows was watching her approach with care and interest? From his office, Professor Spice gazed down intently as she drew closer and closer to the university building, until she was too close beneath him to see, at which point he strode to one corner of the office and rested comfortably against his bookshelf, awaiting her arrival.

As Janine Van Alderdash took the stairs high into the reaches of the building, her heart pounded out her own fears in a rhythmic and threatening manner, as though she might forget how nervous she was and her heart was merely trying to help her to remember. But as she pushed through the door leading to the eleventh floor, a peculiar calm came over her. With a rational acceptance she couldn't explain, she knew that whatever awaited her in the coming moments was a fate she must surely face with courage and accept with willingness.

She didn't even notice the sign posted on the wall indicating that wing P was on the right, while wing H was straight ahead; the unseen, unnamable force that had drawn her this far continued to draw her. Had she been more aware and seen the sign, she may have stared in befuddlement, curious as to the significance of the letters H and P. Whether she ever would have determined them to indicate history and philosophy will forever be an unknown detail. The journey down the corridor was a long one. There was seemingly no one else anywhere within sight or earshot, and all the classroom and office doors were shut tightly. The corridor itself was dim and shadowy, and when, in the darkness, she saw a single rectangular doorway that emitted a crackling, flickering light rather than simply boasting a closed wooden door, she knew quite well that was her destination.

The open doorway revealed an office that resembled a very miniature library combined with an equally small laboratory for an alchemist. Indeed, the shelves that were not filled with very old, leather-bound texts with unpronounceable titles such as *The Destagulatoriationistic Riddles: Volumes the First Through the Third*, *Angular Wizardry and Pre-Saqliospitronic Theory*, and *Counteracting the Divisive Destinatory Conductor Subtexts of Middle English Allegory* were filled with vials, pouches, scales, and many-colored rocks and minerals. In fact, many of the texts seemed particularly placed in close proximity of these items, including *The Many-Faced Elemental Powers* and *Mineralia: The World Inside the Stone*. One such book was open to a particular page atop a small wooden desk, its writing in some places blood-red, in others forest-green, and occasionally dashing brilliant yellows and blues, or fire-raging oranges. Beside this text was a foreign contraption, seemingly a scale of some sort, but with a series of little weights, pulleys, dials, and chains, the purposes of which were beyond Janine as she stared in awe. So engrossed with the contents of the room was she that she never noticed the narrow pair of eyes focusing on her from the shadows.

"Welcome, Miss Van Alderdash." Spice's voice was calm and silky, conveying little of his thoughts. Janine perhaps should have responded with a start, but her reaction was hardly one of someone who'd had a sudden fright. She merely turned to him expectantly and cocked her head in curiosity. "Thank you for honoring my request," the professor continued as he approached her from the corner of the room where he'd been lurking.

"Professor," Janine said, her voice nearly betraying a trace of delight, though her face itself held no evident emotions.

As Spice stepped directly up to Miss Van Alderdash, she followed his intent stare with bewitched indifference. "Miss Van Alderdash," he purred in her face. "Janine. You haven't the vaguest notion of the damage your aloof indifference to my advances has inflicted upon me."

He began circling her, and she watched as he did so, her eyes intent, the corners of her mouth lifting into the slightest of smiles.

"Indeed," Professor Spice went on as he made his tiny journey around her small frame. "You clearly lack the degree of respect expected by society to be impressed upon a gentleman of my stature." Though Janine's expression said nothing as to whether anything the professor was saying was comprehended, he did not seem to care. He merely continued, allowing himself to believe that the attention she appeared to be paying to him was genuine respect, and not a spell he himself had cast upon her.

She said nothing, but continued to watch him, perhaps on some level tragically aware of her inability to respond appropriately, but more likely (and perhaps more tragic yet) entirely ignorant of her state and her true feelings to the situation.

"Janine," Spice continued, "I find it sad that such a lowly and wickedly unimpressive creature such as you should laugh in the face of opportunity, should turn from the finest chance of success it has ever faced."

Had she been herself, Janine Van Alderdash would hardly have tolerated being referred to as an "it." Had she not spat in the professor's face on the spot, at the very least she would have turned on her heels and slammed the door behind her. Do you find it not a bit sad, attentive reader, that the vile professor knew very well that the only way he could secure the "respect" of Janine Van Alderdash was through dark magic and manipulation?

"It is," he went on, his tone altering as he rounded her for the manyeth time, allowing his eye contact to fall directly upon her own, "not entirely impossible to redeem yourself from this sad state, my dear. Indeed, I would find myself rather gratified to find you willing to make amends for your wrongs." And he held himself up high and erect, staring down through eyes of ice. "Should you, say, grovel for my forgiveness, should you fall upon your knees and confess your wicked ways, should you choose to face your true feelings toward myself and your undeserved good fortune to be accepted by one such as I ..." He allowed himself to drift, to seek her eyes for the slightest sign of comprehension, but of course, he found none.

This is, it seems, an appropriate time for me, your constant narrator, to step in and interject an observation. It is difficult, nay, *impossible* to say with any degree of certainty whether Anson Spice had intended to make such an offer to Janine Van Alderdash in that moment. It is further impossible to determine whether there was any sincerity to the offered bargain, any intention of honoring it should she somehow have momentarily escaped the clutches of his magics. Of course, he must have remembered and seen that the young woman was not herself. He must further have been aware that she had no likely way of responding to his remarks, not in her current state. I fear, my dear companion, that we must accept this moment in the poor professor's life as one of unusual weakness and great insight into his stumble from humanity. Either he was so sadistically disturbed in his own mind that he was merely toying with the poor girl for his own amusement, or...perhaps more sadly yet, he was regretting his actions and hoping for a miracle to occur, waiting to see if the power of the young woman's soul might be able to break through the power of his skills. If that truly was the case, how disappointed he must have been.

"It seems to me," he went on, concluding his thought with care, "that it would be reasonable to extend the offer once again and to accept your mistake as one of temporary folly, and trust that you've absorbed your rightful lesson."

He waited for a response, of course, but none arrived. Her blank stare reflected the same careless serenity and oblivion that he himself had injected into her, and with each second of void response, Professor Spice's face grew redder with rage. (Or embarrassment? Sorrow? Regret? Frustration? We can only guess.)

"Very well," he said at last, and he turned his back to her, for, though he could not confess it, not to himself or to anyone else, he could not look at this young woman while doing her harm, not as he'd done to Carlisle Swither, for whom he'd felt nothing more than contemptible annoyance.

The words that slipped from his lips were similar to those he had uttered in the tobacco shop, and had Oliver Booth been present, he may very well have identified them as one and the same. In fact, there were slight differences, differences in intonation and in several of the words and phrases themselves. Some were sung when they'd previously been spoken; some were chanted when they'd formerly been sung. Some words carried an emphasis upon the first syllable where they'd previously done so in the third, and some intoned the vowels in the long manner where in the tobacco shop they had been so uttered in the short.

These differences led to such differences in results as darker hairs bursting forth from the skin than what did so on Carlisle Swither, the disappearance altogether of the ears as opposed to their mere change in shape and size, and indeed the bursting forth and continuous growing of additional limbs even as her entire body found itself shrinking much to the same size as the Swither boy in his post-metamorphosed state.

Oh, how revolting she became! Professor Spice's bitter anguish suffered from Janine Van Alderdash could not be disputed after witnessing what a vile and repugnant form he'd chosen to assign to her. She would later scare many and please few, she would spend her days in the streets surrounding the tobacco shop, sneaking inside for warmth and shelter when possible, only to be discarded with little care and much violence.

Some stories begin with something shocking; some stories begin with something illogical. Some stories venture into the realms of fantasy, while others keep their feet on the solid ground of reality. Some stories end with a tragedy; some stories end with much laughter and joy. Some stories see their characters share in the appreciation of life and its many paths, while other stories hurl their heroes into a perpetual state of despair. Some characters learn a lesson by the end of their story; some characters never get the chance to grow and improve themselves. Some characters learn secrets and accomplish great things through tenacity; some characters do the teaching and help to bring the accomplishments about. Some characters have a destiny we can be envious of; some characters are doomed to be the victims of heinous wickedness. Sadly, in this story it is Janine Van Alderdash's destiny forever henceforth to be Professor Spice's spider.

There is little else to be told of the histories of Misters McGulliver and Spice, and it is perhaps evident what the aforementioned tragic event is that will bring this portion of our tale to its completion.

Millicent McGulliver's unfortunate demise came about as the direct result of a visit she received from Miles Garrish. Garrish, to put it simply, was her murderer.

While the motive may be clear to anyone standing on the outside of the situation (how could Garrish *not* want to bring pain and anguish to Percival McGulliver after the fateful card game?), it was not quite so obvious to the people of West Cuttingsborough, including its constabulary force, which was, historically, quite an accomplished organization. As far as the residents of West Cuttingsborough could see, Millicent McGulliver had not a single enemy. The most likely suspect they ever managed to come to a consensus about was her best friend, Janine Van Alderdash, who had mysteriously disappeared, though that had been some time prior to the murder, so her role as a suspect was never a very solid one. Of course, they never did find Janine Van Alderdash, and the case of Millicent McGulliver's murder remained unsolved for many years afterward.

You may be asking why Mr. McGulliver wasn't suspected in the deed. In fact, he was suspected rather strongly at the first, and had he and his wife not shared their meaningful reunion of emotions (or at least his own, if not genuinely on her part) in their late night meeting in the kitchen of what was now known as the McGulliver mansion, he perhaps would have been convicted for his ghastly indifference toward his own spouse. But Percival had seen this conversation with his wife as a true testament to a new turning point in their marriage and in their lives. His devastation at the robbery of this second chance right out from under his nose was all the testimony anyone needed to believe wholeheartedly in Mr. McGulliver's innocence.

Many who would meet Percival McGulliver after the death of his wife would assume that it had been this event that had turned him into such a nervous and bashful individual; of course, those who had known him all along knew that this was simply his demeanor. Perhaps, some of the more insightful ones would think, the loss of Millicent had merely made it *truer*.

In fact, insightful as such a deduction may have been, it was, in all likelihood, the exact opposite of what had happened to him. If such wasn't the case, how could he possibly have acted in good conscience in paying that fateful visit to Anson Spice and striking such a dastardly bargain?

In the weeks preceding Miles Garrish's visit to his former home, he had made certain to close his clock shop for an hour at lunchtime every day so as to have a rational and reasonable alibi upon the discovery of the murder. Interestingly, this alibi was never required, as Miles was never suspected, and for whatever it might be worth in mitigating the increasingly tragic events of this story, the suspense of always expecting to be found out haunted our Mr. Garrish for the rest of his days, driving him quite insane and earning him the unaffectionate moniker of "The Mad Clocker." Even this escalated paranoia and declining mental state, however, did not point the scent of guilt in his direction; most simply accepted it to be the result of an inability to come to terms with such a tumble in stature as his "gambling troubles" had brought about. Gambling troubles? Heavens, no. Miles Garrish had never been out of his own control at the gaming tables, not until that one night, that is.

As he walked through the streets of West Cuttingsborough, the spring in his step and the smile on his face looked no more suspicious to the people he passed than did the clothes he wore. He carried in one hand a bouquet of orange roses and in the other a large picnic basket. To an onlooker, he may have appeared much like a comically deranged Little Red Riding Hood. The merriness he radiated may have been an overplayed attempt to look unlike someone preparing to commit murder, or it may just as plausibly have been genuine glee at the prospect of what he was about to do. You tell me, dearest companion, which would be more distasteful.

He walked up and down the streets, turning lefts and rights up and down roads surrounding the mansion, awaiting the ripened opportunity when there would be no onlookers to see him enter the McGullivers' abode.

Millicent was only mildly surprised by Miles's knock upon her front door. It wasn't uncommon for her to receive guests during her husband's workday; she was, after all, a very well loved resident of the city. But when she opened the door to see Miles Garrish standing there with a disturbingly toothy grin, her ease faltered.

"Miles," she said, certain that her attempt to sound casual was a decisive failure.

"Good afternoon, Millie," Miles returned, and he extended his arms to present the bouquet of bright orange roses and the picnic basket. She looked at him questioningly, and he smiled reassuringly. "I'd hoped we might chat a while, and enjoy this lunch I've prepared. It's far too much to enjoy on my own, you see, and I feel there is some unfinished business that needs tending to between us."

Millicent didn't take time to wonder what "unfinished business" could exist between them when they'd shared very little interaction at all. Miles had periodically invited the McGullivers to the mansion for dinner, but often there were other guests there as well, and his attention was divided amongst them all. That's not to say that he didn't do his best to tend to her and invite her into the conversation. No matter how clearly pertaining to business and the Council the talk may have been, Miles was always attentive to Millicent's comfort at his home. Then, of course, there were the renowned parties Miles threw at the mansion. However, the McGullivers didn't always attend, and as their relationship grew more distant, they rarely did anything together. But all in all, Millicent did not feel she knew Miles Garrish nearly well enough to be harboring "unfinished business" with him.

She hesitated only for a second before dismissing any cautionary feelings she may have been experiencing. "Yes," she managed to say, ushering him inside, "Yes, of course, I'm sorry. Of course I'd love to have lunch with you, Miles."

And he entered the mansion, looking immediately at his surroundings to see what had been modified since his departure. He did his best to hide his disapproval of these adjustments, merely nodding in feigned interest as they made their way through the corridors to the patio in back of the house, where Millicent set out dishes and silverware and two glasses.

Nodding his thanks, Miles seated himself at the table and presented the contents of the picnic basket. It was cold chicken, cranberries, baked beans, crisp salad greens with raspberry dressing and bacon, and two massive slices of chocolate cake. The final item to be drawn from the basket was a glass bottle containing a very inviting olive green beverage, which Miles identified as pear juice. They enjoyed the meal in peaceful exchanges of pleasantries, neither of them venturing too near the more sensitive subjects they may have had to discuss. Whatever, specifically, their unfinished business was, Millicent noted, Miles was evidently awaiting the end of their meal to broach it.

Sure enough, that is precisely what he did. As they finished their cake and set aside the dirtied dishes, Miles leaned forward, folding his hands in what Millicent assumed was meant to be a "down to business" manner.

"Millicent," he said, looking down at the table as though he found it too painful to meet her eyes. "I fear that there has been resentment between us since…" He trailed off, allowing himself to look up at her and indicate the mansion and its grounds with a wave of his hand.

"Well, Miles ..." Millicent began, but Miles held up a silencing hand.

"Please, Millie," he said, the sincerity thick in his voice. "Do allow me to finish."

Millicent nodded her consent and folded her hands politely in front of her, forcing her face into an attentive smile.

"The truth of the matter is, Millie," Miles continued, "I have always been quite fond of you. In fact," and here he leaned forward to accentuate his point, "I've always fancied that you were rather too good to be married to someone like Percival."

Millicent's eyes crossed, though she maintained her silence.

"You see, Millicent, your husband is a very malicious and devious creature. What he did, how he cost me everything, in my own home, well, I know you must credit it to good fortune smiling down upon him that day. Personally, I have no doubt in my mind that every step of that game was calculated by your husband, executed as perfectly as a staged musical or ... a magic trick." At this last, he arched an eyebrow that clearly invited any knowledge Mrs. McGulliver may have regarding her husband's winnings at the game of Divisor to be shared with him.

She shook her head and said, "I don't know anything about what you're suggesting, Miles." There was a tremor in her voice, and as she peered cautiously at her companion across the table, she felt a sudden rush of nausea to her head. Gripping the edge of the table with one hand, Millicent picked up her glass of pear juice and had a sip of it to cool down with the other.

"I don't expect that will help," Miles said, still leaning forward even more across the table. His smile was unwavering, but his eyes had changed decidedly. There was certainly joy in them, but nothing remotely merry; it was a sinister joy, a thirst.

Millicent attempted to look at him questioningly, but even the slight motion of her head caused the yard and the building beside her to swim and dive and dash mad circles around her. Things suddenly appeared to be upside down or mobile that had no business being in either condition.

"You see," Miles Garrish continued, "the juice itself is the cause of your . . . condition."

Though her thoughts were clouded and her orientation had abandoned her, Millicent was cognizant enough to absorb what she'd just been informed of. Her eyes managed with effort to steal a glance at her guest's own glass, and she was devastated to find that it was still filled nearly to the brim with his own helping of pear juice. All at once she found her maddeningly grappling mind screaming at itself for letting her guard down, for welcoming Garrish in when her senses had warned against it. Of course, at this point she was far beyond any chance of turning back or altering the course of events. Her instincts wouldn't allow her body to surrender to the poison, and she proceeded to clutch the table, to writhe and jerk sporadically in her chair. She wanted to scream; she felt she needed to cry out, if not for assistance, then for the sheer pain of the pear juice as it wormed its way around her insides.

Miles Garrish watched all of this with a patient eye, never once allowing the grotesque contortions of his victim's body to revolt him or cause him to turn away. It is interesting to note with what accepting lack of conscience Garrish managed to watch Millicent's death, while Janine Van Alderdash's metamorphosis was something even the dread Professor Spice could not bring himself to lay eyes upon.

Far too many moments passed before she was gone at last, and her head lay motionless and frozen in terror upon the patio table. Only then did Miles Garrish stand up, straighten his clothes, collect the flowers and picnic items, taking special care to pour the contents of his own glass into the green lawn, and set off upon his way, being careful to take the less populated route through the mansion's backyard so as not to be spotted.

The merry spring was back in his step his entire walk to his clock shop, where he reopened and serviced a handful of customers that afternoon with a welcoming grin and a whimsical voice.

Percival McGulliver was going to Cobble Road. He had planned this visit for some time, but he'd never been entirely certain he would follow through with it. He had tried everything he could think of to cope with his pain, but the loss of Millicent was too strong a blow to his heart for him to deal with. Besides, Percival McGulliver, whatever else he was, was quite a weak man, and if there were any sort of simple solution to this problem, whatever the consequences or stipulations, that was sure to be his course of action.

He had, of course, considered using his own skills to travel backward in time to prevent his wife's murder, but, of course, he was far too cowardly to do this. Uncertain whether he'd be able to bring himself back to the present was enough of a concern, not to mention the notion of coming face to face with a murderer and actually attempting to stop him. This was never a genuine possibility, and McGulliver, a coward but no fool, knew that perfectly well. It was an idea dismissed as soon as it had been conceived.

Once his mind had allowed him to consider that possibility, though, the next option came quickly and clearly. Certainly Anson Spice could help; surely he knew of some manner in which to reverse what had happened. Alas, it was, he truly believed, his only option.

As it happened, Percival missed encountering Scratches O'Hannigan in the streets of West Cuttingsborough by mere seconds. Perhaps if they had met that day, things could have gone quite differently. Perhaps Scratches may have detected a suspicious air in his old friend. Maybe he would have followed him to his destination or distracted him from his plan and his troubles. Perhaps they may have reignited the friendship of their youth and thus relieved Percival of some of the anguish that was leading him to the tobacco shop. But, sadly, this never happened, and the course of events as they played out put Percival McGulliver in the professor's pipe shop that afternoon with a pleading look on his face and a frighteningly amoral willingness in his heart.

"Percival," Professor Spice said, observing the little man as he entered the shop. There were no lingering businessmen in the shop that day, or if there were, they were absent at the time that McGulliver paid his visit. It was only the two of them in the shop, and Percival slowly approached the counter with his hat in his hand and a shake in his step. "I trust you've not come here for tobacco."

It wasn't a question; in fact, the certainty with which Spice stared down at his old rival told McGulliver exactly what he'd expected: that Anson Spice already knew exactly why he'd come here.

Percival didn't respond; he merely stood still, peering up at Professor Spice through timid and pleading eyes. Spice strode out from behind the counter, a contemplative look stealing across his face as he selected his words with care.

"You've come regarding your wife," he asserted, and stood directly in front of the little man, silently awaiting his confirmation.

Percival tore his eyes from the tall man, his face a moistened candy apple. With a degree of effort, he managed a struggled nod.

Spice permitted a chilling sneer to stretch his bony face, and he nodded slight approval. "Very well," he allowed, turning away from McGulliver, his manner suddenly very businesslike. "I can bring your wife back, Percival. I can do so in such a fashion that you may likely eventually forget she was ever parted from you."

Percival McGulliver watched the tall man walk random patterns slowly and catlike around the shop's sales floor. McGulliver's eyes were a frantic mixture of ecstasy and disbelief. Spice went on, "It is not ordinarily in my nature to confess a weakness. However, dear friend..." (These last words contained a wickedly biting sarcasm that made Percival flinch) "...I must confess that you possess an ability for which I have a use."

Percival's expression immediately changed to one of sharp suspicion. "I...uh...I..." he began and could get no further.

Spice promptly interrupted with an expression of detestation and agony. "Stop, Percival. Please, I implore you. If I must communicate with you, you shall spare me your insipid stammering." He turned away with a shake of the head and a mutter of "fool." Percival looked down at his feet, shamefaced, waiting for the professor to proceed.

When he did resume his proposal, it had the sound of a rehearsed speech, as though Spice had been specifically awaiting this conversation and preparing for it from the moment Millicent had died. Indeed, this suspiciously versed behavior would lead Percival McGulliver to draw his own conclusions about his wife's murder. He never approached the authorities regarding this suspicion, however, as he knew that the one man he thought might have been guilty of poisoning his wife was also the only man who could bring her back.

"We will make an exchange," Spice continued. "I have a particular spell that can accomplish your need. It takes time, however. A great amount of time. Each week, on Thursday, I will give to you a pouch of a very special pipe tobacco, a different variety each week. You will combine these one at a time in a secure location; they are not to be disturbed; they are not to be moved. When all of the components have been combined, a recitation of the enchantment, permitting you blended the tobaccos properly, will bring your wife back."

Percival, momentarily forgetting himself, attempted a question. "But will she … that is, when she …"

"She will be restored to precisely what she was before her demise," Spice answered in anticipation of McGulliver's question.

Percival began nodding excitedly, whether simply in comprehension or in some excitable method of accepting the terms, who can say?

"Stop that ridiculous head-bobbing," Spice growled. "I have not finished." McGulliver froze, his face redder than ever. "For every specimen of tobacco I furnish you with, you shall, in return, provide me with a component of the code you've arrived at to manipulate time." Percival McGulliver's eyes widened. "Indeed, I know about it. You're hardly the best secret-keeper, Percival, at least from those perceptive enough to realize there is a secret to be kept. Our final transaction shall consist of the final sample of tobacco and the enchantment on my part and whatever final component there is to the code on your own part. Am I understood thus far?"

McGulliver nodded rapidly but spoke nothing.

"Very well. Once you have recited the enchantment, you will find a portal has opened in the air in close proximity to you. It will be expecting a sacrifice."

McGulliver's eyes widened. He shook his head frantically and once again dove into a reckless bout of attempted questioning. "But it…uh, I…but it…what does…that is…where does it…lead?"

Spice's responsive grin was as coldly dead as Millicent McGulliver and as skeletal as the dead trees that lined Cobble Road. "That hardly matters, Percival. What you don't know can't prevent you from moving forward with your plans, correct?"

Even to Percival McGulliver, now all but devoid of conscience, the morality of such a claim sounded sketchy at best. But he nodded his acknowledgement of its logic.

"Good," Spice nodded in return. "The sacrifice, then, must be… particular." Percival's head turned slightly, questioning. "A person imperfect…someone with…shall we say, a difficulty? A handicap, you see. The sacrifice must be a cripple."

Percival's revolt at the notion must have shown on his face. Spice's grin widened and his eyes seemed ablaze with the mounting excitement he was experiencing from this transaction. "You see, Percival, you must be capable of proving your willingness to go to the most extreme of measures for what you wish. To be willing to sacrifice an already helpless individual to suit your own needs, well, my friend, that is a claim that the powers that you'll be appealing to will gladly reward."

Percival McGulliver was again looking at the floor, his head shaking in a pathetic mixture of shame and despair, for he knew very well that he intended to do everything Professor Spice was instructing him to do. If he still knew that there was the option to decline, to turn around and return to his life and not venture into the dark waters he and the professor were stirring in now, he never gave any indication. He simply stood there staring at the floor and nodding his unconscionable acceptance.

"Very well, Percival. I trust we have a bargain?" McGulliver nodded one last time, and Spice's sneer tore his face into a mask of malice. "There is, however, one last item you'll be in need of."

It was becoming too much for Percival. How many parts to this spell could there be? Where was it to end?

Professor Spice stepped into the back room of the tobacco shop for only a moment, returning with a vial of a swirling, fragrant liquid. It was uncorked and seemed to move within the vial, completely of its own volition. Setting the vial upon the countertop, Professor Spice pulled open his cash register drawer and withdrew a single nickel. Looking up at McGulliver, the professor held up the coin and explained, "This ...will be your earthly payment for your claim on the sacrifice. Once you have determined who that shall be, you are to present this to his caretaker, the one he needs for his own daily survival more than any other."

"Uh ..." Percival stumbled, his brows knitting in perplexity. "He?"

Spice smiled. "Indeed. Of course, you are welcome to select anyone you like, but as it happens, there is a boy in the town by the name of Gerald Gladwell. He lacks the power of speech; that, I would say, should do quite nicely."

And he tipped the vial over the nickel; Percival McGulliver observed as the thick and bubbling liquid seeped upon the silver coin, saturating it in its powerful smell and substance. Once the nickel was quite covered in the fluid, Spice set it upon the counter and indicated that Percival should collect it.

The little man approached the counter with trepidation, certain that the oily liquid must surely still be wet upon the coin. "Take it," Spice spoke with force. "It is dry." And so it was. As Percival McGulliver lifted the nickel from the counter top, he felt nothing of its liquid coating touch his fingers, though he could smell the foreign scent it contained quite unmistakably.

Looking up at the tall man with an expression of fear and doubt, he couldn't help but take the professor's extended hand in his own, making official his entering into a dark business with Professor Spice.

PART FIVE:

Conducting Business

Gerald's hands had begun trembling long before he'd concluded reading his sister's diary, and the shaking had only intensified since he'd closed it. The boy couldn't help himself from looking frantically around the room for some further sign, some indication of what had happened to her. The last thing the diary had told him was Patty's theory that Mr. McGulliver intended to sacrifice him through means of dark arts, most likely in an effort to raise his deceased wife from the ground. To confirm so very far beyond the shadow of any doubt all of the anxieties and doubts he had been having the last couple of days regarding his employer was more than Gerald could handle.

The boy felt certain as he made his way shakily from Mr. McGulliver's chair back to the secret compartment in the wall that at any time he would see his employer's shadow cast itself across him and his surroundings, and that at that time, whatever dismal fate had washed itself upon his unfortunate sister would make its next meal out of him. He put the diary back just as he'd found it, and all the other items he'd removed from the wall, with the exception of the nickel with the foreign scents to it, the one he had seen his sister receive from Mr. McGulliver when they had been McGulliver's dinner guests. With a shudder, Gerald thought of his own gift, the intricate model of the fields and mountains surrounding West Cuttingsborough. How it had always fascinated him! Many were the nights Gerald had studied its details and daydreamed of being small enough to enter into and explore it. Now he wanted nothing more than to go home and destroy it. But something had made him pocket the nickel when he'd first found it, and now, much as had occurred with his sister two years prior, he simply forgot that it was there at all.

Gerald couldn't help poring through his memories, scanning for any other signs over the last two years that would have indicated to him, that *should* have indicated to him that Mr. McGulliver was less than honorable. Had this been his intention all along? Was this why he had come to the house and offered him a job when Patty had disappeared? Was it, in fact, the reason he had hired Patty to begin with? Simply to put himself within arm's reach of Gerald? The thoughts were disturbing, and he didn't know how to cope with such information.

He was remorseful for the way he'd left the coffee shop, leaving his concerned friends to worry about him in his absence. He'd known at the time that the things he was hearing were true; he realized now that his mind had already been made up about Mr. McGulliver. But to have been forced to confront it and deal with it so abruptly, with no warning at all, well, that was something for which he had not been prepared. Nor was he prepared for the rush of urgency he felt now as he came to the unconscious decision to *do* something about all of this. To continue as things had been was out of the question; to stop reporting to work and simply not say or do anything in the hopes that the problem would go away was folly. No, the only thing to do was to confront Mr. McGulliver face to face and put a halt to his plans...somehow.

Hats for All Occasions was every bit as vacated as it had been when he'd sneaked into the back room. Yet its darkness, its quiet, its shadows and night sounds seemed to declare otherwise on his very long and excruciating venture from the office to the front door of the shop. As he let himself out, he took another glance around the store, then quickly swiveled his head back to the street, fearing being spotted by a passerby. But the streets appeared deserted, and Gerald scuttled his way quickly from the store and down the street toward his home.

But the streets only *appeared* deserted; Scratches O'Hannigan had a way of not being seen, and so Gerald never noticed him lurking in the alley near the hat shop, watching Gerald's every move with fixed and intent curiosity. Nor did he see Scratches begin heading in the direction of Cobble Road. Of course, this was how Scratches wanted it; he moved with the greatest stealth, uncertain what he had to share with Molly, but fairly confident that Gerald was beginning to believe that something was amiss with Percival McGulliver.

Scratches had been well aware of that for some time now. Percival wasn't the same as he had been in their youth; his childhood friend was long vanished, and he'd left in his stead a distant, cold, manipulative trickster, though few seemed to recognize that. It was with a silent outrage that Scratches O'Hannigan had watched as Percival McGulliver had remained a loved and respected member of the community. He didn't wish to call attention to his friend's history of lesser-known wicked deeds; he knew such information would be far more valuable if kept secret until the time for its use was ripened to a crisp.

Clutching his one and only possession, his old fiddle, tightly in his hands, Scratches ventured toward Cobble Road, running through a list of plans and ideas in his mind that might successfully protect Gerald from the schemes of Percival McGulliver. Each notion seemed more ridiculous and implausible than the last, and the nearer he drew to the dread road that housed the tobacco shop, the more furious Scratches O'Hannigan became. That his old friend could change was one thing; that he could evolve into someone so clearly lacking in a moral compass (or, worse still, so capable of ignoring it) was quite another, and it was this truth that Scratches was having difficulty grasping.

Cobble Road appeared to loom, to hover in the darkness of the West Cuttingsborough night. The shadows of the buildings seemed to breathe and to pulsate with a living quality that seemed to challenge him to enter their realm at his own risk. Scratches had never been able to understand how it was that businesses on Cobble Road stayed afloat. Few non-residents of the wicked street ever roamed there; even with such cases as the tobacconist, which had no rivaling counterpart in the downtown area, most people would prefer to go without than to visit Cobble Road to meet their needs. Yet somehow, some unseen blessing of nature or the cosmos had granted Cobble Road the ability to live and to thrive, albeit in its own twisted and surreal fashion.

Scratches O'Hannigan was no fool; he was afraid of Cobble Road. He could feel, as he walked along it, slimy, sticky things slithering around his ankles, and he was quite certain that something was breathing warm, acrid breath upon his neck. Yet at the present, his sole purpose was to take care of Gerald, and in order to do that, he needed a plan, and he couldn't rightfully formulate one without the assistance and participation of young Molly.

Stepping with a stride of comfort and ease, fearing to move too quickly or too slowly, Scratches managed to evade the tickles at his arms, the whishing of air past his face, and the moist drips that somehow seemed to touch his legs and trickle *up* them. And as he did so, he kept his eyes focused tightly upon his destination, the rickety, unpleasant, unwelcoming, wooden structure that was the tobacconist's. As he approached, he scanned the night for signs of life in its proximity. He saw nothing, but that didn't necessarily mean no one was there. Perhaps if he—

The arm grabbed him by the jacket and pulled him off the road with alarming force. For only a fraction of a second did Scratches have any opportunity to speculate over who might be grabbing him; almost immediately he detected that the arm's position was lower than where one would expect it to be, as though he were being accosted by a child or a very small person. Then the shine of metal glinted in the faint moonlight and he knew instantly that he had encountered Molly in her wheelchair.

"Molly?" he hissed in the blackness. "Is that you, lass?"

Molly nodded, then realized her error and choked out a hoarse "Yes."

Scratches nodded and took a moment to regain his escaped breath. "Aye, good . . . good." After he'd calmed down a bit, he turned to the girl, whose shadowy shape was slowly coming into dim focus. "What d'ya know, Molly?" Scratches asked.

"Nothing . . . but I've been watching for either you or Gerald to show up, just in case. What's going on?"

The girl couldn't possibly have seen the grim frown on the older man's face, but if emotions can send waves of detectable airs through a night's darkness, then she most certainly felt his warning of impending doom flow from himself and pierce her in the heart, and she knew.

The time of her son's danger was upon them.

When Gerald had arrived at his house, he'd found his father asleep at the kitchen table, patiently awaiting his evening meal. The boy's heart sank with the sight of his vulnerable parent and the mental image of him waiting, innocent and confused, for his son to report home as usual to prepare dinner for the two of them. His heart broke even more at the thought that the man had most likely been expecting Patty this evening as well.

Jefferson Gladwell *always* expected Patty to arrive at home.

Gerald attempted to wake his father as he boiled hot water to add to some oats and toasted a couple of slices of stale bread over the open flame on the stovetop. The father stirred, mumbled something unintelligible, attempted to lift his head and look at the person gently shaking him, found he couldn't come to open his eyes, and allowed his head to fall once again to the tabletop. Gerald smiled his best self-comforting smile and collected the finished food and dished it up for himself. After setting it at the kitchen table, the boy helped the man to his feet and guided him gently to bed, laying him down and covering him up as tightly and snugly as he could with the thin, meager bedding. Then he gave him a kiss on the cheek and returned to the table to mull over the day's events over his warm meal.

He had a pretty good idea of what was going on, of what Mr. McGulliver was up to. What he was uncertain of was just how far along in the process they were at this point. Gerald couldn't help but shudder as he realized that *any* of the preceding Thursdays could easily have been his last. It was an astounding thing to consider how quickly his life had been uprooted, shaken dramatically, and dropped down again in an all but unrecognizable state.

Well, he considered, the first thing to do was to find Scratches and Molly the next day. Together they would pool their knowledge, observations, and ideas and formulate a plan, a way to get him through this. If there was one thing Gerald was certain of right now, it was that he was unwilling to go a step further alone; he had two friends he trusted, and that counted for something.

Then, he wondered, staring off into the starless black sky out the window, did it count for enough?

Percival McGulliver had seen everything.

The little hat salesman knew only too well that little Gerald Gladwell had been searching through his private office and had uncovered the secrets contained in the compartment in the wall. Of course, McGulliver had read Patty's diary, and he could only assume that the boy had read the most crucial parts and learned of his sister's inconveniently accurate assessments of the situation. If such was the case, then the boy would very likely not be reporting to work again, or at the very least he would do so with the utmost escalated caution.

Of course, he will have talked to the fiddler by then. This was something else Mr. P. H. Rutherford McGulliver was quite aware of, the friendship between his assistant and his boyhood friend. It wasn't a union he liked or trusted, and he had made every attempt to evade the fiddler's unwelcome questionings and threats. He had reacted as anyone would expect him to, with trepidation, unfounded levels of nerves and tremors, and had assured O'Hannigan that he meant only the best for the young boy.

Scratches O'Hannigan hadn't believed a word of it.

As you might expect, it had occurred to Percival McGulliver more than once that he might use his abilities to his own advantage in removing the nuisance of Scratches O'Hannigan. However, he had taken enough of a risk in removing Patty from the situation. None had suspected him in the least for her disappearance. Of course, he'd been questioned; he had spent all his days in her company, after all. But he had been so genuinely distraught with what he'd done (what he'd been *forced* to do, as he saw it), that it hadn't been a challenge at all clearing his own name. Why, there had even been tears, something Gerald would recall upon his discovery of McGulliver's hand in what had happened to Patty. Those horrid, cold, and selfish tears had haunted the boy for two years, seeming to be a shared pain at the loss of Patty, and afterward they would continue to haunt him as a nightmarish reminder of what sinister forces he had shared such close quarters with unwittingly. No, McGulliver knew that to remove Scratches O'Hannigan was out of the question. He could only disguise his own ugliness without drawing suspicion for so long.

As it happened, after Percival McGulliver's discovery that the girl Patty had been snooping around behind his back to get to the bottom of his plans, his trust in people declined markedly, leading him to leave his secrets unprotected only on the rarest and most unavoidable of occasions. In fact, McGulliver had already seen what

Gerald was going to do before the boy had even done it. Upon his leaving for the evening, McGulliver had undergone an exercise it had come to be his habit to perform. He would use the code to move time along quickly as he watched from a secure position outside the window of the hat shop, watching to see what may or may not happen in his absence during the night.

Percival McGulliver did this every night.

Ordinarily it was all for nothing, as he found that no out-of-the-ordinary occurrences ever disturbed Hats for All Occasions. On this particular night, however, he watched as Gerald emerged from his hiding place on the sales floor and made his way to the back room. After allowing sufficient time for Gerald to get where he was going and be in the thick of whatever he was intending to do, McGulliver had frozen time long enough to reenter the hat shop, creep in a needlessly stealthy fashion to the office in the back, and to discover Gerald frozen with his hand inside the secret compartment in the wall.

Percival McGulliver was torn between his feelings of panic and ire.

It occurred to the conniving little man to use this foreknowledge to his advantage and prevent Gerald ever from discovering these secrets, at least long enough to move them to someplace more secure. He felt, however, that the matter could be dealt with, that he might be able to resolve this without anything so extreme as altering time or sending the boy away as he'd done to Patty. And of course, were he to do the latter, everything would have been in vain, after all. Gerald was quite indispensable in his plans.

And so he'd allowed the matter to proceed as it was meant to do, and now he was faced with the aftermath of how, exactly, to repair the situation. Of course, his own mind had a tendency to flee from matters of difficulty, and as was the unfortunate way with Mr. McGulliver, he found himself determining once again that the best course of action was to appeal to the wisdom of Professor Anson Spice.

Only having been through a great many trying and taxing experiences could have so coldly and so thoroughly claimed the bright and sharp-witted mind of Jefferson Gladwell. While Patty and Gerald had come to accept the inexplicable nature of their father's decline into almost complete mental deterioration, somewhere deep inside the most uncovered, dank, and indecipherable reaches of his mind, Mr. Gladwell knew truly everything that was going on and just why he seemed so incapable of acting as such. Someday, he hoped, from this secret and distant corner of his innermost self, he would be able to explain everything to his children.

Both of them.

Of course, for the time being, Jefferson Gladwell didn't have any notion whatsoever as to where those two children were at the moment. While one was trapped in a time she was never meant to exist in, the other was departing his little house far earlier than was customary for him, in the hopes that he might be able to sit down once again at the Beanhouse with his friends and share with them all that he had learned the preceding evening. It was imperative, Gerald knew, that this be completed in enough time for him to arrive at work at Hats for All Occasions at his customary time.

The thought of his reporting to work as usual made Gerald shudder. It was the last place he wanted to be, but not to show up there was, he was well aware, the worst thing he could do. He must not only report to the hat shop as always; he must also act perfectly nonchalant and at ease. Anything less than natural could give the boy away, something he didn't like to think on for fear of predicting too real an outcome.

Finding Scratches O'Hannigan was simple. He was hovering right around the proximity of his usual street corner, sipping on a coffee and absently brushing his fingers along the smooth surface of his fiddle. Upon seeing Gerald step up to him, the man scrambled to his feet and set the fiddle and the cup of coffee gently against the wall. Nodding his usual greeting, he began to speak to the boy warily.

"Aye ... mornin' to ya, Gerald." The boy nodded and smiled, and as he did so, tears leapt into his eyes with astonishing rapidity and force. "Oh no, lad! What is it, then? What's eatin' at ya, my boy?" Scratches stepped forward and embraced the silent boy, allowing him to spill his sorrows onto his dirty clothes. "There, there, my boy ... Easy does it, then, lad." As he stroked the boy's hair with gentle care, the fiddler looked around at the still empty streets in desperate helplessness, then started to usher Gerald further down the side street, into an alleyway.

The boy quickly composed himself and shook his head adamantly. He pointed to himself, then to Scratches, then to the empty space beside them, and then made a gesture as if to suggest sipping a hot drink. The fiddler nodded his immediate comprehension.

"The girl, then? You want to find Molly?" Gerald nodded gratefully, and Scratches O'Hannigan pressed his hand gently to the boy's back to lead him on. "Very well, then, lad. Can't say much as how I'd really be all that keen on going to Cobble Road, but if we must, we must."

As they approached the dread corner of West Cuttingsborough, they could each feel the very density of the air around them start to change. If he had known how to put it into words (and, of course, if he'd been able to form those words), Gerald might have said that stepping onto Cobble Road that morning, earlier than he'd ever done so before, was like stepping through a curtain of near-solid gases, commingling to create a stench and a stickiness to help keep intruders out. Indeed, once upon Cobble Road, things looked and felt different. Darker, certainly, but also heavier, almost as though they carried the burden of all the street's dark doings upon their tired shoulders simply in walking along it.

Scratches O'Hannigan wanted to share his senses of foreboding with the boy, wanted to be able to fend off the darkness in the companionship of shared fear. He knew, however, that his role was a caretaking one at the moment and that it was imperative that he remained strong and sure, not to allow Gerald to see that he too was afraid.

Fortunately, they didn't have to walk very far. Only a few yards down the road, they heard a familiar creaking sound as Molly's wheelchair appeared from behind a knobby, twisted, bare tree.

"That's about as far as you two'll want to be going," she said, and an onlooker may have mistaken the words, what with their boldly ascertaining nature and the cold and assertive voice with which they were delivered, as being threatening ones. Both Scratches and Gerald knew, though, that it was not a threat; Molly was warning them.

"What is it, then, lass? What goes on in Cobble Road?" Scratches asked with a good deal of trepidation.

The girl looked up at him from her seat, pursed her lips, and, clearing her dry throat, croaked out, "McGulliver's in the tobacco shop. He's in there talking to Spice."

"Is that out of the ordinary, then lassie?" Scratches asked, knowing full well by her tone and expression that it couldn't possibly be a regular occurrence.

"He never comes here. Never. I think something's wrong."

"Right, then," O'Hannigan sighed, and he turned to Gerald, standing next to him, suddenly trembling and petrified. The boy was looking clearly in the direction of the pipe shop, and with a good deal of fearfulness in his eyes. This time, however, the fear was not for the giant, menacing tobacco dealer; the boy was suddenly quite afraid of his own employer, timid and meek hat salesman, Percival H. Rutherford McGulliver.

"Let's go back to the Beanhouse," Molly suggested, and Gerald instantly nodded his prompt gratitude at the notion.

"Verily well, then, kids. Let's be off," Scratches declared, and they all made a hasty retreat for downtown West Cuttingsborough.

Misters Cromby and Simon were not at the tobacco shop at present. They were actually in the Beanhouse coffee shop when our trio entered there, sharing in a delightfully insipid exchange of ideas that only could have interested the two of them.

"Gratitude is slow coming from the Council, I must say," Simon was huffing over an elaborate pastry and gourmet coffee.

"Indeed," his cohort intoned, "and with such an economic state as this? Intolerable!"

"Quite," Simon confirmed, delivering his cup of coffee a firm and abrupt single nod.

When Gerald entered with Scratches O'Hannigan and Molly in her squeaking wheelchair, the men took little notice other than to be aghast at the disagreeably unkempt appearance of the ragtag group of characters. Indeed, it's quite likely that in their self-absorbed arrogance neither of them even recognized the boy at first sight. Of course, there was little chance of their not recognizing Spice's assistant. There were not many wheelchair-bound people upon Cobble Road, or in all of West Cuttingsborough, for that matter.

Gerald and his companions, however, never even saw the two businessmen, and if their conversation was uttered loudly enough to be shared (willingly or not) by the whole of the clientele at the Beanhouse, then they were too absorbed in their own discussion to process what it was they were hearing.

Until it was too late, that is.

"Now then, Simon...I say," Cromby declared in an only moderately lower tone than he'd previously been using. "Isn't that young chap McGulliver's errand boy? The one over there with the crippled girl?"

"Ah, by Jove, I do believe you are correct there, Cromby. What the deuce would they be doing sharing morning coffee together?"

"A capital question, Simon, a capital question. I wonder if the good professor knows anything of this apparent rapport."

"I should think not. I'm not certain he wouldn't disapprove of such fraternization between business associates."

"Indeed."

"Quite."

"Indubitably."

They went on like this for some time, until they had had their fill of coffee and gossip, at which point they left meager gratuity for their server and excused themselves toward the exit, nonverbally agreeing between the two of them where they would be going now and what interesting information they would be sharing.

As they seated themselves at the same secluded booth at which they had previously spoken, Scratches and Molly exchanged knowing glances with each other. "Well, then, lass...do you want to tell 'im? Or shall I?"

Molly sighed as she stole a glance at Gerald. The boy was looking questioningly from one of them to the other. "I will," she decided, at which Gerald fixed his gaze on his younger friend's face.

With a considerable degree of reluctance, Molly met the boy's gaze and told him, "Mr. O'Hannigan and me...we met up last night to talk about the situation."

A look of only the slightest suspicion dawned on Gerald's face. He looked promptly to Scratches, who nodded his affirmation of Molly's claim. The fiddler took this opportunity to jump in and assist the girl.

"Gerald, lad, I don't know everything that's going on here, but... well, son, ya've most assuredly gotten yerself caught up in a situation that's likely not to be envied much by many. Ol' Percy, he was quite a different man when we were in school together, he was. Now, I'm not certain he wouldn't sell his own mother to the Devil himself for his own pers'nal gains."

Molly nodded her agreement and then resumed. "We don't have much time, Gerald, not much time at all. According to...well, to what I suspect, Mr. McGulliver could be making his move against you within the month. Now, Gerald, Scratches told me he saw you last night…coming out of the hat shop after hours."

Gerald's eyes widened and his gaze shot to the fiddler, who appeared a bit ashamed at having been found to have been spying on his young friend.

"Aye, well, it seems to me that…I…well…I…" Scratches O'Hannigan's voice trailed as he saw the look that rested upon Gerald's face. It spoke volumes as to what was going through the young boy's mind, and in that moment, the fiddler realized that his youthful friend seemed to know more than they'd realized.

Molly must have noticed the look in her son's eye at the same time that Scratches O'Hannigan did, for she suddenly leaned toward the boy and touched his hand in a gesture of concern that indicated deeper wells of affection in the rough teenager than she'd been known to reveal in the past. Indeed, one who knew Molly's true identity and the true relationship she shared with Gerald would have proclaimed with no hesitation that it was her first motherly action toward her son.

"You found something there last night, didn't you, Gerald?" The boy looked at her with a maturity that should not have existed in such a young boy's face. "You really should have let us come with you, you know," she went on, seeing from his expression that she'd guessed correctly. "It was really dangerous for you to do that alone."

Gerald looked down at the table and shrugged a sad admission. His eyes, when they returned to his friends, spoke the burdens of his heart, and in that gaze, they both knew the truth: Gerald knew everything that was going on, possibly more than either of them knew themselves. Molly was certain, at least, that Gerald now knew more than Scratches O'Hannigan did. All he knew for certain were the things she'd told him the previous evening, and those had been quite selective. As things were beginning to progress, Molly couldn't help but predict where the series of events was going to carry each of them, and she had an unsettlingly solidified notion of where (or when) she was going to turn up in the very near future.

Scratches and Molly had Gerald write down a detailed account of his after-hours exploration of Hats for All Occasions, during the writing of which they watched him curiously, awed at the intensity and concentration with which the words seemed to spill from his pencil to the napkin. When he'd finished, they shared the napkin between them to read it simultaneously, uttering little reactions and judgments of the story as they did so.

Once they had a full understanding of all that Gerald had learned the previous evening, they all sat silently for some time, not in an awkward silence, but rather a comforting one. With no verbalization of it, no explanation, no discussion or consensus, they all came to the realization that sudden action was going to be necessary and that it might be some time before any of them had a quiet moment to reflect with no consequences. Therefore, they simply allowed each other to bask in the silence they'd allowed to formulate for a moment.

When they all seemed to start fidgeting with the acceptance that the time for quiet had passed, Scratches O'Hannigan, as the senior member of the trio, attempted to convey a "down to business" demeanor, leaning forward and whispering in his best "this is a serious matter" voice, "I think then, kiddos, we're's needin' a plan."

The best plan of action they were able to devise at the moment, however, was simply for Gerald to report to his job at the hat shop as usual while Scratches and Molly kept an eye on him from a reasonable distance. Gerald attempted to protest that he would be perfectly fine on his own, but both of his friends made it crystal clear to him that leaving him on his own with Percival McGulliver was out of the question. There was still some time, however, before Gerald was due at the store, and not wishing to arouse the slightest suspicion in his reporting for duty too early, they sat and sipped their beverages and partook of a breakfast of assorted donuts before even considering the notion of getting up and departing.

It was during this breakfast that Gerald suddenly began to choke on a donut, grabbed Molly's arm next to him, and gestured frantically toward the Beanhouse's door. Alarmed by this sudden behavior, the girl didn't know whether to dislodge the dry donut from Gerald's throat or look at what the boy was pointing to. In the seconds that allowed him to gain control of the food he'd swallowed whole and prematurely and to swallow it down well enough at least to confirm his safety with a hasty nod, Molly at last turned and looked at the front of the coffee shop just in time to see Misters Cromby and Simon taking their leave.

"Oh no," Molly said, and Scratches O'Hannigan looked confusedly from the girl to the boy, awaiting an explanation.

"What is it, then, lass? Those fancy lads leavin' the place, then, is it? What's the harm, then, kids? I've seen those two gents around about town. They're a wee tad on the bold and arrogant side, I grant, but harmless enough, surely?"

Molly abruptly shook her head in a confident correction. "No," she said. "They're two of the most regular visitors to the tobacco shop."

Understanding dawned on the fiddler's face; only a second later it seemed to melt into further confusion. "But…I don't understand, then, lass. They're just the reg'lar folks of downtown Western Cuttingsborough, ain't they? What'd a couple of downtown gents be doing as reg'lars on Cobble Road?"

The girl's face of panic turned into one of somber frustration. "That's something I've always wondered too," she said. "They hardly ever buy anything there. Occasionally, you know, but not often. They just stand around in there and talk about things that are going on around town. They're loud and obnoxious and they…well…they never really…resolve anything. They just sort of…keep talking until Professor Spice tells them to leave."

Now it was Scratches's turn to appear serious and thoughtful. "That is curious, lass…but if I had to make my best guesses, I'd says as how they're prob'ly most likely as like as not…Anson's spies." Molly and Gerald turned slowly to each other with befuddled expressions upon their faces to communicate each to the other that what Scratches had just said was beyond either of their comprehensions.

Seeing their loss of understanding, Scratches O'Hannigan went on to explain. "See . . . how much of what they say when you're around them do ya kids understand?"

Gerald immediately shook his head while Molly affirmed, "Practically nothing. The words make sense, and if I try hard, I can figure a little out, but it's all so dull, I really never care to."

Scratches nodded, more confident in his theory now. "Aye," he said, "that's the way it's meant to be, lass. The less ya understand, and the less ya care to understand about, the more they can say about the goings-ons in West Cuttingsborough that only Anson understands, see? See, kids, Anson's rarely seen outsides o' Cobble Road since he moved there, and he's a bit now of what some would call a recluse. But he still has potential stock in the city and its business, ya see, and those two gents are most likely as not giving him reg'lar reports on the status o' the types o' things our tobacconist would be wantin' to know about. Most likely, I'd say that the things they're sayin' that you doesn't understand . . . well, they're prob'ly some sort of secret code worked out between the three of them. If they're not there to buy tobacco, kids, then they're there to give information . . . and I'd best be believin' they're most likely collectin' a payment while they're at it."

Once he'd explained his theory, it made perfect sense. In a way, both Gerald and Molly felt a touch of relief. The haughty presence of the two businessmen in the tobacco shop, with their out-of-place appearance unlike the usual to be found on Cobble Road, had always instilled an unsettling disturbance in both of the youths. Now, to know that they were just greedy and amoral and doing dirty work for Professor Spice, their fear of them seemed able to trickle away.

Only a split second later, they both processed the ramifications of the men being spies for Professor Spice. "Wait," Molly said, darting her eyes to Scratches O'Hannigan. "What if they saw us? What if they heard us? They're probably going to tell Spice right now."

Scratches O'Hannigan was already nodding. "There's nothin' we can do 'bout it now, lass. Let's just keep on sittin' here and eatin' our breakfast as best as we can (I know my stomach's not feelin' quite its us'al self, it's not, no sir), and we'll go on to Hats for All Occasions just like we'd planned on, when it's time for Gerald to be there."

The other two didn't like the idea of sitting there idle when Cromby and Simon were about to give up their fraternizing and plotting to the tobacconist, but they also knew that they couldn't stop them, and to follow them to Cobble Road would be foolhardy. And so they sat and watched the time tick itself away, waiting for it to beckon the silent boy to face his danger.

At the same time that our trio of friends was having their discussion at the Beanhouse, our two antagonists were having a talk of their own. Yes, Percival McGulliver had paid his planned visit to the tobacco shop on Cobble Road, where he had found Anson Spice in a less than welcoming frame of mind. The tobacconist led McGulliver to his office in the back of the store and motioned for him to sit down. Once the little man was seated, the professor walked a few paces around the office, stopping behind Percival's chair.

"Really, Percival, how many times must I remind you of the specifics of our arrangement?" he purred in menacing tones.

McGulliver shook the barb off and dismissed it with a wave of a hand. This took Spice by some surprise, so accustomed was he to seeing the little man crumble and bend beneath his corrective voice.

"Well?" he demanded after taking a moment to consider the look of dire panic on the hat salesman's face. "What is it?"

Percival took a moment to be surprised that he was being granted permission to speak, but only a moment. He promptly jumped into as stammer-free of a recitation of what had happened as possible. This, of course, took some time and was less than moderately successful. Spice dealt with the sound of the little man's impediment as best he could, limiting his eye rolls, grumbles, and tooth grindings as much as was within the bounds of his capabilities.

When Percival had completed his narration of the boy's stealthy discoveries in the hat shop, Spice considered what he'd heard carefully. Then he nodded decisively and declared, "So things are soon going to come to a head, it seems." Percival shrugged his agreement in an evident "So it would seem" gesture. Sighing his annoyance, Spice went on, "Very well. I suppose there are three options."

Percival nodded rapidly to show his understanding and attempted to speak. "Yes, well, uh ... what might those, uh ... be?"

Spice glared at McGulliver in contempt, then shook his head and continued. "Well, clearly we can simply leave the situation as it is and continue on in the hopes that we will still be met with success in the end. That, I feel, isn't a wise choice." This last was added with a glance toward Percival as though to assume that it was precisely this idea that the little man had in mind. "Secondly, we might admit defeat and abort the operation altogether."

This was met with an anguished look from the hat dealer, but before he could verbalize a protest, the tobacconist had held up his hand and snapped, "However! I don't intend to surrender this cause so easily."

It is curious to consider that in several years of these dealings, Percival McGulliver never once stopped to consider what the professor needed the code for. Not once did he ask himself, through his own dark and sinister aims, what he might be unlocking or setting free in supplying the code to the wicked pipe seller. Certainly if he hadn't wondered it before, though, a comment such as this one from Anson Spice should have incited such a curiosity in the little man. What did he have to lose or to gain? To what dark end was his collection of the elements of the time code? But no, still Percival McGulliver did not bother to ponder these thoughts. Alas, had he ventured to get to the bottom of so clearly vital a question, many of the tragic events outlined in this narrative very likely may have been prevented.

"And," he said feebly, knowing and fearing what the towering man was going to suggest, "what, uh, is the, uh, the…third… option?"

Smiling, Anson Spice stepped closer to the little man. "Ah," he said, wicked delight evident on the pale face. "The third option, I fear, is our only genuine one, and that is to accelerate the process… perhaps not without certain unidentifiable…complications."

"Uh…complications, then? Of, uh, what…sort?"

"Fool," Spice spat, "if I knew such a thing, they would be identifiable, then, wouldn't they? There is never any telling in the dark magics how or whether a spell may be altered in tampering with its outline." With a sigh and a shrug, he went on, "But with nothing ventured, there shall be nothing to gain, and it is our only true course of action. The boy and the fiddler will undoubtedly attempt to confront you; I have complete certainty on that point. The goal, then, is to be prepared when they do. I will be stepping into the stockroom now to prepare the final week's component for the spell. As I do so, you will document the remainder of the code upon a piece of paper. We are too near our destination to allow a child and his lunatic friend to stand in our way."

It was at this moment that they heard the sound of businessmen Cromby and Simon entering the store. There was to be no question of who had entered, as the men's booming voices carried clearly as crystal to the back room.

Now, let us take a moment to address Scratches O'Hannigan's theory about the roles of Cromby and Simon at the tobacco shop. Of course the fiddler was absolutely correct about their being spies. He was also correct about their collecting payment for sharing valuable information with the tobacconist and speaking in a secret code of sorts to avoid unwanted ears from comprehending. However, this did not change the fact that they were still haughty businessmen who more often than not felt higher of themselves than they perhaps deserved, and that their mundane and insipid discussions and debates usually went on even outside the boundaries of the tobacco shop. Indeed, they had been working for Professor Spice for so long, they often failed to distinguish the line between the real discussions and those that were masked reports of the city around them. This, of course, had made their most recent visits decidedly frustrating and unwelcomingly farcical (a trait Professor Spice had no use for), and so Spice had been reaching his tolerance limit with the both of them rather quickly as of late and had even been considering the possibility of dismissing them permanently. This attitude was altered, however, and his deteriorating opinion of them a great deal repaired with the news they brought.

"In fact," Cromby was saying, "I should think that the investors' fattening bankbooks should more than compensate for whatever inconveniences they faced in the location of the summit."

"True enough, but for the fact that the summit itself proved to be a tiresome affair."

With a shake of his head in disgust, Professor Spice dismissed Percival McGulliver and led him out to the sales floor.

With a questioning look, McGulliver inched his way toward the door. Spice nodded for him to depart, and the little man scurried out with a whimper. The tobacconist then turned to the businessmen and demanded, "Well? Do you have business here or have you simply determined to make yourselves the usual nuisances that you are?"

The men were decidedly taken aback by this uncharacteristic demand for an objective to their visit. While Anson Spice rarely seemed to delight in their routine trips to his shop, it was rarer still that he appeared to be put out by them.

"Well, I..." Cromby began, but Simon stopped him.

"Allow me, old bean," he said, approaching Spice with an overly familiar air that was met with a biting glare. Almost immediately, Simon backed off and turned the floor back to his colleague.

"Right, then," Cromby said. "We were partaking of a morning beverage in that horrid coffee shop downtown..."

"Choices are rather scarce, you know," Simon piped in, apparently some sort of lending of moral support that didn't quite measure up the way he'd intended.

"Well," Cromby continued, spurred on considerably by the impatient stare of Professor Spice. "Yes, well then, we simply thought, you see, that you might be interested to learn where your errand girl whiles her time before reporting for duty here."

"Not considerably," Spice deadpanned, "but proceed nonetheless."

Cromby attempted an undetectable nudge for Simon to continue, which was immediately and unmistakably noticed by Spice. Still, Simon picked up the explanation for his colleague. "She was there with the errand boy from the hat shop, if you can imagine!" At this, Simon attempted a chortle of delight, in the doomed hopes that the tobacconist's spirits might lighten.

The remark did have a visible effect on the professor, though not what either of the men had anticipated.

"What?" he demanded, his eyes widening and his brows furrowing in sudden piercing concentration. "What did you say?"

"She was with the boy!" Cromby declared, reclaiming his role in the discussion. "And they weren't alone, at that!"

"Indeed," Simon concurred. "The street musician was with them also. They were quite a sight!" He too attempted a bit of a chuckle, an action that, under many circumstances, may have spawned impatient ire from the tobacconist, but at this moment was merely met with stunned astonishment.

At the mentioning of Scratches O'Hannigan, Professor Spice's face dawned sudden realization. He had been lackadaisical with the operation to the point of recklessness, and now things were spinning out of control. The boy knew everything and now had allies to assist him. That the fiddler was aiding him was no surprise; that had been suspected all along. But that Spice had chosen to trust the girl and not to suspect her potential for treachery was something he could not forgive in himself.

"Go now," he said to the men, urgency creeping into his voice, urgency that few had ever heard in him before. "Go stop McGulliver. Tell him to return here at once."

The men were quite unprepared for this instruction. The only ones they usually received from Anson Spice were the ones informing them that it was time for them to leave. They hardly knew what to do with themselves in the situation. That is, until he barked a harsh "Now!" at them and they stumbled into each other in a clumsy rush for the exit.

As he watched them hurry down Cobble Road, Professor Spice continued to chide himself for his carelessness. Of one thing he was now certain. However this was all going to end, it would be ending this very day, and if their way had faltered a bit in getting this far, at least Percival McGulliver would be prepared.

The sign in the door of Hats for All Occasions read:

"Closed Indefinitely"

The trio stared at it silently for a moment, considering the implications of the store being unexpectedly closed.

"Those guys have to have talked to Spice, and Spice must have talked to McGulliver," Molly said with sudden conviction. "He must have warned him that we know something, maybe everything." Of course, had they known that Percival McGulliver had already been aware of Gerald's nighttime studying session in the back room of the hat shop and suspected the boy knew everything there was to know (or at least enough to have roused suspicions), they very likely wouldn't have come back to the store at all.

"Aye," Scratches O'Hannigan confirmed. "I think as like as you're right, then, lass." The fiddler turned to the boy, and the look he cast down at him was a serious one. "Gerald, lad," the man said gently, "We need to be makin' a decision then, my boy."

"I think the choices are obvious here," Molly said, more to herself it seemed than to either of them. "It's either a matter of waiting and seeing or active pursuit." She turned to the boy. "It really needs to be your decision, Gerald."

Gerald didn't know what it was that he wanted, or what would make for the wisest course of action. He turned his questioning face to both of his friends, wishing not just their counsel but also their best mental scenarios of how they might not simply face McGulliver but best him as well.

Scratches and Molly looked at one another, and Molly waved Scratches on to share whatever he might be thinking. "Right then," the street musician nodded. "The truth, lad, is that none of us is much too strong. However, then, neither much is ol' Percival. So on that ground we may just be okay."

Molly nodded her agreement. "I don't think he can take you by force, Gerald. But the truth is, we don't know what he can do... through other means."

Both the man and the boy shuddered at this observation, seeing in it the truth that it bore. Gerald looked back to the hat shop and then toward the neck of West Cuttingsborough in which the mansion lay waiting. The other two allowed him his moment of consideration. After all, unless they spotted Percival McGulliver sprinting through the streets toward them, they didn't really see that they were in much of a hurry. Of course, the point now was to gain the upper hand, to beat McGulliver to the punch, to be ready for him before he was ready for them.

Molly pained inside at the sight of her son in such torment. She wanted nothing more than to wheel her chair up to him and hug him as hard as she could and never let go. If she were to do that, however, she knew she would cry, and she needed to maintain her composure until this was finished. And if it was finished the way she hoped it would be, then at that time there would be no need for her composure.

Gerald turned then to meet his friends' eyes. With an attempt at a smile and a shrug of resignation, he looked at them and thought of what he would like to say to them if he were able. He could practically hear it in his mind. He would tell them how afraid he was, how uncertain. He would let them know that he wanted more than anything simply to run away, but he couldn't possibly do that, not with his father so dependent upon him. And that would lead him to share how frightened he was of the possibility that he might leave his helpless father with no one to care for him. He wanted to enlist their promises to see to him if he didn't make it through this alive. He wanted to tell them to let him go on his own so they wouldn't need to endanger their own lives, and at the same time he wanted to beg of them to lead the way, to show him what to do and how to succeed. And then he would tell them, with the best voice of confidence a boy his age and size could muster, that he was prepared simply to march into the McGulliver mansion and face Percival McGulliver right this moment and see this through to its end.

Gerald was ready for this to be over. In such a short time his life had been turned upside down, and yet it felt as though it had been years. There was no indication in the sign on the door of where Percival McGulliver was to be found, or whether or not the hat salesman expected Gerald to hunt him down, but the extravagant and overwhelming McGulliver mansion seemed practically to call to the boy through the crisp morning air, over the buildings and through the roads and alleyways, beckoning him to come and find the man who had put so much work toward bringing Gerald to doom. And while Gerald could not say all of the things he wished he'd been able to, perhaps his friends had received the message nonetheless, either from a look on his face or else perhaps through some greater, indefinable bond, for Scratches O'Hannigan turned to him and asked softly, "To the mansion, then, lad?" The boy looked to his friends and gave a single, abrupt nod.

Molly and Scratches, while each in their own special way felt a parental protection of the boy, both backed up to allow Gerald to take the lead. The young boy didn't protest, but looked through the streets of West Cuttingsborough toward the location of the great mansion, and he took a single step toward it. Allowing him a moment to begin the fateful journey, the other two watched, each with a concern and a heartbreaking fear that compelled them each to chase after him, grab him in a loving embrace, and to take him far away from where he should ever have to face such troubles. But they fought such a desire and watched their little companion make his way down the street without looking back at them.

After a moment, Scratches turned to Molly and said, "Let's go, then, lass…Don't ya fret; we'll get the lad out o' this." As he began walking toward Gerald, he noticed immediately that Molly's wheelchair had not begun to move. Turning back to the girl with a questioning eye, he went on, "Come on, then, Molly, lass…is somethin' wrong, then, dear?"

Molly had distinct tears resting in her eyes. She was watching the boy she secretly knew to be her son with a fear for his safety she'd never known she could feel. Even as she'd grown to know and love him in the time since she'd arrived from her own time in the past, she never could have expected to know a time when she found herself so deep in the throes of unconditional love as to wrestle with the decision she'd known all along she would have to make.

Trembling, the girl looked up at him from her seat and said, in barely more than a whisper, "I need to leave. I can't go with you."

A questioning eyebrow communicated Scratches's confusion, but he still said, "I don't understand, then, lass."

Molly's head began to shake adamantly and she pressed on with what she knew she had to say. "I can't explain. I really can't. I just… I have to leave. I can't stay here for this. It's too dangerous."

"It's too dangerous for the lad too, Molly!" Scratches nearly shouted, enough to cause Gerald, ahead up the road, to stop and turn around to look questioningly.

With a cry of despair, Molly scolded Scratches. "Oh, why did you do that? I didn't want him to see me go! Now he's going to be upset."

"Well, lass, the boy has a right, I think," Scratches declared with a cool confidence the girl was not impressed with. With a glare she pointed an accusatory finger at him.

"If my plan goes right, I'll be back to help, old man! But I can't help by going with you. I can't risk dying in there or everything will turn out wrong!"

Scratches, as ignorant of Molly's identity and where she'd come from as Gerald was, could not fathom what this was all about, and he shook his head in stunned silence. Worse yet, Gerald was clearly distraught by whatever disagreement was not only holding up his friends but also clearly causing them such hostility. True, Molly and Scratches had only met the previous day, and they had greeted each other initially with less than warm sentiments. But that felt so long ago now, and he couldn't go forward knowing that his two closest friends and confidants were at odds with one another, particularly if that disagreement regarded himself.

From where he stood many yards away, Gerald watched as the two spoke angrily but quietly enough to prevent him from hearing anything that was said. That bothered him. He'd half a mind to march right back to where they were and communicate as best he could with flailing arms and angry scowls how much the friction between them was upsetting him. But he didn't. He stood there waiting and watching, and he was more than a little alarmed to find the altercation conclude with Scratches turning away from the girl in the wheelchair and beginning to stride toward him while Molly started to wheel herself in the opposite direction.

When Scratches reached the boy, Gerald attempted to express his confusion through a questioning gesture toward Molly, but Scratches continued past him without a glance, muttering as he went, "C'mon then, lad. We'd best be on with this."

Gerald wanted desperately as he followed the fiddler down the road to demand an explanation; why would Molly take the trouble to guide him toward awareness of his impending doom only to take leave at the crucial moment? But he knew better than to pester

Scratches about it and determined that in order to be best prepared for whatever was going to occur at the McGulliver mansion, he'd best not distract himself with the girl's absence either.

Percival McGulliver was waiting for the three companions. He had no reason to be aware that he would only be receiving a visit from two of them, nor would he have cared. Indeed, he would have been perfectly satisfied to know as much, as that would simply mean he had less opposition to be concerned with. As long as the boy showed himself, his plan could execute as intended. Of course, the girl's handicap made her a worthy candidate to sacrifice to the portal; however, as the physical payment of the anointed nickel had been bestowed upon the boy's sister and the spell clearly called for it being gifted to one of the victim's loved ones, it was too late to consider her as a potential sacrifice.

No, it must be Gerald.

That Anson hadn't come with him to see this through had vexed him no small amount. But the tobacconist had reminded him with a biting edge that he was the superior player in their arrangement and that he knew better than Percival how best to see things through. His place, he had told the little man, was not in the mansion sending the mute boy hurling into a swirling portal to a scathing and vile torment; his place was in the comfort of his own establishment, awaiting word from McGulliver that the process was complete.

So now Percival scurried about the mansion, making all the proper arrangements that would see this task through in the most prepared, organized, and hasty fashion.

The door looked so very large to Gerald.

The boy had, of course, been to the mansion once before, but that had been two years ago, shortly before the no-longer-mysterious disappearance of his sister. Being here again now only emphasized the pain he felt at the loss of her and the ire that had grown within him over so short a time toward his employer, the wicked man who had brought this on his family.

Entering was going to be most difficult, he knew.

Scratches O'Hannigan had softened as they'd neared the mansion. His silent rage at Molly for abandoning them had melted into a somewhat less silent sympathy for the boy. He had to remind himself that as much as Molly's departure angered him, it must have saddened Gerald on a much deeper level. Clearly the two had shared a special bond all this time that Scratches had known nothing of. It made the fiddler feel a bit foolish. He had always felt quite protective of Gerald, but to know that the boy had had Molly looking after him all along made the man feel far less useful than he'd always fancied himself to be.

Now, however, he was quite certainly needed, and he determined that he must take that responsibility seriously. The time for being angry would have to be later. He had an idea for when the time came to face his old friend. He hadn't shared this idea with Gerald, however, believing with ample certainty that the plan sounded much finer in his own mind than it would if verbalized. He didn't have, in his own humble vision of himself, many skills or talents worthy in a mortal conflict with one with abilities such as Percival McGulliver's. He did, though, have talent, and useless as it may seem, he would utilize what he could. His music had nearly been Anson Spice's undoing once, and if Percival had grown to be as similar to the tobacconist as Scratches suspected he had, then perhaps using his one natural gift wasn't as silly a notion as some might think.

The musician watched as the boy eyed the door to the mansion. "I don't think we need to be knockin' then, lad," Scratches whispered in an effort at humor. The boy forced a smile at the man and looked back to the door, nodding agreement. Slowly, Gerald attempted to raise his hand to the door handle, found it shaking uncontrollably, and quickly pulled his hand away and looked up to his friend in a plea for assistance.

Without a second's hesitation, Scratches O'Hannigan nodded, sputtered, "Yes, yes, of course then, lad, of course," and set his own hand upon the cold metal. With only the slightest pressing of the handle down and pushing of his weight into the solid wooden door, the entranceway opened for them and they found themselves gaping in at the dimly lit and finely furnished foyer of the McGulliver mansion.

Dimly lit? The foyer glowed with the wavering light of several candles mounted on the walls and resting on a table. Gerald and Scratches looked around and saw that the sky out the windows was that of the deepest, darkest hours of the night. Where had the day gone? How had it passed from morning to the middle of the night simply with their passing through a doorway? What powers were they in the midst of?

It was very quiet. It seemed contrary to the laws of nature that such a large building so very filled with little worlds of discoveries and treasures at every turn should exude such complete and devastating silence. And yet, the two friends knew that somewhere in the thick of this wicked quietude dwelt Percival H. Rutherford McGulliver, and he was waiting for them.

He was waiting for Gerald.

Lost in taking in the sights of the entranceway, Scratches hadn't noticed Gerald approach the great winding staircase and, indeed, begin to climb it.

"Gerald!" the fiddler hissed into the darkness. "Where're ya goin,' lad?" Gerald turned to look at his friend, and the expression on the boy's face seemed to say, "Why, going upstairs, of course." And the boy motioned with his whole arm for Scratches to follow him. Almost immediately the boy gestured a different communication, emphasizing the foyer and allowing his face to become more questioning and less commanding. "No, no," Scratches replied. "I'm not stayin' down here, lad. If you're goin' upstairs, then I'm goin' up there too, I s'pose."

Gerald allowed his face to mold into an "Are you sure?" expression, and Scratches nodded in return warmly. He couldn't help but smile at the boy's maturity and courage. "Aye," the man responded. "I'm quite certain." Then he became more serious and gestured toward the upper level. "How, though, Gerald lad," he asked, "do ya know we're s'posed to be up there, huh?"

Gerald looked up into the darkness at the top of the winding staircase, then back at his friend and shrugged. He seemed genuinely incapable of answering the inquiry. Then, without giving the matter another thought, the boy turned back again and continued up the stairs, Scratches O'Hannigan following closely behind him. Before they reached the top of the stairway, Scratches reached for Gerald's arm and stopped him. "A second there, lad," he said as Gerald turned to him, puzzled. "Promise me, boy, that when we find him, you'll stay behind me, let me face him first. I've got an idea, Gerald, and it may not be the greatest of plans, true 'nuff, true 'nuff, but…well, just let me protect ya in there, lad. Promise me." Gerald smiled warmly to his friend but, Scratches noticed, did not communicate a positive or negative response to the request. He simply turned back the way he'd been going and continued.

The upper level of the house was equally as dark as the lower. Gerald led them through the twisting and intersecting corridors and past many of the same rooms he recalled from the McGulliver-led tour he'd been on two years ago. They saw the map room and the laboratory, the library, and the costume room. Many of these doors were open for the looking into, while others remained a mystery behind fast-shut doorways. Scratches was often tempted to slow down and peer through some of these rooms, partly because it was next to impossible not to be impressed by them, but also because as far as he could see, Percival McGulliver could have been hiding in any of them.

After some time of this, Scratches realized that the boy didn't seem to be slowing at all, and he even seemed to be making his turns with purposeful confidence. He took another few moments to follow his companion in this manner, watching with a fresh eye for signs of what he was beginning to suspect, that being that Gerald Gladwell knew exactly where he was going.

"Gerald, lad," Scratches called to the boy, who appeared to be speeding up, close to the point of leaving him behind. Almost instantly, he realized he'd probably spoken too loudly and continued in as loud a whisper as he could manage, "Gerald! Hey there, boy! Slow down!"

Gerald paused and looked back curiously at the man, arching his eyebrow in a questioning expression. Scratches gestured his equal confusion as he caught up to his small companion. "Where ya goin,' lad? How is it you're movin' s' quickly, then, Gerald, and know exactly where you're goin,' then?"

Gerald looked up and down the corridor and then back at Scratches and shrugged quite sincerely. Somehow, the man gathered, the boy just knew. The events were spiraling into a madness the man couldn't have predicted, and he wasn't sure he was eager to see where they took them.

"Fine, then, aye," he said, his voice hoarse with the dryness of fear. "Lead on."

And so Gerald did, and before long they had arrived at a closed door on the south side of the mansion, and here the boy stopped and indicated the door.

"This is it, then, lad?" Scratches asked doubtfully, though he made quite certain to keep his tones more hushed than they'd been thus far. Gerald nodded somberly, and Scratches nodded back. "Right, then," he said, and he reached out and turned the knob on the door.

It opened.

They stepped in.

And Gerald found himself once again in the room that had so captivated him two years earlier, the room whose view he saw every night when he retired to bed and every morning when he woke in the form of the little intricate model that sat by his bedside. The room was just as the boy remembered it, the entire southern wall still missing, the floor extending out over the hills and mountains. The wrought iron furniture was still there, as was the wine rack. Scratches O'Hannigan looked at this sight and drew in a breath of awe.

"Well, I've never ..." he started to say, but his voice caught short as the silhouetted image of a man stood from the wrought iron table and nodded in their direction. Scratches cocked his head and tried to make out the figure, but the darkness was too dense.

Of course there was only one person it could be, and Percival McGulliver's voice was like an icicle injected into their blood. "Scratches," came the greeting from the darkness. "Gerald." Gerald swallowed his fear down; he was greatly tempted to look up at Scratches for support, but he determined that such a move would convey fear and weakness. He needed to stand strong and confident before his foe.

"Percy," Scratches managed to say, his voice more hoarse still than it had been only seconds ago. "What's gotten into ya, old friend?" The despair in the fiddler's voice was genuine. "Where'd ya lose your way, man?" Scratches begged to know.

Percival McGulliver scoffed at the inquiries and stepped closer to them both. "Don't pity me, Scratches," the hat salesman said calmly. "I'm doing exactly what I ... what I, uh ... what I want."

Had Patty been there, she would have noticed what neither her brother nor Scratches O'Hannigan was capable of detecting: Mr. McGulliver's voice seemed to fall into its stammering habit when he was attempting to communicate confidence toward his own misdoings.

Having no more need to control his volume, Scratches allowed himself to raise his voice to a level of the severest anger. "Percy, you old fool!" the fiddler shouted. "You're willing to harm a child, you're willing to hurt the people in your life ya rely on the most! And for what? To what end, Perce? So's to dabble in the darkest o' arts that shouldn't be messed around with anyway? Shame, old friend, for shame on ya!"

Percival McGulliver was close enough now to be seen, if only in the wickedest of dim night shadows. The stars in the sky behind him created as ominous a backdrop for his stand of evil as even the darkest of poetic minds could conjure. They could see the sneer on his face that welcomed O'Hannigan's remarks with amusement and scorn.

"You don't know what you're talking about, Scratches. I have no choice in this matter. This was settled…well, a long time ago. The ingredients are in order, you see, and the earthly cost was paid some time ago."

Suddenly Gerald recalled what he'd read in his sister's journal and realized that he couldn't remember what he'd done with the exotic-smelling nickel he'd pocketed in McGulliver's office. Discreetly, the boy thrust his hand into his pocket and immediately felt the cold, hard shape of the coin, left right where he'd placed it the previous day. He left it there, not certain whether it would be useful, but somehow afraid that perhaps Mr. McGulliver had better not see it in his possession.

The little man was gazing thirstily at the boy now, sudden true comprehension dawning on him as he realized that the fruits of his labors, the ends to his plans, the aims of all his actions and deeds were now materializing in crystalline purity and uncompromising certainty. This was where it all was going to end, and he was quite certain it was going to end beautifully.

Ignoring Scratches O'Hannigan now, Percival looked straight down at Gerald and said in as warm a voice as anyone had ever heard from him, "Please, Gerald…I hope that you don't, uh…that is, take this, well…personally. I truly was very fond of you and, uh, well, I think perhaps I will…well, perhaps I will…miss you from time to time. Yes, I think…quite."

Scratches O'Hannigan was snarling at the fiendish remarks of his wicked friend. The coldly precise comments, the attempt at a warm-hearted smile, the unmistakable hunger gleaming in the eyes behind the spectacles, visible even in this black night air . . . they were all signals pointing toward what he believed to be the complete and irretrievable slip of his old friend into complete and unforgivable evil.

"Well, now," McGulliver went on, his tone changing to one of business-like manners, "I suppose we'd best, uh . . . well, begin." Reaching into his breast pocket, he drew forth a piece of paper, which he eyed carefully for a moment before smiling at his visitors and gesturing to the paper in an almost playful fashion.

Scratches O'Hannigan drew closer to Gerald and stepped in front of him. Whispering down to the boy, he said, "Gerald, lad, stay behind me. I don't know much about how to stop this, lad, but I'm going to be doin' my best here, I promise ya, boy." Gerald nodded, though his friend's back was to him and he knew Scratches couldn't see the response. Hesitantly, the boy began to back up in the direction of the door as Percival McGulliver began reading from the piece of paper in his hand. The words were foreign, certainly; at any rate, they held no meaning to those in the room. They seemed to carry a power, those words did, and as Percival spoke them the air behind him, just above the edge of the floor that reached out into the sprawling night sky seemed to shimmer just a touch, the stars behind it fading and clarifying in subtle but genuine ripples.

The little man noticed the boy's movement and glanced up at Gerald warningly. "I, uh, wouldn't be doing that, Gerald. You'd best, uh, stay put." The boy stopped as commanded, though he drew no closer to McGulliver either.

Neither the boy nor his employer noticed Scratches O'Hannigan reach his own hand in turn into his coat to bring forth his cherished little fiddle. McGulliver noticed immediately, though, when he heard the man playing it. His reading of the strange words ceased abruptly as his head snapped up to meet the eyes of the fiddler.

"Stop that!" McGulliver snapped at him, and Scratches paused only long enough to read a distinct emotion in his old friend's eyes.

Quite surely, there could be no doubting it: Percival McGulliver feared the music. O'Hannigan continued to play, gaining confidence now that perhaps this simple demonstration of his own talent held more power than simply to captivate a roomful of avid listeners. He had known what he would play before he had even begun to reach for the instrument, though it took Percival a moment to recognize it.

"I said stop that! Stop at once!" the little man continued to shout. He started to come forward, arms outreached toward the little fiddle, but as he drew closer, suddenly a look of dawning realization cast itself over his eyes. "What is that?" McGulliver demanded. "What is that music you're playing?"

Gerald did not recognize the tune at all, nor did he see any importance attached to it. In fact, he was too absorbed with what he was seeing occur in the air behind Mr. McGulliver to pay heed to some simple music. The ripples that had begun to appear after Mr. McGulliver had commenced the reading of the paper had grown from their first size to one considerably larger. They swam around each other in rhythmic repetition, dancing across a small space in the air, stretching sometimes a bit farther, sometimes a shorter distance, but they had ceased any change in size once Mr. McGulliver had stopped reading and become focused on Scratches's playing.

"That," Percival gasped as he placed the tune he was hearing, "that is the music from the graduation ceremony!" Scratches didn't confirm or deny, but had Gerald been able to see his face, he may have noticed the faintest of smiles materialize on his friend's features. The boy couldn't understand why a song should have such an effect on Mr. McGulliver. Here was a man capable of terrible magic, unthinkable deeds, and some notes on the strings of a little instrument had him trembling and forgetting himself completely.

"Stop it at once!" the man continued to scream, his voice louder and clearly more frightened.

Percival McGulliver, like most of West Cuttingsborough's citizens, never knew where the beautiful music from the graduation ceremony had come from. He had had his suspicions, of course, and he knew of his friend's natural gift for music, but the music of the graduation had symbolized something that neither McGulliver nor Spice had ever been able to understand. It had been a thing of pure beauty, a creation beyond words, something that had moved any and all who had heard it to tears, smiles, and wholehearted bliss. It had become something that had been spoken of ever since, by those who had and hadn't been there alike.

And yet no one had ever claimed responsibility for the beautiful music. No musicians, no conductor, no composer, no one had ever stepped out onto the stage to take a bow or even come forth to the community later on to say, "It was me! I was responsible for that!" This was beyond inexplicable where our two antagonists were concerned. Where Anson Spice was outraged at the anonymity of the accomplishment, the lack of credit to be hoarded for it, though, McGulliver was more befuddled by the selflessness of the music. Someone had worked quite hard to create it solely for the enjoyment of others, whereas all of Percival McGulliver's talents and wisdom had always been put into use to convenience himself only. McGulliver would likely have been even more greatly aghast at this selfless deed if he'd realized that Scratches O'Hannigan actually forfeited his opportunity to walk across the stage that afternoon in favor of providing the music from another room.

"Stop that!" McGulliver was shouting, and now he was actually pulling at Scratches O'Hannigan's sleeves, making his best effort to cease the horrid sound. This effort spoke, however, either for O'Hannigan's physical strength or else for McGulliver's weakness, or perhaps for both. For all his tugging and yanking, the little man could not wrest the fiddle from O'Hannigan's hands, nor stop the man's hand from setting the bow to the strings. In fact, with little more than a shake of his body, Scratches managed to throw Percival aside.

Anger took over the little man. With a lift of his finger, he let out a blood-curdling scream, and suddenly, with no warning at all, both Gerald and Scratches found themselves back in the foyer of the mansion. They barely had time to acknowledge this fact, let alone to share each other's confusion or question what had happened when suddenly they were in the map room. A second later they were in front of the mansion in the road, and a second after that they were halfway up the winding staircase. Just as they were preparing themselves to be completely *un*prepared for wherever they may appear next, they found that they were back in the open-walled room, and they saw Percival McGulliver there with the paper clutched in one hand and the other hand extended high above his head, the forefinger still pointed straight as an arrow into the night sky. The shimmering ripples of air behind McGulliver had, Gerald noticed immediately, grown into a definitive shape. They had now expanded into a circular blend of metallic blues, purples, and greens. The ripples were still there, the bumpings and shakings of air still disrupting the night, but now in the form of what appeared to be a small pool of colorful waters hovering on its side in the air. The thing, Gerald would estimate later, was probably no more than two feet in diameter.

No sooner had they stumbled back into their places from which they'd so suddenly been snatched than Percival McGulliver was shouting at them both, his voice shriller and more hysterical than anyone who'd ever known him had ever heard it to be.

"Don't you see?" the very little man bellowed in a screech that could have scraped actual marks along a pane of glass. "Don't you fools see what I am capable of? I am the Master of Time itself, fools, and you cannot stop me! You have nothing, no weapon, no trick, no talent, no skill, no thought that can conquer the very nature of Time!" Even as the man was shrieking his threats and promises, Scratches O'Hannigan brought the fiddle back to his chin and began once again to let flow the beautiful music.

In an instant Gerald and Scratches found themselves on Cobble Road in the daytime. Promptly they were outside the hat shop at dusk. In a blink, they were in Gerald's own front yard on a frigid winter morning.

And then they were back in the three-walled room of the McGulliver mansion, Percival McGulliver only angrier and more maniacal than before. He was in the midst of screaming the foreign words from the paper, and as he did so, there could be no mistaking the ever-changing growth of the pool of colors in the night air. The shimmering circle had easily grown to ten feet in diameter, and it was continuing to expand as the words flowed from McGulliver's lips.

Scratches O'Hannigan once again drew the fiddle to his face and resurged back into the elaborate tune that continued to vex the wicked little man so greatly. With a flinch of anguish, he clutched the paper more tightly and shouted the ancient-sounding words more loudly still.

As the window of light continued to grow, Gerald cowered near the door, torn between wishing simply to bolt and run for safety and knowing he had a deep-rooted need to see this through to its finish, and certainly unwilling to abandon his friend. The music proceeded to play, the portal continued to grow, and with every word departed from Percival McGulliver's mouth, the little man's grasp on reality seemed to trickle slowly away. A look of manic excitement was housed in his eyes, and his voice had reached such a pitch as to suggest one on the verge of hysteria.

The light from the portal was brightening to the point of being blinding, and indeed, both Scratches and Gerald had turned their faces away from its emanating presence. It was now nearly the size of the entire missing wall; the night sky was only visible around the circular pool's perimeter, and even that was flooded with the brilliance of the mysterious floating pool's colors.

Percival McGulliver's screaming words pinnacled in a crescendo of piercing pitch. When it seemed his voice had frozen in a permanent note of splitting shrill ecstasy, he at last let go of it and allowed his body to relax. They were suddenly enveloped in the still night quiet, the words spoken, the portal opened completely, and not a speck of night visible through its all-encompassing light and color. It continued to shake and shimmer, seemingly almost alive, but now it did so in a silence that was so complete, it was quite possibly eerier than McGulliver's almost possessed screeching of foreign spell-casting.

Even the music had stopped. Scratches O'Hannigan was so taken with the brilliant vision before him, complete with his childhood friend's silhouette painted upon the surface of its alien glow, that he had completely forgotten to continue to play the notes upon the fiddle. It still lay against his chin, the bow perfectly in place, prepared for the instant that its owner may decide to return to it.

Percival's normal, familiar voice broke the silence. "Well, then," he said quietly, satisfied with his first look at the portal he had opened behind himself, "it would appear that, uh, well, that it is... time. Yes, quite. Gerald, if you'd be so kind as to, uh..." Gerald's eyes widened in realization. There was nothing now standing in the way of his being cast into that hole in the sky, and there was no telling what sort of torture, misery, or pain lay waiting for him on the other side of it. Shaking his head in fear and despair, the boy started to reach for the doorknob behind him. As he scrambled to his feet and found his hold upon it, he crinkled his face as he strained to pinpoint something.

Scratches O'Hannigan had noticed it as well. There was a sound that hadn't been there a moment ago. The complete silence was being disturbed, only slightly, that was true, but disturbed nonetheless. Gerald turned his head toward the door whose handle he still held in his hand and was certain the sound (It was a familiar sound, wasn't it? Where did he know it from?) was coming from the other side of it. With no fear, only hope, the boy turned the knob and drew the door open.

There was nothing there.

And yet...the sound was certainly out there somewhere, in the mansion. It was a squeaking noise, pulsing and whining, seeming to grow nearer and nearer. The boy continued to focus on the corridor, attempting and failing to determine what it was he was hearing, what it was that was coming.

So absorbed in the sound was he that he didn't notice that Percival McGulliver was shouting again.

"You will obey!" the little man's voice was belting to the night, and Gerald was awakened from his concentration. Scratches O'Hannigan stepped in front of McGulliver as the little man began to draw nearer to the boy. Blocking the hat seller's path, Scratches O'Hannigan was astonished when McGulliver successfully pushed him with little effort stumbling into the wall. Gerald found himself frozen in terror as the little man, so clearly not the same person Gerald had known all these years, approached him with the speed of one half his age.

As McGulliver grabbed Gerald by the arm, the boy only fought barely, fatigued with the horror of the entire situation and beginning to feel that the best way to escape it might just be to give in to it and have done with it. McGulliver dragged the boy along the floor by the wrist right up to the hovering portal. When they were stationed there, the little man bent down and began to hoist Gerald to his feet, with decidedly more effort than it took to dismiss Scratches O'Hannigan, who was recovering slowly from a nasty bump of his head to the wall. The little man, with the boy now in his arms, glanced up at the swirling mass of colors in the air. With a glance at Gerald, Percival McGulliver felt a chill come over him. He could practically feel the touch of an unseen hand or some other force on his shoulder, encouraging him to put the boy back down. Looking back at Gerald, Percival shook away the feeling, swallowed back any reluctance that may have been intervening, and dragged the boy toward the portal.

As Gerald found himself landed upon his feet in front of the portal, exhaustion settling in upon him, he didn't notice that the creaking sound had reached its peak and then ceased all together.

"Stop."

The voice was clear in the still silence, and all three people in the room turned their eyes to the door, Scratches rubbing his head as he lay upon the floor, Gerald breaking through the spell of fear with a decided struggle, and McGulliver only barely holding up the boy for all the exhaustion that casting the spell had descended upon him. They all had the exact same reaction to what they were seeing: confusion and shock overtook both men and the boy.

It was undoubtedly Molly seated in her wheelchair in the doorway, but something was different about her, and as she wheeled herself into the room and closer to all those inside of it, it became clear what that difference was. This was not the young lady who had taken leave of her friends only a short time earlier in the morning. Those were her eyes, that was her wheelchair, and certainly, though only one word, that had clearly been her voice. But this woman was older than the Molly they knew, many years older. This Molly was no teenager; she was an adult, mature and reserved, calm and sincere.

And loving. The look she gave to Gerald as she wheeled up to him was clearly one of true and blissful love and protection. Again, she said, "Stop."

"What is this?" McGulliver shouted at the woman in the wheelchair. "What do you mean by this? Stay out of my business! This does not concern you!"

Molly smiled a patronizing smile at the man and said, as calmly as if she were placing an order at Lotsa The Pasta, "I don't think this will be necessary, Mr. McGulliver."

McGulliver shook his head adamantly at the woman. "Don't try to stop me, woman! The fiddler tried and found he couldn't do a thing. Best you learn the same right now and save yourself!"

Molly shook her own head in return, but it was a peaceful, serene shake that did nothing to calm McGulliver's nerves. "I have no desire to save myself, Mr. McGulliver. My life has been leading up to this moment for many, many years. There will be no need for you to sacrifice Gerald. And believe it or not, I want what you want just as much as you do. More, probably. Millicent was good to me once. She helped to turn me around and get my priorities in order. It's largely thanks to her that I even have a life worthy of being proud of. She didn't deserve to die the way that she did."

Percival McGulliver's face was painted with his impatience. "What are you suggesting, then?" he demanded.

"Take me," Molly said from the chair, and Gerald started to protest. Scratches forced himself to his feet and began to draw near to the circle of people gathered around the portal.

"What are you talking about?" McGulliver hissed in distaste.

"Take me. I will go in there." She nodded toward the portal. "Willingly. I know you need someone with a handicap. I'm clearly that."

McGulliver sneered and shook his head rapidly. "It's no good, woman. Crippled, yes, you may be that, but the earthly price has been paid already. The coin goes to a loved one of the victim, and I gave it to Patty. She's his sister; it must be the boy."

"I'm Patty's loved one as well," Molly declared, and McGulliver waved her off with scorn. "It's true," she went on, and she purposefully looked to Gerald before she said what she had to explain next. "She's my daughter."

Gerald's eyes widened; his head shook in an expression of entirely perplexed bewilderment. Scratches O'Hannigan, now only feet away from the others, whispered in a hushed voice, "What, lass?"

Completely ignoring the presence of Percival McGulliver and his hovering portal, Molly held her gaze on Gerald's eyes and explained. "It's true, honey. It's me, your mom. I've known it all along." Gerald continued to shake his head in disbelief, but Molly ignored it and continued. "Mr. McGulliver sent her into the past, specifically to my own teenage years. She came to me and befriended me and we formed a plan for your rescue. She's still there."

As Percival McGulliver heard these details, his face paled with the realization of his own mistake. Fool that he had been not to send her further away, to somewhere completely out of reach of assistance. This frustration was promptly displaced by his annoyance that he was being blatantly ignored in the middle of his own ritual.

Molly went on with her explanation, both Scratches and her son held in the fast grip of what she had to say. "Gerald, honey, when I left earlier...well, for me, that was years and years ago. I...I went back. Back to my own time, and I...well, I lived...and waited. I waited for today, when I would come here and do what I could to help you."

Gerald was in utter shock. Of course, Scratches was having some difficulty processing this information as well, and Percival McGulliver was quite perplexed, but Gerald was the one who was truly cast into a whirlwind of confusion and emotion. Could what he had just heard have been true? Could this woman, this person he'd known as a friend and a guide have in truth always been his late mother, the woman who'd always been a stranger to him and his incapable memory? He felt that he could trust what he was hearing, that Molly meant everything she said. But...at the same time, something didn't seem to add up. It was Scratches who put it into words for him.

"Now wait a second, lass," Scratches O'Hannigan said as he stepped up. "You died. If you didn't, if you'd changed things, then why wouldn't Gerald be rememb'rin' things the ways you say they were and not the way they were before ya changed 'em?" That was it exactly, of course. Gerald knew Molly; he didn't know Mom. If what Molly said was true, then why didn't he remember spending his whole life in the warm and loving care of this woman?

Molly's eyes carried pools of tears at this question. She nodded her agreement and looked back to her son. "I know. I know that's true. I couldn't...I couldn't change things. Patty was very clear about that. She was so terrified that her intervention in my past might change the way your lives turned out. She didn't want me to disrupt any more than I had to in order to save you. So...well, so you see... I *had* to die."

Scratches O'Hannigan was shaking his head. "I don't understand, lass. What are ya sayin'?" Gerald was looking to Molly for an explanation. What was she trying to say?

"I left, Gerald…I left and staged a fake death. I did it to keep things in order. I didn't want to, and it was the hardest thing I ever had to do, but I didn't know any other way. I…the day that I had actually died in life before, I left home. I knew that I needed to survive, that I had to be here when this day arrived so that I could be the one to help you to live through it. So I went into hiding and lived a very quiet and very safe life. Not a happy one, though; you must know that, Gerald. It pained me so much to live in secrecy and not be there to see you and your sister. It was more than I could take most days. I've been gone ever since…until now."

"How's that's possible, then, lass? How could you do it?" Scratches O'Hannigan was in awe of what he was hearing.

Molly shrugged and smiled at Gerald. "Because I love my son. I had to live to be able to help him. I love you, Gerald."

The boy smiled back and began to reach out a loving hand.

Before anyone could have known what was happening, before anyone who wished to might have stopped her, Molly wheeled her chair backwards with a sudden thrust of force, and they watched as it careened off the edge of the floor into space and vanished into the swimming pool of color that hovered in the air.

"No!" Scratches shouted, reaching a useless hand toward where Molly had been seconds ago. The vortex sparked and shone, its ripples raged dramatically, and its edges stretched and expanded, and then, as quickly as the woman had disappeared, the portal did the same. All that remained was the black night sky.

If Gerald had had a voice, it would have broken through the night. If he could have screamed his anguish, he would have sent its message to the heavens. If the boy had the one natural gift necessary to announce to the world the grief he was feeling not just for losing his friend but so abruptly losing his mother for the second time in his life, he would have used it to cry out and beg for someone to take the pain away.

Percival McGulliver was looking in shock and disbelief at the space where the portal had been only seconds ago. A smile slowly broke out upon his face. "It's done," he said, jubilation trickling into his voice. "It's finished!" And the little man danced and laughed, cheerier than either Gerald or Scratches had ever seen him.

They looked to the other man with bewilderment. "Perce," Scratches said, "This is madness. Look what ya've done, man! A woman just died! What can there be to be celebratin'?" But Percival McGulliver waved off the remarks, staring into the night with squinted eyes, as though he truly believed he could make heads or tails of anything in the pitch-like blackness.

And then they all heard a sound; instantly, distinctly, the mansion's front door downstairs slammed shut. Percival McGulliver looked to the others in joyous glee. "Percy," Scratches attempted, but the little man had already broken into a run for the door, leaving Scratches and Gerald shaking their heads in disbelief after him. "Come, lad," Scratches said to the boy, and they both followed Percival McGulliver to investigate the sound downstairs.

As they made their way down the spiraling staircase, the dim glow of candles lining the walls illuminated not one, but two people standing in the foyer in front of the door. Percival McGulliver was standing stock still with a look of genuine happiness and near disbelief as he stared unwaveringly at a beautiful woman with dark brown hair and a look of loss and sorrow shadowing her otherwise stunning face.

"I'll be swined," Scratches O'Hannigan breathed from his position halfway up the stairway. "That there woman is Millie McGulliver." Gerald didn't need to be told. He'd seen her picture, and he'd known since yesterday the true objective of the whole arrangement between Misters McGulliver and Spice.

From the spot on the stairs where they'd stopped, Scratches and Gerald continued to watch what transpired between the husband and wife, curious and decidedly disturbed.

"Millie," Percival was saying, visibly awkward in his movements, wishing to reach out and embrace her but uncertain what the proper thing to do in this situation might be. "Millie, I've waited so long for this." The man was crying, his eyes gleaming with the joy that was bursting from within him at the sight of his long-absent wife. "Oh, Millie," he went on, his comfort level increasing with every second. Still Millicent had not spoken, and still she had not betrayed any of what she might be thinking or feeling through her facial expressions. Her face remained a mask of cold and impersonal detachment. Briefly, Percival McGulliver recalled what Spice had said about how rushing the final stages of the process could cause unwanted complications, and a fleeting terror injected itself into his mind, demanding of him, what would he do if it turned out she'd come back wrong somehow? But he quickly forced this thought from his mind and continued to praise his wife.

"Oh, Millie, the things we'll do! We're going to pick up right where we left off and…"

"Shut up." The statement was plain and direct, to the point and entirely without emotion. Millicent was looking at her husband now, but the recognition in her eyes was of anything but a loving reunion.

Percival recoiled at the bold frankness of the statement. "Millie?" he hazarded in the confusion of her first words to him. "Millie, what…?"

"Quiet, Percival." If there was even a hint of a trace of any emotion in her voice and face, it was one of the purest and most vile contempt.

"Millie," Percival attempted again, "you're tired. You've been through quite an ordeal, and…"

"I want you to leave, Percival. I want you to leave now and never come back. You've insisted upon my return, and here I am. I will remain here for the time being, but I will not remain here with you.

I will have no part in your torture of an innocent boy and his family. I will not tolerate what you did to this boy and his sister, what you've only just done to his mother. I have no place with the sickness that you've become, Percival, and you will leave now. Argue with me and I will simply punish you. I have spent many years in the Great Beyond, Percival, and I have learned many things in that time. I have seen everything you have done, but additionally I have acquired strength, wisdom, and power, the likes of which you could never even imagine. Be wise now to your own self and go. Go now from this home, from this city, from the lives of everyone who knows you. And you'd best be avoiding any games with time anymore, Percival, because I will know, and I will make certain you will be punished for it. Now go."

Percival McGulliver was utterly shocked, his mouth agape with the harsh words he had just heard from his beloved wife. Years of anticipating a warm reunion in which she would embrace him and bestow many thanks upon him for restoring her body to the living realm were suddenly and unexpectedly flushed away in a matter of moments. Years of work and planning, preparation and secrecy, treachery and deceit had yielded nothing he had worked toward.

He attempted another pleading look to Millicent, who merely stared back with the vacant stare that had dwelt upon her face since her arrival. With a downcast gaze and a visible pain of heart-wrenching proportions, Percival McGulliver, shocked and distraught, reached a trembling hand to the handle of the door and opened it. Even from their post on the stairs, Gerald and Scratches could see the single gleaming tear streaking down Percival's cheek as the little man stepped out of his home of many years. One last look to his wife proved no more fruitful than any of the others, and she was saying nothing more. Millicent had said all she had to say. She simply waited for him to depart.

Every deed, every decision, every act committed by this misguided and self-serving villain of our tale had been exercised toward one end: reunion with his late wife. In the matter of a mere moment, that same wife had removed any and all purpose not only from his wicked acts, but also from his own existence. And so Percival McGulliver walked out into the cold night air, looking back every few steps in the sad and pathetic hopes that his resurrected wife would be running outside after him with a changed heart and a warm smile. Such a sight never came, however, and eventually he found that he was beyond the view of the mansion's doorway, and there was nothing to be done but to keep on walking. And so Percival McGulliver kept right on walking, over the West Cuttingsborough city line and out of this tale completely.

Back at the mansion, Millicent McGulliver was addressing the two visitors who were still halfway up the winding staircase. "You can come down now, you know," she was saying to them. She looked up at them and, while she was certainly still little more than a shell of the vibrant woman she had once been, she did assert a bit more warmth toward Scratches and Gerald than she had toward her husband. "Don't worry; I won't hurt you. Neither of you."

They made their way slowly, cautiously down the stairs, and as they approached her, she attempted the slightest of smiles. "I've seen it all, you know," she said, shaking her head at the thought of her husband's evil deeds. "I've seen him every step of the way. I felt so helpless, unable to do a thing to prevent any of it. All that kept me from losing my mind was knowing that it was all building up toward tonight."

"Ya mean," Scratches began, "to say that ya wanted to be… brought back?"

Millicent McGulliver promptly shook her head. "No," she said. "Not at all. No, I just knew that only I would have the power to stop Percival once and for all. I knew that if he would go to these lengths and extremes over such a long span of time just to be with me again, then he would undoubtedly take it to heart when I told him I wanted nothing to do with him. I have no interest in being on this mortal plane, gentlemen, but at least I can rest assured that my husband's days of havoc are past." If she noticed the skeptical exchange of glances between the fiddler and the boy, she gave no indication.

She turned to Gerald then and her face warmed at his innocent and tired eyes. "You look like her, you know," she said to him. "She was a wonderful person, Gerald. Your mother and I were very close at one time, and your sister too. You should be proud of your family."

The boy smiled and nodded, the most he could manage in the chaos that this day had become.

"And now, gentlemen, I am quite tired and think I would like to sit down and enjoy a cup of tea by myself."

The two companions understood that they were being politely dismissed, and they hastily made their way to the door, shaking Millicent's hand awkwardly and smiling their gratitude for her assistance. "I, uh ... well, lass, I'll be ... checkin' in on ya ... if you'd be inclined for me to, that is." He was blushing visibly, something Scratches O'Hannigan didn't ordinarily do.

Millicent smiled back at him and said, "I think that would be very welcome, Mr. O'Hannigan. Come by as often as you like." She turned to the boy. "And you too, Gerald. Please."

And they took their leave and stepped out into the night while the fairer McGulliver made her way to her old familiar kitchen and began to boil water for tea.

She knew he was there before he showed himself or spoke. She didn't know how she knew, and she further didn't know why she wasn't as frightened as she probably ought to be. It seemed, she considered, that being deceased once already had rather dulled her emotions and capacity for fear in earthly things. She'd known a perfect world in her restful years since Miles Garrish's fateful luncheon visit to the mansion, and the only thing danger could bring now was her certain return to that peace.

So as she sat at the kitchen table, staring out the window into the dark West Cuttingsborough night and unconsciously allowing her tea to cool, she did not jump or start or cry out when Professor Anson Spice spoke to her from behind her back.

"Good evening, Millicent," Spice purred, and Millicent McGulliver simply continued to stare, not even bothering to turn around.

"Hello, Anson," she said calmly, and it was perhaps a little disconcerting to the towering man that his menacing presence, his unexpected night visit, and his cold tones should have no effect on his prey.

"Do you know why I'm here, Millicent?" the man continued, and he stepped closer to her, still not willing to make the circle around the kitchen table to force her to look at him, however. That would place her in control of the situation. No, he would stand as close as he could behind her until the madness of suspense drew her to turn around and face him.

"I think so, Anson," Millicent McGulliver replied, but said no more. Her lack of concern and her passive melancholy were beginning to wear on Professor Spice. He had waited years for this moment, and the fact that she seemed almost to be welcoming it with open arms was taking all of the pleasure out of the experience.

"You cost me my position at the university, Millicent," Professor Spice hissed in the tone a disappointed parent may have used to reprimand a child. "You cost me the finest array of study materials and the most impressive laboratory in West Cuttingsborough."

"I suppose I did," was all Millicent McGulliver said, and still she did not turn to face him.

Anson Spice could step no closer to her. Had he been lower, she would have felt his stale breath on her neck. His feet were actually beneath her chair, his hands resting now upon its back.

"You are a meddler, Millicent," Spice went on, and had the woman cared enough to consider it, she would have noticed that his voice seemed more emotional now, more frantic, less in control. "You always were."

Millicent McGulliver expressed more emotion toward the situation now than she had at all thus far or would in the remainder of their discussion, and she did so with only the faintest of sighs. It was a sigh of exhaustion, but also one of sadness, of resolve, of disappointment, and of regret. "Why not admit what you're really upset about, Anson? It's not that you lost your teaching position."

Anson Spice glowered at the back of the woman's head. "What are you talking about?" he spat, and she stared for a moment at the wall and out the kitchen window before formulating her response.

"Janine," Millicent said softly, and she realized it had been a very long time since she'd allowed herself to say the name. "You're angry about Janine."

It took all of Anson Spice's power and determination not to erupt into an outrage at the name of the Van Alderdash girl. Millicent wasn't waiting for a response from the tobacconist, but she wasn't attempting to explain any further. She knew Spice understood what she meant, and she knew that, whether he hadn't realized it himself before now, he knew it to be true at this moment.

Finally, she allowed herself to speak further, still allowing not the littlest trace of emotion to enter into her voice.

"Whatever you did to her, Anson, wherever she is now, whatever fear, pain, and torment you put her through, that was your doing. It wasn't mine, and it certainly wasn't hers. You made your decision; punishing me won't change that. I will say, though, that I never did or said anything to influence Janine against you. I suppose that's how you're justifying this to yourself, and I suppose there's a certain logic to it, but unfortunately it's an untrue logic, and I don't know that you're blind enough to allow a fiction to heal your wounds." Millicent thought for a second before building on that thought. "No," she went on, "you're a man of facts. You've always made that very clear. To punish me now would be an unfit solution for you, not knowing for certain if I'm truly the one you're angry at."

Well, now…Anson Spice was unused to this. The calm resolve with which the resurrected woman spoke was of the tones he was accustomed to delivering unto others. To be poisoned with his own mannerisms, his own stillness and coolness of voice, and with the memories of the pains he'd worked so hard to dull over the years was a tool of anguish against the usually stoic and looming man which he was unprepared for.

Struggling to compose his voice so as not to allow a hint of faltering or shaking into it (and perhaps, to a careful listener, failing at this endeavor), Anson Spice proclaimed his intent to the still woman's back.

"I will have all the evidence I need, woman. You see, I have your husband's code for time alteration. I intend to shift time back to those years when your tiresome meddling cost me everything. And I don't intend to allow for your escape this time. I plan to capture you in the act and bring you crying and begging to your knees for mercy before you have the opportunity to write any sort of letter to the university. I intend to kill you before your first murderer has the opportunity."

If his voice seemed at all uncertain or wavering upon the word "kill," Millicent McGulliver most likely detected it.

Anson Spice would later wonder if Millicent McGulliver was smiling at this point in his visit, and it was this thought, amongst the terrible fate that he was forced into, that would cause him rather rapidly to lose his mind completely. Indeed, those who referred to Miles Garrish as the Mad Clocker may have reconsidered the name had they been able to see the state in which Professor Spice found himself.

"Anson," Millicent said quietly, her voice unchanged from how it had remained through the entire talk. "I know the code as well, and I've had a lot more time to perfect it than you have."

Professor Spice hadn't anticipated this. He had suspected, even, that Millicent McGulliver might not have even been aware of the code's existence. That she should not only be aware of it, but, as she was implying now, also be a master of it was rather alarming to the man. What was more alarming still was the clear and unmistakable fact that her claim held the undertones of an unmasked threat.

"It's true, Anson," Millicent continued, and she surely now could *feel* the man's uncertainty, the break in his confidence, and even the fear that now trickled off of his presence as evident as the odor off of a rotting carcass. "In fact, I might even say that I'm better than Percival. Of course, Percival lacks the total confidence and self-control to ever truly master such a thing as that. I like to think that I'm more stable than my husband, and so I can accomplish things using his own magic that he never dreamed of."

Spice was doing little now to control his emotions. He knew now that he was not merely being threatened; he was being toyed with as well, like a mouse paralyzed with fear at the mercy of a sadistic cat. It occurred to him to turn around and flee the scene, but that was not in the style of Anson Spice, and somewhere beneath the cringing and angry exterior, he still believed in that. No, he felt as though all he could do now was wait and see how this meeting played out.

As it happened, he would not have to wait terribly long.

"Anson," Millicent said in her hauntingly detached voice, "You've made your plans clear, and so for reasons of self-defense alone, I have cause to do what I'm about to do. But I think you must realize and understand first that it is not in self-defense that I do it. No, allowing you to kill me would be the most selfish thing I could do. No, what I do, I do to avenge Janine."

Spice started to protest, started to intone his whispers of menace. He even began silently to withdraw the papers with the elements of the time code from his breast pocket and to observe the first line of the sequence.

He never could have been quick enough to best her. She really had surpassed her husband; Millicent didn't even need to wave a finger.

Scratches O'Hannigan and Gerald Gladwell were walking quietly side by side through the night streets of downtown West Cuttingsborough. It had been quite an eventful evening, and both were quiet in their steps, whether reflective or fatigued or both, it was no matter; they needed no conversation. Scratches suspected the boy must have things on his mind, but he was showing no efforts to communicate them to the fiddler, and O'Hannigan knew enough to respect the boy's need for time.

Still, though, something was not sitting well with Scratches O'Hannigan, and perhaps if Gerald had not lacked a sense of speech, perhaps if the quiet had been stronger, more evident in the night, maybe he would have realized that the boy also was attempting to make sense of something and struggling with it. How, they would have asked each other, can you make sense of something when you don't know what it is you need to make sense of?

At long last, as they were drawing toward the street that would take them their separate ways, Scratches stopped walking, held Gerald's shoulders to make him do the same, and looked sympathetically into the boy's eyes. "Yer mother there, she was a brave one, lad."

Gerald tried his best to avoid the man's gaze, not wishing him to see the sorrow in his eyes, spilling out now in salty liquid warmth. He did manage to nod his agreement, however, and in a split second of connected gazes, they each saw what the other was thinking and feeling. They had lost someone tonight, and they hadn't known until it was all but too late who it truly was they were losing. Gerald was mourning the loss of a dear friend, and that alone was more than he should have had to bear; to know that he was losing more than a mere friend was something he wasn't certain he'd ever fully get a mental or emotional hold on. Scratches was thinking of how short a time he had known Molly, and he was regretting the fact that he hadn't taken action in his concerns for Gerald's safety sooner. Had he made the attempt, perhaps he too could have shared more time with thc young lady.

Perhaps it was that they had taken a second to get control of their feelings. Maybe it was that shared second of sympathetic loss. Whatever it was, in the passing of no more than seconds after this moment, both Gerald and Scratches began to come to a realization of just what it was that had been eating at their minds. Scratches, of course, was the one to verbalize it.

"I need to wrap my head 'round somethin,' my boy," he said, scratching his fuzzy chin thoughtfully. Gerald nodded, knowing that he too was attempting to work something out in his own mind. "Percy," Scratches went on, "was jus' tryin' to bring 'is wife back all this time, right?" Gerald nodded his agreement. "Right then…okay. Well then, lad…what exactly was the Professor in the bargain for?" Gerald's head cocked with the shared perplexity, and he found himself forced to shrug a dumbfounded admission of ignorance.

Now, it should be noted no later in this narrative than at this precise moment that, while no one actually *knew* the culprit in the case of the poisoning of Millicent McGulliver, it had always been Scratches O'Hannigan's personal confidence that the murderer was none other than Anson Spice. He didn't have any reason to believe him guilty other than an understanding of the man's dark depths. He knew nothing of Millicent's letter to the dean of West Cuttingsborough University, the one that had led to Spice's dismissal. Indeed, only one person in the world knew for certain who was responsible for not just the end of his teaching career but also the severing of him from the countless resources for his experiments that the school had to offer, and that was the professor himself.

True, Spice had never seen the letter with his own eyes; he didn't even precisely know that a letter existed. So he certainly couldn't have known that Millicent McGulliver had written one. But he had seen her with his own eyes, had seen her through the window in his door, the look of terror painted in terrible colors on her disarmingly beautiful face, and the towering dark man had never once doubted who was responsible.

Neither Scratches nor Gerald yet knew the entire truth of the events which had unraveled as of late, but in an instant, they both shared a sudden understanding that had no foundation in evidence but somehow needn't have any, simply for the utter certainty which each of them felt in the suspicion. That suspicion was instantly spoken by Scratches O'Hannigan with a look of astonished panic darted toward the boy.

"He wanted the McGulliver woman back too, Gerald lad," the man said, and Gerald's eyes widened as he realized that somehow he had been suspecting the exact same thing. "I don't know why, boy, but we need to get ourselves back to the McGulliver mansion quick like. Come!"

The speed with which they dashed for the mansion was incomparable. By the time they arrived at the towering home, they were each winded and pained from the adrenaline-fueled exertion that had carried them to the former home of Percival McGulliver. They knew not what they expected to find when they arrived, but whatever it was, it was not what they found.

The astonishment came for both of them when they encountered Millicent McGulliver herself, seated at the kitchen table with a mug of tea cupped between her palms, a look of either shock or peace (or both?) etched across her face.

As Millicent looked up at them, Scratches warily snuck a darting glance around the room, searching for the slightest trace of any kind of struggle or perhaps that Anson Spice may even be lying in wait behind a piece of furniture somewhere only inches away. Seeing nothing, he turned to Mrs. McGulliver and asked, with only the slightest traces of trepidation in his voice and eyes, "Millie…Are ya okay, then, lass?"

With some alarm, Millicent shook herself out of her trance-like state and seemed truly to focus in on her visitors for the first time since their arrival. With the confusion of one waking from a dream, she made her best effort to think clearly and speak intelligibly, standing up from the kitchen chair and gripping the back of it for support.

"Yes," she managed at last. "Yes, I'm fine…thank you, Mr. O'Hannigan."

Gerald and Scratches glanced at each other doubtfully, then looked back to the lady of the house. "Millie," Scratches said as he took a step closer to the confused woman, "did something happen after we left?"

Millicent looked into Scratches O'Hannigan's eyes with a realization that told Scratches almost all he needed to know. "He was here," she said softly, barely more than a whisper. "Professor Spice. He came here."

"Ah, no," Scratches exhaled as Gerald's eyes widened in disbelief. "What did he do to ya, lass?"

Millicent was coming to herself rapidly now. Seemingly more aware of what she was saying, she shook off her disorientation and said, much clearer now, "Nothing. He didn't do anything. He didn't have a chance."

The world will be a colder place some day. Colder, that is, except in the places that will be unforgivingly hot. There will be darkness and despair when that time comes, and wherever one looks, the terrain and life upon it will look, in all ways, suspiciously reminiscent of the haunting Cobble Road. The twisted branches of acrid-breathed trees, the weeping eyes of dead animals slithering into beckoning underwater graves, the vacant stares of the few living people who will wander aimlessly with frozen grins of terror…All of these things will be housed in a land of anguish, suffering, and regret.

And amidst it all will wander one lost soul, never intended to know such a time or place, for it was into this uncompromisingly desolate wasteland of the future that Millicent McGulliver exiled Professor Anson Spice.

On his journey home, Gerald passed a particular vacated building in West Cuttingsborough. This building was the former home to Odds and Endless Wonders, West Cuttingsborough's only second-hand store, though its owner, Marcia Bottles, ever referred to it as an "antique shop."

Odds and Endless Wonders had never been a favorite of the West Cuttingsboroughians, mostly because of its owner's more than pretentious, snobbish attitude toward her business and wares. Invariably, items such as chipped teacups and puzzles with missing pieces were priced at exorbitant amounts in Marcia Bottles's claim that their incomparable value as representations of past eras' fashions made them incontestable bargains. The fact that most of these items had been purchased brand-new by their original owners, who had then sold them to her themselves, was a fact Marcia scoffed and waved her hand at, with no better retort than a humph and a shush.

So of course it was little surprise to most when the business eventually failed and its vacant building's window found itself housing a "For Lease" sign. What may have been more surprising to most (and alarmingly moving to Patty, in particular) was that Stuart Freeley's HOP fund had generated quite enough money to pay several months' rent on the building and have a substantial amount left over. And as it happened, on that very same day that Gerald found himself passing the building after his encounters with Misters McGulliver and Spice, several hours earlier, Stuart Freeley had claimed the empty property with the cash from the HOP fund.

As Stuart was idling his time walking with little care and overtly conscious perception, he was unlikely to miss the sign in the window of the former Odds and Endless Wonders. Stuart, like most West Cuttingsboroughians, had never been a considerable fan of the second-hand store, but that had little to do with its prices and more to do with the fact that Stuart Freeley was, quite possibly, West Cuttingsborough's least materialistic person. Ever cherishing the simple and natural pleasures of the world to the chagrin of his extremely money-conscious stepfather, Stuart had little need for the garishly ostentatious items for sale in the store.

He did, however, have a use for the vacant building, and he felt he knew what it would be quite perfect for.

In the earliest days of West Cuttingsborough, long before the days of Marcia Bottles and Odds and Endless Wonders, the future antique shop was home to the West Cuttingsborough Players, a troupe of amateurish thespians who would showcase their own decidedly inadequate talents in the areas of drama, music, opera, comedy, and the like on a weekly basis. While their skills may have wanted for a degree of taste and quality, it was the only entertainment the town had in those days, and it had thrived quite nicely. Complete with the structure of a theater, including box seats and a balcony which Marcia Bottles would use for storage and displays, the building still held the appearance of a live stage theater, and the second Stuart Freeley saw the "For Lease" sign in the window, he knew exactly what the HOP fund must be used for.

The money had rested for nearly four years now in between the pages of his own personal library in his bedroom, a location he knew to be quite secure from the greedy hands and eyes of his stepfather. Indeed, businessman Simon never had the slightest inkling of a notion that his son had been so successful in the collection of a large sum of money. Had he been aware of this, he may have been less amused by his wife's suggestion that he give him an apprenticeship.

But an apprenticeship wasn't what Stuart desired. He wanted nothing more than to live a life dedicated to repaying Patty Gladwell for the fine way in which she had treated him in their high school days. And he knew when he saw the sign in the window of the antique shop exactly what purpose the HOP fund could serve. Of course, to use it for Patty to return to school now would be absurd. For one, though unspoken through all of West Cuttingsborough, it was commonly believed by most that Patty had either fled the town forever on her own or met with some horrible end that was in all likelihood too grisly for any of them ever to desire to know its details. For another thing, even if she were to return, they were all older now, and to return her to high school would simply be nonsensical.

But this? Well now, this was something that could be quite beneficial either in the scenario that would see Patty's return to the town or still in the much sadder and much more likely possibility that they had seen the last of her. He would use the money from the HOP fund to purchase the empty building and re-open it as a community theater. It would all be done in Patty's name and with her name clearly imprinted on the front of the establishment. In her absence, he would approach Mr. Batchley with the proposal that he might act as chief director. Then, if Patty ever returned, there would be a fine stage theater waiting for her to own, to operate, to direct, to produce, or to star upon as her own heart wished and instructed her.

It was a plan to be proud of, and it went swimmingly. In a matter of days, Stuart Freeley had signed the papers and paid the money, offering the rest of it to a very obliging Mr. Batchley to put toward the expenses of costumes, sets, and other necessities to open the first performance. As it happened, that first show was Mr. Batchley's own *The Great Culinary Caper* in honor of Patty's final performance upon the stage of West Cuttingsborough High School, and it was a fantastic success, yielding enough profit to continue to put on impressive performances upon that stage for years to come.

Of course, Gerald didn't know any of this as he made his way through the town. In fact, he didn't even take a second's notice of the building he would be hearing about from Stuart Freeley the very next day.

As Gerald drew toward his home, he found his heart sinking with the realization that he didn't know what was to become of him or his father at this stage. He couldn't very well return to school, not and expect to support the two of them at the same time, nor could he go back to work. At least, not at the hat shop, not that he would have desired to anyway, not even under different ownership. The understanding of how fantastic an arrangement had been generated to allow first Patty and then Gerald to depart school and work full time was something that wasn't lost to him. In all likelihood, anyone who wasn't in Mr. McGulliver's desperate situation and who did not possess his unique skills that could be used as tools of manipulation wouldn't give the slightest consideration to taking him on as a full-time employee.

And, of course, he had been forced to mature earlier and more rapidly than he should have been expected to do, first through his entering into the working world, and then even more so in the last several days through his battles with the wicked men. More than anything, Gerald simply wanted to lie down and cry, to allow himself to be a frightened boy and to expect the loving comfort of a warm and protective parent. *Is that too much to wish for?* he asked himself as he stared at the closed door of his house. He didn't think it was, but it didn't matter; nothing changed the fact that he would need to be the one (as he always was) to comfort his father, not the other way around.

Sighing his acceptance of the cold truth, the boy turned the handle and pushed the wooden door open, stepping inside the humble abode. He was perhaps a little alarmed to find his father sitting expectantly on the couch, hands folded in front of him, leaning forward, visibly nervous about something. Upon hearing the boy enter, the man looked up at his son and rose slowly, smiling his recognition at Gerald and greeting him with open arms.

"Gerald," he said, in as collected, aware, and cognizant a manner as anyone could be expected to have. "I'm so happy to see you, Son."

Was this the same man Gerald had known for the last several years? Where was the uncertainty? To what other region had retreated the childlike innocence, the lack of comprehension of all things serious, the wide-eyed mystification over such trifles as buttered bread and revolving windmills?

This man was healthy.

This man was clearly as sharp-witted and aware of the world around him as the father Gerald so fondly recalled from the earliest years of his youth. He didn't wish to allow his hopes to rise too greatly. Surely this must be a dream! Surely he would awake any second and find that he was unconscious in Mr. McGulliver's clutches, or worse yet, that he'd actually died and that this was simply some subconscious illusion that was greeting him on the threshold of the Great Beyond.

But he knew better. His senses told him with every scent in the house, every itch on his body, every tickle in his throat, and surely with every warm, salty tear flooding his eyes that what he was seeing, what he was hearing was quite real.

The man started forward but halted abruptly when he noticed his son's trepidation; the boy had started backward at the sight of the approaching father. Jefferson Gladwell held up his hands in a gesture of innocent, well-intentioned friendliness. "It's okay, Gerald; it really is. It's me," he said as gently as he could manage. Then, after only a second's hesitation, "It's Dad."

Gerald's cocked head and wide eyes asked all the questions that were swirling through the boy's head.

"I know," Jefferson assured him, ushering him with a welcoming hand to the couch and nodding as warmly and reassuringly as his own fears and doubts would allow him to.

As the boy edged his way with a caution his own emotions wouldn't allow him to disarm, his stare never strayed from the welcoming and warm gaze of his father.

Seated beside his son on the couch, Jefferson Gladwell took a moment to collect his thoughts, exhaling deeply and looking down at the floor, hands folded in his lap. At long last, composure regained, he sat up straight and looked confidently in the eyes of his son, youthful, yes, but also aged so far beyond his years without any choice in the matter. Guilty tears leapt to the father's eyes.

"I'm so sorry, Son," he managed, all the confidence he'd built up over the last minutes withered away and swept in a dusty breeze out the window or through the cracks in the wall. The boy waited patiently for more explanation. What his father might be apologizing for and what he could have done to yield such painful emotion toward him was beyond Gerald's ability to fathom.

His look of perplexity must have been enough to allow the elder Gladwell to muster the strength to forge on. Nodding, he said, "Gerald…how I've been, the way I've acted…what you and your… your sister had to do…" The man drifted for a moment, but shortly felt something that woke him directly with a start. His head shooting up to see what it was, his instinctual hopes were confirmed in finding his son's hand lying gently and encouragingly upon his arm.

The confidence that flowed into the man's veins was fueled by the promise that he and his son's relationship held the hope whose return he'd been anticipating for years. Looking into Gerald's eyes, Jefferson Gladwell continued his explanation.

"It's my own doing, Gerald. I did it all myself." Gerald's trademark cocked head renewed the expression of his lack of understanding. Nodding his acknowledgment, the father went on, "Since your mother's death, I didn't know how to deal with it, what I could possibly do without her. Your mother…" Here the man smiled and shook his head, his mind clearly fixed upon a memory ancient and unknown to the boy but only as crystalline as this morning's minutia to the father. "She was quite a person, Son. Oh, she had an edge when we were kids, always getting into trouble, rubbing most people the wrong way, but…well, Gerald…your parents loved each other an awful lot."

The tears in the man's eyes were only proven happy ones by the confident smile of the treasured memories that embraced his face.

"Well," he went on, sighing with the burden of having to move beyond the fondness and into the dark. "When she was gone…I needed…I needed…" Jefferson Gladwell must have swallowed half a dozen times in his attempt to share what was on his mind.

Whatever Gerald was expecting his father to say, it was not what he heard.

"I went to Professor Spice for help, Gerald. And to Mr. McGulliver."

Gerald's eyes widened with the realization of the implications of what he'd just heard. Everything he had just been through, everything that had almost happened to him, everything that *had* happened to Patty…and his father had involved himself in it of his own free will? It was practically too much.

The man did his best to forge on through his son's visible disapproval. "I didn't know what else to do, son. I'd heard things… noticed things. I thought they could help, and I didn't know where else to turn."

The boy managed a shrug of "What, then? What did you do?" and the father nodded his understanding.

"Gerald…I've been back and forth through time, and seen your mother return to and from the grave more times than I can count. Everything I did always resulted in your mother's death. And with each travel, with each spell, with each alteration to time and history and my own life, it became more and more difficult to keep track of what was real and what wasn't, what had happened in the current reality and what was no longer a true event of the past. I lost all account of time and my own place in the universe, and little by little…well, before I knew it, I'd completely lost my grip on reality. I knew what I remembered, and I remembered more than I would have liked to, but I couldn't communicate it, I couldn't fully get my head around it. And you kids were forced to take care of me."

The look of shame in the father's eyes was all too clear to Gerald, and the boy felt instantly remorseful for allowing his face to betray his feelings about his father's confession. He forced a smile to his lips and asserted a nod of sympathy; Jefferson Gladwell was given the strength to continue.

With a degree of thought and visible consideration, the man pursed his lips and studied his son carefully. After a moment, he said with the slightest trace of uncertainty, "You ... you've been ... you've been ... involved with them ... haven't you, Gerald?"

The boy shook his head with adamant denial. Immediately he had more to communicate to his father than he could possibly manage with mere gestures and facial expressions. Looking around the small room, he spotted a miniature pad of paper and a pencil on the counter in the kitchen and jumped up to retrieve them. Then, for the next several minutes, Gerald worked diligently at writing down in as much detail as he could while maintaining a good speed the entire sequence of events he'd just undergone.

From Patty's disappearance to her discovery of Mr. McGulliver's plans, from Molly's warning to her revealing to him of her true identity, from her personal sacrifice to Millicent McGulliver's otherworldly resurrection, from Percival McGulliver's departure to Anson Spice's demise, the story was communicated in all its glory through the boy's rapidly scrawled unspeakable words.

When Jefferson Gladwell had finished reading and digesting his son's tale, the tears leapt into his eyes with a force both he and the boy were unprepared for. "You knew her, then? You've seen her?"

Gerald slowly nodded, his own eyes sympathetic for how difficult such a fact must have been for his father.

The man swallowed, looking at his son expectantly. "And she ... she saved you? She ... she was really a hero, wasn't she?" Gerald nodded and smiled, touching his father's arm and leaning in to him for a warm and comforting embrace. The man attempted a smile and nodded his pleasure at this fact. "That's my girl," he said, wiping the tears from his eyes.

The father glanced back down at his son's narrative again, shook his head, and exhaled his astonishment with a high-pitched whistle through his teeth. "I had no idea," he said. "No idea just how terrible they could be." The boy nodded his regrets, and then shrugged them off in a clear signal that he held his father responsible for nothing and had already begun to move beyond the clutches of McGulliver and Spice. Gerald then contorted his face in a thoughtful scrunch and gestured at his father with a questioning look. The man understood perfectly; the boy wanted to know how it was that his father had come to return to his own self so suddenly and unexpectedly. Jefferson Gladwell shrugged. "It must have been something you did. You or someone else. Something changed somehow and restored me. I don't need to know how."

For some time, they sat in silence, cherishing the realization that they truly were faced with a real second chance, and one that did not rely upon entering into any sort of contract with McGulliver and Spice.

"Well," the father said at long last, after they had sat in silent thoughtfulness for some time, "I suppose this is where we begin to move on. I suppose this is where I accept that she's really gone. If I couldn't change anything in all my attempts, and certainly the things you've done have changed nothing, then there's nothing to do but start living again."

And so they did, expecting nothing and everything. Nothing in the absences of their loved ones, nothing in the alterations made to the flow of time through their interventions, both planned and thrust upon them. Everything in the simple potential that stood before them, a second chance to live again as father and son, as family, and renew their relationship and press on with it into the Great Unknown Future.

It was then that Gerald remembered the anointed nickel he'd been keeping in his pocket. Standing up abruptly, he fished for it and felt his fingers close around its rough metallic surface. Drawing it forth, he held it up to his eye level to examine it more closely, with a certain amount of awe but undoubtedly with a significant degree of distaste as well. The father recognized it instantly and shuddered. "I don't think we need to keep that around, do we?"

The boy shook his head slowly, still eyeing the coin with infatuated distrust. No indeed, if ever the thing could possibly bring about luck, it was, Gerald was certain, not the sort of luck they had any use for. Not anymore.

Now that they'd both survived dealing with Professor Spice and Percival McGulliver, they were quite certain that they were prepared for anything.

What happened next, however, was something neither the boy nor his father could have been ready for. Nor was it anything either of them had experienced before. It wasn't exactly like waking from a vivid dream, but nor was it exactly unlike that either. It was not particularly as though they heard or felt a sudden noise or movement to suggest anything in the universe had been altered. Truly, had Gerald been capable of using words to describe what happened, and had his father ever felt inclined even to attempt to do so, they may have ventured to claim that the world appeared to come suddenly into a clearer focus. It was as though, in unison, the sights in the room, the sounds outside the small house, the scents and sensations in the atmosphere enveloping them were all suddenly distinctly more defined, and they themselves much more aware of them. And as this unannounced and curious sensation admitted itself, there was a mutual hitching of both their breaths as they looked to each other and came to the vivid realization that they both knew something with no uncertainty whatsoever in their hearts.

There was no exchange of questioning eyes between them, for their confidence was so fast and so glorious, any doubts had perished before they could have been birthed. They did not see movement out the one window in their line of vision, nor did they hear anyone coming down the grassy hill outside the house. Yet they knew quite well she was there and nearing them with every passing second.

The young woman, though changed and matured, though grown in worldliness and heavier of heart with the burdens of life's truths and hardships, still radiated the same tenderness of soul, the familiar love affair with the world around her that had endeared her to all the citizens of West Cuttingsborough. It was with tired legs and an open heart that she made her way down the hill and toward the humble little home.

Gerald saw that his father was crying. It was not the helpless and childlike weeping the boy had come to expect from his father in recent years, but rather the happily heartbroken silent tears of a responsible and loving father. Gerald's eyes must have been questioning now, for the father read them as clearly as a book. The man nodded with certainty, gestured him in a shooing manner to the door, and smiled.

"Go," the man said reassuringly. "I'll wait here."

And with that, young Gerald bolted to the door, swung it open, and dashed through the yard and toward the hill. He ran faster than he had ever had reason to before. He'd known fear and excitement, joy and anticipation, suspense and humiliation, but he had never known a feeling such as this, and never had he been inspired to move faster than time itself; that is, he never had until now.

He could see the figure now, coming down the hill, and though an onlooker would have predicted it impossible, his speed quickened. His clenched fists pumped until they broke free of their own form, becoming open palms slicing the air like paddles in a river, begging for greater speed. And as they opened, the scented nickel fell from the boy's right hand, forgotten in the grasses as he collapsed into the loving embrace of his sister.

e|LIVE

listen|imagine|view|experience

AUDIO BOOK DOWNLOAD INCLUDED WITH THIS BOOK!

In your hands you hold a complete digital entertainment package. In addition to the paper version, you receive a free download of the audio version of this book. Simply use the code listed below when visiting our website. Once downloaded to your computer, you can listen to the book through your computer's speakers, burn it to an audio CD or save the file to your portable music device (such as Apple's popular iPod) and listen on the go!

How to get your free audio book digital download:

1. Visit www.tatepublishing.com and click on the e|LIVE logo on the home page.
2. Enter the following coupon code: f138-550f-d154-6d57-a854-8f98-46e1-2633
3. Download the audio book from your e|LIVE digital locker and begin enjoying your new digital entertainment package today!